Sparkledove

A DISPLACED CHRISTMAS STORY

TIMOTHY BEST

ISBN: 978-1-963705-20-1

Published in the United States of America by Harbor Lane Books, LLC.

www.harborlanebooks.com

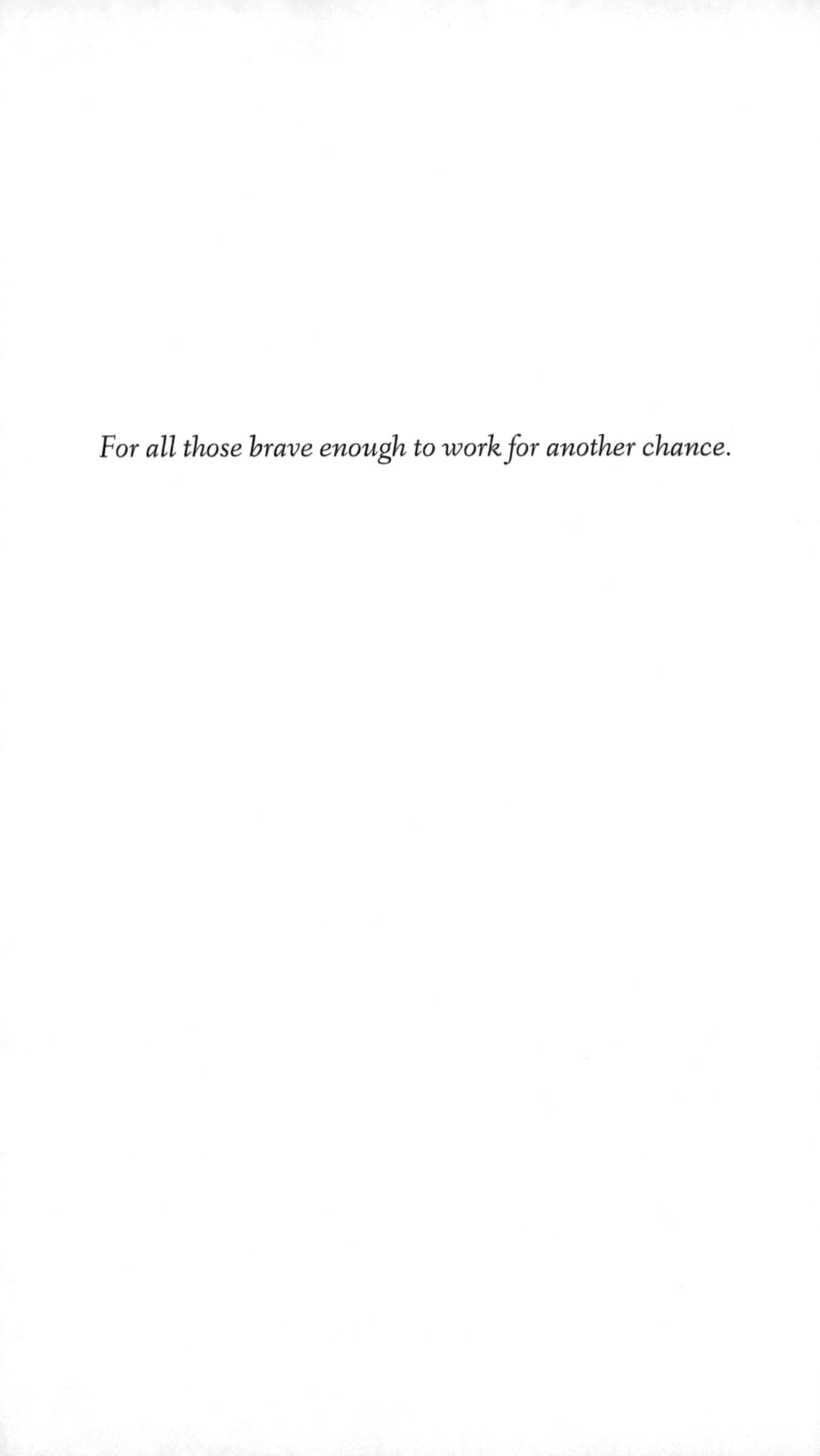

For all those brave enough to work for another chance.

*At the end of the day, it isn't where I came from.
Maybe home is where I'm going and have never
been before.*

— WARSAN SHIRE

One

MERCER STREET

Goldie Maraschino's stilettos clicked through the Delta terminal of JFK International Airport until she stepped onto the escalator that would take her down to baggage claim. Her four-inch heels allowed her to stand at five feet eight. Perhaps they were impractical for the airport, but she cared more about appearance than comfort. As she descended to the lower level, she chewed her gum with an open mouth and watched through Ray Ban sunglasses while a young mother just ahead of her struggled to wrangle two young children. The kids were tired and whining. It was the Tuesday before Thanksgiving, and it seemed like everyone in America was traveling.

On the opposite side of the escalator, she saw a police officer ascending who was giving her the once-over. The cop wasn't looking at her in a suspicious way, but rather in a "Whoa! Very nice!" kind of way.

That's right, Law & Order. Dare to dream, she thought, pretending to examine a bright red fingernail. She didn't like cops, and she had good reason; her boyfriend was one of New York City's rising crime bosses. But then she was distracted by the weary mother, who was trying to soothe her whiny kids, and cracked her gum.

Coming off the escalator, she clicked-clacked her way toward baggage carousel 7. As she walked, she could feel the eyes of other men watching. She was used to this and, in fact, liked it. She was a blonde-haired, green-eyed, twenty-five-year-old in a minidress with a fur-collar leather jacket and a wiggle in her butt that could make a bowl of red Jell-O turn green with envy. Goldie was a babe, and she knew it.

The fur on the collar of her jacket wasn't real. Neither was her blonde hair. Even the name "Goldie" wasn't real. But the gold bracelets that jingled on her slender wrists came from Tiffany's, her shoes were Jimmy Choo's, and the Louis Vuitton tote slung over her shoulder all said to the world that here was a woman with money. Even if that money came from drugs, stolen merchandise, hookers, and payoffs from merchants who sought extra protection for their businesses. Goldie wasn't directly involved in any of her boyfriend's business dealings, but she wasn't ignorant of them, either.

Coming to the baggage carousel as the first pieces of luggage were sliding off the conveyor belt, she glanced around and spied a Skycap with an empty luggage cart. She raised her chin, and the Skycap wheeled his cart over to her.

"You need help with your bags, ma'am?" he asked. He was an elderly man with silver hair.

"Not me," Goldie said, dipping a hand into her tote and then her wallet. "See Mother Goose over my shoulder with the two kids?"

The man eyed the woman and her children. "Yeah?"

She pulled out a fifty and handed it to him. "Help her get to wherever. Just say Santa came early this year. *Don't* point me out. Understand?"

The Skycap looked over at the woman, then at Goldie, and smiled. "You're a good Christian woman."

"No, I'm not," she replied, cracking her gum and speaking with a very pronounced Bronx accent. "But maybe Jesus ain't above a bribe."

As the Skycap stuffed the bill into his shirt pocket, she spotted a large Vuitton bag that matched her tote and hurried over to it. Plucking it off the carousel, she pulled up the handle and started to roll it away as she heard the woman with kids ask the Skycap: "Which one? Who hired you for me?" She was pleased but, at the same time, slightly mystified by the random act of kindness.

Stepping outside where she thought the taxis would be lined up, Goldie realized she had misjudged and was about fifty yards away from the correct exit. Spotting a waiting cab, she gave a loud whistle like a foreman on a loading dock. The cab driver turned on his overhead light and rolled toward her.

Her given name was Karen. But everybody called her Goldie because of her love for gold jewelry. She wasn't formally educated and could have a quick temper, but she was street-smart. She dropped out of high school in the eleventh grade because her then and current boyfriend, Markie Santina, had gotten her pregnant. At the time, Markie was a wise guy in training for the Lombardo family. Being Catholic, Goldie decided to have the baby. One night, when she was seven months pregnant, Markie found himself backed into a corner by three members of a rival family in the parking lot of Rozano's Restaurant just off Mulberry Street in Little Italy. It was a minor skirmish, nothing the family heads would've paid any attention to. Those involved were just teenagers with hormones that needed to establish turf. But when the three guys started to beat Markie up, Goldie, who had just gotten into the car, hopped back out and went after his attackers. She plowed into them, swinging her purse back and forth like a broadsword. The effort helped Markie and caused two of the attackers to back off, but not before the third one kicked her squarely in the stomach. Other departing restaurant patrons helped to break up the fight, but later that night, Goldie had to be rushed to the hospital, where she lost the baby and nearly her life.

Suddenly, the "minor" skirmish at Rozano's wasn't minor anymore. Within six months, all three of the young men who had attacked Markie mysteriously disappeared without a trace, beginning with the one who kicked Goldie. Usually, this would've caused a war between families. But since the bodies were never found and Markie's alibis were so strong, nothing could be pinned on him. This actually elevated his stature in the Lombardo family, where he continued to climb the ranks. It also cemented his relationship with Goldie. They didn't marry or have other children, but Markie promised to take care of her. Being in love and from a family of modest means, Goldie let him. For the past month, she'd been in Las Vegas, which was the longest time she'd ever been away from Markie. Her Uncle Luke, her mother's oldest brother, had died after a long bout with cancer. When the funeral was over and the out-of-town family members departed, Goldie stayed behind to help her Aunt Sophie settle Luke's affairs since they had no children of their own. She was the logical choice for this since she had no job to get back to and knew how to get things done. Back in New York, she was Markie's second set of eyes. She wasn't his accountant, but she had a natural head for numbers and would occasionally double-check the books. She wasn't his head of security, but she was the one who suggested he buy another condo in the same building where they lived under the name of a dummy corporation so he could keep records, cash, and extra weapons close by but off premises in case their home ever got searched. She wasn't his secretary, but she kept diaries that included names and dates of things he sometimes shared with her. She wasn't an active player, but she loved and supported her man.

It was a forty-five-minute ride from JFK to Greenwich Village, where Markie and Goldie had a three-bedroom condo on Mercer Street. It was in an older but completely renovated building, and their place had a value of around three million dollars. For New York real estate, it was comfortable but not overly luxurious. Winter had come early to Manhattan, and a mixture of snow and rain began to fall as the cab passed through Queens. Finally arriving in the Village, she smiled to herself that she was almost home. She and Markie had phoned and texted daily and had even done a few FaceTime calls where all she had worn were a pair of Egyptian earrings, but she was still missing him.

She paid the driver generously, and he retrieved her larger bag from the trunk; then Goldie entered the lobby of their building with her tote slung over her shoulder and her other bag rolling behind. The door was held open for her by a man in a jacket and tie named Larry, who worked the front door and reception counter in the lobby. Goldie greeted him as she came in. He was an employee of the building but was also on Markie's payroll and carried a Smith & Wesson .38 clipped to his belt under his jacket. There was also another beefier man sitting on a sofa in the reception area. He was more casually dressed, and his name was Bruno Carmichael. He was one of Markie's oldest friends and fiercest enforcers. He had a thick neck, curly black hair cut close to his large head, and had a notorious tough-guy reputation. Someone once threw a brick at Bruno's chest to slow down an impending attack, and he hardly flinched as it bounced off. He was reading the sports section of the *New York Times* when Goldie came into the building. Both men were visibly surprised to see her.

"Goldie," Bruno said, setting his paper down and rising.

"Ay, Bruno, how ya doin'?" she asked, setting her bag down momentarily. "Where'd all this cold weather come from? My freakin' ovaries just retreated to my ribs."

"You're back early," he said. "We weren't expectin' you till tomorrow."

"Changed my ticket and came home early," she explained. She walked over to the wastepaper basket behind Larry's counter and, without bending over or picking up the receptacle, spit her gum into it with perfect aim.

"If we'd known you were coming in, we would've sent a car for you," Larry offered.

"A cab was fine," she replied. "Travelin' is already stupid, and it's gonna get even crazier tomorrow, the day before Thanksgivin', so I decided to surprise Markie."

"Sure," Larry said, a little concerned.

"Oh, he'll be surprised," Bruno agreed.

She sensed the hesitancy in both men and looked them over.

"What's goin' on? Everythin' alright?"

"Eh, everything's fine," Larry said. "I-I just think Markie wanted to make some arrangements for your homecoming."

"Oh, I don't want no celebration or nothin'," she waved off. "I just wanna see my man."

"You want help with your bags?" Bruno offered.

"No. Two men in the lobby at all times," she said, reinforcing one of Markie's rules. "He upstairs?"

"Yeah," Bruno answered. "But..."

"But what?" she asked.

After a pause, the bigger man shrugged, "Nothin'."

Goldie grabbed the raised handle of her suitcase and headed for the elevator. As she did, Larry and Bruno looked at one another anxiously, and the moment the elevator door closed with Goldie inside, Larry hurried over to the house phone on the counter.

Markie and Goldie's condo was on the fifth floor, which was the top floor of the building. After using her key and stepping into the foyer of the 1,800-square-foot layout, she immediately noticed a change. There was a narrow wall table in the foyer for holding keys, gloves, and purses. Usually, hanging on the wall above it were six ceramic decorative masks tastefully arranged that Goldie had bought at an art gallery. But now, the masks were gone. In their place was a modernistic Jackson Pollack-style painting she neither recognized nor liked.

"What the hell is this?" she asked herself quietly. "Looks like somebody shook up a can of Cherry Coke.

Hey, baby?" she called. "I'm home! What happened to my masks?"

She rolled her suitcase into the living room and put her tote on a chair. She looked around with a furrowed brow. She was home, but things looked different. A favorite floor vase had been moved. There was an empty shelf near the stereo where she had kept her collection of vinyl albums. They were mostly artists from the 60s, 70s, and 80s, decades of music she particularly liked.

"Hey!" she said, walking over to the empty shelf. "Where's my *Sergeant Pepper*? *Back In Black*? Where the fuck's my *Saturday Night Fever!*"

She looked around, not understanding. "Markie?" she called.

Suddenly, a young woman entered from the opposite side of the living room. She appeared at the end of the hallway that led to the master bedroom. She was a little younger than Goldie, blonde and pretty like her, but much more casually dressed. She had her hair loosely piled atop her head with several strands hanging down. She also wore an oversized NYU sweatshirt, baggy plaid sweatpants, and bright pink high-top sneakers. She carried a long blue down coat over her arm and cracked the faintest of smiles at Goldie as she headed for the front door.

"Uh, excuse me?" Goldie said, taken aback. "Who are you?"

The young woman didn't respond and continued toward the door.

"Hey!" Goldie insisted, her temper igniting while she eyed the other woman's oversized clothes. "Walkin' lampshade: I'm talkin' to you!"

The other blonde opened the front door and tossed Goldie a dismissive look as she exited. Goldie took a couple of steps toward the front door to pursue, but stopped when Markie entered the room, also appearing at the end of the same hall.

"Ay," he said in a Bronx accent as thick as hers. "You're back early."

"That damn well better be the new maid," she snapped.

"Chill," he said, walking over to her. "There's a perfectly logical explanation."

Markie Santina was a good-looking twenty-seven-year-old Italian, six feet tall, weighing 175 pounds, and lean but taut. Some said he looked like a young Richard Gere, although he didn't know who that was. He wore slim-fitting Lucky jeans, a powder-blue Lauren pullover sweater, and some Fly London Chukka black boots. His excellent taste in clothing only accentuated his good looks. He walked over and put his arms around her waist.

"I wasn't expectin' you 'til tomorrow," he smiled.

"Yeah, I can see that," she said suspiciously. "Who just walked out of our bedroom, and why was she in there?"

"We'll get to that," he said. He gave her a quick kiss that she hardly reciprocated, then let go of her waist. "Tell me about Nevada. How's your aunt doin'?"

"Her partner is dead," Goldie answered. "How do ya think she's doin'? Speaking of dead partners, you better start explainin' who that person was that walked out of our bedroom. And where are my masks? And my albums? Why does my house not look like my house?"

"C'mere," he said, moving over to the sofa and gesturing for her to sit. "Sit down."

"What goin' on, Markie?"

"Sit down," he smiled.

She stepped over to their white leather Natuzzi sofa and sat, but didn't remove her jacket with the fake fur collar.

Markie paused a moment, trying to figure out just the right way to explain things, then sat down on an ottoman across from her.

"You know I'm movin' up in the family, right? You know Frank's got his eye on me."

He was referring to Frank Lombardo, head of the largest crime family in the city.

"Yeah, Frank likes you," Goldie conceded. "Who was the blonde that came out of our bedroom?"

"Her name is Kristen DiVarno. She's Charley DiVarno's oldest daughter."

"Charley DiVarno, as in the Chicago DiVarnos?" Goldie asked, knowing they were the largest Italian crime family in the Windy City.

"Yeah," Markie confirmed. "You know Frank and Charley got history, right? Charley's originally from New York, and they hung out a lot back in the day. Anyway, Kristen's in the graduate program at NYU.

She's gettin' her master's in business. Charley asked Frank to have someone check up on her from time to time, so Frank asked me."

"Okay. Swell. But why was she in our bedroom?"

"Well, Frank asked me to look in on Kristen some time ago. I didn't tell ya because, well—I didn't think it was a big deal. But, uh, over time, we got to know one another and, uh, had coffee a few times... and... uh, one thing sort of led to another."

Goldie's green eyes shot daggers at him, knowing where this was going.

"Oh, no," she said, shaking her head. "Oh, no! I've been with you seven years, Markie. *Seven years!*"

"Yeah, I know," he nodded. "And I feel really shitty about this, Goldie. I really *do!* But it was just somethin' that—y'know—*happened.* Nobody planned it."

Tears began to fill Goldie's eyes as her heart sank to the pit of her stomach.

"I thought you were comin' in tomorrow," he continued. "I was gonna meet you at the airport with flowers and give you this talk I been workin' on, then take you to your new apartment."

"My new *what?*"

"I got you this great place on 53rd. The rent is paid up for six months. Your stuff's all there; I got you a car and put fifty grand in a bank account for ya. It's a really nice exit package."

Goldie rubbed her forehead now, actually feeling light-headed, while tears rolled down her face.

"I—uh—I..." She rose, walked out of the living room, and went into the kitchen. Unsure of what to say, she tore off a piece of paper towel from a roll and blew her nose. She was stunned, hurt, and felt betrayed. Everything she knew had just changed in an instant. She glanced around the kitchen and noticed a small, empty space on the wall above the counter where a saying that came from her mother's kitchen used to hang. It read: "The best ingredient to every good meal is love."

She wiped her eyes and tried to regain some composure.

"Exit package, huh?" she finally muttered. "What am I? Some employee who just got canned?"

Her ex looked at her and shrugged slightly. "No... I just felt like I owed ya."

"How long, Markie?" she wondered. "When did all this start?"

"What difference does it make?" he asked.

"How long?" she insisted.

"Eight months."

"Oh, my God," Goldie moaned as fresh tears flooded her eyes. *"Oh, my God!"*

Markie rose and walked over to the counter that separated the kitchen from the living room.

"Look, I'm really sorry about this. I've tried to make things as painless as possible with—y'know—the apartment, money, and car. But, there's no good way to do this kind of thing."

"I dunno," she disagreed. "You're doin' a pretty

bang-up job of tellin' me you've been bangin' someone else."

She paused a moment to try to control her avalanche of hurt. "And, uh... so, I-I guess you're pretty serious about this, eh?" she asked, swallowing hard. "I mean, you moved all my stuff out."

"Yeah," he nodded. "It's serious... actually... we're gonna get married."

Goldie's hurt suddenly shifted into anger.

"*What?*" she asked, open-mouthed. "I'm with you seven years! I lost a baby, lost my sister, I supported ya every step of the way with the family! And now, *now,* after eight months of sneakin' around, you're gettin' married? Just like that?"

"Hey—when it's right, it's right," Markie justified.

"And what am I? Miss Wrong of this year, last year, the year before that?"

"C'mon, Goldie."

"Why her?" she persisted. "What's she got that I don't?"

"Don't do this."

"*No!* I wanna know. I mean, I get that her ol' man is Charley DiVarno, but there's gotta be more to it than that."

He shook his head. "This isn't helpful."

"Gee, Markie. You just Hiroshimaed my life. I wanna know!

"You wanna know?" he asked, raising his intensity.

"*Yeah, I wanna know!*"

"Alright! She's educated for one thing. She's gonna get a master's in business. That'll be very helpful."

"And what? I haven't been? Who double-checks your books? Who reminds you of important names and dates when you ask? Who told you to get a spare condo in this buildin' for your shit in case the cops showed up with a search warrant?"

"She's classy."

"Classy? She dresses like a garage sale!"

"All college girls dress that way," Markie defended. "Plus, she's a natural blonde."

"I take care of my roots every four weeks, and I'm waxed everywhere else. What's the difference?"

"The difference is she don't sound like a beer vendor at Yankee Stadium!" Markie argued, raising his voice and getting agitated.

"You sound exactly the same, Bronx! *Get over it!*"

"It's done!" Markie yelled, raising his hands with finality and taking a few steps back into the living room. "I want this. Kristen wants this. Both Frank and Charley have blessed it. It allows New York and Chicago to join forces and expand into new territories. We're talkin' millions and millions of dollars."

"You sayin' it's just business?"

"No. It's the whole package!" Markie declared. He took a breath to calm down before continuing.

"I love her, Goldie. With you, I-I—"

"What?

He hesitated, then spat out the answer. "I've outgrown you. Okay?"

This last comment really cut her to the quick. She looked at him bitterly while mascara from her eyes caused black streams of regret to run down her cheeks.

"You lied to me," she said with clenched teeth. "You *lied* to me, *cheated* on me for months, then moved me out of my own home while I was burying an uncle and consoling a grieving aunt. *You stole my home, Markie!*"

"Uh, I hate to be obvious, but this isn't your home," he reminded. "My name's on the deed. And I didn't have to set you up with the generous package I did."

"I'm talkin' to Frank about this," she threatened with a pointing finger.

"No. You're not! I told ya, he's given his blessing."

"What? You don't want me to embarrass you?"

"I don't want you to embarrass *yourself*," he countered. "Look, take the package. You don't have to move back in with your mother, you can mend fences with your sister, you can even take the cash and car and drive back out to Vegas if you want. Make a fresh start."

"You're a real bastard, you know that?"

"Goldie, one way or another, you're leavin' the picture."

"What? Now you're threatenin' me?"

"You're *not* going to Frank!" he reiterated.

She turned and hurried toward the front door, forgetting about her tote, wallet, and luggage.

"Oh, *c'mon!*" Markie called. "At least go look at the apartment. Here—" he said, returning to the counter between the living room and kitchen for a pencil and sticky note. "Lemme give you the keys and address."

She ignored him and opened up the front door, leaving her condo keys on the foyer table.

After she slammed the door, Markie continued writing.

"She's takin' it well," he muttered, sarcastically.

Out in the corridor, there was a hallway table across from the elevator with a leafy artificial fern on it. When Markie opened the condo door to chase after Goldie with the sticky note in one hand and a set of keys in the other, his eyes flew open, then he quickly ducked back inside and slammed the door just as the thrown fern smashed into it.

A minute later, Goldie arrived back in the lobby. Her face was a mess from running mascara, her eyes and nose were red, and she was teetering back and forth on the edges of wailing sorrow and seething anger. Stepping off the elevator, Bruno and Larry were both standing at the reception counter and staring at her.

"I'm really sorry, Miss Maraschino," Larry offered.

"You both knew?" she asked, wiping her nose on her sleeve. "What am I sayin'? Of *course* you both knew." She looked at Larry. "I've known you for about a year..." Then her eyes turned to the larger man. "But you, Bruno. You've known me forever. You went to school with my sister. You couldn't have given me the courtesy of a heads-up?"

"Take the package, Goldie," he said simply.

She looked at Bruno, then at Larry, then shook her head.

"Welcome home, Goldie," she said to herself, heading toward the front door. "Welcome home."

Once outside, she crossed Mercer Street and hurriedly walked two blocks before the cold and drizzle started to affect her legs, hands, and wet face. She realized everything was in her tote: money, gloves, ID, and cell phone. She also realized she had no idea where she was going or what she was going to do. She had an older sister named Ellen in Upper Montclair, New Jersey, thirteen miles away. But she highly disapproved of the criminal element Goldie associated with and had cut off all communication with her. They had recently seen each other at her Uncle Luke's funeral in Las Vegas, but Ellen had nothing but harsh words for her at the funeral home.

"Markie Santina sells drugs," she'd said accusingly. "He extorts money, sells stolen merchandise, and he kills people, Goldie. He *kills* people! If you're with him, you're no better!"

Then there was her mother, Carla, who lived in the Bronx. But she didn't make much money, lived humbly, and, frankly, Goldie didn't want to return to the same small bedroom and woman who pelted her with Catholic guilt. She loved her mom, but she didn't want to go back to the same circumstances she had been in at seventeen. She also had a father, Tom. But he had remarried and moved to Pittsburgh, and she hadn't spoken to him in two years. Any friends she had were either wives or girlfriends of Markie's crew, but now she'd be ostracized. So, she finally stopped, looked around at the gray sky, realized how wet and cold she was, and decided to go back to the condo, get her tote, and at least go look at the apartment.

You don't have a single damn option, she thought. *You stupid, stupid bitch!*

Defeated, she slowly turned around and started to walk back toward Mercer Street, sniffling, wiping her eyes, swallowing snot, and trying to think of something to say to Markie that would give her at least a morsel of dignity. She wished she hadn't worn stilettos. She wished she had a hat and gloves and had not worn such a high skirt. She was so absorbed in her thoughts that when she got to Mercer Street and started to cross, she didn't even notice the speeding dark blue Mazda going by. She walked right into its rear quarter panel as it passed. With a dull thud, the impact spun Goldie Maraschino around, and then she tumbled to the pavement, critically injured.

Two

LIKE THE CHERRY

When Goldie's green eyes slowly opened, she had no idea how much time had passed. She remembered being struck by a car on Mercer Street. She remembered pain like running into a brick wall—but, after that, nothing. Now, she was lying on her back, and her eyes were slowly focusing on an overhead light fixture in a plaster ceiling she didn't recognize. The lights were off, but there was enough daylight peeking in from the edges of the drawn curtains to give her an idea of the place. The room wasn't very big. But it wasn't a hospital room. It was more like a room in a boarding house. She was lying in a single bed with a patchwork quilt covering her. She slowly propped herself up by her elbows and looked around the unfamiliar room. Beyond the foot of the bed was a dresser with a rounded mirror above it. To the left was a small table with a chair that was supposed to serve as a desk, but the table had no drawers. She also noticed an overcoat tossed over the seat of the chair, and a purse sitting on top of the coat. There was a hard plastic case on the table.

"Where the hell am I?" she quietly asked. "Why aren't I dead? Why don't I hurt? This can't be the new apartment... unless Markie rented me out some grandma's attic."

There was definitely something off about the room. The furniture looked like antiques, except nothing was scratched or worn. The wallpaper was decidedly retro. It was a floral pattern of pink and red roses that seemed to belong in another time, but there was no faded look to it. Slowly pulling the quilt off her and swinging her legs out of bed, Goldie realized that not only was she pain-free, she was also wearing a one-piece ivory slip with thin shoulder straps that broke about two inches below the knee.

"What is this?" she asked herself.

She slowly stood up, then, seeing an impression underneath the slip below her waist, she raised the garment to her stomach and looked down.

"What the hell is *this*, like, Sheena, Queen of the Jungle?" she gawked.

She looked up and saw a push-button light switch on the wall near a door and walked over to push it. As the overhead lights clicked on, she drank in the old-fashioned look of the room. The fixture above her head had three clear bulbs, each one surrounded by frosted glass that looked like a flower. Violets, she decided.

She shook her head, not understanding. "Toto, I

don't think we're in Kansas anymore. Who decorated this place? Auntie Em?"

She took a few wandering steps around the room and caught her reflection in the round mirror above the dresser. Her hair was still the same length, about five inches past her shoulders, but it was no longer blonde. It was her natural dark-brown color. It hadn't been that color since she was sixteen.

Touching her hair with her fingertips, she suddenly heard movement just outside her door and went over to investigate. Turning a glass doorknob, she discovered a short man with a little pot belly in his mid-forties walking by in a red bathrobe and slippers. He was in a hallway with wallpaper that featured large pothos leaves, and he carried a leather toiletry case. He had a fringe of brown hair around his otherwise bald head and a damp white towel draped over his shoulders. Seeing Goldie, he suddenly stopped.

"You're wearing a robe," she announced, surprised.

He looked her over. "You're wearing a slip," he said, equally surprised.

"*Why are you wearing a bathrobe?*" she demanded with a pointing finger. She was so intense that the man was a little intimidated.

"People usually wear 'em after, y'know, a bath. Or, a shower," he feebly explained.

She looked at the man again, then to her right down the hallway. There were four other doors with numbers on them, two on each side. The number on the outside of her doorway read 9. At the end of the hall was an open door that led to a bathroom.

"Where am I?" she asked.

"Sparkledove," the man replied, puzzled that she didn't know.

"What's a Sparkledove?" she pressed. "Sounds like a Britney Spears perfume."

"It's a town... and this is the Sparkledove Arms."

"What? Like a hotel?"

"Exactly like a hotel," the man replied.

Goldie looked at the short man for another second or two suspiciously, then abruptly closed her door. She had no idea where Sparkledove was or who the man might be. She was thoroughly confused. But after a few more moments, she came to a decision:

"I gotta pee."

She looked around and saw a suitcase and a pair of black shoes with two-inch heels next to the wall where the head of her bed was. On the wall above the suitcase were two hooks. There were three empty wire hangers hanging on one hook, and a dress and underwear hanging on the other. This was apparently her closet, since the room didn't have any other door except the one that led out into the hallway.

"I must be dead," she groaned to herself, scratching her head and picking up the suitcase. Like everything else in the room, the style of the luggage was dated, as if it were seventy to eighty years old. But, like everything else, it didn't show much wear.

She tossed the bag onto her bed, clicked it open,

and looked inside. Right on top of the neatly packed bag was a yellow cloth robe, a toiletry kit, and a medium-sized towel. Underneath were two folded dresses, three blouses, two pairs of slacks, bras and underwear, nylons, and a pair of walking shoes. All long out of fashion.

"I *am* dead," she concluded. "Hell is a place with shared bathrooms and clothing designed by Eleanor Roosevelt."

Goldie put on the robe, took the towel and a toiletry kit, then ventured into the hallway to use the bathroom at its end. She discovered she was on the second floor of a three-story building. She also discovered the toilet in the bathroom had a pull chain instead of a handle, and the water tank was nestled up against the ceiling with a pipe that connected to the toilet. She had every reason in the world to be addled and panic-stricken, but having lived with Markie Santina for so many years, she was used to concealing her emotions amidst the unusual and stressful. Like the time Bennie the Bone was escorted out of their building by Bruno and taken for a ride from which he would never return. Or three different occasions when she had to submit to a full-body cavity search in police stations. Considering these Soprano-like episodes, she figured she would get answers sooner or later and decided to go with the flow.

Within fifteen minutes, Goldie had used the bathroom, returned to her room, and put on the most stylish of her dresses: a black button-up short-sleeve dress with small white daisies on it. She combed her hair and put on some red lipstick that was in her toiletry bag. Then, taking a deep, fortifying breath, she left her room, turned left in the hallway, and went to its end, where she turned right and found a stairway. She went down the stairs to discover it led into the main lobby of what the man in the red bathrobe had referred to as the Sparkledove Arms. It was an odd place. Like her bedroom, the lobby was decorated with out-of-date furniture that didn't look old. There was a circular crimson sofa in the middle of the lobby with a high, 360-degree back. Looking right, there was a dark wooden reception counter with ornate carvings of wildlife on its face and a couple of dozen square mailboxes affixed to the wall behind the counter for room keys and messages. Across the lobby, to her left, were a pair of open French doors with sheer curtains that led into a twelve-table restaurant. It was half full, and all the patrons were dressed like extras from a Humphrey Bogart film. There was sconce lighting on the wood-paneled lobby walls, tastefully positioned here and there. They were fashioned like three candles, with the tallest being in the middle, and the bulbs were shaped like candle flames. Over in a corner of the lobby, not far from the reception counter, was something Goldie had only seen in black-and-white movies. It was a wooden phone booth complete with an accordion-type door and glass windows.

"Good morning, Miss Maraschino," she heard a voice call.

She looked toward the reception counter and saw a woman in her early fifties standing behind it with her blonde hair pinned up in a beehive hairstyle. She wore glasses on her nose connected to a delicate silver chain around her neck. The name tag on her green-and-white polka dot blouse read "Maddie."

"How was your evening?" she asked, smiling. "Was your room comfortable?"

Goldie approached the counter a little hesitantly.

"Y-you know me?" she asked.

"Of course. Room 9. Miss Maraschino. Like the cherry," Maddie giggled.

"And, uh... w-when exactly did I check in here?" Goldie inquired.

"Silly," Maddie teased. "You just got here yesterday. Did somebody have one too many hot toddies last night?"

It was at this point that Goldie noticed the rack of postcards at the end of the counter. They featured a photograph of a western-style main street with printing over it that said: "Greetings from Sparkledove, Colorado."

"Colorado?" she blurted, astonished. "I-I'm in *Colorado?*"

"Sparkledove, Colorado," Maddie verified. "The perfect place for Christmas."

"*Are you shittin' me?*" Goldie bellowed. "*I'm in Colorado? Freakin' Colorado!*"

She turned and saw the push-open double front

doors just eight feet or so beyond the circular sofa, then hurried over to them and went outside.

"You're going to want a coat, dear!" Maddie called after her.

Stepping outside onto the sidewalk, Goldie suddenly stopped, amazed by everything around her. The front doors of the Sparkledove Arms emptied onto a main street, a little less than a quarter mile long, and a town that looked like something straight out of the Old West. The sidewalk where she stood was paved, but that was just in front of the hotel. The rest of the town had plank sidewalks. Some of the buildings were brick with dates on their fronts that read 1866 or 1870. Others were wood and featured squared front facades that hid a cable roof. All were packed together on a main thoroughfare with five cross streets. The collection of businesses ranged from a gift store to a general store, grocery store, bookstore, real estate office, gem store, and others. As if the old-timey look of the town wasn't enough, just beyond the east and west ends of this main street were mountains. Mountains that dramatically shot up several thousand feet at a thirty-degree angle or steeper. As her eyes scanned them, she saw patches of snow at the higher elevations.

"How the hell did I get here?" she yelled. *"I'm in a John Denver nightmare!"*

There were cars and trucks parked here and there, and a couple even rolled past her on the main street, but they were all vintage antiques.

"This-this must be one of them livin' history towns

like that place in Virginia," she decided. "What its name? Williamstown. No. Williamsburg. Colonial Williamsburg!"

Even though she was cognizant of the thirty-six-degree temperature, she ignored the cold, crossed a side street, then stepped up onto a wooden plank sidewalk, stunned by everything around her. She didn't understand how she had woken up in Colorado. Or why she wasn't injured after being struck by a car. Or why everything around her was from a different time. She didn't understand—until she came to a trash container outside of a store and noticed the date of a discarded *Denver Post* newspaper that was sitting in it. It read: Tuesday, November 24, 1942.

"Whaaat?" she exclaimed. "*What?*"

Goldie plucked up the newspaper and read the date again. Then goose bumps appeared on her arms, and she started to tremble. Maybe it was from the cold, or maybe it was the realization that something unbelievable and unexplainable had happened to her. It was a *Twilight Zone* moment. She glanced up from the newspaper and looked around—*really* looked around—at the town again. In the gem store window, she saw a poster that read: "Buy War Bonds." In the grocery store window, she saw a hand-painted sign that announced: "Butter on Friday." She took a few steps down the wooden sidewalk until she came to an artisan pottery store window and saw a picture of FDR on display in the window.

"Jesus Christ!" she said under her breath. "The clothes really *are* designed by Eleanor Roosevelt!"

Letting the newspaper slip from her hand, she wandered down the sidewalk to a shop called Clara's Gifts that had a nice Christmas display in its front window. Now quite aware of the cold, she decided to step inside.

The wooden floor of Clara's was old and squeaked when she entered, but the store was cozy and comfortable. There were glass Christmas tree ornaments, freshly made pine wreaths, shelves of Santa dolls, a display of angels, a cabinet featuring hand-painted Russian nesting dolls, and an assortment of other gifts. There was also an old Philco radio on a shelf playing Bing Crosby's "White Christmas." In a back corner of the store, a woman in her mid to late sixties stood on a ladder with her back to Goldie. She was quite fit for her age, with a dancer's figure and mostly white hair that was nearly as long as Goldie's and tied into a ponytail. She had just begun to hang some holiday roping from the top of a shelving unit, but stopped and started to come down the ladder, hearing someone enter the store.

"We don't open until 10 a.m.," she said. "But if you need something right now, I guess I can make an exception." She turned and saw her visitor. "Say, honey, what are you doing running around in short sleeves without a coat? You wanna catch your death?"

"I think I already have," Goldie replied vaguely. "J-j-just bear with me a second," she asked. "I'm... I'm in Colorado. Right?"

"Right," the lady smiled. Like everyone else Goldie had seen, she was dressed in period clothing.

"And—do you mind me askin' today's date?"

"Wednesday, the 25th," the woman replied. She had nice green eyes like Goldie's and a kind face.

"Wednesday, the 25th?" Goldie repeated, hoping the woman would finish.

"Wednesday, November 25th, the day before Thanksgiving," the woman replied, now looking at her concerned.

"Wednesday, November 25th, in the year of our lord?"

"1942," the woman answered. "Are you alright, honey?"

Goldie's eyes widened. "You're not kiddin' me, right? I-I mean, this isn't one of them theme towns where everybody dresses up in historical clothing and plays their part like in a movie?"

The woman looked her over, now truly worried.

"Sweetie, I think you'd better have a cup of coffee and sit down. You seem to be a little confused." She went over to a chair that had a collection of rag dolls on it, set them on the floor, then brought the chair over to her. She was wearing slightly baggy slacks, a plain blouse, and a gold cardigan sweater.

"Here. You sit down. My name's Clara. I've got a pot of coffee going on the heating plate in the back. I'll fix you a nice cup. You want a little cream with that?

Sorry, but I don't have any sugar. A lot of people don't right now."

The visitor decided to take the advice and sit in the chair provided.

"I'm Goldie," she said, plopping down. "I know this is gonna sound funny, but I don't know how I got here, Clara," she confessed. Her eyes started to become moist. "I-I don't know how I got to this place... to this time. Yesterday, I thought I was dyin'... and today—I woke up here."

"Sshh," the shop owner said, like a mother soothing a child. "I'm sure we can figure it out." She patted her guest on the shoulder, then turned and walked toward the back of the store while Bing Crosby continued to sing on the radio. "Believe it or not," she said as she went, "the exact same thing has happened to me."

Goldie looked up at her. "Really?"

"Really. I was down the street at Clancy's having a drink with some friends a few years ago, and the next thing I know, it's two days later, and I'm over in Golden. And it's not from just alcohol, either. Blackouts can be brought on by extreme stress. You lose someone overseas, honey? Army? Navy? Marci Hurst, here in town, lost her oldest, Jerry, and she walked around for weeks in a daze. She totally lost all track of time. He was in the Navy and died at Midway, but she was never really sure if..."

Goldie's shoulders slumped as Clara continued to tell her story about Marci Hurst's son from the back of the store. But Clara's empathetic tales had nothing to do with the bizarre events that were happening to her. So, she slowly rose from her chair, at a loss, then exited the store.

Back on the wooden sidewalk, she hadn't gone but a few more storefronts further down the street when a 1939 black-and-white Ford with a red bubble light on its roof and a decal on both front doors that said "Sheriff's Department" rolled up to meet her. A man in a brown suede jacket got out of the car. He was maybe her age or a few years older, had short-cropped blond hair and blue eyes, and stood at five feet eleven. He wore a tan police uniform with a matching shirt and slacks and had a star-shaped badge under his open jacket. He also wore black cowboy boots. He wasn't wearing a tie or a policeman's cap, and he didn't carry a gun. As he got out of the car and came toward her, Goldie noticed he walked with a slight limp.

"Oh, Christ," she sighed under her breath, not liking cops in the present, past, or any other time.

"Howdy," he drawled in a low voice.

"Wow. Very *Westworld*," she replied, underwhelmed.

"Excuse me?" he asked.

"Nothin'. What can I do for you, officer?"

"I thought maybe I could do something for *you*," he replied with a little smile. "Drive you back to the hotel? It's pretty cold to be wandering around in short sleeves."

He spoke slowly like a cowpoke in a Tex Ritter movie.

She looked down the street toward the Sparkledove Arms, then back at him.

"How do you know I'm stayin' at the hotel?" she asked.

"Maddie, the owner, gave my office a call," he replied, sticking his hands into his jacket pockets. "Said you got up this morning and seemed mixed up about where you were. If you're ill, being out in this weather without a coat isn't going to help." He stepped over to the driver's side door of his police cruiser and opened it for her. "May I?" he asked, offering her a ride.

"Sure," she shrugged, her arms slapping the sides of her legs.

"Good... wouldn't do to have our most important visitor come down with the flu," he said as she climbed in.

"What does that mean?" she asked. But he didn't answer. He shut the door, then turned to round the car. As he did, Clara came out of her gift store with folded arms over her gold cardigan sweater, apparently looking for Goldie. The officer raised his chin and called out, "I've got her, Clara." She nodded, smiled at Goldie in the car, then went back into her store.

As soon as the officer got behind the wheel and closed his door, Goldie started her interrogation.

"Whatdoya mean, I'm your most important visitor?"

"Well, everybody's excited you're here," he explained, starting the engine. "This kind of thing doesn't happen to us every day."

"Yeah, well, it don't happen to *me* every day, either," she cracked.

He put the car in gear, and they started to head down the street. Goldie looked around for the seat belt and shoulder strap, but there wasn't one. There weren't any in the car at all.

"So, why am I special?" she asked.

"You know, writing a feature story for *Adventure Escape Magazine*. That's big doings for Sparkledove."

Goldie wrinkled her brow and looked at him.

"What're you talkin' about?"

"You're Miss Maraschino, right? Like the cherry?"

"Yeah?"

"So, you're the writer with *Adventure Escape Magazine*." He glanced at her. "I mean, that *is* right, isn't it?"

Goldie tossed her hands up slightly. "Why not?"

They were quiet for another few moments until they pulled up to the paved sidewalk in front of the hotel and came to a stop. The officer put the car in park and turned to her.

"Look, you seem to have other things on your mind. Maybe it's none of my business, but if you want to talk about it, I'm a pretty good listener." He extended his hand. "Name's Eli Johnson. I'm the sheriff here, but don't be too impressed. I'm the entire police force, and I don't think anyone else in town wanted the job."

Goldie took his hand and shook it half-heartedly, but she was really paying attention to something else. Down a side street off the main thoroughfare, she saw a bus from the Rocky Mountain Bus Company idling on the side of the road.

"What's that?" she asked.

"Bus to Denver," Sheriff Johnson replied. "Comes in twice a day and sits there for twenty minutes waiting to take on passengers. Once in the morning and once in the late afternoon."

"Denver? How far is Denver?"

"About thirty-five miles." He looked at her, puzzled. "D-didn't you come in from Denver on yesterday afternoon's bus? I mean, that's what Maddie told me."

Making a decision, Goldie opened the passenger side door. "Thanks for the lift," she said, getting out.

She shut the car door and hurried into the hotel, leaving an intrigued and slightly confused Sheriff Johnson sitting in his car.

"Okay then..." he said acceptingly to no one. He put two fingers on the side of his forehead and saluted in Goldie's direction. "See ya."

Three

DENVER

Although she couldn't explain what was going on, Goldie wasn't accepting it, either. At this early hour in the day, she would've preferred to have awakened in a hospital room, pumped up on drugs and incapacitated. At least that was logical. Expected. What was happening now was too strange. Too weird. She got it in her head that if she could just get out of this small town called Sparkledove, everything would somehow be rectified. She was still clinging to the belief that the community had to be a living history town like Colonial Williamsburg. If that were the case, the sooner she got out of town, the sooner a more reasonable explanation would be revealed.

"Everything alright, Miss Maraschino?" Maddie called out as Goldie hurried through the lobby. "I hope you're not upset that I phoned Sheriff Johnson. I just wanted to make sure you were okay."

Goldie ignored the explanation and hurried up the stairs, remembering that when she left her room, she hadn't even thought to look for a room key or lock her door. But she needn't have worried. When she tried her door, she discovered it was unlocked, and everything inside was just as she had left it. Apparently, Sparkledove was a place of low crime.

Seeing the purse sitting on the overcoat that had been placed on the seat of the chair by the desk, she shut her door, went over to it, and opened it. Inside, she found her room key, plane tickets, sixty dollars and twenty-two cents in cash, and several business cards that read: Karen Maraschino, Senior Writer, *Adventure Escape Magazine* with a Columbus, Ohio address.

"Columbus?" she said to herself, looking at the cards. "I don't know anyone in Columbus. I've never been to Ohio. I've never even liked that song by Crosby, Stills, Nash & Young. And why a writer?"

Goldie never had any aspirations to be a journalist, although she enjoyed writing in her diaries. She started when she was twelve, and it was a leftover habit from her pre-teen days. Digging deeper into the purse, she found an operator's license for a car that required no picture, a compact, lipstick, hairbrush, bobby pins, several folded-up Kleenex, and a small notebook with two sharpened pencils.

She looked at the plastic case sitting on top of her narrow table that was serving as a desk. Opening it, she found a Remington Envoy portable typewriter with fifteen pieces of carbon-backed typing paper inside.

"This just makes no damn sense," she sighed.

Leaving her suitcase and typewriter behind, she put on her overcoat, grabbed her purse, then left her room, locking the door with her room key. Going back downstairs and through the lobby, she saw that Maddie was behind the counter talking to another customer, so she hurried out the front door, hoping her departure wouldn't be noticed.

The bus was still idling, waiting to take on any passengers. It was dark red with white mountains painted on the side, and like everything else in town, it was vintage. Goldie paid the driver one dollar for her fare. The bus left promptly at 9:10 a.m., and there were only four other passengers on board. She breathed a sigh of relief when the vehicle turned onto Highway 70 heading east, but if she hoped to literally drive out of November 1942 and back into the present, it wasn't happening. The highway was a two-lane, and she saw one old car after another drive past, going in the opposite direction. It was too many vehicles to be part of some theme town. Then there were the houses, stores, and occasional billboards she passed. Everything was consistent. Everything was from the 1940s or earlier. Goldie's arms bristled with another wave of goose bumps, and she fought back tears as she realized that somehow, through some unexplained phenomenon, she'd been transported back in time. Even when the Denver skyline came into view, there were no sprawling traffic cloverleafs, cell phone towers, and the skyscrapers weren't much taller than ten stories. It was a totally dated world filled with painted signs on the side of barns for Nehi Soda Pop and Barbasol Shaving Cream.

The interior of the Denver bus terminal was a flurry of activity. When Goldie came through the arrival door, people were coming and going for the holiday. Men wore suits and ties, women wore dresses, and soldiers on leave were in dress uniforms. Everyone wore or carried a winter coat. The place was large and spacious. It had a twenty-foot-high ceiling with big circular light fixtures hanging down on metal poles, and there were several sets of wooden benches where six people could sit facing one direction, while six more seated behind them could sit facing another. The place was upscale and cosmopolitan, and strikingly different from the seedier bus stations of the current day. It was also smoky. Cigarette smoke drifted high in the air throughout the place as people puffed away on Lucky Strikes and Chesterfields. Over by the double front doors, she saw a wooden scaffolding where two painters were starting to paint with five-gallon buckets of light-orange paint.

She weaved through the people and most of the station, then sat down at the end of one of the long wooden benches close to the front doors and scaffolding.

Now what do I do? she thought. "This can't be

real?" she muttered. "No TikTok, *People Magazine*, no *Keepin' Up With The Kardashians*."

She noticed she was sitting next to a three-foot-tall can-like ashtray and, in it, was a broken piece of glass from a discarded soda bottle. Formulating a desperate idea, she picked up the piece of glass and gazed around.

"I've got to be dreamin'," she said quietly, shaking her head. "I've gotta be in a coma... time to wake up, girl."

Without hesitation, she took the piece of glass in her right hand and quickly brought it across the palm of her left. The pain was immediate, and the blood followed a moment later.

"*Shiiiit!*" she cried. "*That hurt!*"

Several people turned and looked at her, but she ignored them, dropped the glass to the floor, and hurriedly dug into her purse for the stash of Kleenex she'd seen earlier.

As she was doing so, she saw someone in her peripheral vision offer her something. She looked up to see a white handkerchief being held by an African American maintenance man who worked at the bus station. She could tell he was maintenance by his gray uniform, lack of an outdoor coat, and the push broom he held in his other hand.

"It's clean," he said.

She took the handkerchief, mumbled "Thanks," and wrapped it tightly around her bleeding palm.

"Go to the bathroom and clean that off," he said. "I'll go fetch the first aid kit."

He didn't order her so much as simply announce the next steps that needed to be done. He was in his mid-thirties, had a little gray in his hair, and seemed neither overly friendly nor uncompassionate.

Reconciled to her situation, Goldie rose, went to the ladies' bathroom, and returned a few minutes later. When she did, the African American man was sitting in the seat next to where she'd been sitting with a metallic box that had a red cross on it.

"Sit yourself down," he invited, "and I'll fix you up."

She said "Thank you" again, sat down, and held out her left hand. The stranger produced a silver tube of antibacterial cream.

"This might smart some," he warned.

He gently removed the bloody handkerchief, then tenderly applied some white cream. As he did, he spoke quietly so others wouldn't hear.

"Saw what you did," he said. "Why'd you cut yourself like that?"

She winced from the sting of the cream, but he blew on her palm to relieve it.

"You've heard of the expression: 'Pinch me, I must be dreamin'?'" she asked. "Same idea."

He nodded slightly as he produced a roll of gauze from the kit and started to carefully wrap her hand.

"I'm in a nightmare," she admitted. "Yesterday, I

was in one world, and today I'm in this. It's like a time-shift reality."

"I see," he replied.

He continued to wrap the gauze firmly until he thought the wound was properly protected, then got a small pair of scissors from the kit and cut it.

"It's okay if you don't know what I'm talkin' about," Goldie offered. "You're a nice man, and I appreciate the help."

Right at that moment, there was an announcement over the PA for a bus departing for Boulder, Loveland, Fort Collins, and then Cheyanne. The maintenance man finished dressing Goldie's wound and didn't speak until the announcement was over.

"Some years ago," he finally said. "I served in the Great War. Went from Denver to Mississippi for basic trainin', then on to France. Before I knew it, I was crouchin' in a mud-filled trench, with men screamin', dyin', and other men tryin' to kill Germans. I said to myself: 'Yesterday, I was in one world, and today I'm in this. It's like a time-shift reality.' I might've even cut my hand with my bayonet just to make sure everything was real."

Goldie looked at him, intrigued.

"So, what'd you do?"

"I adapted to my surroundings, learned from others around me, and decided to survive, to beat the hell I was in. I don't know what's goin' on with you, young lady. But I know if you want to, you can adapt and survive, too."

She looked at him appreciatively. "I'm Goldie. What's your name?"

"Gerome!" a man's voice called. "What do you think you're doin'?"

They were interrupted by a paunchy white man in his late forties. He had a swoosh of blondish hair that came from the back of his head and was combed in a circular style to cover the top and sides of his balding head. He wore slacks and a sports jacket, with a white shirt and a blue bow tie. He seemed very unhappy that the maintenance man was sitting.

"Is this boy bothering you, ma'am?" he asked Goldie.

She was immediately taken aback that the man had referred to her caregiver as "boy," but then remembered it was 1942.

"No," she said, as Gerome closed the first aid kit and silently rose, "I-I cut myself on some glass, and this man was sweet enough to tend my wound."

The man in the bow tie looked down and saw the glass on the floor.

"Oh... I'm terribly sorry, ma'am. You shouldn't have to deal with sharp objects like that in my terminal. I'm Bradley Hammersville, the manager here." Then he turned and spoke curtly to the black man.

"Gerome, get that glass cleaned up right now. Then get into the men's room. A soldier got sick in there."

"Yes, Mr. Hammersville," the other man said

contritely. He started to walk away. As he did, Goldie called out to him.

"Hey, Gerome. Thank you. For the first aid *and* the kind words."

Gerome half-smiled, then turned and went on his way.

"Once again, ma'am, I'm deeply sorry," the manager said.

"Fuhgeddaboudit," she replied with her Bronx accent. "But tell me, when's the next bus for Sparkledove?"

"Oh, that won't be until later this afternoon. Doesn't depart until 3:30 p.m."

She looked at a clock over the front door. It was a few minutes before 10:00 a.m. She had five and a half hours to kill.

"Okay. Point me in the direction of the library," she requested.

It was a seventy-cent cab ride to the Denver Library, but the journey was worth the effort. Goldie decided to take Gerome's advice and adapt to her surroundings. She read several articles about Sparkledove, Colorado, and she also looked at back issues of *Adventure Escape Magazine*, which, oddly enough, had numerous articles written by her. The magazine came out every other month, six times a year, and was dedicated to finding unexpected and delightful places in the country. She assumed since it was on the verge of Christmas, the town of 1,002 residents must be a special place for the holidays. She read that the Old-West-style main street was actually called River Street, and there were over ninety Victorian-style homes situated on side streets. Most of these had been carefully preserved under the auspices of the Sparkledove Historical Society and its President, Charles Banyan, who also happened to be the mayor as well as owner of the city's only real estate company.

Back in the 1860s, just after the Civil War, silver was discovered in the mountains that lay to the east and west of where the town now stood. Since there was a natural flat piece of land with a river in between these mountains, Sparkledove became a booming mining town. Within ten years, it had a population of over four thousand people and mines that ranged from a major operator to several one and two-man claims. The city got its unique name from a combination of the silver that came out of the mines and the cooing Eurasian Collared Doves that favored the tall, scraggly pines so prominent on the surrounding mountains. By the early 1880s, however, a series of events began that all but destroyed the town. In 1881, a mining explosion killed thirty-one men. In 1882, large deposits of both silver and gold were discovered in more accessible areas closer to Denver, and people lost interest in Sparkledove's remote location. In 1884, a dam collapsed upstate, sending a wall of surging water to dramatically flood the river running through town, and over the course of one terrible night, nearly half the city's houses were either seriously damaged or destroyed, and eight souls lost their lives. By 1900, Sparkledove's population had diminished to less than four hundred residents.

Goldie continued her studies of both the city and *Adventure Escape Magazine* until 2:30 p.m. Then she went to a department store across the street, used the bathroom, got some chewing gum and a candy bar, and made a haberdashery purchase. She caught a cab back to the bus station, where she arrived at 3:12. The crowds from earlier that morning had diminished, and only a dozen or so people were sitting on the benches or standing and smoking. When she entered the station, Gerome, the maintenance man, was mopping the linoleum floor around the scaffolding where the painters were working to get any drippings that might've fallen. He smiled at her when she entered.

"Ay, Gerome," she greeted. "How's it goin'?"

"Be a little careful," he advised. "The floor's wet over here."

"I will."

"Back again, eh?"

"Yeah. The bus I want doesn't leave until 3:30."

"How's the hand?"

"Throbs a little. But I'll survive." She stepped over to him and handed him a small blue paper bag from the department store.

"What's this?" he asked.

"A set of three new white handkerchiefs."

"Oh, now—you shouldn't have done that."

"There's lots of things I shouldn't have done," she quipped. "Joey Totino, in the ninth grade, for instance. *This,* I shoulda done."

"Well, it's awful kind of you, ma'am. Thank you."

"Call me Goldie," she smiled.

She walked down to the ticket counter at the far wall and purchased a ticket back to Sparkledove. She still had no idea how she'd turned into a time traveler, but figured there must be a reason why she woke up in that particular town and was trying her best to learn and adapt.

After she'd gotten her ticket and heard a PA announcement that her bus was now loading at Departing Door Two, she heard a second loud voice echoing throughout the station. She turned and saw Bradley Hammersville, the terminal manager, yelling at Gerome. He was chewing him out for only using water on the floor instead of wax, and Gerome was saying it would be better to wait until the scaffolding was down so he could be sure he got up all of the paint drippings first. "Pour wax over any spilled paint, Mr. Hammersville, and it'll be really hard to get out," he explained. But the paunchy man with the blue bow tie didn't want to hear it. He accused Gerome of being lazy and told him he'd better get his "no good black ass movin' with the wax" or he'd be fired. Goldie didn't like that Hammersville was embarrassing her new friend within the earshot of others. She didn't like how he called Gerome "boy" earlier in the day. And she really didn't like the comb-over of his blondish hair that sat atop his head like a deflated cinnamon roll. She found herself determinedly walking toward the men while two painters were coming down from the scaffolding carrying nearly empty five-gallon paint cans. Hammersfield had by now changed subjects and was complaining about smears on one of the glass front doors. Gerome replied that they were just put there by a little boy who had come into the building with his mother no more than five minutes earlier, and he was going to attend to that next.

"Boy, don't you give me none of your sass!" Hammersfield warned with a pointing finger.

As Goldie came up behind him, she saw that one of the painters had set down his can that held about a quart of leftover light-orange paint. Without hesitation, she picked it up and placed it upside-down over Hammersfield's head.

"He's a veteran, you son of a bitch!" Goldie yelled. "He may work for you, but you sure as shit better give him the respect he deserves! Both as a vet *and* as a man!"

She gave Gerome a quick wink, then turned and started to head for Departing Door Two. Removing the bucket and wiping the paint away from his eyes, a shocked Hammersfield seethed while the two painters laughed hysterically, and Gerome tried his best to keep a straight face.

"He's as orange as a carrot," one painter laughed.

"Or a tangerine," scoffed the other.

"Or Gina Deangelo's tanning spray," Goldie called over her shoulder.

Hammersfield started to go after her, but the painters, both of whom happened to be veterans like Gerome, stood in his way and advised him to drop the matter.

Four

DINNER & THE BRIDGE

Goldie returned from Denver and had just stepped inside the lobby of the Sparkledove Arms when she paused and looked around. "You can check out anytime you like, but you can never leave," she muttered, quoting an old Eagles song.

"Miss Maraschino? I've got a message for you," Maddie called. She rounded the reception counter and dug into the breast pocket of her green-and-white polka dot blouse, producing a folded-up piece of paper.

"Your publisher, Mr. Mitchell, called. He wants you to call as soon as possible. He said it didn't matter how late."

Goldie remembered from studying the back issues of *Adventure Escape Magazine* that the publisher was a man named Owen Mitchell. She took the paper and cracked a small smile. "Okay. Thanks."

"You can use the phone over there," Maddie said, pointing to the wooden phone booth in the corner with the accordion door. "But you're going to need some dimes. C'mon over to the counter, dear, and I'll get you some change."

Goldie followed her across the lobby, but not before smelling some wonderful aromas wafting from the restaurant. She realized, except for the candy bar she'd gotten in Denver, she hadn't eaten all day.

Maddie went behind the counter, opened the cash register, and gave her guest ten dimes. Goldie set her purse on the counter and began digging through it to reimburse Maddie with a dollar bill.

"Oh no, honey. That's quite alright," Maddie smiled with a wave. "Mayor Banyan's taking care of everything."

Goldie paused, remembering her research from earlier. "Charles Banyan?"

"Yes, he stopped by around noon looking for you," Maddie replied. "Where were you all day?"

Goldie decided not to answer and changed subjects. "Say, Maddie, I-I want to apologize for my strange behavior this morning. It doesn't happen often, but I occasionally suffer from short-term memory loss. As you might suspect, it's pretty embarrassing when it occurs, and I'd really appreciate it if you'd keep quiet on the subject and be a little understanding of my condition."

"Mum's the word," Maddie agreed, putting a finger to her lips. "And if you can't remember something, you just ask ol' Maddie, and I'll try to help."

Goldie thanked her, then walked over to the phone

booth, stepped inside, and shut the door. As she did, a man appeared from a back hallway behind the counter and saw Goldie go into the phone booth. He was in his fifties, wore a suit and tie, had a name tag that read "Dean," and had a weathered face from years of hunting and being outside.

"That her?" he asked, leaning into Maddie quietly.

"Uh-huh."

"Everything okay?"

"I'm not sure," Maddie replied, slipping off her glasses and letting them hang from the silver chain around her neck. She looked toward the phone booth, then said confidentially to her co-worker, "She might have a drinking problem."

It took Goldie a couple of moments to figure out what she was supposed to do, having never used a phone booth before or having never seen this particular type of telephone. The phone was a rotary dial with an earpiece for listening and a horn that the user spoke into. When she picked up the earpiece and heard a dial tone, she dropped a dime into the coin slot at the top of the phone, and an operator came on the line a few seconds later. Goldie read the number from the paper Maddie had given her into the horn, and the operator placed the call for her. After her boss, Owen Mitchell, answered his phone, Goldie then had to deposit two more dimes for a three-minute conversation before the two could speak.

"Well, it's about damn time," Mitchell began with an irritability in his voice. "I've been worried about you. It's standard procedure to call once you're on-site, Goldie. You know that. I should've heard from you yesterday."

He called me Goldie, she thought. *He knows my nickname. What else can I learn from him?* she wondered.

"How long have I been workin' for you?" she asked.

"What?"

"How long?"

"I dunno... two years maybe."

"And in all that time, have I ever called in late?"

"Constantly!"

"Oh... well... sorry. You're right. I shoulda called earlier. But I went to the Denver Library today and did some research."

"Well, at least you're on the job," Mitchell said, calming down. "You met our sponsor yet?"

"Charles Banyan?" she assumed. "No. But I hear he came by the hotel today lookin' for me?"

"Don't put him off, Goldie. He paid for your plane, hotel, and meals at the Sparkledove Arms. He expects your full attention and a great three-thousand-word article."

"So much for objectivity, huh?" Goldie mused, starting to piece together how things worked with the magazine.

"We're not the *New York Times Book Review,*" Mitchell noted. "We're a travel magazine where people read about idyllic faraway places we hope they'll visit. This should be a great piece for next year's

December issue. Please, God, let the war be over by then."

"No, not until September of '45," she responded unthinkingly.

"What?" Mitchell asked.

"Uh—a, a guess," she responded quickly. "Just a guess."

"Three more years?" her boss considered. "Geez, I hope you're wrong."

"Yeah. Me, too."

"Don't forget, you're having Thanksgiving dinner tomorrow with Banyan and his family."

"I am? I-I mean, I *am*."

"Okay, Goldie. I just wanted to make sure you arrived safely. Check in with me in a few days. And I do mean *check in*."

"Alright, Owen. Uh, boss—Mr. Mitchell," she stammered, not sure what to call him. She wanted to ask him a dozen more questions. Like, how did a young woman from the Bronx wind up working for a travel magazine in Columbus? She supposed that's where she lived since the concept of working remotely was decades away, but she didn't know. Was she married? Did she have a family? She assumed no because she was in Colorado the day before Thanksgiving, but that was just a guess. Who was this World War II version of Goldie Maraschino? She decided to wait and see if she could subtly extract more information from Mitchell when she checked in again. So, she simply said goodbye, hung up, and thought: *This is the weirdest day of my life. If this is even real life.*

She came out of the phone booth, trying to recall how she knew World War II ended in September of 1945. *I musta seen it on Band of Brothers or somewhere,* she figured. It was too random a fact to remember from a high school history class.

As soon as she stepped out of the booth, the delightful smells from the restaurant beckoned to her again. It was only 4:12 in the afternoon, but she was ready for dinner.

The restaurant of the Sparkledove Arms was a cheery room with light-yellow walls and a fieldstone fireplace that hadn't been lit yet for the dinner guests. The twelve tables that made up the place had clean white linen tablecloths, small vases with a few dried flowers in them, and little salt and pepper shakers in the form of a pilgrim couple from the 1600s.

When Goldie entered, there were only three people in the place: a waitress, Sheriff Eli Johnson, who she had met earlier that morning, and a big, barrel-chested, bearded man in his early sixties who was sitting and chatting with the sheriff.

Seeing the officer, Goldie sighed under her breath, "Great. Andy of Mayberry."

The officer smiled as she entered the restaurant, stopped eating, and wiped his mouth with a napkin as she approached. She felt that not going over to his table would be rude, considering how empty the place was.

"Howdy, Miss Maraschino," he greeted. "How're you feeling?"

"Fine," she answered. She looked at the man sitting with him and extended her hand, not wanting to discuss her morning state of confusion. *Adapt!* she thought.

"Hi. Karen Maraschino from *Adventure Escape Magazine*."

"Hello," the man said, rising to shake her hand. He had calloused hands and a ruddy complexion. His thick, white hair was a little unruly, but it somehow suited his bib overalls, shirt, and work boots covered in dry mud.

"Maraschino?" he asked, "like the cherry?"

"Like the cherry," she confirmed.

"Stu Frey. Like the cooking pan," he joked. He noticed her gauze-wrapped left hand. "What'd you do to your hand?"

"Cut it a little earlier today," she shrugged. "No big deal."

"Maddie keeps a first aid kit behind the counter if you want to borrow it and change the dressing," the sheriff offered.

"Good to know. Thanks. So, Stu, what do you do?"

"I've got a ranch a few miles outside of town."

"Stu supplies all the restaurants with meat," the lawman explained. "Steak, hamburger, roasts. Pork, too."

"*All* the restaurants?" she asked, a little amused,

considering the smallness of Sparkledove. "How many is that?"

"This place, Clancy's Bar & Grill, The Pine River Inn, a bed and breakfast just south of town, and then I supply some individual families in town as well," he replied, eyeing her overcoat. "There are pegs over there on the wall if you want to hang up your coat."

Goldie turned to the waitress. "Is it too early for dinner?"

"No, ma'am," the waitress replied. "The special today is meatloaf and mashed potatoes."

"Then I'm hangin' up my coat," Goldie decided, unbuttoning it and heading toward the pegs.

"Why don't you join Eli?" Stu suggested. "I was in the kitchen dropping off some prime rib for tomorrow, and just sat down to say hello. Some people prefer a nice cut of beef on Thanksgiving instead of turkey. Besides, like everything else, Turkeys are scarce this year unless you're a hunter." He followed her over to the wall pegs and retrieved a heavy coat with a wool collar hanging next to the sheriff's brown suede jacket.

"You do your own processing?" Goldie asked.

"No, but I do my own deliveries afterwards," the big man replied. He slipped on his jacket, then nodded at the sheriff. "See ya tomorrow at dinner, Eli."

"See ya," the sheriff replied, giving him a casual salute with two fingers.

"Nice to meet you, Karen."

"Call me Goldie," she corrected. "Everyone does."

"Goldie. I like that. Happy Thanksgiving, Goldie."

"Happy Thanksgiving," she smiled.

Stu said goodbye to the waitress as well, then turned and left through the lobby. Goldie stepped timidly away from the wall pegs toward Eli's table. "I don't have to sit at your table. I can see you're finished."

"No, please," he gestured. "I'll have dessert while you have dinner. I skipped lunch, so I'm making up for it."

She smiled politely and sat down, even though she didn't want to. She had been practically brainwashed to be suspicious of lawmen from her years with Markie.

"So, you're having Thanksgiving dinner with Stu?" she asked.

"Kind of," he replied, offering no further explanation. He gestured to her left hand. "You sure you're okay?"

"You're pretty obsessed with how I feel."

"Wellll," he drawled in his slow, cowboy way. "This morning, you told people you didn't know where you were or how you got here. Then, you went runnin' around in thirty-degree weather without a coat—"

"I didn't run," she interrupted. "I was—curiously exploring."

"Now you've got gauze wrapped around your hand."

"Not my best day," she admitted.

"You also told Clara that, yesterday, you felt like you were dying."

She recalled what she had said to the lady in the

gift shop while he continued: "And on your first day here, you apparently weren't even here. Nobody saw you."

"God, you're nosy," she observed.

"Occupational hazard," he explained.

The waitress came over to verify Goldie wanted the meatloaf. She did, and she also ordered a Coke. The sheriff ordered pumpkin pie. After the waitress had gone, she responded to the lawman.

"I went to the library in Denver to do some research on Sparkledove," she offered. "At the bus station, I cut my hand on a broken soda bottle. Okay? Happy, Officer?"

"We've got a historical society right here in town," he replied. "It's like a museum."

"Run by the guy who is both its president and the city's mayor. I wanted unbiased research. Regarding my confusion this morning, I occasionally suffer from short-term memory loss. It's usually triggered by a traumatic event."

"Interesting," he said. "Did you recently suffer a traumatic event?"

She hesitated before answering, then decided she had nothing to lose by telling the truth.

"My boyfriend of seven years dumped me for someone new," she admitted. "Some young college girl. Wears clothes that look like they came from a locker room hamper. He'd been cheatin' on me for months, but I just found out about it yesterday."

"Ouch," he empathized. "Yeah, I guess that would

do it. Seven years," he mused. "Must've met him when you were quite young."

"I did."

"I'm sorry... I understand heartbreak. Guess these are heartbreaking times for people all over the world," he said.

"Yeah. That's true," she agreed, realizing he was referring to the war.

The waitress delivered Goldie her Coke and Eli his pie. After she returned to the kitchen, he changed the subject. "Let's talk about something different. Something good. Wait 'til you see Sparkledove decked out for Christmas."

"Nice, huh?" she asked.

"Very. My folks used to bring me and my sister to some of the holiday events in town when we were kids."

"So, you weren't born here?"

"No, but I was raised not far away. And the covered bridge at the end of town, have you seen it yet?"

"No."

"Mayor Banyan claims it's the only authentic New England-style covered bridge west of the Mississippi. Don't know if that's true, but it sure is pretty to walk through on a snowy night. It has viewing windows on either side."

Goldie smiled politely and knew what a covered bridge was, but she'd actually never seen one in person. She'd done some traveling, but not as much as other people. Markie had taken her to Mexico a couple of times to meet with drug suppliers, but the month in Vegas for her aunt was by far her longest and greatest distance as a solo traveler.

The rest of the dinner conversation was pleasant but one-sided. She didn't know anything about Karen Maraschino, Senior Writer for *Adventure Escape Magazine,* or the events of November 1942. So, she kept the conversation focused on the sheriff. He was amiable enough and answered her questions, yet he was somewhat vague with his answers. He was raised in a little town "not far away" and went to a community college, but never specified where. He joined the Army Air Corps, hoping to become a pilot, but never got his wings. When Goldie asked why, he simply shrugged, "Didn't work out." He remained in the Air Corps doing what he described as "other stuff" until March of 1942. Then, he was discharged, but again, he didn't explain why. He came to Sparkledove shortly thereafter. He had a local sweetheart named Lila and fell in love with both her and the town's Victorian charm. But by the time he'd returned from service, Lila had moved away. Goldie asked if they wrote to each other while he was in the army, and he responded, "Some." By pure chance, he met the mayor, Charles Banyan, having lunch at Clancy's Bar & Grill, and the two hit it off. Between Eli's community college education, military service, and youth, the mayor decided he'd be a good candidate to replace the town's elderly sheriff, who had recently passed away, and offered him the job. Having no other prospects, he accepted the offer and took to the role and townspeople like a duck to water. That was nine months ago. He was twenty-eight and, according to Banyan, one of the youngest sheriffs in the state. While, in a way, this was a lot of background, it left as many questions as answers.

Eli kept Goldie company throughout her meal, and she was grateful that the conversation didn't involve any further questions about her former boyfriend. After dinner, he said goodbye and limped his way through the hotel lobby and out the front door. Goldie, meanwhile, was called over to the registration counter and informed that Charles Banyan had called and left a message that he'd pick her up at 4:00 p.m. for Thanksgiving dinner the following day. She borrowed the first aid kit, went upstairs, saw that the bathroom at the end of the hallway was empty, and decided to take a long, hot shower. As she stood in the curtained bathtub with the water running down her, she checked her body to see if anything was different. Everything seemed the same except the hair situation. Then she started to think about other things. Did women shave their legs in 1942? Did they shave under their arms? Had tampons been invented yet? Had Pamprin? She obviously had some things to figure out.

After returning to her room, she got dressed in a fresh blouse and slacks, changed the wrapping on her hand, and by 7:30 p.m., she found herself bored out of her mind. She had no internet, cell phone, TV, or radio, and she hadn't even seen magazines in the lobby.

"No wonder men went off to war," she said in ignorance. "There's nothin' to do."

She wondered when she went to sleep whether or not she'd wake up the next morning in Sparkledove, back in present-day Manhattan, or somewhere else in another time.

The 60s might be good, she thought. *The Beatles, Stones, go-go boots, bellbottoms.* She was a devotee of music from the 60s, 70s, and some of the 80s and had a romantic, although not entirely accurate, understanding of those decades.

By 8:10, she couldn't stand to be in her room anymore. Her hair was mostly dry, so she stuck a piece of gum in her mouth from the pack she'd bought in Denver and grabbed her coat. She discovered there were gloves in her pocket as she went downstairs, returned the first aid kit, and then started to take a walk around town.

In the quiet of the evening, and now having had all day to process what had happened to her, Goldie had time to organize her thoughts. She still clung to the belief that she was in a coma, and this was all just an elaborate dream. But her cut hand and the length of time she'd been in this "dream" contradicted that. Dreams were random and flitted from place to place. This had been one long, continuous sequence of events. Then, she thought about praying. She looked up at the sky while walking and quietly murmured: "I suppose there's somethin' really important I should say about now, but I got nothin' except, 'What the fuck?'" Then she noticed all the stars and her breath disappearing against an endless black canvas of faraway twinkling white lights.

"Wow," she admitted to herself, cracking her gum loudly. "Nice."

She walked away from downtown and found herself on a street where old house after old house seemed to have a story to tell. Through the window of one, she saw a man tending a blazing fire in the fireplace and smelled the pine logs from the smoking chimney. She passed another house where children had made turkeys from cut-out handprints on paper and were taping them to a window. Everyone had a home. A sense of place. Everyone except her.

She came to the end of the street that connected to the final cross street of town, which was called Bridge Street, and looked around. Across the street and some fifteen yards beyond it was a twenty-foot embankment that went down to the steadily flowing river that was a major reason for the town being built in the first place, she remembered from her library research. The river was about forty feet across, and just beyond its other side was the tall, looming shadow of a huge mountain, looking black and ominous. *Probably crawling with bears and wolves,* she thought. She noticed the river had a bend about two hundred yards away, and when she turned and looked left to follow it, she saw that Bridge Street led straight into the covered bridge that

Sheriff Johnson had mentioned at dinner. It was fifty feet in length, had a wooden, red-painted exterior, a wood-shingled roof, a nine-foot-high clearance, and a wood-plank floor reinforced by steel girders underneath. From a distance, it looked like a long, skinny barn with two tall, glassless windows on either side of its middle where people walking could stop and enjoy the views. She saw all this detail at night thanks to three large, clear glass two-hundred-watt light bulbs that hung down on metal poles from the wooden rafters, not unlike the circular light fixtures she had seen earlier that day in the Denver bus terminal. She assumed the inside of the bridge was lit so people walking or those with horse-drawn carriages could navigate their way after dark.

Goldie had to admit Eli Johnson was right. The bridge was very pretty. She walked down the street toward it, and although she wasn't one to use words like "charming," she concluded it was certainly that. As she stepped onto the structure and began to walk its length, chewing and cracking her gum as she did, she thought about the movie, *The Bridges of Madison County,* that she and Markie had watched one night on Netflix. She really liked the love story, but her boyfriend thought it was sappy and lost interest.

Her footsteps echoed on the wooden planks as she slowly strolled over the river. The water beneath her didn't babble like a creek or stream, so she assumed it must've been deep. She came to the viewing windows in the middle, then turned left and looked at the downriver view that paralleled the town. The window had a low, wooden windowsill about knee level and was two and a half feet wide by five feet high. Gazing out at the view, she instantly understood why the windows were there. She saw moonlight silhouetting the mountain at the far end of town, but its looming shape blocked out the rising moon itself. Between the backlit mountain, stars above, river underneath, and the Norman Rockwell-like covered bridge, it was practically a magical scene straight out of an animated Disney movie. Goldie stopped chewing for a moment, leaned out of the window slightly, stuck her face into the cool pine-scented air, closed her eyes, and took a deep breath. She didn't know how she'd gotten here, but, at least in this moment, she was grateful. After a full thirty seconds of admiring the view, she turned and continued on her way, walking and chewing her gum. As she did, she saw a dirt road just beyond the far end of the bridge that turned left, then went up a slight incline into some woods, but she didn't see any houses, lights, or signs of civilization.

Maybe that leads to one of the minin' operations that used to be here, she speculated. It had to go somewhere.

She arrived at the opposite end, looked at the dirt road that went left, then decided she'd done enough exploring for one night. Turning to go back the way she came, she suddenly stopped with surprise. Standing at the same viewing window where she had just been was a man in a lightweight, red plaid jacket, blue slacks, and brown lace-up boots. He was standing and looking at the river. He was in his mid-thirties, had a high forehead, and stood looking out the window forlornly. He paid no attention to Goldie and, indeed, didn't even acknowledge she was there. He just looked out of the same window at the evening.

"Oookay. This is awkward," she said to herself. She thought it odd that her footsteps had echoed throughout the bridge when she walked, but she never heard this guy coming. After a few pensive moments, she decided that, of course, other townspeople or visitors would be interested in such a landmark, and she must've been too lost in her thoughts to hear his approach. So, she cleared her throat to let him know someone else was coming, then started to walk back the way she had come on the opposite side of the bridge.

As she came nearer, she wondered if she should speak to him. Say: "How's it goin'?" or, "Happy Thanksgiving." But her New York City instincts told her to keep walking. She figured he was paying her no mind because he wanted to be alone, which was fine by her.

But just as she was passing the stranger, he grabbed the side of the glassless window, raised a leg, and stepped up onto the low windowsill.

"Hey!" Goldie called, stopping.

The man ducked his head to clear the top of the window, then leaned his entire body outside. Only the tips of his fingers from his slightly extended arms holding onto the inside of the window frame kept him from falling forward.

"*Hey, mister! Don't!*" she yelled.

She started to run across the bridge toward him. But as she did, the man's fingers let go, and he fell forward. The bridge was approximately fifteen feet above the river, not high enough for someone to commit suicide unless the person jumping couldn't swim, or the river was shallow, and they struck their head on a rock. Or, possibly, the river had a strong current that pulled people under. All of these thoughts raced through Goldie's mind during the three seconds it took her to reach the window. When she got there, she looked down, open-mouthed. She saw nothing. No man, ripples of disturbed water, nothing.

"Where'd he go? Why wasn't there a splash?" she asked out loud. She looked at the quiet, slowly moving current. "What the hell's goin' on?"

She turned and ran down to the end of the bridge where she had originally started, then rounded its corner and went about halfway down the embankment looking for the man, which was difficult to do considering the darkness, incline, and brush. Grabbing the branches of a bare lilac bush with her sore left hand to steady herself, she looked around the shoreline, searching for the man. As she realized no one was there and the water was quietly serene, the hairs on the back of her neck stood on end.

"No," she said. "I did *not* just imagine that!"

Becoming a little frightened, she turned and went back up the embankment.

"No!" she repeated, chewing her gum rapidly to control her fear. She reached the top of the embankment and turned defiantly to look at the river. "We're *not* doin' this! This ain't no episode of *Supernatural!*"

She brushed some small branches and leaves off her coat and looked back toward the houses she'd passed by earlier to see if there were any cars on the streets or people out walking. Everything was quiet. She briefly considered reporting what she'd seen to Sheriff Johnson, but then decided against it, figuring he probably thought her strange enough already, considering the events of that morning.

"I'm in a Hallmark movie on LSD!" she declared. She took a deep breath, spat out her gum, then turned and started walking back toward her hotel.

Five

THANKSGIVING

Surprisingly, Goldie went to bed that night not thinking too much about the man who jumped off the covered bridge. After all, in one twenty-hour period, she'd discovered that her long-time live-in boyfriend had been unfaithful, she'd been struck by a car, she'd awakened in a different state in a different time, she'd cut her hand to verify what was happening to her wasn't a dream, she'd discovered she had an alternative life and career in the previous century, and she'd attacked a man with a bucket of light-orange paint. So, another man jumping off a bridge—and not even off a high bridge—was a pretty low priority, all things considered.

She awoke to the distant but distinct smell of turkey cooking in the restaurant downstairs, and it briefly reminded her of her youth in the Bronx. When she and her sister, Ellen, were young and their parents, Tom and Carla, were together, her father used to wake them up early and take them downtown to see the Macy's Thanksgiving Day Parade. When the parade was over and they went back home, her mom would be cooking, and the aroma of turkey permeated their apartment. It was the smell of safer and happier times.

After a yawn and stretch, she tossed back her patchwork quilt, revealing a 1940s pointed brassiere and high-waisted panties that she'd gotten from her suitcase. Neither garment was comfortable nor stylish.

Getting to her feet, she looked around at the hotel room. "Yep, still here," she said quietly.

She got her yellow cloth robe, slipped it on, then collected her toiletry kit and the towel off the back of the chair at her desk. Opening the door in her bare feet, the first thing she saw was the short, slightly pot-bellied man in the red robe from the previous day, complete with the towel hanging around his shoulders, passing by. They paused and looked at each other.

"Wow. *Groundhog Day*," she said.

"Nooo," the man replied. "Thanksgiving."

He looked at her judgmentally, then continued on his way while she went in the opposite direction toward the bathroom.

After Goldie had gotten ready for her day in the second of her three dresses, a one-piece deep green outfit that buttoned up the front with a matching belt and puffy shoulders, she went downstairs to a busy lobby. Like every town in America, there were people who had once lived in Sparkledove but had moved away. Now, they all seemed to be back: children visiting parents, sisters visiting brothers, cousins visiting cousins, and a fair number of them were staying at the hotel. Because some families didn't want to be bothered with dinner preparations, not to mention people were using ration books for everything from butter to sugar to canned milk, many families decided to celebrate Thanksgiving at the Sparkledove Arms. The hotel had a steady stream of dinner reservations beginning at noon that continued until 8:00 p.m. Even for breakfast, Goldie had to wait in line just for toast and coffee. While she did, a guitarist and violinist were starting to set up music stands to play a variety of popular tunes, although she learned they didn't begin until 2:00 p.m. Meanwhile, Maddie and Dean hurried around the place, attending to various duties dressed as pilgrims from the 1620s.

After breakfast, Goldie was content to stay in her room for several hours and even started to type up several things she'd learned about the town from her trip to the library. She didn't exactly intend to write a three-thousand-word article about Sparkledove, but she was used to keeping a daily diary and wanted to remember things she'd read the day before at the library. Writing also helped her adapt to her surroundings. She figured if she adapted, answers would come.

At 3:50 p.m., she returned to the lobby wearing her overcoat, and the place was still bustling. While the guitarist and violinist played a nice instrumental version of "Good King Wenceslas," a young woman, about eighteen years old, stood behind the registration counter. She was dressed like a Native American, complete with two long black braids on each side of her head, a headband with a feather sticking up in the back, and a fringe buckskin dress. She also wore a name tag that read "Josie." She was talking to a young man who stood in front of the counter. He had a crewcut, wore a high school varsity jacket, and was about the same age. It was obvious from the way they smiled and leaned into each other that these two were a couple.

"Excuse me," Goldie said, approaching and chewing her gum as usual. "Sorry to interrupt. Do you have a phone book I could borrow? There wasn't one in the phone booth."

"Would you like the Denver directory or the local one?" Josie asked. She had dimples, a fresh-as-a-daisy face, and looked very Anglo-Saxon Protestant for someone dressed up as a Native American.

"The local one, please?"

Josie reached under the counter and produced a very thin booklet.

"There you go."

"Thanks a lot," Goldie said, then she eyed the young woman's outfit again. "Y'know, some people could take offense at what you're wearin'."

"Really?" she asked innocently. "Like who?"

"Native Americans," Goldie replied.

"Who?" the young man asked, apparently not familiar with the term.

"People from indigenous heritage," she explained.

"In-in what?" the young man in the varsity jacket asked.

"Indians," Goldie clarified. "People from Indian heritage."

"Why?" Josie wondered. "It's Thanksgiving. Wouldn't they be more offended if they weren't remembered?"

"It's not about them being remembered," Goldie explained. "It's how they're portrayed."

"What do you mean?" the young man asked.

"Native Americans don't generally like how the white man has represented them."

"I don't understand," Josie said.

"I don't know any Indians," the young man replied.

"Native Americans?" Goldie corrected.

"Oh, wait," he remembered. "Johnny Bodine. He's one, I think. I mean, his dad is a member of that lodge over in Brownsville."

"That's the Elks," Josie corrected. "They don't have anything to do with Indians."

"Native Americans," Goldie corrected again.

"Yeah, but they meet in a 'lodge,'" he argued.

"Barbara Little used to have a tepee in her backyard for sleepovers," the young woman recalled. "That doesn't mean her parents were Apache."

"Apache were really tough," the young man noted. "They'd ride a horse until it dropped and then eat it."

"You guys are missing the point," Goldie said.

Both of them looked at her.

"Native Americans don't want to be portrayed by white people wearing cheesy costumes."

The young man examined the girl behind the counter. "That *is* a cheesy costume," he agreed. Then he smiled. "But you look really cute in it."

"Thank you," Josie grinned with her deep dimples.

Goldie expelled a breath. "I can see that raisin' social consciousness around here is goin' to be challengin'. Kinda like Megan Fox takin' acting lessons." She held up what she came for. "Thanks for the phone book."

She stepped a few feet away to the edge of the counter so the young people could continue their conversation. She wanted the directory to find a local photographer who either already had some holiday photos of Sparkledove or was willing to take some for a price, should she decide to attempt an article. Though she wasn't trying to eavesdrop, she couldn't help but hear what the two teenagers were talking about.

"I get off at 6 p.m.," the costumed Josie said. "You've got to be at my house no later than ten after."

"What time is dinner?" he asked.

"About 7:00. Will you be able to eat again?"

"My Mom's serving about 4:30, but I'll eat light. If your mom's not serving until 7:00, why do I have to be there so early?"

"My Aunt Ami will be there, and she drives me nuts," Josie answered. Then, she affected an irritating older adult voice. 'Josie, are you really going to wear your hair like that, dear? How serious are you and

Dexter? When he finishes high school in the spring, is he going to enlist? Why the army? The Marines are better. Have you thought about college? Have you chosen a vocation? *I* was a teacher, you know?' The woman can ask more questions than a Japanese interrogator. You've got to be there to help me deflect her nosiness."

"Okay," the young man agreed. "6:10, you got it."

"Dexter, promise?"

The young man smiled, then turned and started to walk toward the front doors. As he went, he said, "Just call my name. I'll be there. Just look over your shoulder, honey."

Goldie paused from studying the phone directory and looked up curiously toward the young man as he disappeared out the door.

Whoa. How weird was that? she thought. *That kid just recited a couple of lines from "I'll Be There" by the Jackson 5.*

She turned back to the counter with a bemused smile at the coincidence and spent about thirty more seconds perusing the directory when an older man, whom the young woman recognized, came into the lobby.

"Hi, Mayor," she greeted. "Happy Thanksgiving!"

"Happy Thanksgiving, Josie," the man reciprocated, approaching. "Nice Indian costume."

"It's Native American," she corrected, glancing toward Goldie.

"Uh—okay. I'm looking for Karen Maraschino."

Goldie quickly took the gum out of her mouth and turned to the man. As she did, she subtly stuck it under the counter.

"I'm Karen," she smiled, recognizing him from a photograph in an article she'd seen at the library. "You're Mayor Banyan."

"Call me Charles," he said, extending his hand. "Welcome to Sparkledove, Miss Maraschino, the perfect place for Christmas."

"Call me Goldie," she reciprocated, shaking hands. "All my friends do."

Banyan was about fifty-five, tall, fit, and distinguished-looking. He was handsome for his age, with salt-and-pepper hair combed back, and had the posture of someone who was used to being in charge.

"Maraschino," he wondered. "Is that—"

"Like the cherry, yes," she finished.

"Very good. How are Maddie and Dean treating you?"

"Dean?" she asked.

"Maddie's husband. They own the Sparkledove Arms."

"I haven't officially met him. But I think I saw him earlier this mornin'." She glanced around the lobby but didn't see the proprietors. "They're dressed up like they just got off the Mayflower, and they're treating me fine."

Banyan turned and eyed the crimson circular sofa in the middle of the lobby behind them.

"They should've taken my suggestion and replaced

that piece of furniture with a big boulder. We're right in the middle of the Rocky Mountains, for goodness' sake. There are only a thousand of them around."

"A big boulder?" she asked.

"For Plymouth Rock. Kids would've loved to climb all over it, not to mention it goes with Maddie and Dean's costumes."

She stared blankly at the circular sofa. "Sure," she politely agreed, not really caring one way or another.

"Well, Goldie, if you're ready, my car's just outside. I hope you're hungry; we've prepared quite a feast."

"Eh, great." She stepped back over to Josie behind the counter and handed her the directory.

The Banyan residence was most of the way down River Street, at the opposite end of town from the covered bridge, and then a left turn down a side street called Nugget Lane. During the three-minute drive, Goldie's host asked all the expected questions: How did she like Sparkledove? Had she ever been to Colorado before? Did she have a family who was missing her at Thanksgiving? She replied that the town was very picturesque, that she'd been to Colorado before but never in this part of the state, and that she wasn't married, so her time was her own. She fibbed about being in Colorado before because she figured people expected her to be well-traveled, since she worked for a travel magazine. Her host also inquired about the gauze on her left hand, but she said it was just a small cut and looked worse than it was because of the wrappings.

Banyan's house was easily one of the larger Victorian-style homes in town. Built in 1871, it was a 3,700-square-foot home with a round turret on its right-hand side and a wide front porch that wrapped around the house on its left. The porch featured delicate spindle woodworking, and the windows on the second floor were narrow and rounded at the top, with bricks "soldiering" in the arches. A five-foot wrought-iron fence surrounded the property, and three brick chimneys rose above the roof. Overall, the place looked like a cross between a palace and a life-size gingerbread house.

Banyan was prodigiously proud of his home and talked about its original wood flooring, the original glass in most of the windows, and wallpaper specially commissioned to reflect the tastes of the 1870s. But he also spoke of new piping, insulation, a furnace, and state-of-the-art appliances. "It retains its authentic character," he explained. "But has all the modern-day conveniences a family needs."

The participants at the Banyan house this Thanksgiving were Charles, his wife Stephie, and their twenty-nine-year-old son, Peter. Stephie was an elegant-looking woman with auburn hair who would've easily been a prominent member of the country club if Sparkledove had one. Peter was tall, trim, and handsome like his father. He had wavy brown hair, hazel eyes, and frameless glasses that he used when reading. He was single, had his own place, and was the editor of the local weekly newspaper, *The Sparkledove Wing*, called *The Wing* for short. As soon as Goldie and Peter set eyes on one another, each thought the other was attractive. His weak eyesight had been one of the reasons why he wasn't in the military. Another was two cracked vertebrae from playing football in high school. He made a point of telling Goldie he had tried not once but twice to join different branches of the service, but between his eyes and back injury, he'd been turned down. She was quickly figuring out that if a young man was eighteen to thirty years old, it was the national expectation that they would be in the armed services.

The party had drinks in a nicely appointed parlor while Benny Goodman played on the radio. The refreshments were served by a young Hispanic woman named Lupe, who spoke in broken English and wore a nice but simple dress. She had mahogany eyes, a triangular face, thick lips, and an eager-to-please smile. Charles was slightly embarrassed by the way she mispronounced certain words. She referred to the drinks as "kooktales" instead of "cocktails" and rolled her R's, which, he assumed, made her difficult to understand. But Goldie assured her host she understood Lupe perfectly. Stephie also spoke about a cook in the kitchen named Margarita, but Goldie never saw her.

During drinks and conversation in the parlor, Goldie learned that Charles was a big fan of *Adventure Escape Magazine* and had written her publisher, Owen

Mitchell, more than once about doing a feature article that highlighted his town.

After a while, everyone was called into the dining room for dinner. The dining room had a ten-foot-high ceiling and an impressive crystal chandelier that hung and sparkled over an impeccably set table. Before they ate, everyone bowed their heads, and Charles offered a prayer about being thankful for his family, his prominent position in the community, his beautiful home, and even a writer from *Adventure Escape Magazine* joining them. Afterwards, the first course began. There may have been rationing going on in most homes in America, but one couldn't tell it from the Banyan spread with its polished silverware, china plates, flaky homemade rolls, full butter dishes, salad, and wine.

"So, why do people call you Goldie?" Peter asked.

"Because I have a thing for gold jewelry," she answered. Then she noticed everyone was looking at her bare wrists and neck. All she was wearing were rather plain clip-on earrings. "Of course, I leave it at home when I'm on assignment. I don't want to seem pretentious, not to mention risk losing it."

"Of course," the senior Banyan agreed. "Being in your magazine could mean gold for us, metaphorically speaking. Tourism is the town's largest source of revenue."

"I see," Goldie replied.

"And you said you were single?" the mayor continued.

"Yeah. Um, yes. I'm originally from New York City, but do too much travelin' to settle down. The job, you know."

"But you're based in Columbus now, right?" Stephie asked.

"Eh, yes."

"So, your people are back in New York?" she continued.

"Uh-huh," Goldie answered, having no idea since it was 1942.

"Isn't that fascinating?" Stephie observed. "An ambitious woman writer traveling the country alone. Very brave and independent. Probably would make a great reporter for a local newspaper. Wouldn't you agree, Peter?"

"Could be," he said, buttering a roll. "If it were the right publication. But I don't think Goldie would be interested in a paper like *The Wing*."

"Really?" Goldie asked. "Why's that?"

"You're used to traveling to interesting locations, learning about the history of a place, and covering fun events that travelers would enjoy. I dare say you wouldn't find covering a Sparkledove City Council meeting very gay when the big topic of conversation is the potholes on Fox Cross Way. Or, debating whether or not the city should follow blackout protocol."

"Absolutely not," Charles declared decidedly. "We're in the middle of the country. Too far from any coastal port or any manufacturing facility to be a threat to anyone."

"Yes," Peter replied. "Except President Roosevelt asked that *all* cities take precautions."

"The president isn't taking into account towns like ours that depend on beautiful Christmas lights to attract tourists," Charles justified.

"No. He's taking into account spy planes that could use the town's lights as a landmark to pinpoint the direction of Denver, less than forty miles away. Not to mention the armory just east of it."

"Now, boys," Stephie interjected, "let's not get into a verbal joust over dinner. It's Thanksgiving."

"Quite right, Mother," Charles agreed.

Unfortunately, over the course of the next hour, Charles and Peter found themselves at odds over pretty much everything. Peter mentioned once the war was over, he hoped Sparkledove would get electric streetlights, but Charles proclaimed gaslights would be more aesthetically appropriate. Peter spoke about how families were struggling financially, as loved ones went off to war and manufacturers cut back on everything that wasn't related to the war effort. By contrast, Charles spoke about how the Sparkledove Historical Society needed to impose higher fines on homeowners who weren't keeping up with preservation. The two even argued about what kind of pie was best for dessert. Charles said pumpkin, while Peter claimed apple. Their disagreements got so heated at times that it made Goldie feel uncomfortable. But Stephie intervened again and again, like a referee at a sporting event. Despite this constant difference of opinion, however, Goldie did learn about a schedule of events that she was supposed to cover for her article. This included the lighting of the community Christmas tree, a tour of historical homes—all meticulously decorated —and she was also expected to judge a gingerbread house competition at a community dance. Other events were happening as well between Thanksgiving and December 24th, and Stephie repeated the town's unofficial theme that Sparkledove was indeed "The perfect place for Christmas."

But by 6:10 p.m., Goldie decided the perfect place for her was out of the house. The dinner was first-class, but she'd had enough of being polite, pretending to be someone else, and listening to the bickering Banyans. Peter asked if she'd like to walk off her dinner with him escorting her home, and since it was a pleasant evening, she agreed. She gave her thanks to Charles and Stephie, then thanked Lupe, asking her to also thank Margarita in the kitchen. After she and Peter slipped on their coats, they left the house and started to head back to her hotel. The three-minute car ride was about a ten-minute walk.

"I'm sorry," Peter began, once they were outside the wrought-iron gate, "that my father and I got so testy with one another. I guess you've figured out we're rather like oil and water."

"Oh, really? I hadn't noticed," she lied.

He smiled. "I'm also sorry about my mother's not-so-subtle remark about you making a good reporter and working at my newspaper. Had you taken that bait, she would've had us engaged by the time we had pie."

"Yeah, but that would've been a disaster because you like apple, your dad likes pumpkin, and I'm more of a cherry girl."

"Anyway, thanks for being tolerant."

"It's okay. Families. We love 'em, but we love to argue with 'em even more."

"Right," he agreed. "At least, me and my father."

They continued walking in silence for a few moments, then Goldie's curiosity got the better of her.

"So, why was your mom trying to fix you up? You don't look like you need any help in that department."

"Thanks... she and my father married young, and she thinks I'm getting past my prime. It's just the difference of generations."

"Got it."

"Plus, she hasn't seen any eligible local young ladies she thinks are good enough for me."

"Really?"

"I'm an only child, so I deserve nothing short of royalty," he kidded. "Princess Elizabeth, at the very least."

"You mean Queen Elizabeth?"

"Princess Elizabeth," he corrected.

"Oh... right," she remembered. "She wouldn't be queen yet."

"What about you?" he asked. "I heard what you said to my folks about traveling, but there's got to be more to the story than that. Why hasn't a looker like you been snatched up?"

"Actually, I was snatched for a long time... but he recently decided he didn't want me anymore. Like, *real* recently."

Peter looked her over. "Then he's a fool."

"Yeah. I kinda figured that, too," she grinned.

As they turned onto River Street and continued walking, Goldie determined that not only was Peter good-looking, he had charm to spare. She asked how he had gotten into the newspaper business, and he talked about his love of writing and how he hoped to pen a novel someday. But in the meantime, he also liked that his writing informed a local community and helped people make better decisions about their lives. Even if those decisions were about something small, like the potholes on Fox Cross Way. She had to admit, she liked Peter Banyan. He was, so far, one of the best things about her new, displaced life.

As they strolled by cross street after cross street down the main thoroughfare of town, she looked to her right and saw Sheriff Johnson, his friend Stu Frey, and several other people going into a small Catholic church carrying packages and bags of one kind or another. She figured it was some sort of Thanksgiving service and decided, after Peter had dropped her off back at the hotel, she might keep her coat on, wait a couple of minutes in the lobby, then walk back to the church. After all, it was early in the evening, and what else was there to do?

Six

Before Peter said goodbye to Goldie at the hotel, he promised to see her again soon. She couldn't help but wonder what that meant. Did he mean on a date? Or in his capacity as editor of the newspaper? Or did he simply mean it was a small town, and seeing each other was inevitable? She thought about it while listening to the musicians in the lobby play one of their final numbers for the day, then she left the hotel and walked back to the church.

Saint Mark's was a wooden structure built in 1869 and lined with stained glass windows on both sides. It was small, and when filled, held only eighty-three of the faithful. To her surprise, when she opened the front doors and went inside, she found the plain but tidy church empty. Empty, except for a priest entering from a side hallway to the right of the altar to pick up a cardboard box sitting in front of it. He was very thin and had a baby face with a little acne. He looked like he was about eighteen, but Goldie knew that wasn't the case. Seeing her, he smiled warmly.

"Hello. Are you the lady with the hot buns?"

The comment caught her off guard. She started to look around at her butt, but then stopped.

"Excuse me?"

"The buns. The dinner rolls. Do you need help bringing them in?"

"Uh, no. I'm not, eh, the hot bun lady."

"Oh. I'm sorry. Then, you're here for dinner?"

"No. I've already eaten."

"Oh, now I understand," the priest said. "We're all downstairs."

He walked past the box he was initially going for and stepped forward while extending his hand. "I'm still connecting names with faces, and I don't think we've met. I'm Father David Fitzsimmons, but everyone calls me Father Fitz."

"Karen Maraschino," she reciprocated, shaking his hand. "Everyone calls me Goldie."

"No doubt because you have a heart of gold," the priest assumed.

"Sure. Let's go with that," she agreed.

"Maraschino?" he repeated.

"Yeah. I know," she said.

He turned, returned to his box, picked it up, and then led the way. "I can't recall seeing you in church. Are you Catholic?"

"Yeah, but I don't usually go unless it's one of the big four: Christmas, Easter, a weddin', or a funeral."

"Get all the answers you need going to church so infrequently?" Father Fitz asked, a few feet ahead of her.

"I don't get any," she answered honestly. "Hence the infrequently."

"Well, I'm glad you're here now," he replied good naturedly.

The side hallway led to some stairs that went down to a finished basement. It was a meeting room painted white where about twenty-five to thirty people were gathered: some sitting at tables, some standing and chatting, and small children darting around here and there. Although there was no formal kitchen, a serving area was sectioned off with two long tables covered in tablecloths and several hot plates with extension cords plugged into wall sockets. On the hot plates were platters with three golden-brown turkeys, ready for carving. There were also bowls of mashed potatoes and gravy, cranberry sauce, pots of coffee, pitchers of milk and juice, plates of carrots and celery, cookies, two pumpkin pies and one apple, and a stacked collection of plates, silverware, and napkins from several homes. Over in a corner, a small radio sat on a box while the Andrews Sisters sang "Don't Sit Under The Apple Tree With Anyone Else But Me." It took Goldie just a couple of seconds to figure out she'd walked into a Thanksgiving potluck.

"Hang your coat on the coat rack over there, and there's a clean apron under the serving tables," Father

Fitz instructed. "Once you're suited up, go ahead and start carving one of the birds."

Goldie looked around with a bemused smile, realizing that since she'd told the priest that she wasn't the hot bun lady and that she'd already eaten, he assumed she was there to work.

"Okay, Father," she said gamely. "You got it."

The clergyman thanked her and went to set the box he was carrying down behind the serving tables while Goldie went to hang up her coat. As she did, she noticed some wonderful black-and-white framed photos, evenly spaced and hanging on the walls around the room. There was a photo of two young mothers waving from the front porch of one of the town's historic houses in autumn. There was another of a young girl holding her pet cat up close to her right cheek. Still another of a grandfather and grandson walking away from the camera hand-in-hand in the woods, just as a beam of dappled sunlight struck them. They were just simple slices of life, but they were executed with Annie Leibovitz precision.

Goldie admired them for a few moments, then slipped off and hung up her coat. Next, she went over behind the serving tables and tied on an apron. She also spotted some rubber dish gloves and slipped them on, keeping her cut hand in mind. Then, she removed a turkey from a hot plate, put it on an empty plate, picked up a carving knife and fork, and started to carve it, putting the warm slices on an empty platter. It wasn't until she was well into her carving that Sheriff

Johnson noticed her. He'd been talking to an elderly woman at a table, giving her his full attention. Stu Frey had spotted her before the Sheriff, but he, too, was engaged in conversation.

Finally coming over to her, the lawman looked at her, surprised.

"Howdy."

"Doody," she replied.

He looked at her, not understanding.

"See, I thought we were doin' a Marco Polo kind of thing," she joked, knowing he had no idea what she meant. But then, she waved it off. "Never mind. Happy Thanksgiving."

"Same to you. What're you doing here?"

"I'm workin'," she said, slicing some white meat off the back of the turkey. "What're *you* doin'?"

"I heard you were having dinner with Mayor Banyan and his family."

"I did," she said matter-of-factly. "Now, I'm here."

"How did you even know about this?"

"I'm a journalist with razor-sharp investigative abilities."

Eli looked at her dubiously, so she amended her response.

"I was walkin' home from the mayor's and saw you, Stu, and some people comin' into the church, and there's squat to do back in my hotel room except count the roses in the wallpaper."

He smiled a little. "Okay."

"So, what *is* this?" she asked, wanting his explanation for the event.

"Some people in town don't have much," he explained in a slow, low voice. "Others are alone. Still others work at places like the hospital in Denver but don't get off until late and don't have time to prepare a meal." He glanced around. "This dinner serves a lot of needs so nobody gets left out."

"Including sheriffs who have to work and can't be with their family?"

"That too," he agreed. "It was all Stu's idea, but me and Father Fitz hopped right onto it."

Eli limped his way around the tables to where she was, then grabbed and tied on an apron. As he did, the young clergyman came by.

"Everything coming along all right here?" he asked.

"Just fine, Father," the sheriff replied. "Stu will be over in a minute, and then we can start the serving line. I guess you've already met our illustrious writer from *Adventure Escape Magazine*, eh?"

"*Adventure Escape Magazine?*" Father Fitz said, surprised. He looked at Goldie. "You-you mean, y-you're not a—"

"Worker-bee for this here soiree?" she asked. "No. But I'm glad to help."

"Hot buns!" a woman's voice announced. "Where do you want, Father?"

"Oh, good," the priest replied, turning. "Put them right over there by the cranberry sauce."

A woman carrying a brown paper bag with a

dishtowel over it approached the table but paused when she saw Goldie. It was the young Hispanic woman who had served dinner at the Banyan house less than an hour earlier.

"Ay, Lupe," Goldie smiled. "How ya doin'?"

She approached the table timidly as Father Fitz and Eli looked at one another, wondering how the two knew each other.

"You won't tell Señor Banyan that Margarita made extra buns in his kitchen, will you? I think he'd be angry."

"Your secret's safe with me," she assured. "But I don't think he'd mind."

"You don't know Señor Banyan," Lupe chuckled, rolling her eyes.

Goldie explained to Eli and Father Fitz how she knew Lupe, and they likewise promised to keep silent about the Banyan's cook using their kitchen to make extra rolls, although Father Fitz agreed with Goldie that he couldn't imagine that Charles and Stephie would mind. Within another couple of minutes, Stu Frey came around the tables to join them, and he, Eli, Father Fitz, Goldie, and Lupe stood ready to serve all the people dinner cafeteria-style. Before they did, however, Father asked that the radio be turned off and everyone bow their head for a prayer.

"You know," he began, "the first Thanksgiving back in 1621 was mostly a celebration of survival. Those who came to the New World on the Mayflower had to endure a harsh voyage, a harsher first winter, and disease. Many pilgrims died that year.

"Now, we're involved in another kind of struggle for survival. Some families have felt the effects more harshly than others. So, let's remember those who have died, those who bravely fight on, our leaders, and we ask God to bless this wonderful feast that we're able to enjoy this day with family and friends. Amen."

People came over and lined up as the rest of the servers put on aprons, and Duke Ellington and his Orchestra came over the radio. Goldie was standing next to Father, and they started to chat while they served. She learned that he'd only been in Sparkledove a couple of months and that this was his first assignment as a priest. She also learned the wonderful photographs on the wall were his. He was a passionate amateur photographer who, at one time, intended to become a photojournalist but ultimately had a higher calling. He'd taken the photographs as an excuse to meet his congregants, then hung several on the walls to spruce up the basement. Goldie asked if he'd like to provide the accompanying photographs for her article. She still didn't know if she was going to write one, but she was thinking more and more about trying. She even suggested that Charles Banyan might be persuaded to make a contribution to the church for Father Fitz's services, and the young priest was both complimented and intrigued by her proposal. Goldie was good at this kind of thing: hitting situations cold, then figuring things out, and formulating a plan of action.

After everyone had been served, she stood behind the serving tables with a little smile as she watched people eat. Everyone was talking, chewing, laughing; some of the younger kids had gravy stains on their clothes, and she couldn't help but feel this was what people were supposed to do on Thanksgiving. Stu Frey, about five feet away, was also watching everyone, and she walked over and patted him on the shoulder.

"Good idea," she said quietly. "Nicely done."

"Glad you were here to see this," he said. "Not for your article. But just—well—because."

"Me, too," she agreed.

"See that guy in the blue shirt?" he asked, subtly pointing.

"Yeah?"

"That's Melvin Purdle. Brought his mandolin. Plays a mean "Jingle Bells.""

"I can't wait," she smiled. Then she walked over to Eli, who was helping himself to a chocolate chip cookie.

"Aren't you gonna fix yourself a plate?"

"After everyone else has eaten," he replied, taking a bite of cookie.

She nodded, then changed subjects.

"Hey, I wanted to ask you about the covered bridge at the end of town. Has anyone ever jumped off it?"

"You mean, like, kids in the summer?"

"No. I mean like a grown man committing suicide?"

The lawman looked at her. "Why on earth would you ask that?"

"Well, I checked it out last night, and it's got those two open viewing windows on either side, and I was just wondering."

"It's not high enough for that kind of thing," he decided, taking another bite of cookie.

"Normally, no," she agreed. "But what if the guy couldn't swim? What if the water was low, and he hit his head on a rock?"

The munching sheriff looked at her, confused. "The covered bridge is one of the most scenic, peaceful places in town. Especially for the river views. And *this* is what you thought of when you went over there?"

"Yeah. I'm romantic that way," she cracked. "Do me a favor and look through your incident reports, will ya? Somethin' like this might've happened before you became sheriff, and I'm curious."

"I thought you were here to write about our Christmas festivities."

"I *am*, and I *will*. J-just humor me, okay?"

He looked at her and took another bite of his cookie.

"You're a very strange person," he decided.

Seven

THE TOWN TREE

The following day, Friday, November 27th, Goldie awoke at 7:21 a.m. in her hotel room, thinking about time. Even before she was fully awake, it was on her mind. How long did her publisher want her to stay in Sparkledove for the article she was supposed to write? Until December 10th? 15th? The 20th? Was she supposed to write her article before she left town? What was she supposed to do today? She'd learned from her host, Charles Banyan, that there were some events she was expected to attend, but how many days apart were these, and what was she going to do in the meantime? Then there was the time frame itself that she found herself in after her accident on Mercer Street: November 1942. What was the significance of that? Was time passing at the same speed back in present-day New York City as it was in Sparkledove? Or was all this happening in the span of a few minutes while an ambulance was taking her to the hospital?

She stretched, yawned, climbed out of bed, then looked at the bullet-like brassiere and waist-high, slightly baggy panties she was wearing.

How did the human race continue to propagate? she wondered.

An hour later, Goldie had showered, put on her last clean dress, and eaten a breakfast of blueberry pancakes, sausage, and coffee in the restaurant. Coming back into the lobby, Maddie, wearing her usual glasses with the silver chain, beckoned her over to the registration counter.

"Good morning, Miss Maraschino," she smiled.

"Call me Goldie."

"Uh, Goldie. The McCaw brothers are here for you."

"Who?"

Maddie gestured to the circular crimson sofa in the middle of the lobby. Goldie turned and raised her eyebrows in surprise. Facing her were two very rough-looking men who looked like they lived on the streets. They were unshaven, had long, greasy hair, earflap caps, and wore coats and boots that had clearly never been cleaned. They had dirt under their fingernails, no particular expression on their weatherworn faces, and bad teeth. It was hard to tell their ages, but they could've been in their early thirties. She hadn't noticed them before because when she crossed the lobby, the tall back of the circular sofa had obscured her view. When she turned to them, they both rose.

"Hey," the taller of the two said. "I'm Saul."

"I'm Paul," the other one nodded.

Goldie looked at them, unsure what to conclude.

"Saul and Paul McCaw?" she asked, resisting the temptation to snicker.

"We're here to fetch you to the mountains," Saul said.

"But you're going to have to lose them clothes," Paul warned.

Goldie turned back to Maddie behind the counter.

"Can you interpret this?"

"The McCaw brothers live up in the mountains," Maddie smiled. "The boys have some beautiful pine trees up there and provide the town with its Christmas tree that goes in the little square next to the post office. No doubt Mayor Banyan thought you'd like to be there when they cut down the tree, but you're going to have to wear more rugged clothing. This is quite an honor, Goldie. They made a special trip into town just to come get you."

The visitor turned back to the expressionless mountain men. "Lucky me," she said with reserve. She stepped over and shook hands with each, wanting to wipe her hands on her dress afterwards.

"You'll want to go down to Miller's General Store," Maddie suggested. "Get some boots, pants, a hat, whatever you need. Remember, the mayor's paying for it. Then, send your overcoat and dress back here with Chad, and I'll take care of them."

"Chad?"

"He works at Miller's."

"Okay."

"Also, you got any laundry, honey?"

"A little, yes."

"With your permission, I'll get it from your room, and we'll fix you right up while you're gone."

"That's awfully nice of you, Maddie. Thanks." She stepped back over to the counter and whispered confidentially. "Uh, these guys are okay, right?"

"Oh, no," Maddie replied quietly, slipping off her glasses. "They're as odd as a five-legged dog. But you'll be safe."

Goldie turned back to the grubby-looking brothers and smiled faintly, hesitant but accepting. Then, she went up to her room to get her overcoat.

Miller's General Store was on River Street, three blocks away, and the McCaws drove her down to the store in their 1936 Chevy flatbed pickup. Goldie sat wedged in between the two brothers in the small cab and had to practically hold her breath from the smell of their clothing and body odor. If Charles Banyan intended for this to be a homey excursion into the mountains to select the town's ideal Christmas tree, it so far wasn't having the desired effect. Miller's, on the other hand, was fascinating. Inside, one could find clothing, tools, heavy woolen Native American blankets, paint—a little bit of everything. There was even a glass counter with a selection of candy bars and homemade beef jerky. The centerpiece of the store was a cast-iron potbelly stove with its door swung open and hickory logs burning brightly inside to fend off the morning chill. Sitting in three chairs around the stove was a man in his late seventies named Deke Miller, his son Chad Miller, who was in his fifties, and Clara, from Clara's Gifts, whom Goldie had met on her first day. They were chatting amongst themselves and having coffee when Saul, Paul, and Goldie came in.

"Well, if it ain't the McCaw boys," Deke said. "You got the Christmas tree already?"

"No," Saul replied. "Just came into town to fetch this writer so she could tell about it in her magazine."

"How's your daddy, boys?" Chad asked.

"Hall's fine," Paul replied.

"Your father's name is Hall?" Goldie queried.

"Yup."

"Hall, Saul, and Paul?" Goldie asked.

"Does have a kind of symmetry to it, don't it?" Saul noted.

"How're you feeling, dear?" Clara asked.

"Good," Goldie replied. "Got off to a rough start in town. But I'm doin' fine now."

Clara eyed the gauze on the visitor's left hand. Goldie noticed it immediately.

"This is nothin'," she said, raising her hand a little. "Just a scratch."

"Glad to hear it." Clara smiled. She turned to the men sitting with her. "Gentlemen, this is Goldie, a writer with *Adventure Escape Magazine*. She's here to cover our holiday festivities."

"Sparkledove's the perfect place for Christmas," Deke nodded.

"Yeah. Heard you were coming," Chad smiled, rising to shake her hand.

"Goldie, this is Deke Miller and his son Chad. Deke's father started Miller's way back in the 1860s."

"We were the first business of modern-day Sparkledove," the older man said proudly while Goldie shook one man's hand, then the other. "We were just a little provision store back then for the hill folk and hunters. Forgive me for not risin', young lady. My arthritis acts up sometimes."

"It's okay," Goldie smiled.

"They got good jerky," Saul observed, straight-faced.

"And better coffee than I make," Clara added.

"If you're goin' up in the mountains with these two hooligans," Chad said. "Bet you want some more appropriate clothes."

"Yes, please," the guest verified.

"Yeah—gets cold up there where the good trees are," Deke said. "Although this winter ain't gonna be so bad. The worst winter I ever saw was the winter of '99. Nearly froze my fingers off for some kindlin'. Look here," he said, extending his arm and showing the pinky finger of his right hand. "See that fingernail? Black as coal. That was ten minutes outside without gloves."

"Oh, that's nothin'," Saul replied. He stepped over and sat down in the chair where Chad had been and started to untie his left boot. "The worst winter was 1921. I was up on Tanner's Ledge huntin' with my daddy." He slipped off his boot, then his ratty sock. "Had a worn spot on the bottom of my boot that broke through. Lost my fourth toe."

"Nope, I got both ya beat," Chad said, turning his back and yanking up his long-sleeved shirt. "Look above the beltline. See that scar? That's ice burn from the winter of '38. My jacket and shirt got hiked up from carrying a calf across the grazing pasture."

"Naw, the worst was '35," Paul said. "I was up about ten thousand feet, trackin' a mountain lion that killed one of our horses. I had to relieve myself..." He started to unbuckle his belt. "The wind was really whippin' that day and—"

"*Whoa!*" Clair, Goldie, and Chad all yelled simultaneously.

Just then, Peter Banyan came into the store, dressed for going into the mountains.

"Morning, everyone," he smiled. He looked at Goldie. "Just came from the hotel, and Maddie said you might be down here suiting up with the boys." He looked at the McCaws. "Paul, Saul, how's your mother, Moll?"

"Moll?" Goldie asked.

"Short for Molly," Clara explained.

"Of course," Goldie said, rolling her eyes.

"Good," Paul nodded, unemotional.

"Dandy," Saul verified, equally somber.

Goldie looked at Peter's attire. "Are-are *you* coming to the mountains, too?"

"Yeah. Thought I might. Got my car and camera right outside and thought I'd drive you up. Getting the town Christmas tree is a big deal, and my paper should cover it."

"Yes!" Goldie said, relieved. "Good!"

"Sorry that neither my dad nor I mentioned it last night. Guess we were too busy agreeing to disagree."

"No, it's fine," Goldie said. "It's really fine. Let me just pick out a few things, change, then we'll be off."

She selected an ensemble of heavy woolen pants, a long underwear top, and a plaid shirt to go over that. Next, she selected black rubber boots that clipped shut, gloves, a burnt-orange stocking cap, and a blue jacket. They left the store and climbed into Peter's 1941 Ford Super Deluxe Station Wagon. It had chains on the tires and sandbags in the back to give it more weight to plow through the snow. They followed the McCaw brothers out of town, got onto Highway 70 for less than a quarter mile, then went up a steep dirt mountain road that bent and turned its way past boulders, fallen trees, and hand-lettered "No Trespassing" signs. There wasn't any snow for the first twenty minutes of the journey, but then they seemed to go around a corner, and suddenly, the landscape changed from limestone brown to dazzling white. Goldie was wide-eyed and impressed, never having seen anything like it.

"I'm very glad you showed up, Peter," she

admitted, turning from the view back to him. "Without you, I was afraid of steppin' into a winter version of *Deliverance*."

"What's that?" he asked.

"The McCaw brothers. They're, they're—I don't know what the hell they are."

"They're mountain people," he shrugged. "A little rough around the edges, maybe, but if you asked, they'd give the shirts off their backs."

"And the ticks that went with 'em," she added.

He smiled good-naturedly. "Oh, coming originally from New York, I bet you've seen your share of rough characters."

"You have no idea."

"What part of the city are you originally from?"

"The Bronx."

"I thought with that cute accent of yours, it was maybe the Bronx. Sounds a lot like someone I used to know."

"Cute accent?" she asked.

"Yeah," he replied sincerely.

"The last person that mentioned my accent compared me to a beer salesman yellin' at Yankee Stadium."

"Your old boyfriend?" he guessed.

"Yeah."

"He's an idiot," Peter flatly declared.

Goldie felt herself blush, which she didn't do often. She liked Peter. She'd known him for less than twenty-four hours, but he was handsome, civic-minded, nonjudgmental, except for Markie, and she suspected he liked her, too. In a way, such feelings made her feel guilty because even though Markie had broken her heart with Kristen DiVarno, she couldn't just turn off her feelings for him like a faucet. Then again, she asked herself, what was she feeling guilty about? Markie wouldn't even be born for another fifty years.

For now, at least, she dismissed such thoughts and concentrated on the scenery, loving everything she saw. Within another ten minutes, the vehicles turned onto a snowy road even more primitive than the one they'd been on, covered with about five inches of powdery white.

There was only one set of tire tracks on the road coming and going ahead, and Goldie figured it must've been from the McCaw brothers' original scouting trip for the tree. Slowing down and stopping on a scenic ridge, Goldie looked out her window and ooooed at the view. The world was now divided into two separate horizons: the upper part was clear blue sky as far as she could see, and the lower part was a combination of jagged and rolling mountain peaks covered in white and lined with green pines.

"Wow! Absolutely incredible!" she gawked.

"I'll take a picture of the view if you like," Peter offered, turning off the engine. "But it'll be in black and white, and you won't get a sense of the majestic perspective."

"Yeah. Please do."

She climbed out of the station wagon and

immediately felt the colder temperature and crisp air nipping at her cheeks. The McCaw brothers climbed out of their flatbed ahead of them and walked toward her.

"I wouldn't step too far off the road if I was you," Paul warned.

She looked down at the sparkling, pristine snow around her and took a step toward the edge of the road. "Why?" she asked. Her first and second steps were uneventful, but with the third, Goldie suddenly found herself off the edges of the road, and she plopped into nearly waist-deep snow. The sudden drop-off surprised her, and she gave a high-pitched yelp.

"That's why," Saul said matter-of-factly.

The McCaws just looked at her while Peter put his camera bag on the roof of his station wagon, then came around the hood of the vehicle and stepped out into the snow to help. "Here. Take my hand," he said, extending it. Then he extended his other hand toward Paul. "Little help here, please."

By making a human chain, Saul, Paul, and Peter pulled Goldie out of the snow in a matter of seconds. Resisting the urge to laugh but grinning nevertheless, Peter opened up the passenger side door, got into his glove compartment, and retrieved two items: a whisk broom and a .45-caliber army-issue pistol.

"Here," he said, offering her the broom. "Brush yourself off."

"What's with the gun?" a snow-encrusted Goldie asked.

"Just a precaution," Peter shrugged, sticking it into his side jacket pocket. "Up here, you have to be wary of critters.

"I don't care," she said, brushing herself off. "This is totally awesome. The view, the snow, I'm glad your dad wanted me to participate in this."

"An adventure—I think that's exactly what he was hoping for," Peter confirmed.

"How high up are we?" she asked.

"Around nine thousand feet," Paul said.

While Goldie finished brushing herself off, Peter grabbed his camera bag. He took a photo of the vista while Saul untied two axes from the back of the truck and handed one to Paul. After Peter put the whisk broom away, the brothers led him and Goldie into the woods via a deep trail of footsteps on the other side of the road, where the snow went almost up to their knees.

"How in the world did you ever find this place?" Goldie asked the brothers as they trudged through the white.

"To you, this is a mountain," Paul said over his shoulder.

"To us, it's our backyard," Saul explained. "We know pretty much every tree and boulder around here, whether snow-covered or not."

"It's also our grocery store," Paul added. "And when we're up here huntin', we're also on the lookout for a pretty town Christmas tree."

"We're like Santa's helpers," Saul said, stone-faced.

"Givers... that's what we are," Paul declared, just as emotionless.

After another couple of minutes of plowing through the snow, the brothers stopped and gestured. In a small clearing, amidst the fifty-foot and frequently scraggly long-needle pines, was a twenty-foot short-needle pine that was full, beautifully shaped, and seemed to have Christmas written all over it.

"Whatdoya think?" Saul asked.

"It's perfect," Peter agreed.

"Absolutely!" Goldie voted. "Seems a shame to cut such a beautiful thing down, though."

"Well, it's only beautiful if people can see it," Peter reminded. "Besides, it gets three lives. It's been growing up here in the woods for years, providing a home for the birds. Soon, it'll be the centerpiece of the town's holiday decorations. Then later, it'll be free firewood for a lot of families. So, in a very real way, it'll serve several purposes."

"And we'll plant some seedlings here come spring," Paul promised. "For every one tree we cut down, we plant three."

"Cool," Goldie smiled, admiring its perfect shape. "But, how are just the four of us gonna get that thing hauled through the woods and loaded onto the truck? The truck isn't long enough to hold it."

"Don't you worry 'bout that," Paul said. "My cousins Barry, Larry, and Harry are comin' in on horseback." He looked at the sun. "They'll be here in about a half hour. They'll have ropes so we can pull the tree back to the road, then all of us together will lift it right onto the truck, prop the top over the cab, and we'll hitch the bottom securely to the bed."

"This isn't their first tree wrangle," Peter leaned into Goldie.

"No. No, I guess it sure isn't," she said, impressed.

"Let me get a picture of you and the boys in front of the tree before they cut," Peter suggested.

The McCaw brothers and Goldie walked forward toward the tree, then turned and faced Peter with Goldie in the middle. Peter stayed back several feet to get the entire tree in frame, and everyone put their arms around one another's waist. The McCaw brothers didn't change their expressions, but Goldie smiled widely for the camera. After a few seconds, she said:

"Hey, Saul?"

"Yeah?"

"Move your left hand, or you'll never be able to use it again."

Eight

EVASIVE MEANINGS

Peter, Goldie, and the McCaw brothers spent the next couple of hours cutting down the town's Christmas tree, and hauling it back to the road via ropes and horses, courtesy of the McCaws' cousins Barry, Larry, and Harry. The seven of them carefully lifted and rolled the tree onto the McCaws' flatbed Chevy with the help of the horses. The beautiful scenery eventually morphed into cold, hard work for Goldie, but she thoroughly enjoyed it. By a little after 1:00 p.m., the tree was coming down River Street towards the post office, where a volunteer crew was quickly assembled to set it in place, which they had all done before. Sparkledove didn't have a city park per se, but the post office was set back from the street with a fifty-by-twenty-foot brick-laid courtyard in front of it. Using ropes and long, retractable poles with V-shaped ends, the tree was pushed to an upright position, then lifted into a large tree stand made of lumber waiting in a corner of the courtyard. Next, the base was secured with wooden wedges while the legs of the stand were weighed down with sandbags.

When everything was secure and in place, the McCaw brothers tipped their earflap caps to the local helpers, then returned to their home in the high country. Peter asked Goldie if she wanted to go to Clancy's Bar & Grill for an Elk Burger and a beer, and after a long morning of such physical work, she was more than ready.

By 2:25, Peter and Goldie were coming out of Clancy's when something disturbing caught her eye. She saw Peter's father, Charles, talking to a woman in her mid-to-late thirties outside the Sparkledove City Hall. The woman was distressed, crying, and Charles was gesturing calmly with his arms, apparently trying to explain something. Goldie didn't know the woman's name, but she recognized her from the potluck Thanksgiving dinner at St. Mark's.

"What's goin' on?" she asked Peter, pausing and watching.

"That's Martha Eggleston," Peter replied. "Sad story there. She was married to a man named Bucky. Nice guy. He was a civil engineer and commuted to and from Denver. But a couple of months ago, he was driving home late one night and went off the road. Fell asleep, I heard. Unfortunately, he was killed. Everybody in town was pretty stunned by it."

"She's still cryin' for her husband?" Goldie asked.

"My guess is she's crying because she's about to

lose her home," Peter explained. "She didn't work, and they've got an expensive place over on Falcon Drive just a few blocks that way," he pointed. "Scuttlebutt is she can't afford it anymore, and the bank may foreclose. My father's probably trying to list it for her. He owns the realty company in town."

"Yeah, I know."

"But homes are never worth what owners think they are," he added. "And with the war, there isn't a lot of movement in the market."

"Geez, that really sucks," Goldie observed. "To lose your partner and your home one right after the other. Believe me, I know."

"Sucks," he repeated, slightly amused. "I've never heard a girl talk exactly like you before. But, you're right," he quickly agreed. "What Martha's going through right now is terrible. Sucks."

Not long after, Goldie returned to her hotel, and Peter returned to his office and the business of putting together the weekly newspaper. He didn't spend a lot of ink on the war news unless it was a major development because he figured people could get that from the Denver paper and the radio. He concentrated instead on local stories and interesting tidbits for the tourist traffic that would steadily increase between now and Christmas.

Back at the hotel, Goldie got some fresh gauze from the first aid kit behind the front counter, then called her publisher, Owen Mitchell, to report on her activities thus far. During the brief conversation, she also learned a couple of new things about the Goldie Maraschino of 1942 and her current assignment. She was informed that Charles Banyan had purchased her an open-ended plane ticket and had invited her to remain in Sparkledove right through the Christmas holiday. But nobody realistically expected her to do this. Mitchell figured she'd have plenty to write about by mid-December. She also learned from her boss that she'd had similar assignments for December features in previous years because she was unattached and had no one waiting for her in Columbus. This particular piece of information struck her as depressing. But she couldn't argue about the person she'd been in the past. She could only do something about the person she was now.

She returned to her room, discovered her laundered clothes, and changed into nice slacks and a blouse. After freshening up in the bathroom and putting the new gauze on her hand, she went back to her room and sat at her desk for a long time, writing questions to herself using the pad and pencil she'd retrieved from her purse. The questions were self-analytical, like: "Why 1942?" "Why Sparkledove?" "Am I dead?" "Am I supposed to write a story?" "Am I supposed to accomplish something?" "If I do, can I return to my own time?" "What about the man on the bridge?" "No splash." "No body." It was all very confusing.

At about 7:15 p.m., she went downstairs for dinner: a Coke and a salad. It was during this light meal that she realized the impetus of her being in Sparkledove wasn't because she'd been struck by a car in New York; it was the mayor, Charles Banyan, who had reached out to Owen Mitchell and was paying her expenses. *I need to get to know him better,* she decided. *See what makes him tick. But first, I need to go back to that covered bridge.*

After dinner, she returned to her room and put on her new jacket, hat, and gloves from Miller's General Store, then went back downstairs and borrowed a flashlight from the registration counter. Leaving the hotel, she walked to the covered bridge, hoping to arrive about the same time she had when she first saw the man. She didn't know what to expect, but she had a theory. She believed the man she'd seen jump off the bridge was an apparition. The notion was odd because her entire existence in Sparkledove could be an apparition. But she was basing this theory on what she didn't hear or see. She didn't hear the man's approaching footsteps on the bridge. She didn't hear a splash when his body hit the water or see a disturbance in the water. And she didn't find a body. Furthermore, the man didn't even acknowledge her. Nobody in town had said anything about someone jumping off the bridge. Not Maddie, Peter Banyan, the folks she'd met at Miller's—no one. Being a small town, she figured people would gossip about everything. Especially someone's husband, boyfriend, or son who had come home soaking wet in the dead of winter. But none of that happened. So, it couldn't have been real, right? At least, that's what she was thinking.

It was snowing lightly by the time she reached the bridge. Snow wasn't sticking to the ground yet, but the cold air smelled like it could change at any moment. Everything was still and quiet as it had been the night before Thanksgiving. Goldie walked to the middle of the bridge, her footsteps echoing on the plank wood floor, and looked out at the picturesque view as she had done before. The view from the open-air window wasn't as clear as it had been two nights earlier. She looked down at the quiet, slow-moving river, then walked to the other side of the bridge and looked at the view from the upriver direction where the river turned toward her. The view wasn't as pretty as the downriver direction, but it was still nice.

She stood in the middle of the bridge, looking out one window, then the other, for nearly two minutes. Then, she walked down to its other end, where the dirt road turned left and went up a slight incline into some woods. Now having a flashlight in hand, she decided to walk up the road and into the woods. She went about a hundred yards up the incline until she came to a six-foot-high wire fence and gate with a sign that said: "No Trespassing by order of the Sparkledove Sheriff's Department." The wire gate was held shut by a chain and padlock, but there was enough length on the chain that a person could squeeze through if they really tried. Goldie turned her light one way along the fence, then the other. It stretched in both directions beyond the beam of her light and went off into the dark woods. It wasn't hurricane fencing, but it was still a crisscross pattern of heavy-gauge wire that a construction company might use.

While all sorts of reasons for the fence came into her mind, her thoughts were suddenly interrupted by the nearby groan of an animal. Being from the city, she wasn't quite sure if it was a groan, a growl, or a howl, but it didn't sound friendly. A couple of seconds later, she heard something scurrying through the underbrush coming toward her.

Deciding to make a hasty exit, Goldie turned and ran back down the dirt road. As she did, she used her flashlight and looked behind her, expecting to see anything from a bear to Sasquatch pursuing. But she saw nothing. She was relieved when she saw the lit interior of the covered bridge, and she ran back onto the relative safety of its wooden planks when she abruptly stopped. She stopped because the man with the high forehead she'd seen two nights earlier was once again on the bridge. He was wearing the exact same clothing: a lightweight red plaid jacket, blue slacks, and brown lace-up boots. He stood looking out at the downriver viewing window and ignoring Goldie, just as he had done before.

"*Hey, you!*" she yelled. "*Mister!*"

Not reacting to her call, the man stepped up onto the wooden windowsill and ducked his head to clear the height from the top of the window. Goldie bolted after him as he held onto the inside edges of the window with his fingertips and leaned his body out over the river. She extended a hand to grab the back of his jacket, but just missed it as he fell off the bridge. This time, however, she was close enough that when she got to the window, she should've seen his body hit the water. But it didn't happen. Just a second after the man fell, Goldie was at the window. She peered down and saw nothing.

She clicked on her flashlight and scanned the water. It was calm and moving as slowly as before. Then she looked down the bridge toward the dirt road. There was no evidence of an animal chasing her.

"Damnit!" she cried, slamming a gloved hand against the side of the bridge.

She stuck her head out the window and looked down at the water.

"Who are you?" she demanded. *"What does this mean?"*

Nine

MARTHA EGGLESTON

The following morning, a little after 10:00 a.m., Goldie walked into Clara's Gifts. She was wearing slacks and walking shoes from her suitcase, and her new jacket and gloves from Miller's. "Tangerine" by Jimmy Dorsey was playing on the Philco radio, and the place was now heavily decorated for Christmas. Like the first time she had entered the store, the old wooden floor squeaked, announcing her arrival, and the place smelled wonderful due to the fresh pine wreaths and the open jar of cinnamon sticks on the counter.

"Oh, hey, honey!" Clara called. She was leaning casually on one of her counters and looking at the *Denver Post*. Her mostly white hair was hanging loose today, and she wore an attractive blouse and pants outfit. Except for herself, Goldie noticed that Clara was the only other woman in Sparkledove she'd seen wear pants.

"Morning, Clara," Goldie smiled.

"That's sure a pretty tree you, Peter, and the McCaw boys got yesterday. It's maybe going to be our best one ever."

"Thanks. I enjoyed goin' with them. It was fun."

The older woman gestured to the paper on the counter before her. "Speaking of brothers, I was just reading about those Sullivan boys who died a couple of weeks back. Terrible tragedy."

"Sullivan boys?" Goldie asked.

"The five brothers who went down on the Juneau during the Battle of Guadalcanal." She shook her head. "Their poor mother... all her babies gone at once."

"Yeah," Goldie nodded, remembering the Steven Spielberg film *Saving Private Ryan* and wondering if the Sullivan brothers were the inspiration for the script. "Very sad."

"And the others, too," Clara added.

"Others?"

"Yes. Several other sets of brothers died when the Juneau sank."

"Rrright," Goldie said, not knowing this. "Terrible."

Clara looked at her visitor for a moment, realizing she was unfamiliar with these events. She noted it, then let it pass, remembering she must've come in for a reason.

"What can I do for you, honey?"

"Do you know Martha Eggleston?"

"Sure. There's another sad tragedy."

"I saw her yesterday, and she was pretty upset. I wanted to drop by her house today and see how she's doin', and I thought I'd take her a little holiday remembrance of some sort."

"Angels," Clara said knowingly. "Martha loves angels. Got a nice display of 'em right over here."

Clara led the way to a shelf where a wide selection of decorative angels sat. As Goldie was looking them over, Father Fitzsimmons came into the store.

"Mornin', ladies," he greeted, and the floor squeaked when he entered.

"Morning, Father," Clara smiled.

"Ay, Padre," Goldie greeted.

"I need some wreaths for the church to hang on the outside door and inside over the stained glass windows. I'll need eight."

"Coming right up, Father!" Clara smiled. "I have to get them from the back. Just give me a minute."

As Clara disappeared into the rear room of the store, Father Fitz came over to where Goldie was and looked at the angels.

"Getting yourself a souvenir?"

"No. A gift for Martha Eggleston. I saw her talking to the mayor yesterday, and she seemed distraught."

"Yes," he nodded. "I've heard about her troubles. You getting her something to lift her spirits is very nice, Goldie."

She picked up a white ceramic angel holding a small hand harp and singing.

"What do ya think of this one?" she asked.

"Quite lovely," the priest agreed.

She looked at the figure for a moment. "Do you think they're real, Father? Angels?"

"Of course. They're written about in the Bible from beginning to end," he noted. "From the Book of Genesis right through to the Book of Revelation. We're told angels were present at the birth of Christ."

"So—if angels exist—then demons must, too, huh?"

"Sure, I'd agree with that," he said.

"What about ghosts, Father?" she wondered, thinking about the man on the covered bridge. "Souls that are neither angel nor demon? Do you think God lets ghosts wander around the planet?"

"I think there are a lot of things in the universe we don't know about or understand," he replied. "First Corinthians tells us that God's wisdom is not man's. Now, you can either conclude that's a very convenient piece of scripture priests pull out of their pockets to explain away things, or, if you're a person of faith, you can accept it."

"I don't know what I am," she admitted.

"Well, either way, I still think the angel is pretty and that Martha will like it."

Just then, another customer came into the store. He was about Clara's age and wore slightly dirty work clothing as if he worked in construction.

"Morning, Father," he greeted, coming in.

"Hello, Herb," Father Fitz reciprocated. "How was work?"

"Oh, fine. I want to get a certain type of Christmas

music box for Sharon before they sell out again. She saw them here last year and went crazy for them. But by the time I got to my shopping, they were gone."

The clergyman nodded, then gestured to Goldie. "You probably haven't met our esteemed writer from *Adventure Escape Magazine*. This is Goldie Maraschino. Goldie, Herb Pontz."

"Also known as Karen Maraschino, like the cherry," Herb proclaimed, extending a hand. "I've read your work, young lady. I love *Adventure Escape*. Never miss an issue."

"Really? Great," she said, shaking hands with him and hoping he wouldn't ask her anything about a past story.

"Oh, hi, Herb," Clara called, reappearing from the back room with her arms encircled by green wreaths. "You just getting home?"

"Yeah. And I wanted to get one of them music boxes for Sharon this year. You said you'd be ordering more, remember?"

"Yep, and I already put one aside for her. So, don't you worry. You can get it now or whenever you want."

"Oh, thanks. If I picked it up in a day or so, could you have it gift wrapped for me?"

"You bet," Clara smiled.

"Great. I'm off tomorrow, but going out of town. So, I'll come by first thing Monday morning."

"Herb does the night shift at the brass works in Denver," Father explained to Goldie. "They're running twenty-four hours a day, seven days a week."

"Brass works, eh? That many people need candlesticks?" she quipped. "Or is Colorado more spittoon country?"

"Munitions, dear," Clara clarified. "Brass casings for our boys to fight our enemies."

Goldie's face turned red with embarrassment. "The war... of course..." She looked at Herb.

"I didn't mean any disrespect. I'm sure your efforts are helpin' to save hundreds of lives."

"Or end hundreds of lives, depending on how you look at it," he replied. He turned back to Clara. "Anyway, thanks for doing the gift wrapping. I'm not very good with that kinda stuff."

"Especially after working all night," Father said empathetically.

"True enough," Herb agreed. "It's been a hard day's night, and I've been working like a dog."

"What?" Goldie asked, surprised.

"Hey, isn't that Sharon across the street?" Clara asked, looking toward the front window.

Herb, Father Fitz, and Goldie all turned, looked out the window, and saw a woman walk into a store called Summit Grocers.

"Geez, it is!" Herb said. "She's probably getting groceries for breakfast. I gotta scoot. If she sees me in here, she'll figure out what I'm doing. She really made a thing out of wanting one of them music boxes last year."

Herb started to hurry toward the door. "Gift

wrapped by Monday morning, right?" he called over his shoulder.

"Promise," Clara assured.

"Hey, Herb," Goldie said, "where'd you come up with that—"

But it was too late; the munitions worker was already out the door.

"That's the second time that's happened," she muttered, more to herself than Clara or Father Fitz.

"What's that?" the priest asked.

Goldie paused, thinking about how to respond. She couldn't exactly say she'd heard a young man named Dexter use a line from a Jackson 5 song in the lobby of her hotel, nor could she say that Herb just recited lyrics from a Beatles song. After all, nobody knew about the Jackson 5 or the Beatles in 1942.

"Nothin'," she said, figuring it must've been another odd coincidence.

"How about gift wrapping for *you*, honey?" Clara inquired, gesturing to the angel.

Fifteen minutes later, Goldie was walking up the sidewalk of the Eggleston residence on Falcon Drive with the boxed and gift-wrapped angel in hand. She'd gotten the address from Clara, although Peter had mentioned she lived on Falcon Drive the day before. Like so many houses in town, it was a lovely two-story Victorian. It was built in 1879, and although the house was wood, it had a distinctive fieldstone chimney that ran up the right-hand side of the house. It also had a nice rectangular stained glass window over the front door and a red Sparkledove Realty sign in the front yard.

Martha Eggleston was trim, in her mid-to-late thirties, and had black hair that she wore in tight curls on the sides of her head that got longer and looser toward the back; Victory Curls, people called them. She wore a plain blue dress with a white cardigan sweater. Goldie asked for a few minutes of her time to give her a little gift. Martha recognized her from the potluck dinner at St. Mark's and invited her in for coffee. The house had very few lights on, but Goldie could see that it was nicely decorated, although not for Christmas.

While water was heating up in a tea kettle on the stove, the women sat at the kitchen table, and Goldie presented her gift. Martha was both pleased with and saddened by the ceramic angel.

"It's beautiful!" she exclaimed. "But my heart's just not into decorating this year. In fact, I've asked to withdraw from the Tour of Homes."

"What's that?" Goldie queried.

"Homes are opened up to visitors on the second Friday and Saturday evenings in December," she replied. "Just the first floors. Everybody on the tour decorates their home in the style of the 1860s to 1890s. Except, no candles on the Christmas trees. That's too much of a fire hazard."

"Right," Goldie recalled, "the mayor mentioned something to me about that."

"Yes," she said, disgusted. "Just another one of his

many ways to drive us homeowners into the poor house."

Martha caught herself and stepped back on her attitude. "Sorry, Goldie. You're here to write a tourism story. Not hear the gripes of an angry widow."

"It's okay," the younger woman reassured. "Anything you say to me is off the record and won't have any effect on the article. Part of the reason I'm here today is that I thought you might need to vent."

"Vent?"

"Talk things out. Believe me, I understand having no one to talk to when things turn to crap."

Martha rose from the table, folded her arms, and went to her kitchen window, staring out pensively at the overcast day.

"We moved here six years ago because of the charm of the town and the beautiful old houses, nestled in between the mountains and the river. We liked the idea of living in a place where people wanted to go for the holidays... the Fourth of July, Christmas... things like that.

"But the town's historical society really expects you to keep your houses just so. Especially on the outside. Owning an old home is like owning a boat. You just keep pouring more and more money into this big hole. Exterior painting, a new roof, landscaping, and even the type of curtains we hang are dictated. Besides the upkeep, we were also paying dues to the historical society for street maintenance, upkeep of the covered bridge, flowers in common areas in the summer—you name it. With Bucky commuting and me not working, we never saved a dime."

"Did you ever think about goin' to work?" Goldie asked.

"Of course. But I've got no car now, and that really limits work options. I also have no skills. I never worked before because Bucky wanted his wife to be a homemaker like his mother. We were hoping to raise a family. We tried for years to have kids, but it never happened. Actually, in an odd way, that turned out to be a blessing. We had to take out a second mortgage because we weren't keeping up with things. Mayor Banyan actually makes home inspections. Did you know that?"

"No, I didn't," Goldie replied.

"I wouldn't be surprised if he's taking some of those historical society dues and lining his own pockets."

Just then, the tea kettle started to whistle.

"When the war broke out, things got even tougher," Martha continued, rising and going over to the stove. "There were manpower shortages at Bucky's office. He was working longer and longer hours."

"Yes. I heard he'd fallen asleep and gone off the road comin' home one night," Goldie said. "I'm so very sorry."

Martha stopped in mid-reach for two coffee cups and turned to her visitor. "He didn't fall asleep," she said with certainty. "He called me just before he left the office that night and said he'd been drinking coffee all day. I distinctly remember. It was a Wednesday, and he joked on the phone about how he'd be up until Friday. He *didn't* fall asleep."

"He could've been drinkin' decaf?" Goldie suggested.

"Bucky hated decaf," the hostess replied. "Said there was a big taste difference."

Goldie paused and thought while her hostess turned back to get the coffee cups.

"Okay... so, what do *you* think happened?"

"I think he either swerved to avoid something on the highway, or..."

"Or, what?"

"Or he was purposely run off the road. Maybe by another car following or an oncoming car from the opposite direction. Possibly a drunk driver that weaved over the centerline."

Goldie paused again and considered what she was hearing while Martha spooned coffee from a can into the cups, poured in the hot water, then stirred."

"I don't have any milk or sugar," she said. "I'm sorry."

"It's okay... was there any evidence to suggest Bucky was run off the road?"

"No," Martha admitted, still stirring. "There were no skid marks on the pavement or damage done to our car that suggested he was rammed from behind. But then, the car was also a mess, so how could they tell? It went off the highway at a steep embankment and rolled over several times before—" she stopped as tears filled her eyes. She set her spoon down, excused herself, then went into the bathroom to get some toilet tissue and blow her nose. While she was gone, Goldie got up and brought the filled cups over to the table. She put Martha's cup in front of the chair where she'd been sitting.

"Sorry," Martha said, returning about a minute later. "I still fall apart rather easily."

"Totally understandable," Goldie assured. "So, the cops suspect no foul play, huh?"

"No," Martha said, shaking her head and sitting down again. "And now the house is sold. I mean, I *had* to. I was destitute."

"Sold?" Goldie queried. "But there's a For Sale sign in the yard."

"Yes. It's for sale because I sold it yesterday to Sparkledove Realty. You probably saw me bawling my eyes out on the street with the mayor."

"Yeah, I did."

"We'd just finished signing the paperwork at city hall. Then he put up a sign in the yard late yesterday afternoon. The bastard sure didn't waste any time, if you'll pardon my language."

Goldie took a sip of her coffee. So did Martha. The two women were quiet for a few moments. Finally, Goldie asked:

"Look, it's not any of my business, but what do you mean you were destitute? Didn't Bucky have life insurance?"

"No. He was only thirty-eight. Everything went into the house. Like I said, we had no savings, I have no job, and we had a first *and* second mortgage. My parents offered to help for a little while, but they live out of state. Bucky certainly didn't come from money, so selling was my only option."

"Well—did you at least get a good price?"

"During a war, when no one can afford to buy houses? Ha!" Martha exclaimed. "I sold it for a little over half of what we paid, even after all the improvements. That Charles Banyan, he shakes your hand in friendship with one hand while his other is reaching for your wallet. He's a snake! I can't believe he and Peter are even related. They're so different. You should've seen the beautiful obituary Peter wrote for Bucky. It was actually more like a short story. He wrote about how everyone liked him, about how he helped the local scout troop here in town and taught boys to fly cast down at the river." She looked around. "I've got a copy in the other room if you'd care to see it."

"I would," Goldie said.

Martha rose and got a copy of *The Sparkledove Wing* from another room, then returned and handed it to Goldie. As the visitor read it, she agreed with Martha's assessment. The obituary read more like a four-hundred-word compassionate short story about a local resident who was well-liked and went out of his way to be a part of the small town, instead of the gory details of his death. Goldie certainly appreciated learning more about Bucky through the obituary, but the thoughtful way it was written also made her all the more attracted to Peter Banyan.

After another twenty minutes of visiting, Goldie left the Eggleston house and stepped back outside and onto the sidewalk of Falcon Drive. She hadn't noticed it before, but when she returned to the sidewalk, something caught her eye. Falcon Drive was a short side street with only ten houses on the street, five on each side. There was a red Sparkledove Realty For Sale sign in the front yard of the Eggleston house, but there was also another one in the yard of the house next door. There was no sign in the yard of the next house, but there was in the yard of the house after that.

Three out of five houses are for sale on the same side of the street, she thought. She didn't know what that meant, but she didn't think it was a mere coincidence.

Ten

CLAUDE BOLTON

It was a short walk from Martha Eggleston's house back to River Street. Spotting the storefront office of Sparkledove Realty, Goldie decided to see if Charles Banyan was there, and without insulting him or putting his patronage at risk, see if she could learn anything more about what Martha Eggleston had claimed.

The realty office was small. It consisted of an outer office for a secretary and a larger and more richly appointed rear office, which was Banyan's. There was also a beautiful five-foot-high Christmas tree in the front picture window of the office that Banyan, himself, was decorating with tinsel and wooden ornaments. Seeing Goldie approach from outside, he smiled warmly and gestured for her to come inside.

"Good morning, Goldie," he greeted as she entered. "How are you?"

"Fine, Charles. How're you?"

"Good. Say, that was a beautiful tree you and the McCaw brothers brought to town. Just beautiful. It's nearly decorated, and we'll have the official lighting ceremony tomorrow night. I hope the McCaw boys behaved themselves with you up in the mountains."

"They were fine," she replied. "And gettin' the tree was fun."

"Well, I'm glad you had an adventure," he said, hanging a small wooden sled on the tree and reaching for another ornament. "I meant to tell you about it at Thanksgiving dinner. But the conversation got a little sidetracked. Peter and I push each other's buttons sometimes."

"It's all good," she assured.

"I'm sorry, I don't have coffee or a soda to offer you," he said, hanging another ornament. "My girl called in sick this morning, and I wanted to get this tree decorated. I know most people don't do their tree trimming until closer to Christmas, but the holidays mean big revenue for the town. So, everyone hops right into Christmas after Thanksgiving."

"No problem. I actually just had coffee with a new acquaintance, Martha Eggleston."

The mayor paused, seeming concerned, but then recovered, smiled, and picked up another ornament from a box.

"Oh? How is Martha today? She's had a pretty rough time of it as you've probably heard."

"Her emotions are fragile," Goldie agreed.

"How do you know Martha?" he asked, hanging the next ornament.

"Actually, we met at St. Mark's. When Peter walked me home after dinner at your place, I saw some people goin' into the church, thought there might be an evenin' service, and went back there to check it out."

"I see," Banyan said. "It's very sad what happened to her husband."

"And likewise sad she's so financially strapped."

"She told you about that, huh?"

"*All* about it," Goldie confirmed.

"Well," Banyan shrugged, "she's not as strapped as she used to be. This company just bought her house yesterday. So, come Monday, she can go to the bank and have access to funds. I'm also allowing her to stay in the house rent-free through the holidays. So, she'll have plenty of time to make new plans."

"Yes," Goldie agreed. "But I'm sure *you* did well on the deal, too."

"Not right now," Banyan chuckled, reaching for a little wooden fire truck. "The housing market is very slow, and now I'm in charge of its upkeep. But we can't have Martha out on the streets. And that's where she was headed had I not stepped in and offered to buy her place."

"She tells a little different story about you coming to her rescue," Goldie replied, realizing she was taking a bit of a chance and upsetting her host.

"I'm sure she does," Banyan replied, hanging the

truck ornament and apparently unfazed. He looked out the window and saw a couple walking across the street. The man of the couple was the one in the red bathrobe that Goldie had run into a couple of times outside of her hotel room door. "C'mere. I want to show you something."

Goldie stepped over to the window as he pointed to the pair.

"See that couple? They're from Fort Collins. They come here every year for a week or so. They have a nice Thanksgiving dinner at the Sparkledove Arms, shop, take a scenic train ride, and maybe take a couple of evening walks to the covered bridge. Kicking off their holiday season in Sparkledove has become their tradition. Over the next four weeks, hundreds of other families will do the same. Christmas is our biggest money-making time of the year, Goldie. Eli Johnson's family brought him here when he was a boy, and Bucky and Martha Eggleston likewise fell in love with the town during our Christmas season. And it's not just the mountains or the quaint stores on River Street that keep bringing people back. It's also the Victorian homes and how wonderfully they're preserved. It's tradition. Continuity.

"But those homes require a lot of maintenance. This is harsh country. The elements are tough on structures. Everyone who buys a historic house in Sparkledove consents to live under conditions set by the historical society. Homeowners have a responsibility to their properties as well as monthly dues. Dues, incidentally, that are paying for your room and meals. As both president of the historical society and mayor, I suppose I'm the enforcer of those responsibilities and dues. Over time, some people may become a little resentful of my role. I understand that. But let's also keep things in perspective. Martha and Bucky agreed to the terms of the historical society. Nobody prevented Martha from working and bringing in a second income except her husband, and Bucky chose not to protect his wife with life insurance. So, once again, my buying the house from Martha really actually saved her skin."

Goldie had to admit, Banyan made a persuasive argument. But some things still didn't sit well with her. Martha Eggleston's resentment of him was pretty strong, suggesting maybe he'd badgered her and her husband. Lupe's comment of, "You don't know Señor Banyan," also stuck out in her mind. Then there was the way he and Peter had fought over almost everything at Thanksgiving dinner. Her years with Markie had taught her to smell hidden intentions from a mile away, and although she wasn't sure why, Charles Banyan was beginning to stink to her.

As she was leaving the realty office, Eli Johnson drove down the street and pulled up next to her in his Ford sedan. He beeped his horn, which caused her to stop and turn. He smiled and rolled down his window.

"Howdy," he said.

She waited for him to say something more, but then realized he expected her to greet him. "Howdy," she replied, a little impatiently and tiring of his Roy Rogers routine.

"Got a second?"

"Sure."

"Hop in."

She rounded the cruiser and climbed in on the passenger side.

"What's up, Dick Tracy?" she began.

"I did what you asked. Looked back at the incident reports, and there *was* someone who jumped off the covered bridge and committed suicide. Happened about five years ago."

"Really?"

"Yep. Man's name was Claude Bolton, and it was kind of a strange circumstance."

"What do ya mean?"

"He came into town one afternoon in September. According to witnesses, he was very disoriented and confused. Claimed he didn't know where he was or how he got here." Eli paused and raised an eyebrow. "Sound like anybody we know?"

"What? Are you tryin' to make a connection between a man who wandered into town five years ago and a journalist who was invited?"

"Not necessarily. But it *is* curious you both seemed to have been confused when you first arrived."

"It's only curious if he wound up staying in room 9 of the Sparkledove Arms," she replied. "Eh—he didn't, did he?"

"No. He had identification and money in his

pocket, and he stayed at the Pine River Inn for three nights. On the fourth, he jumped off the covered bridge."

"What did he do during those three days?" she asked.

"The report's not that detailed," he replied.

"What time of day did he jump?"

"Coroner put it between 8:00 and 8:30 p.m. But his body wasn't found until the next morning."

Eli looked out the front windshield and down River Street, shook his head a little, then continued.

"The funny thing is that the water isn't that deep. The report said about six or seven feet. But one of Bolton's hands was jammed in between two boulders on the riverbed. Meaning, he didn't want to come up. Matter of fact, Jason Shirk, the sheriff I replaced, speculated that—based upon the bruising on his wrist and arm—Mr. Bolton might've had to dive to the river bottom repeatedly to find just the right place to get his hand stuck."

"Jesus," Goldie murmured. Partly because it was a terrible way to die and partly because she was right. What she had seen on the bridge was indeed an apparition that apparently appeared every night at the time Bolton originally jumped.

She looked at Eli. "Can you meet me on the bridge at 8:10 tonight?"

"How did you know a man committed suicide from that bridge?" he asked seriously.

"I didn't. It was a guess because of the glassless

viewin' windows. But people like jumpin' off bridges. In New York City, where I was raised, you could practically set your watch to the bodies fallin' off the Brooklyn and George Washington bridges."

He gave her a suspicious look. "Are you somehow connected to this guy?"

"No. Why would you ask?"

"Because he listed a home address in Taos at the Pine River Inn that was a dead end. Same thing on his identification papers. Meaning, we had no way to contact the next of kin. Bolton's buried right here in town."

"Strange," she said, under her breath.

"He could've been on the run from something," Eli speculated. "Is there something you know about this guy that I don't?"

"Can you meet me tonight, or not?"

"Yyyeah," he drawled, "I figure I can."

"Good," she said, opening the car door and getting ready to hop out. "Bring the report with you and a flashlight. Don't be late."

At 6:20 p.m., Goldie came downstairs from her room in the Sparkledove Arms to find something new. A nine-foot-high Christmas tree had replaced the crimson circular sofa that usually sat in the middle of the lobby. Standing on a step ladder and decorating the tree was the young woman named Josie, who'd been dressed up as a Native American on Thanksgiving. Now, she was dressed up as one of Santa's elves, complete with green pointed shoes, green leotards, a long red top with a wide black belt, and a red pointed hat with a white snowball-like pom-pom. With her Indian wig off, Goldie could see she had light-brown hair in a pageboy cut that accentuated her dimples.

"Ay, looks nice," Goldie said, approaching the tree. "Josie, right?"

"Yes," she said, tucking some lights into the branches. "And you're Miss Maraschino? Room 9?"

"Call me Goldie."

The young lady came down the ladder. "Can I help you with something, Goldie?"

"Naw. I just think it's nice how you dress up for the holidays."

"Maddie and Dean pay me extra if I dress up as an elf." She looked at the guest, then suddenly remembered. "Or, should I say, 'Native Northpoler.'"

Goldie smiled. "If that's the title Santa's helpers prefer. I'll have to check with Will Ferrell about that."

"Who?"

"Never mind."

"I prefer the title of broke, overworked high school student," the younger one noted. "But I don't think that would fit on a nametag."

Goldie smiled again as she headed for the restaurant. "I like your ambition, Josie. It's cool. See ya later."

A little after 8:00 p.m., after she'd had a delicious pork chop dinner with green beans, Goldie approached the covered bridge. A young couple was just leaving the bridge arm in arm, and this was the first evidence she'd seen that the place was a romantic stop, as Eli Johnson had once suggested. It was another cold night in Colorado; the temperature hovered in the mid-thirties, but with her outerwear from Miller's, she was fortified for it. She slowly walked the entire length of the bridge. At the other end, near the dirt road that went up and into the woods, she heard footsteps behind her. Turning around, she saw Eli Johnson walking toward her. He was wearing his brown suede jacket but not his police uniform. Instead, he was wearing slacks, casual shoes, and a crewneck sweater. As she'd requested, he carried a flashlight, and as he came toward her, she couldn't help but think he'd cut a nice figure were it not for his limp.

"Howdy," he greeted in his usual way.

"Oh, my God," she moaned under her breath, weary of his country song manners. "How ya doin', Sheriff?" she called. She looked him over. "You're out of uniform."

"Got off duty at 6:00," he replied, coming closer. "Supposed to be at my parents' tonight. My mother's making pot roast."

"You blew off your parents for me?" she asked. "I'm honored."

"Wellll," he drawled, "you've never had my mom's pot roast. If we could mass-produce it and bomb Germany, the war would be over within days."

"Pretty bad, huh?"

"Yeah, but she keeps makin' it. She *is* determined," he grinned. "Like you." He was now standing next to her at the far end of the bridge. "So, what's goin' on? You wanted me here at 8:10, and here I am."

"You said the coroner said Claude Bolton jumped off the bridge between 8:00 p.m. and 8:30."

"Right. But that was in September. This is November. You gonna ask me to re-enact the event?"

She gestured to the overhead lights. "Was the bridge lit five years ago?"

He turned and glanced at the lights, thinking. "Y'know, I don't rightly know. But what difference would it make?"

"I don't know," she admitted. "Maybe none."

He turned back to her. "Why'd you want me to meet you here, Goldie?"

"Did you bring the incident report with you?" she asked.

"Yeah," he said, patting the inside pocket of his jacket. "Why are we out here?"

"Did the report say anything about how Bolton was dressed?"

"Dressed?"

"Yeah. What was he wearin'?"

Just then, at the other end of the bridge, Claude Bolton came walking out of the shadows and silently stepped onto the bridge with his footsteps making no sound. His hands were in the pockets of his lightweight plaid jacket, his face was emotionless, and his eyes were fixed on the glassless window to his left in the middle of the bridge. Goldie saw him but didn't react and waited for Eli, facing her, to answer her question.

Eli dipped a hand into his inside jacket pocket and pulled out the incident report. Even though the bridge had overhead lighting, he clicked on his flashlight and used it for additional illumination.

"A plaid jacket and blue slacks," he replied, reading.

"How old was he?" she asked.

He checked the report again as Claude Bolton arrived at the viewing window and looked out at the river.

"Thirty-six," he replied.

"And which side did he jump off?"

Eli clicked off his flashlight, then turned and used it as a pointer while Bolton was stepping up onto the windowsill. There was no possible way the lawman could miss seeing him. Unless he couldn't see him.

"The downriver side," he answered.

It was at this precise moment that Goldie realized something she suspected but didn't know for sure until now. Claude Bolton was committing suicide every night at the exact same time that he'd originally committed suicide five years earlier. Furthermore, no one in Sparkledove could see his routine of misery. No one except her. That's why she needed Eli Johnson on the bridge at this precise moment: to verify she was the only one who saw him.

Having lived with Markie for years and also having found herself in dozens of situations where she had to conceal her emotions and be as cool as a cucumber, Goldie's green eyes shifted from Bolton silently falling through the window back to Eli.

"As you know, I write for a travel magazine," she said. "I like my job. I'm grateful to have it, and I'll write a wonderful story about Sparkledove that'll be everythin' your mayor is payin' for. But there's always been this other part of me that wants to do investigative journalism. Crime stories, or maybe a war correspondent. The thing is, there aren't opportunities like that for women. So, when I saw the bridge with its open windows, I played a hunch. And since my hunch was right, I wanted to be here at the time of his death to sort of—I guess—feel Claude Bolton's desperation. Try to understand it. Especially since none of his friends or family know what happened to him. Does that make sense?"

Goldie could lie with the best of them. But, in all fairness to her, what else could she say? She didn't know why she could see something nobody else could see, but she felt like she was on some kind of mystical mission. A mission she had to figure out.

Eli's blue eyes gazed into hers, and he nodded a little.

"Sure. I get that, I guess." He hesitated for a moment, then asked: "You, uh, you maybe want to go get a drink?"

"Is this in your official capacity as sheriff?" she asked.

"No, ma'am. Uniform's off," he replied.

She, likewise, hesitated before answering, but then smiled slightly.

"Okay, copper. Let's go."

Eleven

THE PINE RIVER INN

The Pine River Inn was another hotel in town that was smaller than the Sparkledove Arms, but it had a full bar next to its restaurant, so it was every bit as popular. The walls of Pine River's bar were pine logs, and mounted animals sat on wooden perches, staring down at customers. A mountain lion here, a horned ram there, and a moose head with Christmas tinsel hanging from its antlers behind the bar. The place was pretty busy, and Eli and Goldie got the last available booth. She ordered a whiskey on the rocks, and he ordered a beer.

"Since you're missin' dinner with your folks, go ahead and order somethin' if you're hungry," Goldie offered.

"I made a sandwich at my apartment," he said. "But if you're hungry—"

"No. I ate at my hotel."

He nodded, and they were quiet for a moment. Finally, Goldie asked:

"So, your boss, the mayor, you like him?"

"He hired me, so sure."

"And you're the only cop in town?"

"Yeah. As you may've noticed, Sparkledove isn't exactly a hotbed of crime. It's actually more of a PR job."

"And the guy you replaced?"

"Jason Shirk. He passed away after a heart attack. I never met him, but from what I understand, he had a great background as a lawman. He was a state trooper before he came to Sparkledove.

"And Banyan just hired you out of the blue?"

"Well, I did have military training, I'm pretty good with a weapon, plus, I'm taking a correspondence course in law enforcement."

"You mean, you're not even a real cop? You're a pretend cop?"

"No. I'm a real sheriff. But I'm trying to improve myself by learning more. Nothing wrong with that, is there?"

"No," she said. "'Course not. I'm just surprised."

The waitress brought their drinks. After she left, Goldie took a sip, nodded her approval, then changed directions. "Did you ever investigate Bucky Eggleston's death?"

He looked at her, surprised. "Bucky Eggleston? How do you know about—" Then he remembered. "Oh, Martha. She was at the potluck dinner."

"And I had coffee with her today," she added.

"Uh, no. I wasn't involved in the investigation," he answered, sipping his beer. "The state police handled that."

"What'd they say?"

"He fell asleep and went off the road on an embankment. His car rolled over several times, and he was killed. Very tragic, but pretty cut and dry."

"Have you spoken to Martha about it? She thinks otherwise."

"What does she think happened?"

"She thinks he didn't fall asleep. She thinks there's more to the story, and she might have good reason to believe that. You should talk to her."

"You saying it was foul play, or something?"

"I'm sayin', you should talk to Martha, and don't discount a woman's intuition."

He thought for a moment and took another sip of beer. "Okay. I will."

She likewise took another sip of her whiskey on the rocks, then continued:

"I also wanted to ask you about the road at the end of the covered bridge. It goes up into the woods, but there's a fence and a gate that says, 'No Trespassing.'"

"It leads up to the old Maynard Silver Mine," he nodded. "It was the biggest mine in town back in the day. There's the mine itself, an office, even a house where the director of operations used to live. They say it used to be every bit as nice as some of the homes here in town, but it's all dilapidated now."

"Why is the area fenced off?" she asked.

"Safety. The main mine entrance leads into dozens of tunnels and can go down a quarter of a mile into the mountain. The entrance is sealed off, but you know how tourists or kids can be. If someone got in there, they might never find their way out, and the town doesn't have the resources for a search and rescue. Then there's the buildings. Like I said, they're falling apart. It's too much of a temptation for wannabe explorers, so the entire area is fenced off."

"Can I go up there?"

"What? No. I just told you, it's dangerous."

"Yeah, but the mining history of the town is part of what makes Sparkledove, Sparkledove."

"No, Goldie," he insisted, taking another sip of beer. "The mayor's got pretty strict instructions about that."

"Aw, pleeease," she said, batting her green eyes. "I mean, if the big, strong, handsome sheriff goes with me..."

"Look, I've only been up there twice myself. There's nothing to learn that you can't learn at the historical society. The mine was played out and abandoned years ago. End of story."

Goldie shrugged and took another sip of her drink while glancing around the busy bar. As she did, Eli looked her over.

"You, uh, you don't like your job very much, do you?"

"What do ya mean?

"I mean, you seem to be more interested in sensational things: people jumping off bridges, car accidents that you suspect might not be accidents—"

"I never said it wasn't an accident," she interrupted. "I simply said you should talk to Martha."

"Now you want to go explore a dangerous mine filled with more holes than a piece of Swiss cheese. You're about a hundred miles off course from what brought you here."

"Well, I wasn't wrong about Claude Bolton jumpin' off the bridge," she defended.

"No, you weren't. But it's kind of odd that you'd visit a beautiful covered bridge and come away from the experience thinking about suicide instead of the scenery and the job that brought you here."

"So, you tellin' me what to think?" she asked, becoming prickly.

"I'm saying Claude Bolton was a lucky guess, but he's ancient history. He's got nothing to do with why you're here. Same with Bucky Eggleston. I was told you're supposed to be writing a feel-good piece. You know, 'I'm dreaming of a White Christmas in Sparkledove?'"

Goldie's quick temper flared up, and she stiffened her back.

"Well, excuse me for carin' about the teary-eyed concerns of a sufferin' widow. Excuse me for bein' concerned about a man who died here years ago, and his family has no idea of what happened to him."

"Now, c'mon," he said. "Don't get your nose out of

joint. You said yourself, you're hungry to do a more investigative type of journalism, and I simply meant—"

"I know what you meant," she interrupted. "Don't wonder about things that might interfere with the flow of-of whatever the hell it is you *do* around here! Don't ask questions, Goldie. Don't think. Just go to the historical society, talk to the mayor, and write a nice fluffy piece about all the holiday fun in Sparkledove: 'The perfect place for Christmas.'"

"It's not fluff to the merchants," he reminded. "Or your readers who are hungry for other news besides the war."

She picked up her glass, tossed her head backwards, and finished her whiskey. Then she brought the empty glass firmly down onto the wooden table.

"Thanks for the drink, Sheriff. Sorry I kept you away from your folks."

With that, Goldie grabbed her coat sitting next to her, slid out of the booth, rose, and left the bar, leaving Eli Johnson with a half-finished beer and a furrowed brow.

If she were being totally honest with herself, Goldie wasn't exactly sure why she went off so hard on Eli. Everything he said was reasonable and true. But she didn't like being told no. Especially since she was on the scent of something but didn't know what it was. Or maybe it was because Eli was a cop, and she didn't like cops. Or maybe it was the cowpoke laissez-faire tone of his voice. Or perhaps it was because of the whole time-travel conundrum she was caught up in. Whatever it was, he bugged her.

Twelve

THE TREE LIGHTING

On Sunday, November 29th, the 1,002-person population of Sparkledove seemed to double as people arrived from Denver, Golden, Idaho Springs, Brownsville, and a half dozen other hamlets and villages to witness the community Christmas tree lighting. In addition to tourists, pickup trucks pulled trailers into town that sold everything from cotton candy to funnel cakes to a new snack quickly becoming popular in America called the corn dog. Goldie couldn't imagine where all the people came from, but come they did, and it gave her a much better understanding of the hundreds of families that Charles Banyan had spoken of earlier, as well as the commerce for the town. Christmas in Sparkledove clearly meant serious business.

At 6:50 p.m., Goldie walked down a crowded River Street, chewing her gum and seeing the main thoroughfare in all its festive glory. The street and all of the side streets that turned onto it had been closed off with wooden barricades at both ends. This allowed the overflow of people to walk the street as well as the plank sidewalks. All the stores were open, the vending trailers were decoratively lit, and several people carried lit candles in glass lanterns that were for sale at Clara's Gifts. Goldie even heard someone say that pine roping had been hung on both sides of the covered bridge. Even though the temperature was thirty-three degrees, the crowd made it feel warmer. She spotted Father Fitzsimmons, and they briefly chatted. He had his camera and promised to take photos of the crowd and tree for her. She saw Maddie's husband, Dean. She recognized Melvin Purdle, who'd played his mandolin in the basement of St. Mark's. It was odd to see so many people that she knew compared to an event on the streets of New York, but she liked it. She spotted Sheriff Eli Johnson at a distance, putting up the last side street barricade with the help of two other men she'd never seen before. One had short black hair and a day's worth of black stubble on his face. The other had red hair and a bushy mustache. They weren't young; both were in their forties, but they were big, physically fit, and foreboding with no-nonsense looks. Because of her years with Markie, she couldn't help but think they looked like enforcers for somebody's family.

The courtyard of the post office was the centerpiece of the downtown activity. It featured the decorated but still unlit Christmas tree. There were choir rafters not far from the tree that held an eight-member choral group, singing "Carol of the Bells." Josie was one of the singers, wearing a lovely red-and-white ankle-length Victorian hoop dress, complete with a bonnet. Her boyfriend, Dexter, was smiling proudly from the crowd, wearing his varsity jacket. On the other side of the courtyard was a podium and microphone where the mayor would say a few words. Next to the podium was an overly large prop light switch. It didn't connect to anything, but once thrown, a nearby city engineer would turn on the real power.

Weaving her way through the crowd and cracking her gum as she did, Goldie spotted Paul and Saul McCaw near the courtyard of the post office. They were wearing the same clothes she'd seen them in when they took her into the mountains. They stood there like totem poles, staring unemotionally at the tree and apparently unaffected by the people and holiday spirit in the air. Standing with them were five younger children, ages six to thirteen. Like the brothers, they were dressed in somewhat ragged clothing and looked like they'd all been cast in a production of *Oliver*. They likewise stood looking at the tree, stone-faced, waiting for something to happen.

"Ay, Paul, Saul," she greeted. "How ya doin'?"

"Hey, Goldie," Paul acknowledged.

"Hey," Saul said, straight-faced.

"Come to see your tree all decked out?"

"Yeah," Saul replied. "And to get the kids some jerky from Miller's."

"They got good jerky," Paul noted.

"Yeah, I remember," she said, smiling and looking at the kids. "And who do we have here?"

"Nieces and nephews," Paul said.

"They called us and wanted to see the tree all lit," Saul explained.

"Not to mention hang out with us," Paul added. "We're the fun uncles," he said blankly.

"They 'called' you? You have phone service in the mountains?"

"Maybe," Saul replied. "Depends on the day and whether or not the line is up."

"We're in the phone book," Paul announced, as if it were an accomplishment.

Goldie looked at the deadpan faces of the entire family and took a deep breath. "Alrighty then. You crazy kids try to keep it to a low rumble tonight. Merry Christmas."

"Yup," Saul said.

"Adios," Paul nodded.

She continued moving through the crowd toward the podium and got about ten feet in front of it when Mayor Banyan stepped up to the microphone.

"Could I have everyone's attention, please?" he asked.

The choral group stopped singing, and everyone quieted down. Peter came up next to her with two paper cups of hot chocolate and a strap slung over his shoulder for his camera bag. He and Goldie didn't have a prearranged date, but she was secretly hoping she'd run into him.

"Hi," he greeted. "Thought you might need this."

He handed her a cup, and she smiled, delighted.

"Ay! Thanks!"

"I always want a drink when my father makes a speech," he joked. "But I admit, it's usually something stronger."

She laughed, then dipped a hand into her jacket pocket and pulled out a tissue to dispose of her gum.

"I want to thank everyone for coming out," the mayor began, "as we celebrate the beginning of the Sparkledove Christmas season with the annual lighting of the community tree." He spotted and gestured to Goldie. "Being covered this year, I might add, by Karen 'Goldie' Maraschino, a famous journalist from *Adventure Escape Magazine*."

The crowd applauded as Goldie's face turned red.

"Oh, Jesus," she moaned. "Hundreds of people just saw me spit my gum into a Kleenex."

"Congratulations," Peter said quietly. "You've just become a PR tool."

"As we've done in years past," Banyan continued. "We've got music, food, plenty of holiday cheer, and all the stores are staying open until 10:00 p.m. for your shopping convenience. And be sure to get a Calendar of Events flier being handed out by our volunteers listing the dates and times of all the other activities coming up in town over the next few weeks."

Goldie glanced around and saw a few people starting to pass fliers out amongst the crowd. Peter's mom, Stephie, was among them.

"As everyone knows, this is a very unusual Christmas with so many of our boys serving far from home. So, to honor them, and in accordance with President Roosevelt's recommendation, we'll be turning off the tree at 10:00, then imposing blackout conditions. But, until then, please enjoy yourselves and the wonderful hospitality of Sparkledove."

The crowd applauded again. As they did, Peter leaned into Goldie.

"Notice how he totally ignored the president's recommendation yet made it sound like he didn't?"

"He's a smoothie," she admitted.

"That comment, incidentally, was off the record," he reminded.

"Of course," she agreed.

"And now," Banyan smiled. "I'd like to invite six-year-old Patty Bellows and her folks up to the stage. Patty asked me months ago if she could throw the big light switch this year, and I said yes. So, I want her to grow up knowing there's at least one politician who keeps his promises."

The crowd laughed and applauded as a curly-haired girl who looked a little like a young Shirley Temple was carried up to the stage in the arms of her father, with her mom following close behind.

"Hold this, will you?" Peter said, handing Goldie his cup. As she took it, he slid the camera bag off his shoulder, opened it up, and took out his camera. He also took out a flash attachment and connected it to the camera.

"Time to go to work," he smiled. Then he moved away from her, heading closer to the stage.

Goldie sipped her hot chocolate as the mayor continued his show.

"Dad—make sure Patty's hand is on the big switch. Now, let's all count it down together, shall we? Here we go. Three! Two! One!"

The little girl threw the switch, which meant the city engineer watching her threw the real switch. In an instant, the twenty-foot-tall dark shadow of the tree came to life with hundreds of large-bulb multicolored lights. The crowd made a collective "Ooooo," several flashbulbs popped, and a popular version of "Santa Claus is Coming to Town" started to play over the PA system. Goldie chuckled, sipped her hot chocolate, and drank everything in like a kid just discovering the North Pole. She let the Christmas bug nip at her toes just like the other tourists. After about a minute, she saw the sheriff moving through the crowd, followed by the two tough-looking men who helped him with the barricade. About ten seconds after this, Peter returned to her and retrieved his hot chocolate.

"I'm sure I could arrange a couple of minutes with our young Switcher of the Tree if you like," he offered.

"In a minute," she answered. "Who are those two guys over there with the sheriff?"

He looked in the direction she was pointing, then shrugged. "Tully and Crosby. Tully's the one with the black hair, Crosby's got the red hair and mustache. Tully worked in town for a while at a breakfast place, but I don't think either one lives in town now. They do stuff for my dad."

"Yeah? What kind of stuff?"

"I'm not sure. But between him being the mayor, president of the historical society, and owning a realty company, he's got a lot of things going on."

"I bet," she agreed, slightly suspicious.

"C'mon," he said. "I'll introduce you to Patty."

Goldie and Peter weaved through the crowd. Peter made the introductions, then Goldie spent a couple of minutes talking to Patty and her father. When she was finished, Charles Banyan came over to her. In the interim, Peter paused to take a photo of the happy faces in the crowd.

"So, Goldie. What do you think?" he asked.

"I gotta admit, Mayor, you throw a heck of a party."

"And this is just the beginning. You go on and have fun now, and if there's anything you need, just ask."

As Banyan stepped away, she was sorely tempted to inquire about the two men Peter identified as Tully and Crosby, but her instincts told her not to. In any event, she noticed that the sheriff was now chatting with visitors some distance away, and the other two were nowhere to be seen.

Before Peter rejoined Goldie, his father caught his eye and subtly gestured to have a private word with him.

"Nice job with the speech," the younger man began.

"I don't think what you're doing with Goldie is a good idea," his father said flatly.

"What's that?" Peter asked innocently.

"You know perfectly well what I'm talking about. Coming on to her, walking her home after Thanksgiving dinner, going with her into the mountains to get the tree, taking her out to lunch."

"How do you know we had lunch?"

"It's my town, Peter. I know everything. Now you're sipping hot chocolate with her."

"Don't worry. We're practicing safe sipping," the younger one joked.

"I mean it," Charles said seriously. "She could conclude you're being attentive just because you're my son and I want a good article out of her."

"Oh, and she *wouldn't* conclude that from the plane tickets, free hotel, meals, and clothing you're providing?"

"That's different, and you know it. That's a business arrangement for the good of the community. A publication like hers expects a certain amount of preferential treatment. What you're doing is personal."

"Not as personal as I'd like it to be," Peter smiled.

"I'm telling you, leave her alone!"

Peter turned and went back to Goldie. As he did, he noticed she'd observed some of the conversation with his father and, even though she was out of earshot, he could tell she knew it was a tense exchange.

"Everything all right?" she asked.

"Yeah. Just the usual guff from my ol' man," he

downplayed. "I swear, I could win a Pulitzer Prize for literature, and he'd say: 'What? You don't keep it dusted?'"

She smiled, then they turned and started to meander toward the lit tree.

"Speaking of Pulitzer, that was quite a nice obituary you wrote for Bucky Eggleston."

"You saw that?"

"Yeah. His wife showed it to me. You have a terrific sense of prose."

"Well, thanks. I've read some of *your* articles, and you're not too bad yourself. Although who you are in person and who you are on paper seem to be two different personalities."

"Huh. Interesting," she replied, a little coquettish.

As they came closer to the tree, Peter pointed out some of the historical ornaments on it and their significance to the community. They talked, smiled, and sipped their hot chocolate like two people clearly attracted to one another.

Observing them from a distance was Eli Johnson. He and Goldie hadn't spoken since she left him in a huff at the Pine River Inn, and the regret of the episode was clear on his face. He slowly leaned forward and rubbed a gloved hand up and down his bad leg that sometimes got irritated by the cold weather until he heard a voice behind him.

"Someone steal your girl?"

He turned to see white-haired Stu Frey standing there and smiling.

"Oh... hi, Stu. Uh, she's not my girl. She's just a lady here to do a job."

"Looks like Peter has other intentions," Stu observed.

Eli glanced at Goldie and Peter again. "Yeah—well—they're both adults. I gotta go make my rounds. I'll see ya."

Later that evening, at about 10:40, the streets of Sparkledove were mostly clear. The Christmas tree was off, the barricades used to close off River Street had been moved, and the vendors who had brought in their trailers were buttoning up their rigs for the drive home. At the back of the corn dog trailer, Charles Banyan, Tully, and Crosby came up to the trailer's owner.

"Good night tonight, Lou?" Banyan asked.

"Not bad, not bad," Lou answered. He looked around to make sure no one was watching, then dipped into the pocket of his winter coat and handed Banyan a white letter-sized envelope.

"There ya are, Mr. Mayor," Lou said. "My vendor fee for settin' up on River Street."

Banyan opened the envelope, ran his thumb over a stack of bills, then closed it.

"I'm afraid you're a little light, Lou. I'm going to need another fifty."

"Fifty dollars more?" Lou blurted, astonished. "For *what*?"

"Proximity to the post office, hook-up to power, and we had a larger crowd than last year."

"Yeah, but that don't mean people bought more corn dogs. With the war, I had to pay extra for all my food staples. If you charge me an extra fifty, it will have *cost* me money to come here."

"Fortunes of war," Banyan replied. "You want to come back for other festivities, don't you? We'll have a new crowd of tourists for the Tour of Homes, and you can make it up then."

"Until you charge me even more the next time."

"Let's see what the next time brings," the mayor smiled. "But, for now, I'm going to need that fifty. All the other vendors kicked in extra; you should too."

Lou looked at Banyan's menacing associates, then shook his head, took off a glove, and dug a hand into his trouser pockets.

"This ain't right," he complained. "This ain't fair at all!"

Lou produced a wad of bills, peeled most of them off, then handed them over to the dapperly dressed mayor. As this was happening, all of the men were unaware that Goldie was watching from a darkened doorway.

I knew 'dem boys were muscle, she thought to herself. *I knew it!*

Thirteen

MAYNARD "22"

"Why are we doing this so early?" Father Fitzsimmons asked, walking with Goldie up the dirt road toward the No Trespassing sign and chained gate that led to the Maynard Silver Mine. He was wearing a black overcoat, earmuffs, gloves, and carried his Kodak folding camera in one hand while looking at his wristwatch with the other. "It's not even 7:00 a.m."

"The light," she replied, making up an answer as they continued, "It's, uh, y'know, ambient." She was wearing slacks and the jacket, gloves, and stocking cap she'd gotten at Miller's.

"That means absolutely nothing," the priest said. "That's like saying, 'The water's wet.'"

"What kind of bird is that?" she asked, changing subjects and hearing a pleasant sound. "I love its song."

"It's actually cooing," the clergyman answered, his

breath visible in the frosty morning. "It's a Eurasian Colored Dove. You know—'Sparkledove?'"

"Oh. It's pretty."

"Goldie. Why are we out here?"

"Minin' is a big part of the town's history, so I have to get a photo of the old Maynard operation for my article."

"Okay. But why so early?" he repeated, adjusting his earmuffs.

"Well, I was actually anxious to talk to you," she answered honestly. "Besides grabbin' a picture, I also want to do an open-face confession while we're alone. Is that okay?" She looked around. "Would it count here?"

He smiled. "Oooo, I've never done one of those before. It's unconventional, but here in the Lord's woods? Yes, it counts."

They came to the chained gate and paused.

"Then—bless me, Father, for I have sinned," she said, making the sign of the cross with a hand. "My last confession was in the tenth grade. So, it's been a while."

She spread the two chained sides of the gate apart with her arms and slid through its opening.

"Let me guess, the first thing you want to confess is trespassing?" he assumed.

"No. I asked the sheriff about coming up here."

"Oh—good," he replied, likewise spreading the gate open and slipping through after her. "That makes me feel better."

"But he said no. He said it was dangerous."

"Goldie!"

She saw the road continued up and around a bend, so she kept walking. "C'mon," she urged.

The young, thin priest expelled a heavy breath, then trudged after her. "My first open-face confession is a misdemeanor."

After a couple of moments, she continued: "I lived with a man for several years."

"I see," he nodded.

"But that's not what I wanna confess."

"It isn't?"

"No... this man, he was—*is*—a criminal. A gangster. Part of a very powerful crime family. He steals, extorts money, sells drugs... even kills people."

An open-mouthed Father Fitz stopped walking, so she did too.

"Have you participated in any of these crimes, Goldie?" he asked seriously.

"No. Most of the time, I didn't know any of the specifics. But I knew who he was. What he did. And he sometimes told me things. Y'know, after like: 'Hi, honey, how was your day?' So, you could say I-I enabled him."

They started walking again in silence while she looked around, still hearing the doves coo.

"It's funny," she finally offered, "all the things you tell yourself to justify the decisions you make. Like, we grew up in a crime-ridden neighborhood, so we really didn't have a choice about our lifestyle. Or all the people he either killed or had killed were scumbuckets anyway. I mean, *I* didn't make 'em criminals, right? Or, sometimes, I thought, maybe I could steer him away from the family. Go legitimate... have a house in the suburbs... kids."

"So—what's happened to make you re-examine this relationship?" Father asked.

"He threw me over for another woman," she replied, her green eyes a little moist with embarrassment. "I-I wasn't educated enough... classy enough. So, that's part of it, but not all of it. Bein' here... meetin' the people I've met... th-there's another way to go, y'know? Another way to live. I've seen that in the time I've been here."

The priest thought for a moment, then looked at her with kind eyes. "You've associated with gangsters. Jesus associated with adulterers, prostitutes, thieves, and tax collectors. He said: 'I have not come to call the righteous, but sinners.' Could be, Goldie, he's calling on you now."

"Yeah—well—it's a pretty damn weird call," she said, referring to the time travel which she'd purposely omitted, fearing Father would think her a lunatic.

They rounded the bend in the road, then they both suddenly stopped.

"Whoa!" Goldie exclaimed.

What lay ahead of them was a three-acre section of forest that had been cleared some seventy years earlier. Replacing the wilderness were old buildings with pieces of abandoned mining equipment like wheelbarrows and tipped-over push carts. The closest structure to them was a two-story house with faded white paint and a partially open front door. It had a single-story wing on each side, but the roof on one of the wings to the right had collapsed. Despite decades of neglect, it still made a statement of prominence. A hundred or so yards beyond the house and to the left was an unpainted wooden building with a faded sign over the door that read "Office." Twenty yards to the right of the office was a section of railroad track with a long wooden ramp that went up to a height of nine feet, then abruptly stopped at a gate directly above the track. Looking left again, and some thirty yards from the office, was the chiseled-out large mouth of a mine that went into the side of a mountain. The opening was approximately ten-by-ten feet, and it had a smaller set of tracks coming out of it for push carts that carried ore. It was sealed up with wooden boards and old railroad ties that had been stacked and nailed together. On them, in newer red paint, were the words: "Danger! Do Not Enter!" On either side of the mine entrance were thin but tall buildings with open doorways, no doors, and rusting machinery inside. Any windows that may have once held glass no longer did, and even though the acreage had been cleared away, a few trees had sprouted up here and there over the years. Goldie and Father surveyed this ghostly scene and half expected John Wayne to ride out of the woods at any moment and use one of the two old hand pumps to fill his canteen.

"Pretty amazin', huh?" she asked.

"I knew an old mine was up here," Father said, "but I had no idea the size of the operation."

"Let's put my sins on hold for a minute, eh, Father?" Goldie suggested. "Get a nice shot of the mine entrance, will ya?"

"Uh, sure," he agreed, opening his camera.

He walked toward the sealed-off entrance and looked around for a good angle. "I wonder how all this worked?"

"The director of operations lived in the big house we passed," she replied. "The office, over there, was where the men checked in and out in the morning and evening, and maybe a doctor had a room there too in case of an accident." She pointed to the mine entrance. "There were usually two sets of tunnels in the mines. One larger series of tunnels was where the men extracted the silver, then there was a smaller, interconnecting series of tunnels, also called spurs, with tracks laid for the ore carts." She turned and pointed to the long ramp that ended above the railroad tracks. "Once the carts were full of ore, they were either hand-pushed or, more likely, pulled by horses or mules up that ramp, then the carts were emptied into hopper railroad cars. The railroad track connects somewhere with a line that goes out of the mountains and into Denver."

"How do you know all this?" he asked.

"Read about it at the library. Not this particular camp, but the bigger operations sorta ran the same."

Father Fitz found the angle he wanted, then clicked off a picture. As he was turning the film knob on the camera for the next shot, he looked at the two thin buildings on either side of the mine entrance. Both were about twenty feet high.

"And those?"

"Probably one building pumped fresh air into the mines, and the other provided power for any machinery like drills or even a shaft elevator. The machinery was most likely steam-powered."

"Mayor Banyan told me the mine stopped producing in the early 1880s," Father recalled. "But in its heyday, Sparkledove had over four thousand people, almost exclusively because of mining."

"Yeah, I read that, too," she said, going through the open doorway of the building on the right-hand side of the mine.

"Uh—I don't think going in there is a good idea," the priest warned, deciding to remain outside. "It could fall down on your head."

"This buildin' has been standin' for decades, Father," she replied. "I don't think the walls are gonna collapse at this particular moment."

She saw the large, rusted boiler of a steam engine, an iron wheel that once drove a large piston, and some old exhaust piping that ran from the engine up through a hole in the roof. "Yeah," she called to her companion. "There's an old steam engine in here."

"Fine. C'mon out now," he urged.

As Goldie scanned the roof, something

suddenly caught her eye. Over in the corner, there was a second newer exhaust pipe. Her eyes followed it down behind what was left of the original engine to a smaller tarp-covered piece of machinery over in a shadowed corner of the building.

"Hey, Father," she called. "I found somethin'."

"What?"

"C'mere and check it out."

The priest reluctantly entered the building while Goldie produced a flashlight from her pocket, clicked it on, then walked over to the tarp.

"Where'd you get the flashlight?" he asked.

"I borrowed it from the front desk at the hotel. They've let me borrow it before."

The priest nodded as Goldie lifted the tarp, stiffened by the cold, looked under it with the light, then pulled it aside. Underneath was a gasoline-powered Kohler 4-cylinder portable generator that was clearly a new piece of equipment. Next to it was a five-gallon gas can.

"It's a gas generator," Father said, surprised. "My brother is in the signal corps, and I've seen demonstrations where they were used to fill up hot air balloons."

Goldie examined the machine for a moment, then saw a rubber-coated electrical cord plugged into the generator. The cord ran across the dirt floor, then disappeared through a crack in the wooden wall and went outside.

"Now why would an abandoned mine need a generator?" she asked.

"I've no idea," Father Fitz said. "I've never heard of any activity up here since I've been in town, but that's only been a couple of months."

Goldie looked at the cord again, then turned and clicked off her flashlight. She walked out of the building and moved around to its side.

"What're you doing?" Father asked, going after her.

"Followin' the line," she replied, slipping the flashlight back into her jacket pocket.

"Goldie, this isn't our property. This isn't our business."

"No? Then whose business is it? The sheriff's? He told me the mine was played out. You just said the mayor told you the mine dried up in the 1880s. So, whose generator is it and what's goin' on up here?"

"I don't know. Probably some renegade prospector hoping to find one more vein of silver. We got the picture we came for, you were in the middle of a confession, and I think we should continue with that while heading back to town."

"Look," she said, pointing. "The line goes through a little openin' in between those railroad ties and straight into the mine. That means..."

Her voice trailed off as she walked over to the wall of wooden boards and railroad ties sealing off the entrance and started to feel around.

"That means what?" he asked.

She pulled on a particular board, but it didn't budge. Then, she tugged on another. Nothing happened. "That means somebody's gotten into the mine," she said, pulling on a railroad tie. "There must be an arrangement of boards or ties that *look* like they're solidly sealed, but are actually loose."

The railroad tie didn't give way, so she tugged on another, shorter tie that was once used for the push carts. It moved slightly and squeaked. Pulling again with all her might, four stacked shorter ties suddenly fell away, revealing a small square opening about three feet off the ground. Goldie jumped back quickly to avoid the tumbling ties and fell on her butt.

Father ran over to her. "You okay?"

"Yeah," she answered.

He helped her to her feet, and she brushed off her backside, taking the flashlight out of her back pocket and peering into the opening.

"Hey, Father, you think you can figure out how to fire up that generator?"

"No. This is a very *bad* idea," her companion said.

"C'mon," she urged. "I can see the wire connects to lights that have been strung up inside. Where's your sense of adventure?"

"There's a difference between a sense of adventure and common sense," he advised.

"Okay, then..." she said, raising a leg slightly, bending down, and going through the square opening, "if you won't help me, I'll go it alone with my little flashlight. 'Course, I don't know how far I have to go, or how long the batteries will last. Without proper lightin', I might lose my way and fall down a shaft to a horrible death in the middle of a confession without gettin' absolution. But that's okay. You just stay outside where it's safe and don't help me. I'll let you know what I find, Father. If, y'know, I ever get back."

She started walking into the darkness.

"Goldie. I *can't* go in there," he called after her, bending over and peering inside. "I suffer from claustrophobia. I keep my eyes closed half the time I'm in a confessional. Really! I'm *not* kidding!"

She didn't answer and kept walking, turning her light slowly to and fro to get a sense of where she was.

"Jiminy Cricket!" the priest said angrily, turning and running back toward the generator.

Goldie smiled to herself, hearing his departing footsteps. "Catholic guilt. It's the best!"

She continued walking and moving her light around, surprised by the high, solid rock ceiling. The tunnel she was in went steadily downward at a twenty-degree angle, and the further she went, the less fresh the air became. She also noticed rails on shorter railroad ties for the push carts that carried ore paralleling her to the right.

"It's like bein' in the bat cave," she observed. "Please let Robert Pattinson pop out from behind a rock."

She came to an intersection of tunnels that went right and left. In very faded white paint on one rock wall was the number "4." The tunnel going in the other direction was labeled "17." As she studied the numbers, an endless string of interconnected single clear lightbulbs, each about three feet apart, and hanging on the left-hand side wall via a series of metal spikes, came fading up like someone had slowly turned on a rheostat. Obviously, Father Fitz had figured out how to turn on the generator.

"Let there be light," she mused, thankfully.

Goldie didn't know how many strings of lights had been interconnected, but she guessed there were dozens. The lights on the left-hand wall descended, going straight across the opening of other tunnels, almost as far as she could see. Then, they seemed to turn abruptly left, illuminating the entrance of another tunnel.

"Goldie?" she heard the muted voice of Father Fitz call. "Are you alright?"

"Yeah," she yelled back, clicking off her flashlight. "I'm gonna follow the lights. See where they lead. I might be gone for a few minutes. So, if you don't hear from me, don't worry. Okay?"

"You shouldn't be doing this!" Father called. "But, since you *are,* be careful!"

Usually, Goldie knew she would never be this brave. But her being in Sparkledove was anything but normal. She'd awakened in a different state, in a different time. She was watching the spirit of someone commit suicide daily, and no one else could see it. She'd heard people use the lyrics of songs that were decades away from being written. She figured she had inherited a set of circumstances and a mystery that she was supposed to solve. And since she was sure of this, she didn't believe that dying in a mine was going to be her destiny. She didn't consider herself brave so much as desperate for answers. She was further bolstered by the fact that a priest was waiting outside for her.

She went deeper and deeper, descending lower and lower into the mine. Passing tunnels on either side labeled "7," "13," "11," and "2." Some were large enough to accommodate a group of miners, while others were smaller and clearly just for push carts. There didn't seem to be any rhyme or reason to the numbering system. *Maybe it refers to the order in which they were dug,* she thought. *Or maybe it had something to do with an overall mapping system.*

She finally came to where the lights turned left into yet another tunnel that continued to go down. It was labeled "22." At this point, she'd been steadily descending for nearly seven minutes, and the air was getting thinner. She slipped off her stocking cap and gloves, then stuck them into her pockets.

"I don't know how much miners make," she said, looking around. "But whatever it is—it ain't enough."

She continued into tunnel "22." About a minute later, she noticed little trickles of water on the rock walls. Just a couple at first. Then, a few more, and a few more until there was a small puddle of brown water on the tunnel floor.

"Where's *that* comin' from?" she wondered out loud.

About a hundred yards further down, she came to a tunnel to her left labeled "12" where the lights were strung straight across its entrance. Some ten feet beyond that, she came to the first real thing that truly bothered her on this trek.

Straight ahead, she saw that the rock floor of tunnel "22" had partially collapsed. The tunnel was about nine feet wide, and approximately eight feet of the floor had fallen away, leaving only a foot or so of ledge to her left that continued for a distance of about eleven feet. More disturbingly, she didn't know where the floor had fallen to.

"What the hell is *this*?" she complained. "This ain't no freakin' Indiana Jones movie!"

She slowly approached the drop-off to the floor, got out her flashlight, clicked it on, and pointed it down. The beam of light stretched into only darkness.

"Oh, this isn't good," she decided.

She saw a small rock by her foot, picked it up, and tossed it into the abyss. After she did, she counted: "One Mississippi. Two Mississippi. Three Mississippi." She finally heard the echoing "clack" of rock striking rock at "Seven Mississippi."

"*Oh, shit!*" she sighed. "This isn't good at all!"

Goldie thought about turning around and going back. But after having come all this way, she still didn't have any idea where the lights led. And despite the collapsed floor, the lights were still leading on to somewhere. Meaning, somebody had gotten safely across and strung them. So, she stood there for nearly a minute, considering her options.

Studying the tunnel wall to her left, with the metal spikes holding the connected cords of lights, she took off her jacket to give her arms more movement, then stuck her flashlight into a front pants pocket. Moving to the left-hand side of the tunnel, she raised her foot and put it on a protruding piece of rock, then grabbed another protruding rock with her left hand. She began to scale the seven-foot-high tunnel wall, traveling sideways and carefully maneuvering herself around the string of hot lights. She figured if she fell, she still had that foot-wide ledge of floor to land on, although she didn't know if that would give way as well. This side-stepping process was slow going, a strain on her muscles and balance, and caused her to stretch her arms and legs like a large, brown-haired spider. But finally, after ninety seconds and traveling a mere eleven feet, she hopped safely to the other side of the tunnel floor.

"*Ha!*" she cried, victorious as she landed. She turned and looked down at the blackness she had just traversed.

"*Marco's Fifth Avenue Gym and Climbing Wall, bitches!*" she yelled.

She heard the echoing return of "*bitches-bitches-bitches*" from the emptiness below. Then turned toward the tunnel before her, leaned over, and rested a hand on each leg, trying to catch her breath, which was now becoming quite difficult to do. The air was very stale, and she could see from her cold breath that she was exhaling less oxygen.

"Damn!" she realized. "I gotta do that wall all over again on the way back."

Putting that challenge aside for the moment, she looked ahead and down where the lights still led.

"Doesn't this ever stop?" she wondered.

She forged on, although more slowly and carefully watching the ground in front of her. She also noticed something else: she was now seeing miscellaneous holes that had been drilled into the walls that she hadn't seen before. Each hole was circular and about two inches in diameter. She knew they were relatively new because there were little mounds of loose dirt from the holes on the tunnel floor. After another five minutes, the tunnel and lights finally came to an end. The end of the tunnel had no less than six drilled holes in it, spread out from ceiling to floor. And there was a big red X painted on the rocks.

"Finally," she said to herself, now starting to feel lightheaded from the cold and lack of air. "X marks the spot," she muttered. "And unlike the white tunnel numbers, it's new paint. Meaning, somebody wants to resurrect Maynard tunnel 22."

She still didn't have all the answers, but she figured she had at least a piece to her puzzle.

It was several more minutes before Father Fitzsimmons, sitting on the edge of an old water trough for horses and holding a rosary in his hand, saw Goldie emerge from the small square opening of the main entrance. He rose, looked at his wristwatch, then slipped his rosary into his trouser pocket.

"Twenty-eight minutes," he announced, unhappily. "At thirty minutes, I was going into town for help."

Goldie didn't answer. Instead, she sank to the ground on her hands and knees and took several deep breaths of fresh air. The stale air deep inside and scaling Tunnel 22's side wall twice had really gotten to her.

Concerned, the priest hurried over.

"Goldie! Are you okay? Tell me what's happening?"

"J-j-just gimmie a minute," she said breathlessly. "Lemme rest here while you go turn off the generator."

"Right... okay," Father agreed.

He was gone about sixty seconds while she stayed motionless on her hands and knees and waited for the dizziness in her head to cease. When he returned, the clergyman helped her to her feet.

"Where the heck did you go?" he asked.

"I-I don't know," she replied. "A long way down the main shaft. Th-then there was a connecting tunnel where the lights turned left and kept going. There must've been hundreds of light bulbs in total. It had to have taken a long time to string 'em all up."

Father Fitz looked at the mine. "The main entrance faces east. Did you go in a straight line?"

"Yeah. There were other tunnels on either side, but

I followed the main shaft until the lights changed direction."

He looked to his left. "Then, you must've been traveling north when you turned."

"I don't know. The incline of the tunnel floor just kept going down. Not sharp, but gradual and steady. After I turned, I eventually passed some water running down the tunnel walls and a puddle on the ground."

Father looked to his left again. "Holy cow. You must've gone right underneath the river!"

Goldie looked in the same direction. "Yeah. Yeah, maybe I did. But there was a lot more tunnel after that. All in a straight, descending line. Then the tunnel ended with a solid rock wall and a big red X painted on it."

"You had to have been heading straight north," he repeated.

"Okay... so, what's north of here?"

"Depends on how far you went down before you turned," Father replied. He paused, thinking. "Let's see... from where we are, St. Mark's is north. The mayor's house is, too, but that would really be more like northeast... oh, and Falcon Drive is north."

Goldie's eyes suddenly widened.

"Falcon Drive? Where Martha Eggleston lives?"

"Yes," Father said. Then he second-guessed himself and looked around to check the position of the sun. "At least, I think so. Yes... yes, I'm sure it is."

Fourteen

PENANCE

Father helped Goldie stack the short railroad ties at the mine entrance back to the way they were before. She was still a little dizzy from her journey into the mine, so they worked slowly. By the time they were finished, the generator had cooled down, so they replaced the tarp just as they had found it. While they worked, Goldie didn't say anything to Father Fitz about what she was thinking. After all, she wasn't sure about her thoughts. They were half-baked at best. Her guts told her that Mayor Banyan was shady, and she suspected his fingers were in a lot of pies, but that didn't mean anything. All she truly knew was that Martha Eggleston didn't like him, felt pressured to keep her home maintained when she and Bucky owned it, and she also had to sell her house out of desperation at a loss, which certainly made her like Banyan even less. Then, she'd seen a street vendor hand him an envelope that looked like a payoff, but she had no proof. She'd noticed that three of the five houses on Martha's side of the street on Falcon Drive were for sale, and now she'd discovered that a tunnel in an old abandoned mine apparently went under the same street. But how did it all add up? She definitely had to get more answers.

"I'm glad you're okay," Father Fitz said. "You certainly have a reckless side, and that probably made you attracted to that gangster boyfriend you told me about."

"*Ex*-gangster boyfriend," she clarified. "But, yeah. You could be right."

"Well, since everything is back the way it was, can we please get out of here now? I *do* have other things to do today."

"Sure. Okay. Thanks for your patience and taggin' along. I do appreciate it, Father."

They started to head down the dirt road back to town.

"Is there anything more you want to talk about regarding your confession?" he asked.

"Only that bein' with this guy for so many years gave me a very heightened sense for smellin' when somethin' was wrong. And I think somethin' is *very* wrong about what we discovered here today."

At that instant, Goldie looked ahead and saw a strange sight. A woman, about her age, was coming around the bend in the road ahead of them. Her long blonde hair was messy, and several strands were hanging in front of her eyes as if she'd been running through the woods. But that wasn't the oddest part. She was wearing only a long, thin, short-sleeve white nightgown and was barefoot. The temperature was about thirty-four degrees, and here was this woman walking barefoot in a thin gown in winter, yet her body didn't seem to be affected by the cold. The woman didn't look at Goldie or Father. Her stare was a combination of forlorn and emptiness; it was almost trance-like. But that still wasn't all. She also carried a rope in her right hand. A rope with a noose at its end.

"Not necessarily," Father Fitz said, replying to his companion's last comment. "As I said before, the generator could be from a lone miner hoping to strike it rich. Or maybe Maynard Mining is considering resurrecting the site. I'm sure the mayor would probably know."

Goldie looked at the woman, then at the priest. If she could see her, he certainly would've seen her by now, too. *Unless,* she thought, he couldn't see her. Then she realized she'd seen that same lost expression on someone else's face in Sparkledove. She'd seen it on Claude Bolton.

"Uh, that's a good thought," she responded, still waiting for Father to acknowledge the woman. "Maybe Maynard Mining *is* considerin' doin' somethin' with the mine again. But let me look into it, Padre, please. I think this needs to be done very discreetly."

"What am I going to tell folks?" he asked. "That I trespassed up here with a visitor, then let her break into a mine?"

The woman turned off the road and walked up the pathway that led to the partially open front door of the director of operations' house.

"That's a cool lookin' house," she said. "Mind if I take a moment and peek inside?"

Father looked at the house and directly at the woman going into it through the open door.

"Now *that* place really *could* fall down around your head at a moment's notice," he answered, oblivious to the woman. "Part of it already has. See?" He gestured to the right-hand side of the house and the single-story wing where the roof had collapsed.

"I'm just gonna look through the front door," Goldie said, now convinced that Father wasn't seeing what she was. "I'll be right back."

As she walked toward the door, the clergyman shook his head and muttered. "'I've got to look at the mine. I've got to look at the house,'" he said quietly, mimicking Goldie. "This must be why husbands hate to go shopping with their wives."

The inside of the house featured a large foyer and a staircase. At the top of the stairs was a railing and landing that was about six feet wide and led to the upstairs bedrooms. By the time Goldie peeked around the partially opened door, the blonde-haired woman in the nightgown was most of the way up the stairs. Goldie watched wide-eyed as the woman reached the top of the stairs, then walked to the middle of the railing directly above the center of the foyer. She took one end of the rope and started to tie it to the railing. It was obvious what she intended to do. Once the rope was secure, she was going to put the noose around her neck, climb over the railing, and jump. Goldie was halfway tempted to either call out to her or run up the stairs and try to stop her. But she also somehow knew such efforts weren't going to make a difference.

"Goldie," Father Fitz called. "I think I've been a pretty good sport about all this. But I really need to get on with my day."

She sadly watched the woman for a few more seconds, then turned and walked away, not wanting to see the inevitable. "Okay... comin'," she agreed.

She was noticeably distant as they rounded the bend in the dirt road, returned to the gate, slid through the chain opening one at a time, then headed down the road toward the covered bridge with pine roping that now hung on either side. As they neared it, the priest finally spoke up.

"You okay? You seem to be lost in thought."

She took a beat before answering. "Since I arrived in town, things keep occurrin' in my life that I can't explain. Not, 'What's goin' on at the mine?' although I want to know—but—other things. Things that trouble me. Things where I can't connect the dots."

"Maybe the dots aren't supposed to connect," he suggested.

"Whatdaya mean?"

"Let's say, you're driving down the highway and you see a dead dog on the side of the road. You saw it. It's sad. But it's not really connected to you. It's just something you saw. The only thing that connects you and the dog is a road that goes on for hundreds of miles."

"Compartmentalization," she realized. "You're saying to compartmentalize."

"Maybe it would help," he nodded.

She looked at Father Fitz. "Y'know, for someone young, you talk like you been doin' this priest stuff for years."

He smiled appreciatively. "Thanks. But I have to ask: Is that it? Are we done with your confession?"

"Yeah... I think so."

"Good." He blessed her with a prayer of absolution, then added: "For your penance, say a rosary, stay away from your old boyfriend, and don't ever bring me up here again."

Fifteen

ANSWERS & KISSES

As soon as she got to her hotel, Goldie went to work. The first thing she did was go up to her room and write herself some instructions in all caps that read: SEPARATE THE SUICIDES FROM THE FAMILIAR SONG LYRICS! SEPARATE THE TIME TRAVEL FROM WHAT YOU SAW IN THE MINE! Then, she wrote out a list of questions to help identify possible connections. Questions like:

- Where was the headquarters of Maynard Mining?
- Are they still in business?
- Why did they leave Sparkledove?
- What happened to the mineral rights?
- Who made the holes in tunnel "22" and why?
- What was in that envelope given to the mayor?

And since she saw Eli Johnson and the mayor's two

tough-looking associates, Tully and Crosby, cordoning off streets together, she wrote one more question:

• Does Banyan have Sheriff Johnson in his back pocket?

She figured that if she could get the answers to these questions, a lot of other facts would start to fall into place. *This has to be my mission!* She thought to herself. *Otherwise, what am I doin' here?"*

Realizing she still had time to catch the morning bus to Denver, she changed into a dress, made sure she had her pencils and notebook, then grabbed her overcoat and gloves. She grabbed a cup of coffee for the road from the restaurant, returned the flashlight she'd borrowed, then looked in the Denver phone book to see if there was an address for Maynard Mining. There wasn't, so she got the address of another mining company, as well as the address of the Denver Mining Museum. She also wanted to return to the Denver library and verify a couple of things she'd read about Sparkledove. She caught the bus just before it left at 9:10 a.m., ready to research.

First, she went to the Big D Mining Company, flashed her business card, and met with a man named Matt Colvin. He was very knowledgeable about the state's mining history and informed Goldie that Maynard Mining had gone out of business in 1930 after nearly eighty years. Colvin also verified facts that Goldie had read during her first visit to Denver. The most important of these was in 1882, when new, larger deposits of both gold and silver were discovered closer to Denver, and it was simply more profitable to mine those deposits than the remote and harsher location of Sparkledove. Large and smaller operations may have moved away, but that didn't necessarily mean Maynard's mine in Sparkledove was totally played out, as both Charles Banyan and Eli Johnson had said. In fact, after meeting with Colvin, Goldie returned to the Denver Library to reread the articles about Sparkledove. The articles only said that companies moved on to more lucrative opportunities. She concluded that that could certainly mean there was more silver to be found. But so many years had passed that nobody in town realized it.

Next, she went to the Denver Mining Museum. She learned that the usual way mining companies negotiated for mineral rights in a populated area was to contact homeowners and offer them a lease contract where they would receive a small percentage of profits for any ore mined on their land or transported underneath it. According to the law, a landowner's land was his or hers, whether silver was found six inches or six hundred feet below the ground. So, standard contracts were offered to homeowners who, in most cases, were only too happy to lease their mineral rights since they had no way of finding, extracting, or separating the ore. To them, it was free money. If a mining company ceased operations for a certain period of time or went out of business, it invalidated all leases.

But the best way to assure absolute mining rights was to purchase the homes outright.

She also learned that one way to find additional veins of silver in a mine was to drill small holes, then extract samples and look for silver ore. Once a sample of silver ore was found and weighed, the size of the vein could be determined, and a likely yield from the vein could be estimated. Such estimates held no guarantees, but estimates done by geological engineers did provide circumstantial evidence of potential wealth. She asked someone at the museum about the current price of silver. Since she was used to double-checking Markie's books, she was a whiz with numbers and did some quick calculations. At a 1942 price of $1.29 an ounce, a ton of silver was worth $41,280.00. Five tons would be worth $206,400.00. Adjusting for inflation, she figured that would be worth over $3,200,000.00 in present-day money. And when one considered that gold was often found with silver, very serious money could be made, depending on the tonnage, if there was a forgotten vein in tunnel "22."

She returned to the Denver bus terminal at 3:15 p.m., where she stopped and chatted with her friend Gerome, the maintenance man. Fortunately, she didn't encounter his irritating, racist boss, Bradley Hammersville.

The day had been very productive, and she'd gotten several answers to her questions. It was about 4:15 in the afternoon when Goldie was walking from the bus stop back to the Sparkledove Arms. A little to her surprise, as she was approaching the lobby door, Eli Johnson came out of it. He was wearing his usual tan uniform and brown suede jacket and gave her a nod. She wasn't particularly pleased to see him. Partly because he'd refused to let her go see the Maynard mining operation, partly because he thought her queries about the covered bridge, Claude Bolton, and Bucky Eggleston were off track with her reason for being in town, and partly because she'd seen him associating with two men that she instinctively knew were goons for the mayor.

"Howdy," he greeted in his Gene Audrey way.

"What can I do for you, Sheriff?" she asked, unenthused.

"I was just looking for you. Took your advice and had a chat with Martha Eggleston. She told me about all the coffee Bucky had been drinking the day he died and how he hated decaf."

"Yeah?"

"Yeah. She also told me where their wrecked car was. So, I drove out to the junkyard and looked it over. Saw a couple of things that were interesting."

"Like what?"

"His front wheels were turned to the right, like he swerved to avoid something. When his vehicle went off the road, it rolled several times before stopping. So that *could've* caused the wheels to be in that position. But..."

"But what?"

"Bucky's car is a light tan color, and there's about a

three to four-inch scratch of black paint on the driver's side door. His wheels were turned right, and the scratch is on the left. Meaning, it's possible another vehicle went over the centerline, he swerved to avoid the oncoming vehicle, and as they passed, the other vehicle grazed Bucky's car. That swerve could've been the impetus for all those rolls when he went off the road."

She looked at him, surprised. "And the state police missed all this?"

"I went to the outpost that handled the call that night and spoke to a sergeant. He said there were a lot of things that could've caused the dark scratch on that door. A rock or a fallen tree limb that the car rolled over."

"But you didn't buy that?"

"No, ma'am. I used to work at a body shop in high school to make a little extra money, and I know black paint from another vehicle when I see it."

"Did you tell the sergeant this?"

"Yep."

"What'd he say?"

"He said I was young and he understood why I'd like to sink my teeth into some real police work, considering I was the sheriff of a sleepy little tourist town like Sparkledove."

She looked intently at him for a moment.

"That's it? That's all he said?"

"That's it."

"Un-freakin'-believable!" she exclaimed. "So, he's not doin' nothin'?"

"The official conclusion is it was a single car accident," he confirmed. "But *I* think there's a good possibility another vehicle was involved. How and why, I don't know."

She thought for a moment. "So, what's your next move?"

The lawman rubbed his chin. "I'm not sure I *have* a next move. The incident didn't happen in my jurisdiction. I shared my findings with the state police and could maybe talk with Martha about 'em. Then, she and her lawyer could pursue it if they want. Beyond that, all I can do is keep an eye open in town for a black vehicle with about a three to four-inch scratch of light-tan paint on the driver's side. If another car was involved, it might be local. But that's a big might."

She pursed her lips, frustrated. "If that's all you can do, why'd you tell me this in the first place?"

"You asked me to talk to Martha and I said I would, then I looked into things as best I could."

She nodded, reluctantly acknowledging his efforts, but was still suspicious of him. He glanced over his shoulder back at the hotel.

"You cold? Y-you wanna cup of coffee, or hot chocolate, or something?"

"No," she said, moving past him. "I gotta go. But thanks."

At about 7:50 that evening, Goldie, now back in

slacks and her new jacket and stocking cap, decided to go for a walk. It was snowing outside, and other than flurries, this was the first substantial snowfall she'd seen since she'd arrived in town. She wanted to be somewhere with lots of sky around her, considering she started the day in the bowels of an old mine. She'd packed a lot into this day and was tired. She wasn't bored anymore by a lack of internet, social media, or TV.

She focused instead on trying to figure out her mission and how everything fit together. But she wasn't focused on this at the moment. She was simply enjoying the snowflakes falling on her eyelashes, walking past the beautiful Victorian houses, and noticing how the decorations had changed from Thanksgiving to Christmas. Tomorrow was Tuesday, December 1st, and she couldn't help but think of kids getting more and more excited with each passing day. Christmas lights on bushes or lampposts were noticeably absent because of blackout restrictions, but many houses had a lantern with a candle in their front window that matched the lanterns from the town's Christmas tree lighting. She passed a man walking his Golden Retriever. He greeted her by name. She was embarrassed that she didn't know him, but delighted to be in a place where people were starting to recognize her, even if it was under the guise of a journalist for a famous travel magazine.

Even though she didn't start out heading for the covered bridge, by 8:12, that's where her feet took her.

She decided she wanted to try an experiment. She knew that Claude Bolton would appear soon, and she wanted to stand directly in front of the window which he always jumped through to see what would happen. Would he acknowledge her? Push her aside? Use the window on the other side of the bridge? *What's he gonna do?* She wondered. *Kill me? For all I know, I could be dead already.*

As her footsteps echoed on the wooden planks, she thought about the war. With everything she had to adjust to, and her purpose in Sparkledove still unclear, the world being at war seemed like almost an afterthought. Yet, it was everywhere around her: in war bond posters hanging in shop windows, in food shortages at the grocery store, in blackout restrictions and the town's Christmas tree and covered bridge lights being illuminated only from 6:00 to 10:00 p.m.

Within a minute of her coming to the middle of the bridge and stopping to stare out of its glassless viewing window at the beautiful snowy night, she looked left and saw Claude Bolton walk onto the bridge. He wore the same clothes he always did, had the same forlorn look, and walked straight toward the window and Goldie without giving her any recognition.

"Ay, Claude," she called. "How's it goin'?"

She started walking toward him. "That was probably a dumb thing to say, huh? I mean, I *know* how it's goin'. And *where* you're goin'. Sorry, man. But I need to talk to ya. So, if you could delay your daily self-destruction for just one minute—"

She extended her hands, intending to stop him with a hand on each shoulder. But it didn't happen. Bolton passed right through Goldie's body as if he were smoke. When he did, a sharp, chilling pain shot through her head like a Slurpee brain freeze. It was so overwhelming, she lost her balance and fell to her knees. But Claude Bolton just kept on walking, then did what he did every night. He stopped at the window, looked out at the view, looked down at the water, and after a few moments, raised a foot and stepped onto the windowsill.

Goldie closed her eyes, put her gloved hands on the sides of her head, and waited for the rush of cold pain to subside, which it did in another thirty seconds. During this time, she was unaware of the glare of headlights coming down Bridge Street toward her. She muttered *"Shit!"* as a car door opened and the silhouette of someone came running toward her.

"Goldie! Are you alright?"

She looked up to see Peter Banyan. His Ford station wagon with an open driver's door was behind him at the entrance of the bridge.

"Ay, Peter," she smiled weakly.

"What happened?" he asked. He put a hand on each of her arms and helped her to her feet. "Are you ill?"

"No. J-just tripped over my own two big, dumb feet," she fibbed. "I'm okay."

"Are you sure?"

"Yeah... what're you doin' here?"

"I went by the hotel to ask about your day and see if you wanted some dessert and coffee. Maddie said she'd seen you leave. So, I figured maybe you were out walking."

"And you came here, huh?"

"Well, the bridge *is* a likely destination."

"Yeah. Sure," she said, rubbing her forehead.

"You *sure* you're okay?"

"Yeah," she said, glancing at the empty viewing window where Claude Bolton had jumped. "Just got the wind knocked out of me."

"C'mon," he urged. "Let's get you to my car. Does dessert sound good?"

"I think I'm gonna take a rain check," she said, going with him toward his station wagon. "I'm okay, but I got up real early and am dead tired."

"Fair enough. Hey, can I ask you something?"

"Sure."

"Ever since we met, you may've noticed that I've been spending some time with you."

"Yeah. What about that?" she asked, a little teasingly.

"For the record, my father highly disapproves of me chasing after you," he said with a certain twinkle in his eye. "He's afraid you'll perceive my attention as just a ploy so you'll write a nice article about the town."

"Oh. Like him flyin' me out here and puttin' me up *wasn't* that?" she asked.

"He says that's different. That's a business

arrangement, but me spending time with you—eating with you, walking with you—that's personal."

"Well, it does beg the question: Why are ya doin' it?"

Now at his car, he opened and held the door for her while she climbed inside. After he closed it, he rounded the vehicle and slid in behind the wheel.

"I don't know," he said, shutting his door. "I mean, I like you. And I know we come from different places and live separate lives. I know your stay here is only temporary. But—I don't know—there's something different about you. It—it's almost otherworldly."

"Otherworldly?" she asked, taking off her stocking cap and shaking out her hair a bit.

"Maybe that's the wrong word for it," he conceded, his hazel eyes searching. "Unexpected. Special." He looked at her tousled but attractive brown hair. "I can honestly say, I've never met another woman like you."

"Timeless," she offered, jokingly.

"Yes. That's a good description for it. You're timeless."

He reached over, cupped her face with his left hand, then leaned over and kissed her. She suspected this might happen sooner or later, and if it did, it would complicate things. But she still let it happen. And she still liked it.

Sixteen

THE HISTORICAL SOCIETY

The following morning, Goldie called her boss, Owen Mitchell, in Columbus and gave him an update. She told him she'd learned about silver mining and had even explored a silver mine to get some historical context. She filled him in on the tree lighting ceremony and its almost county-fair-like significance to the area. She talked about the charming stores on River Street, how the Victorian houses in town were strictly maintained, and how lots of people had made visiting Sparkledove part of their Christmas tradition. Mitchell was pleased with the report and said it sounded like she was gathering the makings of an excellent feature article. Goldie ended the conversation by trying to learn more about her life in Columbus. She asked Mitchell if he recalled what he liked about her when they met and how she came to work for the magazine. He jokingly responded that it was because she didn't waste his time with stupid questions and said he had to run to a meeting. So the call ended without her gaining additional insight about her life in 1942. This was frustrating, but at the moment, she didn't know what she could do about it. She figured that if her stay in the 1940s was permanent, she'd eventually find out about her background.

After the call, she headed for the Sparkledove Historical Society, which was just two storefronts down from Sparkledove Realty. This was the first day she wasn't wearing gauze on her hand since cutting herself in the bus terminal seven days earlier, and the injury was healing nicely. The community was now covered with a two-inch blanket of sparkling snow, and even though her entire existence in Colorado was a hugely bizarre magical mystery trip, she couldn't help but think how pretty the mountain town looked. She was also greeted by familiar faces as she walked. Clara of Clara's Gifts said hello as she was shoveling the plank sidewalk in front of her store. Deke Miller of Miller's General Store waved to her while standing outside with a cane and giving instructions to his son, Chad, who was inside and decorating the store's front window. It was nice to be known, she thought.

While she walked, she thought about her kiss with Peter Banyan. She had enjoyed it and liked feeling desired again, especially after Markie's rejection, but she really couldn't explain or justify it beyond that. Truth be told, she didn't want to.

What the hell? Life's messy, she concluded.

The historical society was run by a white-haired woman who introduced herself as Harriette Noise. She was in her eighties, wore a dress with a lace collar, moved slowly, and joked with Goldie that she, herself, was a historical artifact. She'd taught at the area high school for thirty-five years and claimed she hadn't traveled more than two hundred miles in any direction from Sparkledove. She had a sweet, creaky, grandmotherly voice that was as comforting as a porch swing on a summer's day. "I've seen the town at its most crowded and most desolate," she told her visitor. Once upon a time, the building where the society was located had been occupied by a saddle maker. Now, it was a mini museum with historical pictures on the wall, antiques in glass cases, and mannequins wearing period clothing. The centerpiece of the place was a six-foot-square three-dimensional balsa wood replica of the town circa 1878, complete with painted houses, horse-drawn carriages, trees, and small figures on the wood-plank sidewalks. Goldie was frankly impressed and pleased with the displays.

She pointed to the Maynard Mining operation, where she had just been the day before. But in the model, the woods around the buildings were much thinner.

"So, this is where Maynard Mining was?" she asked Harriette, pretending ignorance. "They were the biggest mining company in town, right?"

"That's right," she replied. "But you can't go up there anymore. It's all fenced off because it's not safe."

"And what's this buildin' right here?" she questioned, pointing to the director of operations' house."

"That's where the mine director lived. He was in charge of everything Maynard did in town. It was a beautiful house, but very near the mine, so men and wagons passed in front of it all day, kicking up dust. I doubt his wife was much pleased with the location."

Goldie grinned at the old woman confidentially. "Do you have any interestin' stories about the Maynard grounds? I know there was a tragic explosion that killed thirty-one men in 1881, but anything else?"

The old woman thought for a moment, then remembered. "Well, there *was* one strange incident that happened in 1902. A woman came into town one day. Nobody had ever seen her before. She was young. About your age. Claimed she didn't know where she was or how she got here. But she had money and wound up taking a room somewhere. She wasn't in town very long, but she went plum crazy. Got up early one morning, walked up to the director's house in her nightgown, which by then had been abandoned for twenty years, and hung herself in the front foyer."

"That's terrible!" Goldie said, empathetically.

"It sure was," Harriette agreed. "I was teaching at the time and raising my family. So, I didn't pay much attention to the gory details. But I *do* remember it was a big deal. The town's population was only about four hundred people. No police, newspaper, and certainly no tourism business like there is now."

"Did anyone find out who she was?" Goldie asked.

"No. Not that I recall. *The Denver Post* even ran a picture of her poor deceased face to see if anyone knew her. But no one came forward."

Goldie's goosebumps flared, and she became momentarily light-headed. The parallels between this woman, Claude Bolton, and, to some extent, herself were undeniable.

"W-what time of year did this happen?" Goldie asked.

"Summertime," the white-haired woman answered. "Either late July or August."

That would explain the short-sleeve nightgown, Goldie thought. She nodded, then changed subjects, looking at the model of the town. "And where's Falcon Drive?"

"Oh, that's over here," her hostess replied. "North of the mine."

Goldie looked at the miniature houses on the street, then pointed to one in particular. "So this one would be Martha Eggleston's house?"

"Yes, that's right. Although she just sold it."

"So I heard. I went to visit Martha the other day and noticed the house next door was for sale, too."

"Yes, George and Susan Ash," Harriette answered knowingly. "Lovely people. Lived in town for years. But after their kids were grown, they wanted something smaller and closer to Denver. They had their house up for sale, but with the war and all, it's a very depressed market. So, Mayor Banyan, bless his heart, took it off their hands so they could get on with their lives."

Goldie looked at her, surprised. "Wait. You mean to say he *bought* the Ash house?"

"That's right. Now he's the one selling it."

"Didn't he just buy the Eggleston house, too?"

"Yes, that's right. But Martha sorely needed the money. From what I understand, she was almost destitute. So buying it was practically an act of charity. Plus, he's letting her stay there through the holidays."

The wheels in Goldie's head were spinning furiously like the cylinders of a three-window slot machine, where one of those cylinders had just stopped at BAR.

"So, he owns two houses on Falcon Drive that are next door to each other?" she asked, needing verification.

"No. He owns *four* houses on Falcon Drive next door to each other," the old woman corrected, chuckling. "I've told him he ought to rename the street Banyan Lane."

Goldie paused and looked closely at the five houses on Martha Eggleston's side of the street. She pointed to the house next to the former Ash residence. "I didn't see a for sale sign here," she said.

"No, but that's the mayor's. He's owned it for about six months and intends to rent it out as a source of extra income. But there are some restorations he wants to do inside first."

"How did he come to buy *this* house?" Goldie asked.

"It was owned by a widower named Nathan Louis. Nice man, no children, but bad arthritis. Said he always intended to move to warmer weather, and after twenty years, he did."

Another spinning cylinder of the slot machine in Goldie's head suddenly stopped. Now two windows read BAR-BAR. She pointed to the house next to that.

"And this one? That had a for sale sign."

"Yes. That used to be Jason Shirk's."

"The previous sheriff?"

"That's right. He had a heart attack in late October of last year. About ten days before Halloween."

"And the mayor owns *that* one, too?"

Harriette nodded. "He didn't want Jason's daughter in Idaho Springs to have to deal with the sad business of disposing of the property. Again, with the war and the slow economy, that could take some time."

"Where's Idaho Springs?" Goldie asked.

"About fifteen miles down Highway 70. That's where Sheriff Shirk was buried."

Goldie nodded as the final cylinder in her mental slot machine stopped. The windows now read: BAR-BAR-BAR.

"Wow! That's a lot of property to have money tied up in," she observed. "And all on the same side of the same street."

"Yes. I suppose it is," the older one agreed. "I don't want to gossip, but I've heard the mayor and his son,

Peter, argue about it. Peter thinks his father has greatly overextended himself, and the mayor says the war won't last forever and he'll eventually make his money back plus a profit. Meantime, he said he was happy to remove the worry of a slow real estate market from the shoulders of others. Mayor Banyan's quite a Christian gentleman."

"Yeah, a regular Jerry Farwell Jr.," Goldie observed.

Harriette looked at her, not understanding, but Goldie smiled and continued her line of thought. "So Peter doesn't approve of all the real estate his dad has gobbled up, eh?"

"I think it's just one of many things they disagree about. But it's none of my business."

Goldie looked at the model again, then pointed to the final house on the Eggleston side of the street.

"And what about this one? Who owns that?"

"Why, that's my house, dear."

Goldie's eyes widened. "Your house?"

"Yes," Harriette verified.

"You're not thinkin' of movin' anytime soon, are ya?"

"Oh, goodness no. I should say not. I raised my family there. That's where I'll die."

Things were now clear in Goldie's mind. She knew what was happening. Charles Banyan was buying up houses on the Eggleston side of Falcon Drive to obtain mineral rights to the land. And what was under that string of houses was tunnel "22" of the old Maynard mine. A tunnel he believed still held a valuable silver vein. But how, she wondered, was Banyan's attention drawn to that particular tunnel? Within another minute, she discovered the answer. She turned away from the model of the town and started to examine the antiques displayed in the glass cases on tables that nearly outlined the entire floor of the society. There were pistols, canteens, mining hats, pickaxes, and mixed in among them was a booklet of some kind. There was a handwritten date on its cover that read May 10, 1882.

"What's this?" Goldie asked.

"That's one of the society's newer acquisitions. It's the final geology report done by Maynard's engineers. Maynard Mining went out of business in 1930, and we obtained this from one of their former employees in late '39. Maynard shut everything down in Sparkledove in June of 1882. There wasn't anything left in the mine. The yields had been getting smaller and smaller for some time."

"Do you mind if I see that report?" she asked.

"I'm sorry, dear. But the mayor has strict rules about the artifacts. He's actually the only one who has the key to the case. But I could ask him about it if you want?"

"No," Goldie waved off, downplaying it. "It's not important. I was just curious. But—the yields getting smaller and smaller, the mayor told you this?"

Harriette nodded. "Oh, yes. He was fascinated with the report. Read it over and over again when we first got it. He's quite the authority. He told me everything at Maynard was played out."

Yeah, Goldie thought. *Everything except for tunnel* "22."

Just then, the two women heard what sounded like a gunshot and a woman screaming on the street outside.

"What was that?" Harriette wondered, looking out the front window.

They heard what sounded like another gunshot, then somebody ran by the front picture window going in the opposite direction from the sound.

"You better stay here," Goldie said. "I'll go check it out."

As she stepped outside onto River Street, she saw two more people across the street running away from the sounds she'd heard. In another couple of seconds, she understood why. On the same side of the street where she'd seen the people running, but a block down, was a man in his early thirties standing on the plank sidewalk. He had a few days' growth of black beard, was wearing a winter coat, and was aiming an old-style Winchester repeating rifle at a pretty but frightened woman crouched behind a car on Goldie's side of the street. The woman was about the same age as the man, wearing an open overcoat, and was taking cover behind a 1938 green Dodge sedan parked in front of Miller's General Store.

"Horace? Put that damn thing down!" Deke Miller angrily yelled, poking his head out of the store's front

door. *"Alice? Come here, dear,"* he ordered the woman, extending an arm. She was only about seven feet away from the front door.

Just then, Charles Banyan came out of the realty office without his winter coat to see what was happening. Across the street, and running toward the man with the rifle, he saw Stu Frey hurrying down the sidewalk toward the shooter. Banyan then glanced behind him, saw Goldie watching this unfold twenty feet away, and muttered, "Oh, shit." Meanwhile, the woman named Alice behind the green Dodge took a crouching step toward Deke Miller. But the man with the rifle quickly cocked it, took aim again, and fired. The glass in the driver's side window suddenly shattered from the .40-caliber shell, and Alice shrank back behind the car as if being pulled by a magnet. A second after that, Deke retreated inside and shut his store door. Two seconds after that, the man named Horace with the rifle abruptly turned and pointed it at an oncoming Stu Frey.

"Stop or die!" he ordered.

Stu halted his advance but shook his head disapprovingly at the man with the rifle.

Turning his attention back to the Dodge, Horace stepped off the plank sidewalk and onto the street. There were only a few cars on the street at the time, and all of the drivers saw what was happening and stopped.

"Horace Mason!" a voice authoritatively yelled.

Eli Johnson appeared from one of the cross streets

a block away on Goldie's side of the street and walked onto River Street. He wore his usual jacket and uniform and limped slowly but steadily past the stopped cars toward the man with the gun. He was also, as usual, unarmed.

"What's all this about, Horace?" he asked calmly.

"*Stay back, Sheriff!*" the gunman warned, turning the rifle toward Eli.

"Now you know I can't do that," the blond-haired, blue-eyed lawman smiled, still coming. "Look yonder up the street. The mayor's watching. You don't want to get me in trouble with my boss, do ya?"

Horace quickly cocked his rifle again.

"*You take one more step and I swear I'll shoot you down!*"

Eli stopped and raised a conciliatory hand. "Well, if you're going to shoot me. Can I at least know why?"

"That slut of a wife of mine," Horace said, taking another step toward the green Dodge. "I just found out she's been sleeping around with Benny Hudson."

"Uh-huh," Eli said. "So, naturally, that means you should shoot *me*."

"I will if you try to stop me. I'm gonna kill her!"

Horace suddenly turned and fired another round at the Dodge. Alice screamed. The front driver's side tire burst, hissed, and the car listed to the left.

Immediately after that, Horace cocked the Winchester again and pointed it back at the lawman.

"She's gonna die and *you* ain't gonna stop me," he growled.

"Okay," Eli nodded. "You go ahead and shoot her. But, in a way, she's already dead."

"What're you talkin' about?"

"In about ten minutes, everybody in town is going to know what she did. So, her reputation will be as shot up as Ed Peterson's Dodge over there. Her life in Sparkledove will pretty much be over. Who's gonna trust a person who doesn't keep their word, Horace? That Jezebel reputation will follow her. 'Course, if you shoot her now, it's over in a second. She'll be free, and you'll go to prison for life. That doesn't seem like justice to me."

Horace's angry eyes squinted, considering what Eli had said.

"You're just sayin' this so I won't shoot you."

"Well, there *is* that," the sheriff agreed. "But that doesn't make what I said any less true."

Horace's eyes started to get moist. He stiffened his chin, looked toward the Dodge, then back at Eli. It was right at that moment that Goldie noticed the barrel of a second gun; a Sedgley Springfield hunting rifle was poised over the hood of a 1937 maroon Olds parked on her side of the street about a block and a half away. The barrel was pointed at Horace Mason's heart, and Paul McCaw, in his earflap cap, was crouched behind the Olds, ready to fire. A few seconds later, Stu saw the barrel, too.

"You don't know what it's like to be rejected like that," Horace said quietly.

"By a wife? No, sir, I don't," Eli said, just as quiet.

"But, by a woman? Yes, sir, I do. You remember a girl who used to live in town named Lila Hemmings?"

Horace thought for a moment. "Heard the name, don't know the family," he said, keeping an eye on the Dodge.

"Lila was my age," Eli explained, taking a limping step toward the gunman. "We met in junior college, and I fell hard. Far as I was concerned, she was it. But I also wanted to be a pilot. So, I joined the Army Air Corps."

"What happened?" Horace asked, interested but still aiming the rifle at him.

"Math," Eli said, taking a couple of steps and speaking confidentially so others wouldn't hear. "See, when you're a pilot, you've got to be good at math. Calculating fuel consumption, armament weight... I was pretty good, but not good enough. I failed the math requirement. Didn't get my wings."

He took another few steps toward Horace.

"Wound up being a mechanic, working on planes instead of flying 'em. Got sent to Pearl Harbor and actually worked for a squadron where some of the pilots were guys I went to flight school with. Talk about embarrassing! They were now officers and up there in the clouds, and I was a grunt changing their oil and filling their tires."

"If it wasn't for the math, you could still fly with that leg?" Horace wondered.

"Oh, I had two good legs back then," Eli explained, taking another step. "But that all changed on December

7th last year. As you know, Japanese planes attacked Pearl. I was at Hickam Field, and pilots were trying to get their planes into the air to fight back. One plane got shot up pretty bad just as it was rolling out of the hangar. The plane caught fire, the pilot's canopy stuck, and I ran out to get him. I got the canopy opened and pulled the fella out, but Zeros were strafing the field. He got cut in half by machine gun fire, and I took a round in the leg."

Eli rubbed his bad leg for effect and took another couple of steps toward the gunman.

"Boy, some days it still hurts terrible... Lila was disappointed enough that I wasn't an officer and a pilot. But when I got that bum leg, that was the straw that broke the camel's back. She wrote me and said she didn't want a—well—she didn't want me no more. By the time I got discharged and came back here, she was gone. Moved to California, they said.

"So, no, Horace. I don't know what it's like to be rejected by a wife. But I *do* know a thing or two about rejection. By the Air Corps, by a woman, and I promise you, I *promise*, there *is* life after the hurt goes away."

He was now close enough to the shooter to extend an arm.

"You still want to shoot me? Or, can I please have the rifle now?"

Horace looked at the Dodge again, then slumped his shoulders and handed the gun to Eli.

"Oh, hell. I suppose I ain't no First Prize at the country fair, myself. But I was never untrue to her."

"To be continued," Eli said, slipping his right arm around Horace's left. "But not out in the middle of the street."

Goldie looked down the street and saw Paul McCaw stand from his crouched position behind the Olds and raise his rifle barrel. Then, he walked down to the next side street, turned, and disappeared.

As Eli walked Horace back to the sidewalk on the opposite side of the street from Goldie, he called, "Alice? Go inside Miller's, get a cup of coffee or a soda, and sit by the stove. Don't talk to anyone about this, and I'll be back directly as soon as I've taken care of Horace. Deke?"

The elderly Miller stuck his head out of his front door. "What do you need, Eli?"

"Keep Alice warm and undisturbed until I come fetch her. And I *do* mean undisturbed."

"Okay, Sheriff."

"You know where Ed Peterson is?"

"Yeah. He's inside the store. He was doing some Christmas shopping."

"Okay. Tell him I'll call him this afternoon about his car."

Charles Banyan watched Eli walk Horace to the sheriff's office, which was at the opposite end of town from the covered bridge. Goldie slowly came up to stand beside him, and both watched as Eli and Horace passed by. Eli glanced at both of them but didn't say anything.

"That's the bravest thing I've ever seen," the mayor conceded, referring to the sheriff's actions.

"He's got a pair. I'll give 'im that," Goldie agreed.

"What was Eli saying to him out there? I couldn't hear."

"Me, neither," she said, now moving past him and continuing down the sidewalk toward Miller's.

"I, uh, I-I hope this unfortunate incident won't impact your article about how special Sparkledove is at Christmas," Banyan called.

"Relax, Mayor," Goldie replied over her shoulder. "Shit happens."

Banyan looked at her, surprised, having never heard the expression before or a woman being so blunt. But he got the gist and was visibly relieved.

Within another two minutes, Goldie had walked down to the side street where she'd seen Paul McCaw disappear. She spotted him stowing his rifle in his parked Chevy flatbed pickup. His brother Saul was there too. The bed of the pickup was filled with cut Christmas trees. Goldie and Stu Frey approached the brothers at the same time, coming from different directions.

"I saw what you were ready to do," Stu began.

"Oh, hey, Stu," Paul said straight-faced.

"Me, too," Goldie confirmed.

"Hey Goldie, Stu," Saul acknowledged, equally deadpan. "We got trees for the Boy Scouts to sell. Then we're gettin' jerky."

"You wouldn't really have shot Horace, would you?" Goldie asked.

"If I thought he was going to shoot the sheriff? Dead as a doornail," Paul replied.

"It's the mountain code," Saul explained.

"The mountain code?" she asked.

"Ya can't shoot an unarmed man," Saul said. "No matter what."

"Well, Alice was unarmed!" Goldie reminded. "Why didn't you stop him from shootin' at her?"

"Wives is different," Paul justified.

"Oh, good lord," Stu said, rolling his eyes.

Goldie looked at the brothers, then expelled a reconciling breath. "Well—in your own weird way, you were tryin' to help. So..." she reached out and patted the dirty arm of Paul's coat.

"You're a good man."

Paul's expression didn't change, but he stood up straighter and his chest puffed outward a little with pride.

"That's me," he agreed. "A silent sentinel on a mission to do good."

"And get jerky," Saul added.

Seventeen

HYPOTHETICAL

Eight minutes after leaving the McCaw brothers and chatting for a few moments with Stu Frey, Goldie walked into St. Mark's Catholic Church to find Father Fitzsimmons hurriedly putting on his overcoat and getting ready to leave.

"Goldie!" he said, concerned, taking his earmuffs out of his coat pockets. "I just got a call from one of my parishioners. She said there was gunfire down on River Street."

"Yeah," she confirmed. "I just came from there."

"Everyone alright? What happened?"

"Some guy named Horace Mason went postal on his wife Alice."

"Went what?" Father asked, never having heard the expression before.

"Everything's fine," she assured. "The sheriff diffused it. No one was hurt."

"Oh. Thank goodness!" he said, relieved. "But where did you say Horace went?"

"It was a domestic thing," she replied. "They're both goin' to need some counselin', but not now. Right now, they've just gotta calm down."

The young priest thought for a moment. "I don't know the name Mason. They're not congregants, but maybe I can get their information from the sheriff and offer to lend an ear to one or the other this afternoon."

"Yeah. That'd be good," she agreed.

He started to slip off his coat. "So, what brings you here today?"

"I-I need to talk to you about somethin'. At first, it might sound a little crazy."

"Oh, you mean like living with a gangster, trespassing onto closed city land, or going into a dangerous abandoned mine?"

"Yeah. Like that," she confirmed.

"Okay," he said, putting his coat and earmuffs aside and sitting in a pew, "then I'd better sit down."

She likewise took off her coat and glanced around the simple, quiet church to make sure no one was in earshot, but remained standing.

"Since she was here at the Thanksgiving potluck, I assume Martha Eggleston told you she has doubts about the circumstances of her husband's death."

"She's a woman in grief," he nodded.

"She told you about all the caffeine Bucky drank the day he died, didn't she. So he couldn't have fallen asleep."

"I don't like to repeat what people tell me," he replied. "A priest has to be a strong holder of confidences."

"That means yes."

"No, it doesn't."

"Yeah, it does. Otherwise, why make such a big deal about how you keep confidences?"

Father looked at her, slightly exasperated, knowing she was right. "Go on," he urged.

"You ever been over to the historical society?"

"Yes."

"Ever noticed a geological report they've got there in a glass case?"

"I-I can't recall."

"It's a newer acquisition, obtained in late 1939."

"I don't know. Maybe."

"What about Mayor Banyan?" she queried. "Priests are kinda like cops and trained to smell insincerity. You think this guy's a stinker?"

"Goldie, what are you trying to say?"

"I'm sayin' I came to town to do one kind of story, but I've stumbled onto another."

"What kind of story?"

She started to pace slowly up and down the center aisle of the church.

"Okay," she began. "Let me run a hypothetical by you. Let's say, there's this mayor in a small town that was once known for its silver minin'. This mayor is *really* into power. He likes to lay down a lot of rules, telling people how to live and how to maintain their homes. He also imposes a lot of historical society dues on them. Maybe he even extorts money from street vendors and skims from city accounts. He *definitely* used other people's money to bring in a journalist to write about the town."

"I'm not sure I—" Father started to say.

"Everybody in town, includin' the mayor, thinks the local mines are played out," she continued, still pacing. "That's what they've thought for years. But if you do some research, you'd learn that's *not* what happened. More profitable ore deposits were found in other places, and the minin' interests simply moved away."

"Really?"

"Really. I verified it twice at the Denver library. Then, one day, the mayor, who also happens to be president of the historical society, gets and reads through an old geological report from the largest minin' company that used to operate in town. And the report says there's one particular tunnel that might still have a large silver vein worth a pile of dough. Let's say, he hires some mining geologist from another county or state to explore this tunnel, drill some holes, and get ore samples. And lo and behold, he discovers the report is right.

"*Now,* let's say this tunnel runs under five houses on a particular side of a particular street. Needin' to obtain the mineral rights, he starts to acquire these houses one by one. Some he acquires legally, like from a couple who wanna downsize and be closer to Denver, and another man who had arthritis and wants to move to warmer weather. But others he acquires perversely. Like runnin' a guy with no life insurance off the road and committin' murder. And remember, this mayor most likely *knows* about people's finances and securities because he's the mayor, president of the historical society, *and* a realtor. Let's even say, maybe he's killed more than one person. Because another homeowner, the town's former sheriff, lived on that same side of the street and died about a year earlier. Now the mayor owns all of the houses on that side of the street except one."

She stopped pacing and turned to him.

"What do you think?"

The clergyman was emotionless and quiet for several seconds before answering.

"I think you said, 'Let's say' four times, 'maybe' three times, and 'most likely' once," Father noted, a little sternly. "That's a *lot* of wild conjecture you've stitched together, Goldie. Not to mention, you're accusing the town's biggest public servant of committing murder."

"Well, he may not have actually killed anyone, but he most likely gave the order."

"Again with the 'most likelys,'" Father groaned.

"I grant you, there's some additional proof I need to find," she admitted. "Like, does he own the land where the old Maynard mine used to be? But the sheriff himself thinks the circumstances of Bucky Eggleston's death are sketchy. And there's *no* historical evidence that says the Maynard mine went totally dry. *And* tunnel "22" *does* run under Falcon Drive. *And* ore samples *have* recently been taken. *And* the mayor *has* acquired most of the houses on the Eggleston side of the street since the geological report showed up. *And* he who owns the houses above *also* owns the mineral rights underneath."

"Yes," Father conceded. "But the houses you're talking about are for sale. I've seen the red signs in their yards."

"Cover," Goldie dismissed. "Smokescreen. It's a depressed market. If someone *were* interested in one of those houses, as owner, he could set a ridiculously high price. Plus, you gotta admit, the guy's a megalomaniac."

"What's that?"

"Someone obsessed with their own power."

"One could also say you're obsessed with your own conspiracy theory."

She took a deep breath, went over to the pew behind him, and sat down. "So, you think I'm wrong?"

"I think you're a fearless, spirited woman who's accustomed to suspecting the worst in people because of that former boyfriend of yours."

"But—"

"Look," he interrupted. "I've only been in town a couple of months. This is my first assignment. I was lucky to get it. I've worked hard to build positive relationships. If you're going to pursue this kind of hypothetical, you're going to need more proof than what I just heard if you want my support."

She thought for a moment. "The best proof would be to have a deed with Banyan or his company's name on it for the old Maynard mine. But those records would be down at city hall, and since he's mayor, I couldn't go makin' inquiries without him findin' out. Other workers at city hall probably feed him information unintentionally all the time. I bet nobody can take a crap in this town without him knowin' about it."

She looked at the priest, then remembered her language. "Sorry, Father."

"No," he agreed. "You could be right. During my time in seminary, I had to do a title search for a piece of property next to our campus that my school was interested in buying. I did it as extra credit for a business class. When I was conducting the search, I had to sign a logbook with my name and the property address I was interested in. If Sparkledove has the same type of procedure..."

"What about the former sheriff?" she wondered. "Jason Shirk? Did you know him?"

"No. He passed away before I arrived. But his funeral was held here. I just reorganized my predecessor's files and remember seeing the contact information for his family. He was a widower but has a child who lives around here."

"A daughter in Idaho Springs?"

"Yes... yes, I think that's right. However would you have known that?"

"Harriette Noise at the historical society mentioned it. I, uh, I don't 'spose you could give me her phone number, could ya?"

"Goldie, you can't go stirring up trouble."

"What trouble? You just told me to find more proof, and me going to city hall would be like an air raid siren for the mayor."

Father shook his head. "I-I'm not really comfortable with this."

"If you don't give me the daughter's number, I'll just get it from Peter Banyan. I'm sure he wrote the obituary and has her contact info. But I'd rather get it from you. As a newspaperman, Peter will ask all sorts of questions, and something like this requires discretion. Delicacy. Don't you think?"

The priest looked at her, then breathed out a heavy sigh.

"I suppose I could... but I want you to keep it quiet."

"Hey, quiet as a church mouse, Padre."

"Anything else?"

"Yeah. Could you shoot me a nice daytime photo of River Street for my article? Preferably from a high elevation. One in color and one in black and white?"

"You mean, for the Christmas article that supports the mayor whom you're trying to prove is a skimmer of city funds, a land defrauder, and a murderer?"

"Yeah," she grinned. "Now you're gettin' it. I'm multitaskin'."

About ten minutes later, Goldie went into the offices of *The Sparkledove Wing*. It consisted of a twenty-by-twenty-five-foot storefront divided into different sections by waist-high bookcases and worktables. One of these sections was Peter's office. The place smelled of paper, ink, and old wood. But it had a sense of purpose and efficiency.

As Goldie came into the office, Peter was typing at his desk in his frameless glasses and a suit with no tie. There was also another, older man with white hair and glasses getting letters out of the printer's drawer for an old printing press. He wore slacks, a dress shirt with arm bands just below the elbows, and a buttoned vest.

Upon seeing her, Peter smiled, slipped off his glasses, and rose.

"Hey, good morning. How are you?"

"Great."

She looked around as she walked over to his desk. "So, this is where the magic happens, eh?"

"Yes. Welcome to the world headquarters of *The Wing,* with a circulation of fifteen hundred to the entire community and surrounding hamlets and villages. Over there is Jack, he's the chief spokesman for the staff. Jack, meet Goldie."

"Ay, Jack. How's it goin'?" she greeted.

"Fine, ma'am," the older man smiled.

"How big's your staff?" she asked Peter.

"Jack," he grinned.

"I see," she nodded.

"Would you like a tour?"

"Oh, you give tours? Like the *New York Times?*"

"Absolutely. We're standing in the executive offices." He pointed to another desk. "Over there is our circulation and advertising department." He pointed to the printing press. "Our printing operation features equipment dating back to 1898." He pointed to some shelves with an encyclopedia, a dictionary, and a few phone books, "The research department is over there." He turned and pointed to the table in the corner with a hot plate, a tea kettle, and coffee mugs. "Staff lounge."

She looked around. "I must say, it's a first-class operation," she kidded. She looked at Jack, then at Peter. "I'm surprised you boys are here. I would've thought one or both of you would be trying to interview Horace and Alice Mason."

Peter casually slid his hands into his trouser pockets. "Yeah. I heard about that. There's really no story there."

"Alice has been sneaking around behind Horace's back for some time," Jack explained. "Benny Hudson was just the latest in a long line."

"Pretty much everyone in town knows about Alice except Horace," Peter continued. "So, the only thing a story would do is make Horace even angrier or feel more ashamed. Wouldn't do Alice any good, either."

"So, she really did cheat?" Goldie asked, needing verification.

"Let's just say, they're a couple with problems, and

writing about them doesn't help anyone solve anything," Peter concluded.

Goldie thought for a moment, then nodded in agreement. "Well, you should've at least seen how the sheriff handled Horace. It was pretty impressive."

"Yeah. Heard about that, too." Peter replied. "When my father first hired Eli, I wasn't for it. I mean, the guy had zero experience in law enforcement and a bum leg. But, as time has gone on, I think I was wrong about him."

She smiled, liking that he could admit to a mistake. She also liked that he chose not to profit from Horace and Alice Mason's problems. She and Peter looked at one another, their smiles and sparkling eyes practically lighting up the room.

"I've got to run down to Miller's," Jack abruptly announced. "Collect the payments for this week's ad."

"Good idea," Peter agreed. "Clancy's hasn't paid us for their ad, either."

"I'll take care of it," Jack said, buttoning up his coat and slipping a fedora on his head. "Nice to meet you, Goldie."

"Good meetin' you, too, Jack," she reciprocated.

She and Peter watched as Jack left the office, then they turned back to one another.

"Hey," he noticed, taking and examining her left palm. "Your wrapping is off. How's the hand doing?"

"Except for a little scabbing, good as new," she informed.

He brought the injured palm to his lips and kissed

it. Then, still holding her hand, pulled her close and kissed her on the mouth. Like the first time he kissed her in his car, she enjoyed it. But she also noticed that both times he didn't use his tongue. She wondered if French kissing even existed in the 1940s. After the embrace, Peter smiled boyishly and ran his fingers through his wavy brown hair.

"I don't know if I should apologize for kissing you or take you in my arms and kiss you again."

"Well, when you make up your mind, let me know," she smiled teasingly, then slipped out of his arms and stepped over to his typewriter to see what he was working on.

"Wow," she said, reading. "'Anna Paskins has a new ingredient in her eggnog that has her bridge club delighted but stymied.'"

"People read every day about crime, or someone's son or brother dying far away overseas," he explained. "What I write about is close to home, slice-of-life. After all, isn't preserving that way of life what we're fighting for?"

She turned and stepped over to the bookcase behind his desk. She tilted her head to the side and read some of the author's names on the spines. "Pearl S. Buck, John Steinbeck, Ernest Hemingway... man, you really *do* want to be a novelist, don't ya?"

"I've got a ways to go," he said. "So, are you here to see where I work, or are you *really* here to ask me to the dance this weekend?"

"Dance?"

"The Christmas dance at the community center Friday night. It's another big area draw. There's also a gingerbread house competition I believe you're judging."

She thought for a moment. "Yeah, your dad mentioned something about a gingerbread house competition during Thanksgiving dinner."

He smiled and picked up a Calendar of Events flier off his desk.

"Here. I guess you didn't get one of these at the tree lighting."

"No, I didn't," she admitted, embarrassed. "But thanks."

She stuffed the flier into her overcoat pocket, then changed subjects. "Actually, I'm here because I need a favor."

"Name it."

"I wanna explore some of the surroundin' area on my own and was hopin' I could borrow your car tomorrow."

"Sure. But I'd also be happy to be your chauffeur."

"Thanks. But in every article I write, there's got to be a certain element of self-discovery. Oh, I don't mind bein' spoon-fed stuff with a calendar of events, but there also has to be some self-exploration. Otherwise, the piece won't read as authentic. Does that make sense?"

"Perfect sense. Okay. Just let me know what time you want it, and I'll have it all gassed up for you. Damn the rationing," he grinned.

"Great. Thanks, Peter."

"So, what're you up to for the rest of today?"

"Father Fitz is doing some photography for me, I have notes to type up from a visit to the historical society, I've got to call my publisher—lots of things."

These last two items weren't really in Goldie's plans, but she wanted to create the illusion that she was a busy journalist with an agenda. She also wanted to slow things down with Peter and was afraid that if she said she was free for the rest of the day, he'd invite her to do something. She liked Peter. She really did. But she didn't see the wisdom in turning up the heat on having a relationship. For now, a low simmer was fine.

Within a half hour of Goldie leaving Peter's office, Charles called his son to meet him at Sparkledove Realty and had sent his secretary out on an errand so they could have some privacy.

"She saw everything between Horace and Alice Mason!" the senior Banyan complained, seated behind his desk. "It's a public relations nightmare!"

"No, it's not," Peter assured. "She knows all towns have drama. Especially small towns. Believe me, she's staying focused on a nice, positive article."

"Harriette *did* say they had a good chat before all hell broke loose, but I don't know."

"I spoke to Goldie, and I really think you're getting worked up over nothing."

"What do you mean, you spoke to her?" Charles said with renewed anxiousness. "When was this?"

"Not long after Horace went to jail," the son

replied. "She stopped by my office and both Jack and I told her the Masons weren't really news."

"And she bought it?"

"She bought it because it's true," Peter reminded.

"Why was she at your office?"

"She's a fellow journalist and was probably curious about the paper," he shrugged. "She's also borrowing my car tomorrow."

"*What?*" Charles bellowed. "To go where? To do what?"

"Her job!" Peter answered impatiently. "Jesus Christ, relax, will you? Stop trying to manage everything."

Peter spoke with his father for a few more minutes, trying to alleviate his concerns, but failed. After he left the realty office and returned to his own, Charles made a call from his desk. When a voice answered on the other end of the line, the mayor began with:

"Got a job I need you to do tomorrow."

Eighteen

KIDS & A TRAIN

Midland Elementary School had a rural address and accommodated children from a half dozen small towns and villages, including Idaho Springs and Sparkledove. Through a pre-arranged meeting with Jason Shirk's daughter, Evie Hines, Goldie drove Peter's Ford station wagon to the school and arrived at 12:15 p.m. Hines was Evie's married name, and she was a second-grade teacher who had been teaching for seven years, but she was new to Midland Elementary. She agreed to meet with Goldie while she was on playground duty, watching a couple of dozen first and second-graders. The children swung back and forth on swings, bobbed up and down on teeter-totters, and ran around with the crackle and energy of several lit fuses despite the thirty-three-degree weather. Though Evie and Goldie had never met, they had spoken on the phone the day before and were really looking forward to seeing one another.

Evie was shorter than Goldie, slightly overweight, but had a pretty face, blonde hair, a clear complexion, and gave the immediate impression of a woman who could take care of herself. No doubt the result of being a cop's daughter.

"Ay," Goldie greeted, after one of the school's secretaries walked her out to the playground.

"Ay, how ya doin'?" Evie greeted, in a Bronx accent just as pronounced as Goldie's. The two women shook hands.

"I can't tell ya how nice it is to talk with someone who sounds—y'know—*normal!*" Goldie said.

"Well, ya can take the girl outta the Bronx, but ya can't take the Bronx outta the girl," Evie replied. Then she spotted something happening on the playground. "Timmy?" she called, "Leave Mary Ellen's hair alone!"

Goldie recalled how Peter had said her accent reminded him of someone he used to know, and how he had specifically mentioned the Bronx. Now she realized he was talking about Evie's dad. "Thanks for seein' me," she said. "I really appreciate it."

"My pleasure. So, writin' a story about Sparkledove?" Evie asked, keeping one eye on the kids.

"Yeah. As I said on the phone yesterday, I'm with *Adventure Escape Magazine* and we're doin' a feature on Sparkledove for next year's Christmas issue. The current sheriff has been on the job for about a minute and a half, and since your dad was part of the town for much longer, I thought I'd get some backstory on him. I'm sure he helped make the town's Christmas season what it is today."

"Oh, he loved that town," Evie agreed. "I just took my kids to the Christmas tree lightin'."

"So, tell me about your dad?" Goldie asked.

"Hold on," Evie replied with a raised finger. Then she called out to a little girl. "Hey, Kelly. C'mere, sweetie."

A little red-headed girl in a pea-style navy coat, hat, and mittens timidly approached.

"You're doin' that thing with your knees. You gotta go to the bathroom?"

The little girl nodded.

"Then go on. Run inside," the teacher instructed. Then she turned her attention back to Goldie's question. "Like I said yesterday, my ol' man was one of New York's finest for eighteen years. But he always had a bit of the wanderlust in him. He fancied himself a cowboy and talked about movin' out west. When I was twelve, that's what we did. First to Denver, where he was a state cop for ten years, then to Sparkledove for nearly eight more. He had a lot to do with what are now annual traditions in town. Like, the tree lighting, the community Christmas dance, and even an ice sculpture contest, but that got discontinued. He was also the first to encourage some area farmers to sell sleigh rides to tourists in the evenings."

"How is it he wound up being buried in Idaho Springs?"

"My mom's buried here. There's a place they used to picnic that overlooks the cemetery. It's very picturesque, and she decided that's where she wanted to be laid to rest. My husband is in the war now, so I wanted to get out of Denver and be near them."

"What branch is your husband in?"

"The army; last I knew, he was near Casablanca."

"Is he okay? Safe?"

"As far as I know, but he doesn't write a lot of details. It's more general stuff."

Goldie nodded. "Was it hard for your dad to go from, y'know, investigatin' big city crimes to arrangin' sleigh rides?"

"No. He got a lot of what he called his humanity back after movin' to Sparkledove. He really liked bein' sheriff there. Except for maybe the last couple of years."

"What happened the last couple of years?" Goldie asked.

"Scott?" Evie called out. "No, sir! Your hands don't belong there." Then, she answered the question. "A certain pain-in-the-ass city council member became the new mayor, and he and dad locked antlers a lot."

"Charles Banyan?" Goldie asked.

"Yeah," Evie realized. "Guess you *would* know who he is since you're writin' a story 'bout the town, huh? *Scott?*" she called out again. "What did I just say?"

"Why didn't they get along?" Goldie asked.

"I don't know for sure. My dad and me were close,

but we had a million other things to talk about. My mom got sick and died of cancer, I got married, moved to Denver, and had a couple of kids. So, I wasn't exactly followin' the day-to-day events of my dad's job. But I *do* know he thought Banyan was kind of sleazy and only out for himself. He mentioned it more than once. And I *do* remember Dad sayin' he thought he might have somethin' on him."

"Really? Like what?"

"Don't know. He died not too long after that. But it could've been anything, y'know? From not havin' a huntin' license to a DUI charge in another state." She looked at Goldie apologetically. "Geez. I'm sorry. You want happy stuff about Dad and Sparkledove, huh?"

"No, actually. This is exactly the kind of stuff I want."

The teacher looked at Goldie quizzically. "Why?"

"Lemme ask you somethin'," the visitor continued. "When your father passed away? Had he been sick? Was it a surprise?"

"He was in his early seventies, but—yeah—it was. We *were* surprised. Dad always took care of himself. He'd been fightin' some sort of bug before he passed, but other than that..." Evie called out to a little girl on the playground. "Georgia? Keep your coat buttoned, please. And where's your hat?"

"What kind of bug?" Goldie asked. "How long had he been fighting it?"

"A week. Ten days, maybe. It was some kind of stomach virus. Aching. Vomiting. I guess his weakened condition made him more vulnerable to the heart attack." She looked at Goldie curiously. "Why're you so interested in how my dad died?"

"One more question, then I'll tell ya," Goldie persisted. "After your father passed, why'd you sell his house to Charles Banyan? A man who, according to you, your dad thought was shady?"

"Convenience," she shrugged. "I've got two small kids and a husband overseas. With the war on, nobody was buyin' houses in Sparkledove, and Banyan had cash in hand. The sale of the house and Dad's life insurance provided a very helpful cushion for us to move and get settled here. It didn't matter to me if Dad didn't like the guy. Sellin' our house gave me options."

"Yeah," Goldie nodded, understandingly. "As a mother alone on the home front, that makes sense."

"So, what's goin' on?" Evie asked. "What's this *really* about?"

"Evie, to tell ya the truth. I'm not sure. I came to town to write one kind of story, but seemed to have stumbled onto another. But I can tell ya this, Charles Banyan has been buyin' up all the houses on the side of Falcon Drive where you used to live, and I have reason to believe another homeowner on the street recently died under suspicious circumstances."

The teacher looked at her. "Wait—are you sayin' my dad *didn't* die from a heart attack?"

"I don't know. If you told me he had a history of heart problems, or had been sickly for a long time, or was in poor health generally... but that's not what I'm hearin'. Right?"

Evie looked at Goldie as the color slowly drained from her face. "Are, are you sayin' my dad was murdered?"

"Charles Banyan has been buyin' up houses on your parents' side of the street. There are questions about another neighbor's death. Your father had some suspicions about Banyan and even told you so. And I've recently discovered that a tunnel from an old silver mine runs under Falcon Drive that might not be played out like everyone in town assumed it was. So, am I takin' two and two and coming with thirty-seven? Or four? What would *your* conclusion be?"

Evie thought for another long moment, then gazed at the kids on the playground and called, "Five-minute warning, everyone."

Then she turned to her visitor with slightly moist eyes. "Whatdoya want from me?"

"Did your dad have an autopsy?"

"No. His doctor said it was a heart attack."

"I'm sorry to ask, but would you consider one now?"

"What? You mean, dig him up?"

"It's the only way to be sure his death was natural," Goldie pressed. "Look, Evie, I know you don't know me. I'm just some broad who showed up. But I didn't start out lookin' for any of this. I got no secret agenda here other than the truth. I understand what I'm askin' is emotionally upsettin' and will cost you money. Plus, it might not reveal a thing. But then again, it might reveal your dad's death was wrongfully caused. For a man who made a life out of protectin' the rights of others, doesn't he deserve the same?"

Evie didn't answer with a definitive yes or no, but she did agree to think about it. All things considered, Goldie couldn't ask for more. She made sure Evie had her contact information, requested absolute confidentiality, then left the school.

As she followed backroad directions to Sparkledove that Dean at the reception counter had given her, she mocked herself over her visit with Evie.

"I just asked a woman to exhume the body of her father. Geez, Goldie, why not ask her to do something simple, like believe the Dodgers have left Brooklyn?"

She came to a railroad crossing that cut across some pine woods. The poles at the crossing were flashing and ringing, so she stopped and waited. Within thirty seconds, she saw a long, continuous chain of puffing gray smoke belch into the sky. Underneath it was an old steam locomotive that looked like it had just come out of the 1870s.

Cool! she thought. It reminded her of the train from the Will Smith movie, *Wild, Wild West.* It had a black smokestack that sprouted out of its front boiler, a clanging brass bell, and a wooden cowcatcher that fanned out over the tracks in front of the locomotive like a huge rake. An engineer with a puffy gray hat leaned out a side engine window despite the cold. This was followed by a black coal car, two brightly painted green-and-yellow passenger cars, then a red caboose. The engineer waved to Goldie as the train rolled by, and she noticed it was slowing down with squeaking brakes as it did. After the train passed, she saw a turn-off about an eighth of a mile ahead for the Rocky Mountain Western Railroad Company. She remembered passing a sign that read "Scenic Old-Time Train Rides" on her way to the school, but she didn't give it much thought. Now, however, having seen the iron monster from the past go by, she was intrigued. She took the turn, which, after a short drive, led into a half-full parking lot and a historic-looking train depot complete with a water tower. Tourists could buy tickets and snacks, then board the train for an eighteen-mile loop that went through a picturesque mountain landscape that hadn't changed since Chinese laborers built the railroad in the 1860s. The train used to connect with mining operations and convey ore. Now it carried parents with cameras and kids holding bags of popcorn.

Goldie purchased her one-dollar ticket, then climbed the two iron steps onto one of the passenger cars. Since it was a weekday, the car didn't fill up with tourists, but there were still enough visitors to make her feel like she was on vacation. Each car had a conductor dressed in a three-piece dark suit, complete with a gold watch-chain hanging from his vest pocket and a stiff-brimmed conductor's hat. His purpose was to act as a tour guide during the one-hour ride. When everyone was on board, and with two deep, "ROO-ROOS" from the throaty whistle, the train slowly chugged its way out of the station. Goldie sat back in her leather seat and couldn't help but feel like she was on an American version of the Hogwarts Express.

During the ride, Goldie didn't think about time travel, the war, Charles Banyan and his schemes, where things might be going with Peter, or anything else connected with her strange circumstances. Instead, she listened to the conductor talk about the locomotive that was pulling them and the laborers who built the railroad. She listened to stories of card games, shoot-outs, and grimy-faced prospectors who struck it rich while others died in tragic cave-ins. The scenery was breathtaking and dusted with snow.

The highlight of the trip was when the train went over a forty-foot gorge on a wooden bridge built in 1869. The engineer slowed down so the passengers could get the full impact of just how narrow the iron rails were, how open the bridge was since it had no guardrails, and how, if you looked straight down, you could find yourself suddenly dizzy and disoriented. Even though it was all tourist fodder, a city girl like Goldie found it fascinating.

She got off the train and returned to Peter's station wagon with the same satisfied smile most of her fellow passengers had. After referring to her written directions, she started up the car and pulled out of the parking lot.

Two men were watching from a vehicle in the distance. They were Tully and Crosby. Tully, with his short-cropped black hair and days' worth of stubble, sat behind the wheel, and his red-haired companion with the bushy mustache watched from the passenger seat. The beefy pair stared like ravens from the cab of a black pickup truck. A truck with a three to four-inch scratch of light tan paint on its driver's side front quarter panel.

Nineteen

MAYBE A LOT

After she returned Peter's car and accepted a dinner invitation from him to go to Clancy's Bar & Grill, Goldie returned to her room and attempted a first draft of an article for *Adventure Escape Magazine*. She wondered if she should go back to the Denver Library, obtain a library card, then check out a few issues to use as a template. But that was a question for tomorrow. Today, she wanted to attempt a draft partly because she was used to writing a little every day from keeping diaries for years and missed it, and partly because she'd now been in town for eight days and, frankly, had a lot to write about: the town's history, the preservation of the downtown area and its houses, and going into the mountains to select the town's Christmas tree. Then, there was the tree lighting ceremony, the sincere friendliness of Sparkledove's people, and the awesome and humbling beauty of the Rocky Mountains. It was, admittedly, a

180-degree turn from the other story she was pursuing about Charles Banyan's land grab and his possible involvement with murdering people. But one story was something she was supposed to do, while the other story was something she felt compelled to do. She wrote about eight hundred words. What she wrote wasn't exactly AP Style, but at least she made an honest attempt, and the exercise helped to organize her thoughts.

After changing from a dress to slacks, she rendezvoused with Peter at Clancy's Bar & Grill at 6:30 p.m., which was across the street from the town's volunteer fire department. Whereas the restaurant in the Sparkledove Arms was airy and inviting with its light-yellow walls and fieldstone fireplace, and the bar at the Pine River Inn was woodsy chic with its pine log walls and taxidermy wildlife, Clancy's was just a hole in the wall. It was small, dark, and had no décor to speak of other than some framed black-and-white photos of hunting and fishing trips the owner had taken over the years. There was a photo of an ice fishing trip with a dozen or so strung-up bass, another with a dead black bear, yet another with a dead elk. Despite the documented death, they shared an intimate booth, and Clancy's made an outstanding hunter's soup. They also had crispy French fries that were delicious.

Goldie told Peter about her train ride, an attraction he was very familiar with, as well as starting a first draft of her article. But she didn't tell him about Evie Hines and Midland School. She didn't believe he was mixed up in anything his father was, but Charles was Peter's dad, and she felt like she had to tread very carefully. As their meal was wrapping up, Peter slipped off his frameless glasses and asked if Goldie would like to see his house and perhaps have a nightcap.

She smiled with her red lipstick glistening from one of the few lights in the place, and tossed her brown hair playfully. Then she picked up and took a final swallow of her second whiskey on the rocks.

"So, *now* we're down to it at last, huh?" she asked. "Are we gonna have a fling or not?"

"It's just a nightcap, Goldie," he replied innocently.

"Yeah, and Harvey Weinstein wanted just a back rub," she noted.

"Who's Harvey Weinstein?"

"Doesn't matter. You know what I'm talkin' about."

"Okay," he admitted, "I'm not going to lie to you. I *like* you. Maybe a lot."

"I like you too," she shared. "Maybe a lot. But there is no possible way we can have a relationship. I'm not gonna fall into bed with you just because you're cute and it's the holidays."

"I'm cute?" he asked, pleased.

"You know you are, so let's not bullshit each other."

"Okay," he agreed. "I'm cute and you're timeless. I don't want to make you feel cheap by suggesting anything temporary and tawdry, but I don't want a maybe once-in-a-lifetime chance to slip away, either. I wasn't kidding Goldie when I said I've never met anyone like you. I really wasn't."

"Look, Peter—" she started to say.

"I hear about soldiers falling in love with girls overseas all the time," he cut in. "Men are fighting and dying, yet some still find a way to fall in love with women on the other side of the world and plan a life. If they can be brave and say: 'Screw the odds'—if you'll pardon my language—why can't we? I mean, unless you don't see the same potential."

She smiled appreciatively at his sincerity, reached across the table, and took his hand. "Peter, it's not just that you live in Colorado and I live in Ohio. There are other factors that complicate things."

"Like what?" he asked.

"I-I don't wanna get into it."

"Please, Goldie."

"Well... frankly... your father. Yes, he's the one who brought me here, but now that I am, I see his controlling nature and snake-oil-salesman personality. Honestly, I don't like it. I need to separate that from the article—and I *will*—but you and me gettin' involved only muddies things."

"Welcome to the club," he replied, unfazed. "I don't like him much either. I suppose in the end, he and I both want the same thing: for Sparkledove to be a sought-after tourist location and a great place to live. But we've got very different ideas on how to accomplish that. You're right. He's got more than just a controlling nature. He can sometimes be an out-and-out bully. He grasps things so tightly that he chokes the life out of 'em, like he and I having a good relationship. So, don't think your perceptions about him create an obstacle with *me*. If anything, they only reinforce to me how smart you are."

"Thank you," she said sincerely.

"So, what else do you have that complicates things?" he asked, wanting to meet things head-on.

"I think that's enough for now," she said, reaching for her jacket sitting next to her.

"Wait, you're not leaving, are you? It's early."

"I need to walk and get some air. I spent all afternoon hunched over a typewriter."

"Me too," he said. "I'll go with you."

"No, I need to think things over," she said. "You just said some pretty heavy-duty things. If you were lookin' for a fast lay, that's one thing. But if you're speakin' with your heart and not your crotch, then that's somethin' else, and I should give it the consideration it deserves."

"Fair enough," he agreed. Then he raised an eyebrow. "But maybe you could consider both?"

She smiled and rolled her eyes. "Jesus... men!"

"There's no women without men," he reminded impishly. Then, he got more serious. "Just remember, Goldie, I am *not* my old man."

Ten minutes later, she was strolling alone down River Street, chewing a fresh piece of gum. She was taking her time to carefully peruse the store windows, which was something she really hadn't done before.

The idea of truly trying to have a relationship with Peter was something akin to driving his Ford Super Deluxe Station Wagon. It was beautiful, intriguing, and even fun, but it didn't have much to do with reality. Or at least, what she knew as reality. She came to the window of a bookstore, and a coffee table book caught her eye. The book was called *The Architecture of New York City,* and on the front cover were pictures of the Empire State Building, the Chrysler Building, and the Flatiron Building.

"They've hardly changed," she sighed, simultaneously feeling comforted and lonely by things that were familiar yet distant.

She cracked her gum and felt herself becoming emotional, then she gazed down the street toward city hall, which was in the opposite direction from her hotel. She noticed the lights were on in the sheriff's office next door, and Eli's police cruiser was parked out front. Making a decision, she decided to walk down and pay him a visit.

Like most of the stores and businesses in town, the sheriff's office used to be something else. It was somewhat long and narrow, with a squeaky wooden floor, and was originally built to be a law office for two attorneys, with one office being downstairs and the other being up a narrow flight of stairs on the second floor. Since 1919, however, it had been the sheriff's office, and the upstairs had been converted into a two-cell jail with a bed, toilet, and sink in each cell. As she came through the front door, Eli Johnson was just coming down the stairs to her far right, carrying a tray with some used dishes and an empty glass on it. As usual, he wore his tan sheriff's uniform and carried no gun.

He looked at her, somewhat surprised. "Howdy, Goldie."

"Sheriff," she acknowledged.

She took off her gloves, unzipped her jacket, and looked around while chewing her gum.

There was a chair and a desk, two chairs in front of the desk, a filing cabinet with a radio sitting on its top, a locked, glass gun case, and a half-bath. The only decorations on the walls were a calendar, a wall clock, and a photo of FDR.

Eli cracked a faint, polite smile, then set the tray with the glass and dishes on the corner of his desk. Besides the tray, the desk held two law enforcement textbooks, a typewriter off to the side, and a phone. He turned and limped over to the stairway he had just come down, then shut the door that separated the upstairs from the downstairs.

"If you've come to interview Horace Mason, I'm afraid you're a little late. He just finished supper, and I'm buttoning things up for the night."

"No, I didn't come for that," she said.

"Oh? I thought, with your penchant for the big scoop and sensationalism—" he stopped himself, knowing this direction of discussion wouldn't be productive. "What can I do for you?" he asked, somewhat formally.

"Mind if I sit down?"

"Help yourself," he said. "So long as you don't mind if I rinse out these dishes."

She shook her head, stuck her gloves in her jacket pockets, then slipped off her jacket while he picked up the tray and went into the half-bath to use the sink.

"So, off the record and out of curiosity, what's goin' to happen to Horace?"

He began rinsing things off while the door was open and his back was to her.

"Well, Alice has decided she doesn't want to press any charges. I suppose because she feels guilty about carrying on with Benny Hudson. So, Horace is only going to face charges of discharging a weapon in a public place and property damage. He may get a fine and spend a little time in jail, but that's a whole lot better than five to ten years for attempted murder."

"Absolutely," she agreed.

"I'm taking him over to the county jail tomorrow, and from there it's a circuit court matter. But I'll remind the prosecutor of his clean criminal record."

"I don't know if you heard, but somebody had your back with a rifle pointed at Horace while you were tryin' to disarm him."

"I *didn't* hear that," he said, leaving the dishes to dry on a small table kiddie-corner to the sink. "Who was it?"

"Paul McCaw."

"What was he doing in town? Wait—" he remembered, "Christmas trees for the Boy Scouts."

"Yeah. And Stu Frey tried to come to your rescue, too."

He came out of the bathroom, wiping his hands on a paper towel.

"Well, people can't take the law into their own hands," he said, tossing the paper towel into a wastepaper basket. "Still, I appreciate the consideration."

"Yeah," she agreed.

He stepped over to the chair behind his desk and sat down. "So," he said, rubbing his bad leg, "if you're not here to interview Horace, what can I do for you?"

"I saw what you did on the street. How you approached Horace and disarmed him. What did you say to him?"

He gestured to one of the textbooks on his desk. "Just used what they call Empathetic Psychology."

"I thought what you did was really brave, and believe me, I don't compliment cops."

"Aw—it wasn't as brave as you think," he downplayed. "Horace was riled, but he's no killer."

"If you say."

"Hey," he said, changing subjects, "did I see you driving around earlier in Peter Banyan's car?"

"Yeah. He lent it to me so I could do some explorin' of the area."

"You two seem to be hitting it off pretty good," he observed.

"Yeah, we're friends."

He nodded slightly, then his eyes drifted away to

nothing in particular while she looked at the leg he was still rubbing.

"Your leg hurt?" she asked.

"It acts up sometimes after a long day. Especially when it's cold."

"So naturally, you live in Colorado," she quipped.

"Naturally," he agreed.

She looked at the leg for a moment, then asked, "What happened?"

His blue eyes shot down to the floor, as if embarrassed, then he rose.

"I appreciate you coming in tonight and your kind words, Goldie. If I can help in any way with the story for your magazine, just let me know. Would you like a lift back to your hotel?"

Clearly getting the message that Eli didn't want to talk about his leg, she likewise rose and slipped on her jacket.

"No. I'm good, but thanks," she smiled, zipping herself up.

There was an awkward silence while she pulled out her gloves and put them on. Finally, she asked, "You stayin' here tonight?"

"No. But I don't live far."

"Just goin' to leave your prisoner here alone?"

"Well, we're not talking John Dillinger, and I'll turn the light off before I go so he can sleep."

She nodded and smiled.

"Okay then. Goodnight, Sheriff."

"See ya," he said, giving her a small salute with two fingers.

She walked out the door and back into the night. As she headed toward her hotel, she chewed her gum slowly, feeling that even though she had spoken with Eli, they hadn't really communicated.

At the same time, Tully and Crosby were now standing in the mayor's dimly lit kitchen, having beers. Stephie Banyan was over at the community center, helping to get it ready for the annual Christmas dance.

Tully was Greek, forty, and usually wore a black leather thigh-length overcoat. Crosby was forty-two, Scottish, born and raised overseas, and had a Scott's temper. His red-haired bushy mustache was only accentuated by his plaid woolen winter coat. Both men looked like they might work in a Denver factory, and indeed, as Peter had once suggested, neither was a resident of Sparkledove. As Goldie had correctly guessed, these two did the mayor's bidding, whether it was legal or not. Like the McCaw brothers, neither one was particularly emotional as they conferred with their employer. But unlike the brothers, there was nothing quirky or humorous about their lack of emotion; it was just stone-cold and threatening.

"And you have no idea why she was at the school?" Charles wondered.

"Since she's a travel writer, she's likely been to Colorado before and knows someone at the school," Tully reasoned, taking a swig from a longneck bottle. "She was probably visiting an ol' pal."

"Aye, that makes the most sense," Crosby agreed with his Edinburgh accent, also holding a longneck.

"Maybe," Charles replied. He was still wearing his suit from work, leaning against the stove with a glass of beer on the counter next to him while his eyes searched for another explanation. "But, if she wasn't visiting an old acquaintance, why would Goldie Maraschino go to a school? The scenic train ride makes sense. But the school…"

"Have Peter find out," Crosby suggested. "They seem to be getting more and more chummy."

"I originally didn't want Peter to, well, 'be Peter' with another pretty face," Banyan mused. "But now, there may actually be an advantage there."

"We could always break into the school," Tully suggested. "There's bound to be a staff list in someone's desk at the front office. Maybe we should get a copy. See if someone's name means something."

"Excellent idea, Tully," Charles smiled. "Let's make that happen."

"Sunday night," Crosby suggested. "Almanac's predicting snow. Nobody will be out."

Just then, they were interrupted by the sound of something being dropped on the stairs that led down to the basement. Charles looked at the basement door, just a few steps away, walked over, and opened it. He found Lupe on the other side, standing on the top basement step with the lights on. She was holding a bucket of dirty water in one hand and had just picked up a scrub brush with the other. She appeared just as surprised to see him as he was to see her.

"Lupe!" Banyan barked, displeased. "What the devil are you doing here?"

"Ola, Señor Banyan," she replied in her heavy Spanish accent. "Señora Banyan said I can leave early tomorrow and get ready for the dance, if I stay later tonight and clean the pantry shelves downstairs. They mucho dirty!"

She held up the bucket of brown water for proof. Banyan wrinkled his nose and waved it away. "How long have you been lurking on those stairs?"

"You want I should wash the stairs?" she asked, misunderstanding. "Okay!"

"No," he corrected. "I didn't hear you coming up the stairs. Were you standing just outside the door?"

"I was coming to open—but I dropped my brush," she explained.

She came up the final step and into the kitchen, then went over to the sink. "I'll change the water, then wash the stairs for you."

"That's not what he asked," Tully said, setting his beer down and stepping over to the sink next to her until he was uncomfortably close. "Were-you-listening-on-the-stairs?" he asked, pronouncing each word slowly and distinctly.

"L-listen?" she asked nervously. "W-what should I listen for?"

The three men looked at one another for a moment, then Banyan, deciding her appearance was inoffensive, gestured with his head for Tully to step aside.

"Okay, Lupe," the mayor said. "Put your stuff away and go home."

"But I should still wash the stairs, yes?" she asked.

"Do them tomorrow," he replied. "And Lupe, you know that anything you hear in this house is private, right?"

"Private? Oh, sure, sure! Private, Señor."

"Good. Because if, by any chance, you repeated something that you know you shouldn't, that could be very bad. Very bad for you."

"*And* for your family," Tully added, accentuating the point.

The domestic servant looked at Tully with clear brown eyes that conveyed both her understanding and fear.

Twenty

THE LION IN WINTER

The next morning, Thursday, December 3rd, was Goldie's ninth day in 1942. It had started snowing about 6:00 a.m., and fat flakes had been blowing by the windows at a twenty-degree angle ever since. Combined with the two inches of snow that were already on the ground, Sparkledove was now snuggled in a solid four-inch blanket of white while most of its residents were still sleeping. But Goldie wasn't one of them. By 7:30, she had already walked across the covered bridge, trudged up the road that led to the Maynard Mining operation in her new rubber boots, and had slipped through the gap in the chained gate. She rounded the bend in the road, then looked around at the old mining operation. She had returned partly to see if there were any further signs of activity at the camp, which there weren't, and partly to see if she could run into the barefoot woman in the white nightgown again.

While she looked around and waited, keeping close to the road in front of the director of operations' old house, she thought about her unexplained circumstances. It was always there in the back of her mind, but some moments were more prominent than others. Right now, with the color of the morning being a whitish-gray, dilapidated buildings surrounding her, and tilting snowflakes crashing and melting onto her face, the queries of her predicament were particularly loud: Was she dead? Asleep? If so, how could she be feeling the snowflakes? How much time had passed in New York City? Why was she in 1942? Was her discovery about what Charles Banyan was doing her true mission? Was Harriette Noise's life in danger? What was she supposed to do about it? Did the spirits of Claude Bolton and the woman in the white nightgown connect to any of this? Or should she put them in separate mental compartments? And then there was Peter. What was she going to do about Peter? What was Evie Hines going to do about her father? She thought about these questions and reshuffled them again and again in her head as if that might provide some form of order.

After what seemed like a long time, she looked up and finally saw the woman in the nightgown coming toward her. Like the first time she'd seen her, her long blonde hair was messy and tangled, her feet were bare, and she carried a rope with a noose. Also like before, her body didn't seem to react to the cold, and the blowing snow did not affect her nightgown or hair.

Goldie noticed that as the woman came toward her, her feet left no imprints in the snow. Her stare was a combination of blank and forlorn, and since they appeared to be about the same age, Goldie couldn't help but feel sorry for her.

"Oh, honey. What the hell happened to you?" she asked. "What brought you to this?"

She stood there quietly as the woman walked by, seemingly oblivious to her presence. As she passed, Goldie tried to run a sympathetic gloved hand down the woman's bare arm, but it was like the glove was passing through fog. She touched nothing, although she shuddered from a sudden cold chill that shot through her head, but since she barely touched the woman, it wasn't as bad as when Claude Bolton's entire body had passed through her.

"God, why don't you help these poor souls?" she asked. She watched as the apparition turned, walked up the pathway to the director's house, then slipped through its partially opened door and disappeared inside. If nothing else, at least she now knew that this unidentified woman, like Claude Bolton, was recreating her death every day at apparently the same time as her original death.

She shook her head with sadness and frustration, then turned to go back into town. She walked around the bend in the road in silence, then continued for about another half-minute before she heard a low growl. Stopping and looking to her right, she saw a maple-brown mountain lion standing on a fallen tree trunk in the snowy woods, about one hundred and sixty pounds, staring at her threateningly. Instantly, Goldie realized this must've been the same animal she heard the evening she walked up the road with a flashlight and discovered the gate and fence. She quickly calculated she was closer to the gate than the director's house. Maybe she could run to the gate, slip through the chained opening, then hold it tightly shut, keeping the animal on the opposite side.

While this thought raced through her head, the mountain lion screeched at her, baring its three-inch fangs.

"*Hey!*" she called defiantly. "*I ain't no Meow Mix!*"

The cat jumped off the tree trunk and rushed toward her.

"*Oh, shit!*" Goldie yelled, breaking out in a full run toward the gate.

As she ran, she thought: *Find a branch! A rock! Something to fight back with!* But she could either look for a weapon or do her best Usain Bolt impression. She couldn't do both. Then she told herself: *Don't look around! Keep your eyes on the gate!* After ten seconds, however, she couldn't help it. Realizing the snow was slowing her down and she wasn't going to reach the gate, she thought: *It's better to face the animal head on. I'll go down, but at least I'll have my arms in front of me to fight back.* She stopped, turned, and crouched slightly, preparing for the impact of the lion about to pounce onto her.

"C'mon, you fucker!" she screamed.

But just as she did, a loud crack pierced the quiet of the morning, and the mountain lion tumbled over itself, then slid to a stop in the snow at Goldie's black rubber boots, dead.

She looked down at the animal. Its eyes and mouth were still open, but blood was coming out of the back of its head, staining the snow. Looking around through the falling flakes, she finally spotted Eli Johnson pointing a bolt-action rifle about sixty yards away. After waiting a moment to make sure the lion wasn't moving, he lowered the gun and started to come toward her.

Goldie patiently waited until the lawman limped over, which gave her adrenaline and heart time to return to normal. She was obviously relieved and grateful, but she also knew she was going to get chewed out for trespassing.

"Hi, Sheriff," she meekly greeted as he came within earshot.

"What the hell are you doing out here?" he asked. "I told you not to come here! This is exactly why!"

"Because there are mountain lions?" she asked.

"Because it's dangerous!" he reiterated. "What if I hadn't been here?"

"How *did* you get here?" she asked, looking down the road. "There aren't any footsteps in the snow except mine."

"There's another bridge besides the covered bridge

about a quarter of a mile downriver and a few houses on the south side of the water," he explained. "A family named Nelson has a backyard that backs up to the woods and fence. They keep chickens that were disappearing. Mrs. Nelson finally figured out that a mountain lion was probably living in an old tunnel access, and when it was out hunting, it would use one tree to get over the fence and into her yard, then use another on her property to get back over the fence again. I went over the fence at the Nelsons' with a ladder and was following fresh tracks that led to guess where?"

Goldie nodded, understanding. "Well... I'm sure glad you were armed today."

"Wouldn't make much sense to go after a mountain lion if I wasn't," he observed. "So, what're you doing out here?"

"Bein' nosy," she admitted. "Like I told ya, seein' some of the town's minin' history is helpful for my article." She held out her hands for imaginary handcuffs. "You wanna take me in?"

"As a matter of fact, I *do,*" he said seriously. "But I've got to find that tunnel access. There might be an entire family of lions living there. I also have to transfer Horace Mason today. If I did arrest you, the mayor would just get mad at me with you being his golden girl and all."

"So—does that mean I'm free to go?" she asked, a little tentatively.

"Yeah. That means you can go."

"What can I do to thank you for savin' my life?" she asked.

"Just please don't come up here again."

"You got it," she promised.

She looked down at the dead animal. The snow around its head was now heavily soaked in dark red.

"You're a hell of a shot," she complimented. "I mean, that was amazin'!"

"Let's keep this out of the article, huh?" he requested. "And don't say anything about it to the folks in town, either."

"Why not?"

"'Cause you're trespassing, and I don't want kids coming up here thinking they're Davy Crocket."

"Oh. Yeah," she realized. "Okay. Maybe you should tighten up that space at the gate with the chain."

"You can bet on it," he assured.

She nodded, looked at the mountain lion again, then stepped back toward the gate.

"Right... I'm gonna go now. But, Eli, really—thank you! That *was* an amazing shot."

She had never called him by his first name before, and although she thought nothing of it, he noted it.

"Eh, maybe..." he began.

"Maybe what?" she asked, pausing.

"Maybe... you could save me a dance tomorrow night?"

She remembered the community Christmas dance

and gingerbread house contest she was supposed to judge.

"Uh, yeah. Sure."

"I figure Peter's going to be dancing with you most of the night," he qualified. "But, if there's a slow number—"

"No. A dance. Absolutely! Promise!" she agreed.

He nodded once, then she turned, approached the gate, and slipped through its opening.

Eli watched her walk down the road in the snow toward the covered bridge, then turned his attention to the mountain lion.

"Sorry, pal," he said. "But you can't go eating other people's property. It's the mountain code."

Later that morning at 10:12, Mayor Banyan walked into the doors of the historical society carrying two cups of coffee. As usual, he was dressed in a suit and tie and looked very debonair.

"Good morning, Harriette," he greeted.

Harriette Noise was dusting one of the glass displays as she looked up.

"Oh, good morning, Mr. Mayor. How are you?"

"Fine. Brought you some coffee," he said, offering her a paper cup. "Milk and sugar, right?"

"Oh, how thoughtful. Thank you," she said, setting her dusting wand aside. "You found both milk *and* sugar?"

"Being mayor has its privileges," he grinned, unbuttoning his overcoat. "I wanted to ask you about Goldie Maraschino's visit of the other day."

"Yes. Nice young lady," she noted.

Banyan took a sip of his coffee. "What did you two talk about?"

"Oh, all the usual things I talk about with folks," the old woman replied, sipping her coffee. "The mining history, the artifacts, she was quite taken with the model of town, but then, everybody is."

"Was she interested in anything specific?" he asked.

The white-haired woman thought for a moment. "No... I don't think so. She asked about the Maynard operation and the director's house, and I told her about a woman who committed suicide there in 1902. But I doubt that's going to wind up in her story. It was just one of those little side bits of trivia."

"Hhm," he nodded, not particularly pleased she had shared that. "Anything else?"

The old woman took another sip of coffee and thought for a moment.

"Well, she did ask about—" she was interrupted by a middle-aged couple coming through the front door.

"Hello," the woman of the couple greeted. "Is this the Sparkledove Historical Society?"

"It sure is," Harriette said, setting her coffee down. "How can I help you?"

"We're from Wyoming and wanted to learn something about the town," the man said.

"We've got neighbors who have been here before, and they just went on and on about Sparkledove."

"Well, that's great to hear," the mayor beamed.

"Welcome. This lovely lady can tell you anything you need to know about the town and our upcoming events, like a big Christmas dance tomorrow night if you're staying over."

He looked at his associate. "Harriette, I'll leave you to it. Again, folks, very glad you're here."

Taking his paper cup, he stepped over to the door and exited.

"Goodbye, Mr. Mayor," Harriette called. "Thank you again for the coffee."

"The mayor," the woman said, raising impressed eyebrows and looking at her husband.

As Banyan walked through the still-falling snow to his realty office, he was more or less satisfied that Goldie and Harriette hadn't spoken of anything significant that might interfere with his plans.

Twenty-One

DRUNK ON POWER

I t stopped snowing about noon, and by 3:00 p.m., most of the town's merchants had shoveled the plank sidewalks in front of their stores. So, Goldie walked down to Clara's in search of some information. Even though it was a weekday, there was a war on, and Christmas was still twenty-two days away, the stores of Sparkledove were busy. The town had a great reputation for boutique shopping and nostalgic surroundings, although nobody really used the term "boutique shopping" in 1942.

Upon entering Clara's Gifts, Goldie had to wait a few minutes to speak with the store's proprietor. Both Clara and another woman in her early fifties, whom Goldie had never seen before, were busy assisting customers. So, she contented herself by looking around while the radio played "Winter Wonderland." Finally though, Clara came over to her wearing baggy slacks and a sweater.

"What can I do for you, honey?"

"Maddie at the hotel says you're a whiz with gingerbread houses and have even judged the annual gingerbread house competition."

"True," she said. "I've also won it three times. But I haven't entered in recent years. I mean, how many times do you have to climb Mount Elbert to prove you know what you're doing?"

"Mount Elbert?"

"The highest mountain in Colorado. Gosh, Goldie, with you being from a travel magazine and all, I thought you'd know that."

The visitor took a beat, thinking fast, then replied. "17,448 inches."

"What?"

"The height of the Empire State Buildin' in New York. I know that because I wrote about it once. I haven't written about Mount Elbert yet."

The statement wasn't true. She remembered the number of inches from a trivia site she'd seen online. But it sounded good.

Clara smiled. "Uh, okay. How can I help?"

"I don't know anything about gingerbread houses. The only thing I've ever baked is a potato. But the mayor wants me to judge the gingerbread house competition tomorrow night, and I want to be fair to the people who've worked hard on their creations. So, I was hopin' you could give me some tips. Things to look for."

"Be glad to. There are four big things to consider

right off the top of my head. First, there is the complexity of design. A house with a couple of turrets and a porch is more complex than a design with just four walls and a roof."

"Sure," Goldie agreed. "Makes sense."

"Then, there's the application of the frosting. It's got to be neat. Even."

"Okay."

"Third, would be originality. Houses and churches are pretty common. But what if it's a whole main street of buildings? Or maybe a house set in the mountains surrounded by trees?"

"Do they get that ornate?"

"They can... then there are the little details that make a difference. Like smoke coming out of a chimney. That can be stiff cotton. Or little frosting birds sitting on a fence. Or putting the house on a frame with a small light so it can be lit from the inside."

"It all sounds as complex as the wood model of the town over at the historical society," Goldie observed.

"Precisely," Clara agreed. "Same idea. Only you're working with gingerbread, frosting, candy, and gumdrops. Plus, unlike the historical society, you don't have to deal with the—" she suddenly stopped. Realizing she was talking to a journalist.

"Plus, you don't have to deal with the what?" Goldie asked.

"Uh, er, you know," Clara said, trying to hide thoughts she almost revealed. "The wood, paint, a-all the stuff that went into the model over at the historical society."

"You were *goin'* to say somethin' else, weren't you?" Goldie asked, knowingly.

"No, I wasn't."

"Yes, you were."

"Uh-uh," the store owner denied.

"You said: 'Plus, you don't have to deal with the'—you were *about* to say 'the mayor'—right?"

"No, I wasn't," Clara defended.

Goldie looked at the older woman sincerely. "Totally off the record, Clara, was it the mayor?"

Clara paused, then relented in a quiet voice. "Every place has people that some people don't get along with."

Goldie's green eyes widened. "So—it *is* the mayor!"

Clara looked around nervously, then took Goldie by the arm and stepped to the rear of the store so the two women could have more privacy.

"People in this town work really hard to make it the tourist attraction it is," she practically whispered. "I've poured my life's blood into this store. Sparkledove is a good place! Filled with good people! Your article will be a real help, especially with a war going on. So, I can't drag any of that down because I don't happen to like one individual. You understand?"

"Of course," Goldie said, empathetically. "Clara, of course! I'd never hurt the town because Banyan happens to be a dick."

The store owner giggled. "God, Goldie. The things you say." Then she looked at her quizzically. "H-how did you know who I was talking about? More importantly, what led you to your conclusion?"

"That's not important right now. Just please know my opinion about him won't affect my article in any way."

"Thanks... 'cause if he ever found out I'd spoken badly about him, he could make my life a living hell. He could post a No Parking sign in front of my store, have my business or home assessed for new taxes, find a problem with my business license, or fine the store for some sort of code violation."

"He'd *do* all that?"

"In a heartbeat. Somewhere along the way, and I don't know where or how, Charles Banyan became drunk on his own power. People smile and go along with him because they're intimidated. But he's *not* the whole town."

"Understood," Goldie acknowledged.

"The thing is," Clara said, "I may not personally like the guy, but there's no denying our tourism business has increased since he's been mayor. He gets things done. You being here, for example. Still, any good he does is counteracted when he imposes controlling rules and makes people feel small."

"Agreed," Goldie nodded.

Clara had a notebook in her back room filled with gingerbread house designs and photographs of some of her past creations. She lent it to Goldie to study and refer to. But as important as her assistance was with gingerbread houses, her opinion of the mayor was even more helpful. It cemented in Goldie's mind that he was no good. Besides Clara and Martha Eggleston, she couldn't help but wonder how many other people in town felt the same way.

Twenty-Two

EARLY AT THE CENTER

The following morning, Goldie had an early breakfast, then caught the bus to Denver. It was a Friday, and the Denver Bus Terminal was particularly crowded with weekend traffic. She grabbed a cab to the Denver Library and, for the third time since she'd awakened in 1942, conducted more research. She read several recent issues of the *Denver Post* to gain a better understanding of the war and the world around her. She also re-explored previous articles she'd written in *Adventure Escape Magazine*. When no one was looking, she even tore the pages of one of her articles from an issue, folded them up, and stuck them into her purse. Next, she explored a craft book with a chapter on gingerbread houses.

She stayed at the library until 2:00 p.m., then walked around the city for over an hour. Even though she was in Colorado's largest city, the air definitely smelled cleaner in the 1940s. Reminders of the war were everywhere. Forty-eight-star American flags hung from buildings, she saw posters in store windows reminding people to send Christmas care packages to servicemen, and she walked past several city homes where there was a small gold star flag hanging in a window to indicate a family member's ultimate sacrifice. She thought about how some people in her own time longed for the past. But the problems and challenges of 1942 were just as big and deadly as they were in the present.

Nostalgia ain't what it used to be, she decided.

Then she thought about her mother in Brooklyn, her sister in New Jersey, even her father in Pittsburgh. Did they know what happened? Were they praying for her and missing her?

She returned to the bus terminal at 3:10 and purchased her ticket back to Sparkledove. Then she sat down at one of the long wooden benches with seats on both sides and waited for her bus to be called over the PA. While she waited, Gerome came up to her carrying a bucket in one hand and a mop in the other. He was wearing his gray maintenance uniform and smiled when he saw her.

"Miss Goldie, nice to see you again. How's your hand?"

"Ay, Gerome," she smiled back, holding up her left palm. "Good as new."

He looked around, slightly nervous. "Mr. Hammersfield's somewhere about. You best take care he don't see you. He said if he ever saw you again, he was going to call a policeman and have you arrested."

"He's got it wrong," she replied. "He best take care *I* don't see *him*. I'm likely to take that bucket of water you got there and give him a second baptism."

The maintenance man smiled and chuckled. "I believe you."

"Why do you work for a guy like that?" she asked. "He insults you, belittles you."

"I can't get no factory job," he explained. "They all cryin' for manpower, but they won't hire negroes. At least here, I got a big space to work in and I get to see and sometimes meet interestin' folks like you."

"If you had your druthers, what would you like to do?" she asked.

The man with the tinge of gray in his hair thought for a moment.

"I got a brother who sells shoes. It's a store in a part of town you wouldn't go into, but he gets to wear a tie, talk to customers, and find out what their needs are. Some want work shoes. Others want snow boots. Others want somethin' dressy for Sunday go-to-meetin'. He measures their feet, feels the fit, I swear, that man knows everything about shoes: whether or not a shoe's collar will rub up against the ankle, how long laces will last, he can even identify brands by impressions the soles make. You might not think much about a shoe salesman as an occupation. But he helps people. It's professional."

Just then, her bus was announced over the PA and was loading through Departing Door Number Two.

"What you do here helps people," she reminded, rising. "You sure helped me."

"So, you're adapting okay to your time-shift reality?"

She smiled, appreciating that he remembered what she said the first time they met.

"I'm gettin' better at it. Merry Christmas, Gerome."

"Merry Christmas, Miss Goldie."

She started to head for her door, but as she did, she turned back and said: "Talk to your brother about puttin' in a good word for you at that shoe store."

"Oh, believe me," he answered, "I have."

She returned to Sparkledove to find both the town and her hotel pretty busy. Indeed, on the ride back to town her bus was nearly full. It didn't take long for her to figure out that the community Christmas dance, like the tree lighting ceremony, was a big deal, and the more people she passed on the street and in the lobby of her hotel, the more she wished she had sprung for a new dress. She had to wait to get a table for an early dinner, then wait again to get access to the bathroom on her floor. But by 6:20 p.m., she was headed over to the Sparkledove Community Center.

The center was the newest building in town, built in 1928. It was designed to look like a horse barn with a single-story section on either side, then a taller two-story section in the middle. But it was much larger than a traditional horse barn. The exterior was painted red to look like a barn, complete with a fake hayloft door on its upper middle section. It was almost too far to walk from Goldie's hotel, and thankfully, she didn't have to. Maddie told her employee, Josie, to take Dean's car and drive her to the center. Josie was working behind the front desk, dressed up as a reindeer, and had to remove her antlers and fluffy white tail to put on her coat and take the hotel's special guest to the dance.

As they rode, Goldie lamented her appearance. "I only packed three dresses and I've worn all of them," she complained. "I didn't bring any jewelry to speak of or pack curlers for my hair. I feel dowdy."

Josie smiled. "I'm wearing a brown terrycloth jumpsuit that's supposed to look like fur. From where I sit, you're Miss America."

Goldie looked her younger friend over, recalling. "I've seen you dressed up as a Native American for Thanksgivin', an elf decoratin' the Christmas tree in the hotel lobby, a Charles Dickens caroler for the community tree lightin', now a reindeer—don't you ever wear regular clothes?"

"I wonder that myself sometimes," Josie replied.

The car pulled into a circular drive and up to the two front doors of the center. The building was outlined with hundreds of colorful Christmas tree lights. It was an ornamentation Goldie had seen hundreds of times before in her New York life, but in 1942, it was a novelty. It was also against blackout restrictions, so the lights were only on for a limited time.

After thanking Josie for the ride and walking through the front door, the first thing Goldie did was get a layout of the place. To her immediate right was a ticket table and coat check area. Near them were bathrooms and dual swing-open doors that led into a kitchen. In the taller middle section, some white linen-covered tables and chairs could accommodate up to two hundred guests. They were spread out in a square horseshoe around a dance floor. On the far side of the middle section was a stage where a thirteen-piece band was setting up. On either side of the stage were Christmas trees that Stephie Banyan and some friends had set up and decorated. To Goldie's left were more bathrooms and a storage and supply closet with a temporary bar set up in front of it. Up against the exterior wall of the bathroom was a line of more white linen-covered tables where no less than twenty gingerbread houses were displayed. Some were houses modeled after real houses in town, others were churches, one depicted Santa's North Pole workshop, and another was the Statue of Liberty that sat on a five-sided star base and featured a lit torch. All in all, the collection of offerings was very impressive and smelled wonderful.

Even though the doors didn't officially open until 7:00 p.m., Goldie wanted to get there early and find out what her duties were regarding judging. No guests had arrived yet, but the center was bustling with activity.

"Good evening, Goldie," Stephie called. She had just walked through one of the swinging doors of the kitchen and looked fabulous in a red cocktail dress that had white sequins outlining her waist and the bottom of her skirt.

"Ay, Stephie," she greeted. "You look killer!"

"Killer?"

"Eh, really nice," Goldie corrected.

"Um... thank you."

"I wanted to stop by early and find out what I'm supposed to do as a judge tonight."

Stephie walked her over to the display of entries on the other side of the center. "Just look over each design one by one. There's a number beside each entry, and simply pick the one you like best. Most people understand this is just a subjective call. You'll announce the winner at 8:00 on the stage over there, and there's a nice golden cup trophy that goes with it. Charles will go up first and introduce you. Before announcing the winner and presenting them with their trophy, remind participants that they can bid on any entry by completing a form that includes their name, phone number, address, the item number they're bidding on, and their bid amount. There are boxes for the bids, paper, and pencils at both ends of the gingerbread tables. Winners won't be announced tonight, but all winners will be contacted by the historical society, and they can pick up and pay for their houses here this Sunday between 2:00 and 4:00 p.m. For those who don't have a phone, volunteers will deliver them within three days and collect the money upon delivery. That's it."

"Okay. Sounds simple enough," Goldie decided. She looked at a few women who were putting finishing touches on their gingerbread creations. All of them smiled at her warmly with high expectations, like a bunch of high school girls flirting with boys at a soda shop.

"I hope those who don't win won't hold it against me," she quietly said to Stephie.

"Well, everyone's got an opinion," Stephie replied. "But since you don't live here, you won't have to put up with anyone's disappointment. Besides, oftentimes, people bid a lot more on houses that don't win. So, there's consolation in that."

Goldie looked behind her at the ticket table. "And you sell tickets to the dance?"

"Yes. Then there's a cash bar, plus a photographer who'll roam around, take photos of each table, and people can buy them from him here on Sunday as well. All in all, we traditionally make a pretty tidy sum on the dance. People come from all over. Of course, the band's a big draw too."

Goldie looked at the kitchen. "Are you serving food?"

"No. Tonight, the kitchen is acting as the second bar."

Goldie nodded, then slipped off her coat. She was

wearing her black dress with the daisies and short sleeves, which was definitely out of season.

"Hhm... that dress is very lovely, dear. But aren't you going to be cold with those sleeves?"

"Yeah," she admitted. "I'm not sure what I was thinking when I packed, but it's the nicest thing I brought."

Peter's mother looked her over. "We're about the same height, close to the same weight, I bet we could wear the same dress size?"

"What?"

"Come with me to the kitchen," Stephie said, taking her by the hand. "Two years ago, Charles got a little tipsy and spilled a drink all over my dress, and since then, I bring a spare."

"Yeah?"

"As the mayor's wife, people consider me the hostess. So, I try to be ready for any contingency. It's black, long-sleeve, has built-in cups, and I even bought jewelry to go with it. I don't mean to be presumptuous, but if you wouldn't mind having an alternative outfit..."

"Mind?" Goldie asked. "That's like Cary Grant sayin', 'Can I buy you a drink?'"

"Great. C'mon," Stephie said.

Goldie truly appreciated the offer and liked Stephie. She hoped that, like Peter, she was unaware of her husband's plans. Within another six minutes, Goldie was standing in front of a full-length mirror hanging on the wall in one of the women's restrooms and wearing an ankle-length long-sleeve black dress that made her look statuesque. It featured what appeared to be a plunging neckline but was actually sheer, flesh-colored organza. Still, the effect was convincing and was made even more so with a long gold chain necklace and matching earrings. The dress also had a wide black sequin belt and matching shoes that were a little big for her, but she could wear them if she stuffed toilet paper into the toes. The waist was a little large as well, but could be folded over and handstitched, then the belt would hide the fold-over.

While she stood in front of the mirror, Lupe sat in a folding chair that had been brought into the restroom from one of the tables and was doing the stitching on Goldie's dress. While she worked, Stephie looked at Goldie and nodded approvingly. "On me, that dress looks good. On you, it looks amazing!"

"I can't thank you enough, Stephie," the recipient gushed. "I was concerned about what I was wearing tonight and *so* appreciate this."

"I'm just glad I had a spare. But I'm going to keep away from Charles after his third martini."

"Lupe," Goldie asked, "how is it you've got a sewing kit?"

"Men step on dresses, tablecloths get torn, zippers break. Señora Banyan hears all, and I learn from experience to be ready."

"And both of the women's bathrooms have full-length mirrors for the wedding receptions held here," Stephie added.

"Well, I'm grateful to both of ya," Goldie smiled. "I'm gonna be the belle of the ball."

"Speaking of which," Stephie said, glancing at her wristwatch, "time to open the doors. Excuse me, Goldie. I know Lupe will take care of you."

"Sure. Do what ya gotta do," Goldie replied.

After Stephie exited, Lupe rallied her courage.

"Señorita Goldie, I need to tell you something."

"Shoot."

"Did you go to Midland School this week in Señor Peter's car?"

Goldie looked at her.

"How did you know I went there?"

"Because Señor Banyan had two men follow you."

"*What?*" Goldie asked, stunned.

"He had men follow you. Two of them. They know you went to the school, but they don't know why. So the men are going to break into the school Sunday night and get a list of the people who work there."

"What? Why?"

"To see who you saw. To see if they recognize a name. Or, maybe you could just tell them."

Goldie turned around and gestured for Lupe to rise so they could speak face to face.

"Lupe, I *don't* want to tell them."

"No?"

"No. Señor Banyan may have done something very wrong, and I'm tryin' to get to the bottom of it. You once said: I don't know him. But I'm tryin' to learn. So, no. I don't want to tell them. But I *do* appreciate you tellin' me. How did you learn about this?"

"I was working late at the Banyans in the basement and heard men talking in the kitchen."

"These two men. Were their names Tully and Crosby?"

"I don't know."

"Were they in their forties? Muscular. One has red hair and a mustache?"

"Si. These are bad men, I think."

"I think so, too. Listen, let's keep this between you and me. It's our secret. Don't tell Stephie, Peter, or anyone about what you heard. It's *really* important, Lupe. Okay?"

"Okay, Señorita Goldie. I promise. Our secret!"

Twenty-Three

MISSED NEARNESS

Forty minutes later, as the band was playing a spot-on rendition of "I've Got A Gal In Kalamazoo," Goldie was slowly walking by and examining each gingerbread house lined up on the tables. She carried a little pad and pencil that she'd taken out of her purse before she checked it with her overcoat at the coat check. She really didn't need to take notes, but it made her look like an official judge. As she paused and looked at each offering, some contestants stood nearby and watched her anxiously, which made her feel self-conscious.

While she judged, a dressed-up Clara and Stu Frey were also watching her from a distance.

"I'm telling you there's something off about her," Clara confided.

"What do you mean?"

"Don't get me wrong," Clara qualified. "I like Goldie, okay? But when she first got to town, she didn't seem to know where she was, or the month, or the year. Then, another time, she came into the store, and I mentioned I'd just been reading about the Sullivan boys. You know who I'm talking about?"

"Sure. The five brothers who went down on the Juneau."

"She didn't know that. I mean, she *acted* like she did. But she didn't. It was obvious."

"Not everyone keeps up with the news, Clara," Stu suggested. "It's mostly depressing."

"Yeah, but she's a journalist," Clara noted. "She didn't know that a brass works would make munitions. She didn't know Mount Elbert was the tallest mountain in the state, yet she's in Colorado writing for a travel magazine. It's like—she's totally disconnected with what's going on."

The big man thought for a moment, then queried, "Who's having the best Christmas season? Sears & Roebuck, Woolworth's, or Macy's?"

"What? I-I don't know that."

"Gee, Clara," he smiled. "But you're a retailer."

She looked at him and pursed her lips but got the point.

After Goldie had carefully examined all of the entries and made the last of her notes, a woman approached her. She was blonde and in her mid-fifties. She was naturally attractive, carried a small black patent leather purse with handles, and wore a nice but inexpensive dress with a cardigan draped over her shoulders. She was naturally attractive, wore little make-up, and looked like someone Goldie had already met, but she couldn't place

"Miss Maraschino?" she began.

"Call me Goldie."

"I'm Mary Louise Johnson," she said, extending a hand. "Eli's mother. We're from Brownsville, about eight miles away."

"Oh, hey!" Goldie smiled, now realizing why she looked familiar. "So nice to meet ya!"

The two women shook hands while the band started to play a somewhat jazzy version of "The First Noel."

"I just wanted to introduce myself," she said with a soft voice. "You've made quite a positive impression on Eli."

"Yeah, I bet," she chuckled. "'That irritating journalist.'"

"No. Quite the opposite," the older one assured.

"Really?" she asked, looking around. "Where *is* our illustrious sheriff?"

"Over there, with his father," Mary Louise gestured. "They've just ordered drinks and are holding down our table so we don't lose it. Our daughter and her boyfriend are roaming around somewhere as well."

Goldie spotted Eli in a suit and tie sitting at a table near the kitchen on the other side of the center with an older man also wearing a suit. She noted he looked a lot like his dad and cleaned up well. She was tempted to tell Mary Louise how Eli had saved her life with the mountain lion, or how brave he'd been with Horace

Mason, but considering his penchant for downplaying things, she decided not to.

"I can't imagine how I've made a positive impression," she observed. "He's spent half his time telling me I'm not focused on the job that brought me here, and the other half saying no to areas I want to explore."

Mary Louise smiled politely. "Well, I don't know about *that,* but I *do* know he hasn't spoken to me so enthusiastically about any other young lady except his former girlfriend. That is, until he got a Dear John letter from her while he was in the service. So, you've gotten his attention somehow."

She glanced over towards the sheriff again. "Yeah. What happened there, if you don't mind me askin'? Eli said somethin' about a girl when we first met but was pretty vague about it."

"Lila Hemmings," Mary Louise replied with an exasperated sigh. "She was Eli's first serious love and grew up here. She was very pretty, and they both were full of high hopes and expectations. He wanted to be a pilot in the Army Air Corps, and Lila was certainly attracted to the glamor of a pilot and officer. But Eli failed his math requirement during training. He became a mechanic and a sergeant instead. That didn't sit well with Lila. He was stationed at Pearl Harbor, and almost exactly a year ago, took a round in the leg from a Japanese Zero."

"He never told me any of this," Goldie said, interested.

"No, he wouldn't," his mother said, knowingly. "He was trying to pull a pilot out of a disabled plane at the time. The pilot was killed, and Eli—well—he was actually very lucky. He spent a month in a Honolulu hospital bed, then another learning to get around with crutches first, then a cane. He was given a medal, discharged from the army in March, and came straight back to Sparkledove. He knew Lila had already moved away by then, but he always liked the town and found a job instead. He could finally walk without his cane in August. Just a little over three months ago.

"So, Banyan hired him with a cane?" Goldie asked.

Mary Louise nodded. "He really gave him a second chance and a sense of purpose. I'll always be grateful to the mayor for that."

"And Lila? What happened to her?"

"Oh," the sheriff's mother said, rolling her eyes, "she went out to California with a girlfriend. They went to Hollywood with the intention of meeting and marrying movie stars. She had the audacity to write Eli and tell him she deserved a 'whole man.'"

"Jesus! That's terrible," Goldie gawked.

"Yes, well, selfish, superficial people with immature minds think that way."

"He's well rid of the bitch," Goldie declared.

Eli's mother was surprised at the word "bitch," but agreed.

"I think so, too. Anyway, I just wanted to meet you. He turned down one of my pot roast dinners to stay in town and do something with you one night, so I was naturally curious. He *loves* my pot roast."

Goldie just smiled, not having the heart to tell her the truth.

Within a minute of Eli's mother returning to her table, Goldie ran into Father Fitzsimmons, who was carrying his camera with a flash attachment.

"Ay, Padre," she said. "Gonna shake a leg tonight?"

"Hi, Goldie," he greeted. "Actually, I'm working. I'm taking table photos for the mayor."

"Really?"

"I ran into him on the street with my camera, and he asked what I was doing. I told him I was taking pictures for your article, and he asked if I'd like to take photos of people at all their tables and the festivities. Apparently, it's a big crowd pleaser. I'm here tonight, then I'll also be here Sunday afternoon to take orders if people want copies. I'm sure this isn't exactly what my bishop had in mind for community involvement, but it gives me the opportunity to meet a lot of people. And you were right, Mayor Banyan said he'd be happy to make a donation to the church since I'm taking photos for your article."

"That's great! Where is Banyan?" she asked, looking around.

"Over there, by the ticket table, talking to those two men."

Goldie looked and saw a very dressed-up Charles Banyan conferring with Tully and Crosby, who were decidedly not dressed for the dance. Seeing them together, she got an idea.

"Hey, Father. Without them knowin' it, can you get me a couple shots of the mayor talkin' with those two dudes? But be subtle about it."

The wiry priest looked over at the ticket table. "Still think he's your evil villain, huh? Did you ever speak with Evie Hines?"

"Yeah. I'm working on things."

"Tread very carefully, Goldie," he advised.

"I will. Can you get those pictures? A close-up, and maybe a full-body shot?"

The priest gave her an unenthused look but headed toward the ticket table. Goldie started to weave through the guests, looking for Peter. She got distracted by chatting with Deke and Chad Miller and their family at one table, then another couple she had met at the Thanksgiving potluck, who wanted to chat. During this time, Father Fitz successfully took the pictures she requested, and shortly after, Banyan was handed the golden cup trophy for the gingerbread contest. He took it over to the stage, stopped the music, and started his introduction of Goldie. Caught off guard, she headed to the stage with her pencil and notepad in hand. She looked truly radiant in her borrowed long black dress as she climbed the four steps to the stage. The mayor finished his introduction, and she stepped over to a large, square-head microphone while the audience applauded.

"Hi, everyone," she began. "It—it was really an

honor to be asked to judge the gingerbread competition tonight." She smiled politely at the mayor standing nearby with the cup, then turned back to the crowd. "So many beautiful offerin's... I hope everyone got a good look at all the spectacular creations and will bid on their favorite one. Most of you have been here before, so you know the drill." She pointed to the line of gingerbread display tables. "Submit your bid in the boxes over there with your name, phone, address, the number of the entry you're biddin' on, and the bid amount. If your bid wins, someone from the historical society will call you. You can pick up your gingerbread house right here, this Sunday between 2:00 and 4:00 p.m. If you don't have a phone, a volunteer will come by your place with the gingerbread house you won within three days. So, keep your piggy bank close by. You can also buy table pictures of the fun tonight. If you'd like a copy, our photographer, Father Fitzsimmons, will be here on Sunday to take your orders.

"Before I announce this year's winner, allow me to say thanks for makin' me feel so welcome. Sparkledove is really a—a cool, special place. My words don't do the town, or all of you, justice. But please know I'm very grateful."

She held up her notebook.

"Y'know, I took notes on all the entries, hoping to come up with some sort of expert baker rationale to explain my choice for first place. I certainly get that this time of year has different meanin's and traditions to different people. But we get to enjoy those different meanin's and traditions because we live in a free society. A society that a lot of our sons and husbands have bravely fought for this past year. Whether it's been on supply ships crossin' the Atlantic, in the Battle of Bataan, the Battle of the Coral Sea, Guadalcanal, and too many other places to name. They stand and fight to preserve our right to come here and dance, make gingerbread houses, and send our kids to school where they can learn about George Washington, Ben Franklin, and Paul Revere. I admit, when *I* was a kid, I didn't pay much attention to those American heroes. But I'm sure payin' attention to 'em now.

"So, with that in mind, it's only fittin' that first place for this year's gingerbread competition goes to entry number sixteen, a gingerbread rendition of the Statue of Liberty complete with a lighted torch. Whoever you are, come on up and get your trophy."

A joyful scream of *"Eeeeeeeee! That's me. That's me!"* came from the back of the center. While some laughed and others applauded, Lupe scurried past tables and ran across the empty dance floor with her face beaming like a thousand-watt lightbulb and her hands excitedly waving in the air. As she climbed the stairs to the stage, Charles Banyan muttered to himself under his false smile, "Christ. She can't even speak proper English!"

Meanwhile, sitting next to one another at a table, Stu Frey leaned over to Clara.

"Goldie seems pretty connected to *me*," he said.

After the winner received her trophy and the band started up again, Charles walked with Goldie and Lupe over to the stage stairs, where Peter was now waiting.

"Thank you so much, Señorita Goldie!" the winner gushed.

"Hey, all the entries were anonymous," Goldie replied. "You won it entirely on your own merit."

"I just hope nobody thinks there was something nefarious going on since Lupe works for me," the mayor said.

"Yeah, that's right," Peter smirked, glancing at his father. "Take her victory and make it about yourself." He turned and smiled warmly at the winner. "Congratulations, Lupe."

"Thank you, Señor Peter," she said. "Thank you!"

"Okay, okay," the senior Banyan replied dismissively. "Run along now."

Lupe nodded, then turned and hurried away with her trophy.

Charles looked at Peter. "It's a legitimate concern," he emphasized. Then he turned to the visitor. "Very nice speech, Goldie. And that dress. My goodness. I know it's Stephie's, but you really give it, uh, a whole new interpretation."

"Finally. We agree on something," Peter quipped.

"Thank you both," Goldie smiled.

"And where have you been?" Charles asked, turning his attention to his son. "You're only an hour late."

"Well, unlike Tweedledee and Tweedledum over there," Peter said, nodding toward Tully and Crosby still standing out of place by the ticket table, "I don't have a lot of helpers and have a newspaper to get out. What are they doing here anyway?"

"As you'll recall," his father replied. "Last year, it was very cold and snowed heavily during the dance. Some people couldn't get their cars started. One or two others got stuck in the snow. They're the cavalry since our sheriff has the night off and is here with his family."

"Hmm," Peter mulled. Then he looked at Goldie. "Would you like a drink?"

"That'd be wonderful. A whiskey on the rocks, please."

"Coming right up," he smiled. "Anything for you?" he asked his father.

"No, thank you. And why aren't you taking pictures of the dance for *The Wing?*"

Peter pointed at Father Fitz as he headed toward the bar in front of the storage closet, not far away. "I'll get 'em Sunday," he called.

The mayor humphed and turned to Goldie.

"Whiskey on the rocks, eh? Pretty strong drink."

"I'm a pretty strong lady," Goldie answered.

"I, uh, I understand you borrowed Peter's car and did some exploring of the area."

"I did. I was a tourist for an hour on the Rocky Mountain Western Railroad, and it was fabulous."

"Good. Good. Go anywhere else?"

"Yeah, actually. An old acquaintance of mine teaches at Midland Elementary, and I dropped by to say hello. We hadn't seen each other in years."

"Oh. Lovely. And who was that?"

Goldie picked the first name that popped into her mind.

"Um, Diana Ross," she answered, leaning on her penchant for 60s and 70s music.

"Teacher there?"

"Yes," she lied. "She's brand new. Just started," she added, to explain away why her name wouldn't be on a staff list if Banyan's men ever obtained one.

"It's always great to reconnect with old friends," he agreed.

"Absolutely."

"Well, I'd better get back to Mother," he said, referring to Stephie. "Once again, nice comments on stage. Enjoy the dance."

After the mayor left, Goldie spotted one of the few still unoccupied four-seat tables, went over to it, and sat down. Within another minute, and with drinks in hand, Peter found her.

"Great, you got a table." He set the drinks down. "Whiskey on the rocks for you. Gin and tonic for me."

"Thank you," she said.

"And again, for once, my dad and I are in sync. You look fabulous! Although psychologically, there might be something wrong with me. I'm having a little fantasy about you in a dress that belongs to my mother."

"As long as the fantasy is about me and *not* your mother."

He smiled. Then they took sips of their drinks.

"So, why were you so late tonight?" she asked. "I thought you'd be roaming around getting tidbits about the dance?"

"You know how you get in the swing of writing something and you don't want to stop?"

"Yeah."

"That's why I'm late." He reached into the inside pocket of his suit jacket and pulled out a piece of typing paper. It was folded in threes like a letter, and he handed it to her.

She took it, opened it, and read the headline aloud:

"Visiting Writer Merits Her Own Story."

She looked at Peter, surprised, then continued reading.

"By now, many people in town know that a writer from *Adventure Escape Magazine* is visiting Sparkledove to write a story about how we celebrate the holidays. Although this article won't be published in *Adventure Escape* until next December's issue, a few words have to be written about its author. By doing so, this reporter is well aware he could be accused of priming the pump in an effort to encourage a complementary magazine article, but this journalist will risk it.

"Her name is Karen Maraschino. Yes, like the cherry, and she has a penchant for diving into things.

She served dinner to community members at a Thanksgiving potluck held at St. Michael's Church..."

She looked over at Peter. "How do you know about that?"

"I'm a reporter," he shrugged. "I know a lot of things."

She turned her eyes back to the paper and continued: "She braved the elements to go into the mountains and be part of the team that harvested the community Christmas tree. She thoughtfully purchased and delivered a small holiday gift to a community member who recently suffered a tragic family loss. She sought out advice and expertise about gingerbread houses when asked to judge the annual gingerbread house contest at the Christmas community dance. As one can see from these examples, this isn't a person who is just observing and reporting. This is a person who is investing. She's putting herself into the community and making some good friends along the way."

There was more to the piece, but an embarrassed Goldie stopped reading, becoming emotional.

"Peter... th—this is incredibly nice. I-I'm not used to such nice things bein' said about... but, you can't publish this."

He took another sip of his drink. "Why not? It's true."

"Y-you just can't, that's all."

"Why don't you read the rest of it?"

"Because I'm afraid I'll start cryin' like a baby and it'll mess up my makeup."

"Okay," he agreed warmly. "Read the rest later, then we'll talk."

He was distracted when a dapper Ed Peterson walked by their table.

"Hi, Ed," he said. "How are you?"

Ed was nearly forty years old, thirty pounds overweight, single, and had a round, friendly face. He had a nice-guy reputation and owned the gem store in town.

"Hi, Peter," he greeted. He smiled at Goldie and extended his hand. "Ed Peterson."

"Ay, Ed. I'm Goldie."

"Yes. I just saw you on stage, and the mayor also pointed you out at the tree lighting."

"Sure," she remembered. "I was on River Street when Horace Mason used your car for target practice. I'm really sorry about what happened."

"Yeah," he agreed, "that was a strange morning. But Horace is paying for the damage, so everything will be set right again. At least, with my car. Don't know about Horace and Alice, though."

"Well, *you* sure look pretty good tonight, I must say," Peter noted. "You're puttin' the rest of us bachelors to shame."

Ed smiled, pleased with the compliment. "Thanks. It's a new suit, and you can tell by the way I use my walk, I'm a woman's man, no time for talk."

Peter chuckled while Goldie's mouth fell open.

"Okay," she said, slamming an open hand down on the table. "That's *it!*"

"That's what?" Peter asked.

"Where did you get that expression?" she asked Ed.

"What?"

"'You can tell by the way I use my walk, I'm a woman's man, no time for talk.' Where did you *get* that saying?"

"I don't know. But it's kinda funny, huh?"

"It's kinda *Saturday Night Fever,*" Goldie replied.

"No, honey. It's Friday," Peter corrected.

"I know it's Friday!" she answered.

"You have a fever?" Ed asked.

"No. *No!* The expression comes from a song that's in a movie. It's right at the beginnin' of the film when John Travolta is walkin' down the sidewalk and this great Bee Gees song is playin'..." her voice trailed off when she saw that Peter and Ed were a little concerned about her intensity.

She took a pause and a breath to calm down, then continued, "Ed—just tell me—please! *Where* do you know that saying from? *When* did you first hear it?"

The round-faced man thought for a couple of moments.

"Huh, I don't honestly know. I just remember thinking to myself when I heard it: 'That's cute. I gotta remember that.'"

"Okay," Goldie nodded reluctantly, taking a sip from her drink. "Fine."

"Well, I gotta go," Ed smiled a little nervously. "See you two later."

"See you later, Ed," Peter smiled.

"Hope your fever's better, Goldie," he said, moving on.

She rolled her eyes. "I don't have a freakin' fever," she mumbled, totally frustrated.

"What was all *that* about?" Peter asked.

"Doesn't matter," she said defeatedly. She picked up her glass and finished her drink with a long gulp.

"Do you, eh, maybe want to get out of here?" he suggested. "You never have seen my place."

He made the offer at a moment when Goldie was feeling moved by what he had written, frustrated about all the things she didn't understand, and lonely since it was the Christmas season and everyone around her seemed to be with loved ones.

"Yeah," she agreed. "Let's get out of here."

Peter likewise finished his drink, then they rose and headed for the coat check. As they went, Charles Banyan, Tully, and Crosby had now huddled in another corner of the center and were talking.

"She went to the school to visit an old friend named Diana Ross," Charles explained.

"So, no need to break into the school Sunday night?" Tully asked.

The mayor considered for a moment.

"No, go ahead with the plan," he decided. "Let's confirm it. Get a copy of the staff list."

Within a few seconds of Peter and Goldie leaving

the dance, the band struck up the romantic Hoagy Carmichael number, "The Nearness Of You," a slow dance tune. As they did, Eli was just coming out of the men's bathroom and went over to his table where his mother, father, sister Dinah, and her boyfriend, an army soldier in uniform, were seated. Upon his arrival, Dinah, a twenty-two-year-old blonde-haired beauty, rose.

"C'mon, Eli, I want a dance with my big brother."

"Sorry, sweetie," he said. "I'm taken for this one. But the next slow dance is all yours."

His sister turned to her boyfriend, who rose, getting the cue that she wanted to dance. Eli's parents did the same. As his family moved toward the dance floor, he limped past table after table, scouting the place for Goldie with a smile of anticipation. But after nearly two minutes of the three-minute song, the smile withered.

While the female vocalist sang:
"I need no soft light to enchant me
If you'll only grant me
The right to hold you ever so tight
And feel in the night
The nearness of you"
He realized Goldie was nowhere to be found.

Twenty-Four

PETER'S PLACE

It was a little past midnight when Goldie awoke in Peter's bed. He was breathing heavily, tired and satisfied from their lovemaking. He was fit and smooth-skinned with little body hair and a smaller penis than Markie's, but his experience and knowledge in bed were certainly equal. Not wanting to disturb him, she slowly got out of bed, spotted a dark-green V-neck sweater lying across a chair, and slipped it on. It covered a few cute moles on her stomach and her round bottom and stopped about six inches above her knees. She had a slight case of bedhead, but her unruly dark-brown, long hair looked sexy. With her arms crossed, she looked over her shoulder at her sleeping lover as a naughty new headline popped into her head for the article he'd written about her:

Reporter dips pen in journalist's inkwell.

She smiled a little, then stepped out of the bedroom.

Peter's house was built in 1868 but wasn't one of the larger Victorian-style two-story houses like his parents, or Martha Eggleston's, or Jason Shirk's. It was a single-story miner's cottage, and the town still had about a dozen of them standing. Most had been washed away during the dam collapse and flood of 1884. The cottage was about 900 square feet and consisted of a living room with a fireplace, a small kitchen in the back, an added-on bathroom with a shower but no tub, and a bedroom. The living room had once been divided into a living room and a second bedroom for children, but this second bedroom had been removed to expand the living room. Peter told Goldie that once upon a time, a family of five used to live in the small house. But now, half of the living room had a sofa facing the fireplace where pine logs still glowed with subtle orange heat, while the other half had been converted into an office with a desk, chair, telephone, radio, typewriter, and a bookcase filled with books. Between the books at his office and home, it was very obvious that Peter was a voracious reader.

Goldie looked at the fire for a moment and decided to add another log from the brick hearth. She wandered around the living room, trying to get a better sense of Peter's life. Her knees and bare feet were a little cold on this December night, but her curiosity about the man she had just had sex with superseded the chill. She noticed he had no Christmas decorations up but made no judgment about that. She wandered into the kitchen, figuring he probably had some liquor somewhere. After turning on a light and opening a couple of cabinets, she found a bottle of Jack Daniel's and made herself a whiskey on the rocks. After that, she left the lights on in the kitchen, went back into the living room, and, just as she had at his office, began to examine some of the books on his shelves.

A couple of Manila folders were sitting on top of the books. She picked one up, set her drink down on the desk, and then sat in the chair behind it. She reached over and pulled the chain of a small desk lamp for light. Opening the folder, she looked inside. It was apparently the beginning of either a short story or a novel Peter was writing. Interested, she picked up her drink and started to sip and read while the fire on the other side of the room began to crackle back to life.

About thirty minutes later, Peter awoke, realized he was alone, and rolled out of bed. He went to his closet and slipped on a blue robe, then emerged from the bedroom to see Goldie standing with her back to him in the living room. The room was now dark except for the light from the fire, and she was staring out at the night from one of his two living room windows on either side of the front door. The evening was still and frozen with the snow occasionally sparkling from a waning moon that peeked in and out of clouds. He saw that the fire had been resurrected and that there was an empty glass sitting on a small table at the end of the sofa. Then he glanced over at his desk. The desk light was off, and everything was as he had left it.

"Hey," he said warmly. "What're you doing?"

She looked over her shoulder and smiled. "Just watchin' the night. It's so peaceful and there's a few snowflakes floatin' around here and there; romantic and forbiddin' all at once. It's like we're the only two people in the whole world."

He came up behind her while she continued to look out the window and cupped her breasts with his hands, then noticed she was wearing his sweater, which really appealed to him.

"You were absolutely incredible tonight," he said softly, kissing her neck. "You took my breath away."

"Did I?" she asked with uncertainty. "I haven't been with another man except my former boyfriend for a long time. I don't know what you must think of me now."

"What do you mean?" he asked, still holding her close.

"I don't know about the morality of this—" she was going to say "time," but paused and changed it to "town."

"It's pretty much like anywhere else," he replied softly. "There are liberal views and conservative views. The norms of society might say that a 'good girl' waits until marriage to be intimate with a man, but that doesn't always happen. Especially with a war on. It certainly doesn't mean the good girl is anything less. It just means she's human."

"You're a gentleman to say it." She patted his hands, still holding her breasts, but wanted to move away, so he let go.

"I have no idea if I'm a good girl or not," she continued, "but I certainly needed tonight. There's been a lot of weird things happenin' in my life and I—well—it was nice just to be desired and held for a while."

"Oh, you were definitely desired," he affirmed.

She looked toward the bedroom. "I've gotta get dressed. You've gotta get me back to the hotel."

"What? No. Stay the night."

"I can't. People are already goin' to talk about how late I returned to my room. I don't even know if the front doors at the hotel are still open this late."

"I think somebody is usually at the front desk all night," he said.

"Then, I need to get back."

"Well, wait a minute," he implored. "Can't we talk about a few things first?"

"Like what?"

"Uh... did you... I mean, was I..."

"Yes, Peter. You're a wonderful lover," she assured.

He smiled and tightened the belt of his robe. "Good... ah, that's good. Eh... do you have any idea how much longer you're going to stay in town? Not-not that I want you to leave, or anything."

"My understanding is I'm supposed to stay until I believe I've gathered enough material for my article, and I've pretty much done that. I don't think I can impose on the historical society's generosity much longer. It's time to use the rest of my plane ticket."

"Well, you at least have to stay another week. The

Tour of Homes is next weekend. That's the pinnacle of the Christmas season."

"I don't know. Maybe."

In truth, she wanted to stay longer to see what Evie Hines was going to do. But she couldn't admit that.

"Then there's us," he reminded. "I just slept with you, Goldie. I have no desire to be two ships passing in the night."

"I don't see how we could be anything else," she replied honestly.

"Yes, I know. You've said you've got concerns. One was distance. But planes fly all the time. Trains are always available, too. Then you said you didn't care much for my dad. Well, I don't either. We've laid those cards out on the table. We can work around them. At least, *I* want to."

"There's more to it," she said, starting for the bedroom. "C'mon. We've got to get dressed."

"Like what?" he asked, following after her. Then an idea came to him.

"Oh, I get it. Your old boyfriend. You're still keeping a candle in the window for him."

Goldie turned on the bedroom light and pulled Peter's sweater up and over her head. Now seeing her naked as she looked around for her underwear, he started to become aroused again, but wanted an answer to his question.

"No," she said, seeing her waist-high panties and slipping them on. "God, these are dreadful," she mumbled, referring to the underwear. "No. I have no desire to keep a candle in the window for my old boyfriend. Unless I use it to set him on fire."

"Then what?" he pressed. "Unless you just don't want the bother of a long-distance relationship."

She spotted his white boxer shorts on the bedroom floor, picked them up, and handed them to him.

"Get dressed, please."

The following morning, after breakfast, Goldie came out of the hotel restaurant and into the lobby, which was decorated to the hilt for Christmas. There was a nine-foot Christmas tree that Josie had decorated where the rounded crimson sofa had been, big red bows hung from the candle-like wall sconces, and pine roping was draped in graceful dips and tacked under the registration counter. Behind the counter, Maddie lowered her glasses at Goldie as she approached.

"I hear somebody came in very late last night," she noted in a sing-song voice.

"Yes, but it was all perfectly innocent," Goldie offered, feeling like she had to say something diffusing. "Did you and Dean go to the dance?"

"No, we were here. But I heard it was a big success. And I hear a woman named Lupe won the gingerbread contest."

"She did, and she was thrilled," Goldie confirmed. "It technically wasn't a gingerbread house, but it was very patriotic and appropriate. Oh, that reminds me. Stephie Banyan lent me one of her dresses for the dance. Would it be possible to get it cleaned before I return it to her?"

"Sure thing, honey. Is it up in your room?"

"Yes, a long black dress with long sleeves hanging on one of the hooks."

"I'll make sure it's taken care of."

"Thanks, Maddie," Goldie smiled.

Just then, Josie appeared from a doorway behind the counter, dressed in a long black wig, a full-length blue-and-white gown that looked like it was from biblical times, and a pillow tucked under her outfit so she looked very pregnant. In addition to her costume, she carried a winter overcoat.

"Ah, Mary," Goldie recognized. "Heading off to Bethlehem?"

"If Joseph ever shows up," she replied.

"Josie and her beau, Dexter, are doing a nativity play over at the Episcopal church," Maddie explained. "She even rides a real donkey."

"Sound like fun," Goldie enthused.

"Depends on the mood of the donkey," Josie replied.

"Last year, it kicked one of the performers, and we had to get by with only *two* wise men," Maddie recalled.

Just then, Josie's boyfriend, Dexter, came through the front doors of the lobby. He was wearing biblical robes, his high school varsity jacket over them, and had a beard with a string tie hanging loosely around his neck.

"Hi, everyone," he greeted.

"You're late," Josie answered disapprovingly.

"Eh, sorry. Ran into a troop of Roman soldiers." He smiled at Goldie. "Some biblical humor there."

"An oxymoron if ever there was one," she quipped.

"Have you got your father's camera?" Josie asked.

"In the car," Dexter said.

"With the flash attachment?"

"Yes."

"And color film. They want color film this year."

"Yes," her boyfriend replied wearily.

A guest came up to the counter, so Maddie excused herself to wait on them. "Well, good luck. Break a leg or whatever you're supposed to break."

As Josie came around the counter, Goldie formulated an idea.

"Hey, would you guys be up for a little adventure? Not today, but soon. There's money in it for you."

"Extra money? Sure," Josie said. "Do I have to dress up as something?"

"No. Not this time."

"What do we have to do?" Dexter asked.

Twenty-Five

CHESS

Two days later was Monday, December 7, 1942, and the first anniversary of the attack on Pearl Harbor. Goldie was aware of the anniversary and realized it was the day Eli Johnson had been wounded. She felt bad that she hadn't kept her promise to slow dance with him after he saved her from the mountain lion. Especially after having met his mother, Mary Louise. She had no excuse for the blunder other than being preoccupied with Peter and the article he wanted to run about her; an article she persuaded him not to publish when he drove her back to her hotel early Saturday morning.

She slept in on this Monday, grabbed a late breakfast, then called her publisher.

"Been expecting to hear from you," Owen Mitchell began. "You've been in Sparkledove for thirteen days. I figure you're about ready to wrap things up."

"For the article I was sent to do? Yeah. But what if there was another story I found?"

"What kind of story?" he asked, intrigued.

"The story of a man who uses his position to bully people and impose his will on others. The story of a man buyin' up a row of houses to obtain valuable mineral rights underneath them, but the people who own those houses don't know what they're sittin' on. The story of a man who—when he couldn't buy these houses from some of the owners—resorted to murder so he could buy them from relatives in distress. The story of a man who, if he succeeds, stands to make millions and millions of dollars. And if we don't publish this story, he'll get away with it."

"Who are you talking about?" Mitchell asked.

"My host, Mayor Charles Banyan."

"*What?*" her publisher gawked. "Holy Toledo! Are —are you sure?"

"Yeah. Well—pretty sure."

"Goldie, with these kinds of accusations, you can't be 'pretty sure.' Your evidence has to be one-hundred percent rock solid!"

"I'm workin' on getting' more proof. But I'm right, Owen. I *know* I am. I'd stake my career on it."

"Believe me, if we do something with a story like this, you are! W-what in the world led you to these accusations?"

"It's a long story. I spent half the night typin' up what happened and everythin' I found. I'm mailin' it off to you today by special delivery as an insurance policy."

"Insurance policy? Do you believe you're in some sort of danger?"

"I believe I'm playin' a type of game with a pretty cagey opponent, and things are about to heat up."

"I don't like this, Goldie," Mitchell protested. "I don't like this at all!"

"What am I supposed to do? I didn't ask for this. I just stumbled across it."

"Go to the local law."

"I can't."

"Why not?"

"The town's sheriff might be Banyan's boy. The mayor hired him."

"I-I've got to think about this," Mitchell said, the wheels in his head spinning. "*Adventure Escape Magazine* can't publish a story like what you've described. I mean, we're a travel magazine for God's sake. But I *do* have a good friend at the Associated Press. You could call him with the details. Still, Goldie, if you're wrong, you could be sued. *I* could be sued. This could be a nightmare!"

"I'm not wrong!"

"Okay... here's what I want you to do: Give me a little time. I need to talk to our attorney, then call my buddy at the AP. In the meantime, continue gathering information, but absolutely *do not* put yourself in a dangerous situation. Understand?"

"Got it."

"Alright. Call me back in two hours. Also, is there anyone in town you can trust with what you know?"

"Yes. A priest at Saint Mark's Catholic Church named Father Fitzsimmons."

"Saint Mark's, Father Fitzsimmons," Mitchell repeated, writing it down. "Good. Make sure he knows what you know, give me two hours, then call me back."

At nearly the same time that Goldie was hanging up the phone with her publisher, Charles Banyan was sitting in the cab of Tully's black pickup truck. It had snowed the night before, and there was now a solid six-inch base of snow in Sparkledove. Tully sat behind the wheel while the mayor reviewed a piece of paper he and Crosby had taken from the Midland Elementary School the previous night.

"No Diana Ross listed among the staff," Banyan said, staring at the paper.

"The magazine writer told you her friend was a new hire," Tully recalled. "Maybe she's too new to be on the employee list."

"I suppose," Banyan said, still reading. Then, his eyes recognized a name. "Wait a minute. She didn't go see Diana Ross. She saw Evie Hines."

"Who?"

"Jason Shirk's daughter. She's a teacher who used to work in Denver."

"What do you think the writer knows?" Tully wondered.

"She knows *something*," Banyan realized. "She's seen Martha Eggleston, she's been to the historical society, now she's seen Evie Hines... she obviously has suspicions. But how much does she know? That's the question."

"What do you want me to do?" Tully asked.

"I think I need to have another talk with Harriette Noise about Miss Maraschino's visit with her. I'm missing something. Go find Eli Johnson. Tell him I want to see him. I want to know if our guest has asked him about the old Maynard site or has been poking around it."

"I can put wheels in motion to do containment," Tully suggested.

"But who do we contain?" Banyan responded. "Evie Hines? Goldie Maraschino? I need to gather more information before we put plans like that into action. Goldie knows something's going on with me, but *I* know she lied about Diana Ross, so that's an advantage. We've got ourselves a little chess game, Tully, and I'm a very, very good chess player."

Within a half hour after Tully and Banyan spoke, Goldie walked into the sheriff's office to find Eli studying one of his correspondence course textbooks behind his desk. "Light A Candle in the Chapel" by the Tommy Dorsey Orchestra, featuring a young Frank Sinatra on lead vocal, was playing on the radio. She came in carrying a dozen wrapped roses and a gift-wrapped package.

"Hi," she said. "How ya doin', Sheriff?"

He leaned back in his chair and cracked a faint smile.

"Goldie, good morning."

"What? No howdy?" she asked.

"What brings you in?" he queried, keeping things businesslike.

"Embarrassment. Humility. Contriteness. And roses, I bought you roses to say how sorry I am that I missed our dance Friday night."

"Oh, right. Our dance. I kinda forgot about that," he lied.

She stepped forward and placed the wrapped bundle of flowers on his desk. He looked at them, not quite knowing what to say.

"I, uh, I—nobody's ever gotten me flowers before."

"First time for everything," she said, unzipping the jacket she got at Miller's. "I also wanted to say I met your mom Friday night, and she was really nice. I liked her a lot."

"Yes, she mentioned you two met."

"I *also* wanted to say I know this is an unhappy anniversary for you. Well, for everyone in the country, but especially you. So, that's another reason for the roses."

He looked at the flowers again, realizing his mother must have explained how he was injured at Pearl Harbor.

"Well, this is very nice, but it really isn't—"

"I messed up, Eli," she said, cutting to the chase. "I

should've never forgotten my promise to you, even if you did, and I'm sorry."

He rose from his chair.

"It's thoughtful, but I don't have a vase for these."

She handed him the gift-wrapped package.

"Yes, you do."

He unwrapped the offering to find a nice hand-thrown gold, blue, and bright-yellow vase with a mountain landscape on it. He recognized it from one of the storefront windows in town and remembered liking it.

"This was very kind of you, Goldie," he said sincerely. "Thanks." He took the vase to the bathroom to fill it with water, and on the way, turned off the radio. "So, eh, is that what happened Friday? Our dance slipped your mind?"

"I left early," she confessed. "Peter Banyan wrote this really nice article about me that he wanted to publish in *The Wing,* but it was inappropriate. I'm not the story. Sparkledove is. I needed to talk him out of it."

"I see," he said, filling the vase with his back to her. "I agree with you. You're not the story."

"I think he wrote it just to have his way with me," she joked.

"Hmm," Eli acknowledged, still with his back to her.

She looked at him curiously. "So, aren't you going to ask?"

"What?"

"*Did* he have his way with me?"

"Nope. That's as inappropriate as the article you said he wanted to publish about you."

"Yeah, it is," she agreed. "But it would still be the next question a typical guy would ask."

"Would it?" he answered, coming out of the bathroom and heading back to his desk.

Goldie watched him as he set the vase down, then carefully unwrapped the roses. "It's good that they bundled them from top to bottom instead of just the stems," he observed. "The petals are very sensitive to weather like this."

She watched as he carefully separated the flowers, then one by one placed them in the vase. His silence spoke very clearly to her that he was not a typical guy.

"I don't get you, Sheriff," she admitted. "I really don't."

"What do you mean?"

"I met your mom. You apparently come from a great family. You're brave. You tried to save that pilot at Pearl Harbor and faced down Horace Mason. You keep your cool. Like when that mountain lion came after me. You study to improve yourself. You clearly care about this town and its people. So, why are you working for a man like Charles Banyan?"

"I don't understand," he replied, putting a rose in the vase.

"Did you know there are three houses for sale on Falcon Drive?"

"What?"

"There are three houses for sale on Falcon Drive on the same side of the street. Did you know that?"

He cracked another smile. "A fella could get whiplash trying to follow your stream of conscience." He inserted another rose into the vase. "Of course I know that. I patrol every street."

"Did you know Charles Banyan owns all of those houses?"

"I know his realty company listed them."

"Not just listed, Eli. He *owns* them. Plus another one he says he wants to restore and rent out. That's a total of four houses in a row. Did you know that?"

The lawman inserted another rose. "Why would I know that? And how do *you* know he owns all of those houses?"

"He bought Martha Eggleston's house because Bucky had no life insurance, and she was strapped for cash. He did the same thing with Jason Shirk's house in the name of helping his daughter. One by one, he's bought up four of the five houses on the same side of the street, except Harriette Noise's place. Take care, Sheriff, she doesn't suddenly become ill and die."

Eli put another rose into the vase, thinking, then another.

"Well, I didn't know that he actually owned all of those houses. But, so what? Buying houses isn't against the law. And what do you mean about Harriette Noise?"

Just then, Tully opened up the front door and walked in. He was surprised to see Goldie, and she was equally surprised to see him. But they both covered it quickly.

"Mayor wants to see you, Sheriff."

"Where is he? City hall or his office?"

"Realty office," Tully said, looking Goldie over.

"Have you two met?" Eli asked Goldie.

"No."

"This is Tully."

Eli looked at the man with the black stubble on his face and realized something: "You know, I'm embarrassed to say, I don't know your first name."

"Just Tully," he replied, nodding at Goldie and keeping his hands in the pockets of his black leather coat.

"And what do you do, Mr. Tully?" she asked.

"Odd jobs for the city. This and that."

"I'll be down directly," the lawman replied, putting some more stems in his new vase.

Tully eyed the roses and vase, slightly amused. "Considering a second career as a florist, Sheriff?"

"I'll be down directly," Eli repeated. "Thanks."

Tully looked at Goldie straight-faced, nodded at her, then left the office. His appearance only reinforced in her mind that the sheriff was, at worst, complicit with Banyan, or at best, ignorant about what was going on. She just didn't know which was which.

"Charming guy," she noted, insincerely. "Lots of personality."

He shrugged slightly in agreement, then continued with the roses.

"I gotta go," she announced abruptly, zipping up her jacket.

"Okay... thanks again for the flowers."

She turned and headed for the door. When her hand was on the handle, he decided to make an observation:

"Hey, you ever notice how our conversations start off going one way, but then stop and go another?"

She paused and considered. "Yeah," she agreed. Then she walked out the door.

He stood there for another few seconds, arranging his bouquet.

"Okay then," he said to himself. "See ya."

Six minutes later, Eli walked into Charles Banyan's office. He greeted the secretary in the front office, then went into Banyan's office in the back. He noticed that Tully was nowhere around.

"You wanted to see me?" he began.

"Yes. Have a seat."

The sheriff unzipped his brown suede jacket and sat in one of the two chairs in front of Banyan's large desk.

"Tully told me Goldie Maraschino was down at your office."

"Yeah. She dropped by to apologize for not saving a dance for me Friday night. She left the festivities early with Peter."

"Oh. Actually, she's what I want to talk about. Has she expressed any interest in the old Maynard operation? She ever been up there?"

At this moment, Eli Johnson had to make a quick decision. On the one hand, the mayor was his boss, the man who hired him without giving prejudice to his injury or lack of experience. He certainly felt he deserved the truth. On the other hand, Goldie had demonstrated a clear talent for discovering things that others didn't immediately see and bringing those things to light. Like, Martha Eggleston's belief that her husband didn't fall asleep behind the wheel. Or, finding out about Claude Bolton and a suicide he knew nothing about. Now, she had questioned Banyan's character and brought to Eli's attention the fact that he had not only listed numerous properties on the same street, but also owned them. So, at this particular moment in time, Eli decided to withhold what he knew.

"No, not to my knowledge," he replied. "But it's interesting you mentioned the Maynard site. I just shot a mountain lion up there the other day that was getting chickens from the Nelson place. I also tightened up the chain on the main gate so critters and people couldn't slip through."

"You didn't change the padlock, did you?" the mayor asked.

"No, just tightened up the chain."

"Good," Banyan nodded. "Alright. Let me know if she asks about the place. Eh, maybe we can arrange a tour. But only if she asks. Personally, I'd rather not. Lots of dilapidated buildings up there."

"Sure. Understood."

Banyan rose from his chair. "Okay. I'm off. Going over to Harriette's place to see how she's doing?"

"Harriette?" Eli asked. "What's wrong with her?"

"Didn't come into work today. Called and said she was under the weather. I thought I might take her a nice fresh cup of coffee.

LEAP OF FAITH

"These are really fabulous!" Goldie exclaimed, looking at a collection of photographs that Father Fitz had taken for her article. It was now Tuesday afternoon, December 8, and she was downstairs in the basement of St. Mark's. The photos were all on eight-by-ten-inch photo paper and were lined up on long tables. The young priest stood behind them, smiling proudly with his hands behind his back.

"You really think so?" he asked, wanting to relish the moment.

"You know these are great," she affirmed like a supportive kid sister. "You've got a truly gifted eye for faces, lighting, and angles. You're like Andy Warhol without the weird hair."

"Thank you! Uh, who's Andy Warhol?"

"Some guy back east. It's not important."

In no particular order, Father Fitz had captured a

six-year-old Patty Bellows throwing the oversized light switch at the community tree lighting with a smile to match the tree's wattage, a four-year-old boy looking mesmerized at the tree, a couple holding hands while walking through the covered bridge, an overview of the town taken from a serious hike up one of the mountains, the sealed-up entrance to the main Maynard mine, the pastry chef from the Pine River Inn presenting his homemade streusel-topped cherry pie to the camera, the line of gingerbread houses Goldie had judged at the community dance, and several others.

"Wow, this is going to be hard," she said. "We're probably only going to use four to six of these, and you've given me three times that many."

"Well, I wanted to give you a choice of color or black-and-white," Father said. "I've seen both in the magazine."

"The photos are still predominantly black and white," she noted, having reviewed several issues. "Color ain't all that cost-effective yet."

She picked up and handed him the photo of the sealed-up mine entrance. "Better put this one away. After me draggin' you up there, I'm not sure I'll use it. If you get a photo credit for the article, people will know you trespassed to take it. Better to use a photo from the historical society from when the mine was still active."

"I wish you'd thought of that in the first place," Father said, taking the photo and slipping it into a thin box for photography paper. "So, you're going to write a complimentary story about the town, but *still* go after the mayor?"

"One doesn't have anything to do with the other," she replied. "I mean, yes, there's a connection, but why should an entire town be damned because of one guy? So, yeah, my magazine is gonna run a story about Sparkledove bein' the perfect place for Christmas next year, while the Associated Press might run a story about Banyan much sooner. I mean—that's the plan, anyway."

"And Evie Hines is going to exhume her father's body?"

Goldie nodded. "She called the hotel, left me a message, and we spoke last night. She's gonna petition a judge who happens to be an old friend of her dad's to have his body dug up and perform an autopsy."

"What are you expecting to find?" Father asked.

"That he was poisoned," Goldie said with certainty. "Arsenic, rat poison, drain cleaner or somethin'. Once we determine that, I think the Associated Press story is a lock."

"Can they determine that from an autopsy?" Father asked. "After all this time? After the body has been embalmed?"

"If the doctor knows what he's lookin' for, absolutely. Findin' poison in embalmed bodies dates back to the 1880s. I researched it at the library."

"Amazing," the priest said.

"And if poison *is* found, that sure supports Martha Eggleston's suspicions about Bucky."

"I have to admit, Goldie, I challenged you to find more proof. The mere fact that Evie Hines is even *considering* her father might've been poisoned is very compelling. It's also very disturbing. Like somebody wanting to hear the mass in English instead of Latin."

"Yeah. Don't get too attached to that, Father," she advised.

About five minutes later, Goldie stepped out the front door of the church and into a gleaming white winter's day. A nice nativity creche with plastic figures had recently been put on the small front yard of the church, and she turned to look at it before noticing that Peter was waiting for her. He was dressed for work in a suit with no tie, wearing his winter overcoat, and leaning against his station wagon parked on the street.

"You've been avoiding me," he said as she approached.

"How did you know where I—" but then she stopped and realized. "Maddie," she said. "I told her I was walkin' to St. Mark's."

"What's the deal, Goldie?" he said seriously. "We slept together Friday night, but ever since then, I haven't heard a peep out of you. I came by your hotel on Saturday and dropped off the dress you left at the community center. You weren't in your room, so I left a note at the front desk to see if you wanted to have dinner Saturday night. You never called."

"I know," she conceded.

"I dropped by Sunday morning to see if you wanted to have brunch at the Brown Palace in Denver, but again, you weren't around. I also got my mom's dress and returned it to her. Thanks for getting it cleaned, by the way."

"You're welcome."

"I totally left you alone on Monday, figuring you probably wanted some space. Now, it's Tuesday afternoon and *still* no word? This isn't fair. This is: Get-out-of-my-life-Peter-I-never-want-to-see-you-again stuff. I mean, not to sound crude, but ever since you opened your legs for me, you've totally closed me out of your life."

"That *does* sound crude," she agreed.

"Okay, I'm sorry," he said. "I've been standing out here waiting for you, thinking about what I might say and liked the word play of it; opened, closed—doesn't matter... I haven't *done* anything to you that you didn't agree to. All I'm guilty of is liking you."

Her shoulders slumped. "Yeah—I know... and I've never lied to you. I like you, too. But—"

"I know," he interrupted. "There are complications. I have a theory about that. Want to hear it?"

"Peter—"

"I don't think you want to get back with your former boyfriend. I don't even think the distance thing between us bothers you. *I* think you're a smart journalist who maybe unintentionally uncovered something that doesn't have anything to do with your story but involves my ol' man. And if we're a thing, then that creates a conflict."

Her green eyes widened as her mouth slowly fell open.

"Is that it?" he said, noticing her reaction. "Jesus! I was guessing. You mean—*that's it!*"

"W-we need to go somewhere and talk," she decided.

"Okay, let's go to my office."

"Not your office. Or my hotel. Or your house. Somewhere neutral."

"Are we suddenly at war?" he asked, surprised. "We need a Switzerland?"

"Please, Peter."

He looked behind her at St. Mark's. "Okay. How 'bout the church?"

She turned and looked at it. "Yeah... if Father will leave us undisturbed for a few minutes. Why don't you go ask him? He's down in the basement working on a spread of photos for my article. There's a hallway to the right of the altar that'll lead downstairs. He's got a selection of photos spread out that he's taken for the article. You should go see 'em. They're wonderful. You should also arrange to get him the negatives of the photos you took when we got the community tree. That way, I've got one keeper of all the photos for the article."

She glanced around at the day.

"I'll wait out here while you talk to him. I want your honest opinion of the best photos and don't want to influence you."

"Yeah, okay," he agreed. "Be right back."

After Peter reviewed the photos, Father said he had some errands to run and agreed to let him and Goldie speak in the church. So, they took off their coats and talked for about twenty minutes. Knowing she was risking any type of future relationship they might have, Goldie decided to take a leap of faith and tell him her suspicions about his father, Bucky Eggleston, Maynard "22," Jason Shirk, and the likely millions Charles was going to make. But she left out the part about Father Fitzsimmons going with her to the mine for the sake of his reputation. All in all, Peter absorbed the information about his dad potentially being a land swindler and murderer better than she expected. He didn't get indignant, argumentative, or vehemently deny her allegations. He mostly just sat in a pew and listened with folded arms and eyes that seemed to occasionally fight back a tear.

After Goldie was all talked out, she waited for several seconds for a quiet Peter to respond. He stood, slipped his hands into his pockets, and looked at the large crucifix hanging over the altar.

"We're not Catholic," he finally said. "In fact, we're not much of anything." He turned and looked at her. "I don't want to believe a damn thing you're saying... but... what you've said *does* fill in some gaps I've long wondered about. My father actually came from money... my grandfather made some good deals in Denver real estate. He's taken that money, plus his own savings, and sunk most everything he has into buying a string of houses on the same side of the same street.

Believe me, he's not that concerned about helping destitute widows or anyone else in a slack economy. I couldn't understand why he was being so generous. It also fills in possibilities about Tully and Crosby. I honestly don't know what they do for him, although as I've said before, Tully worked in town for a while."

"So—you believe me?" she asked a little timidly.

"I-I don't *not* believe you... I also now understand your hesitancy about a relationship with me."

"I didn't want this, Peter. I didn't want *any* of this! I didn't even want or intend to come to Sparkledove."

"This geologist's report, have you seen it? Studied it?"

"No. It's in a glass case under lock and key at the historical society. Harriette Noise told me about the contents."

"But this tunnel, number 22, that you have seen?"

"Yeah. There's a chain that locks the two gates going up the hillside to the Maynard site that I could slip through. But I think it's recently been tightened up by the sheriff."

"He knows about this?"

"No. He doesn't know I went into the mine. He just mentioned the gate to me one day and said he was going to tighten the chain. I asked him if I could go to the Maynard site, but he said no."

"I want to see this tunnel 22 for myself," Peter decided.

"We can't," she reiterated. "I think the chain's been fixed."

"Let's go talk to Eli and tell him the whole story. Then we can all go up there and investigate together."

She grit her teeth with hesitation. "That might not be the best idea."

"Why?"

"Because he was hired by your father. I've seen him with Tully and Crosby. He might also be one of your dad's minions."

Peter looked at her disbelievingly. But then, started to give her the benefit of the doubt.

"Okay... I know a place on the other side of the river, past a house owned by a family named Nelson, where we can cut the wire fencing and slip through. It's pretty wooded. Nobody will notice if we go early tomorrow morning."

"That's breakin' and enterin'."

"My father's reputation is at stake. Not to mention the biggest scandal in the history of the town. Besides, you've already broken the law by going up there."

"I don't like this, Peter."

"I've got to see it for myself, Goldie. If you don't want to involve the sheriff, you're not giving me a hell of a lot of choices."

"Why not just wait and see what the autopsy on Jason Shirk reveals?"

"Because this is *my father* we're talking about, and I want to see for myself!"

She paused, then nodded slightly.

"Yeah, I get it... I'm sorry to ask, but do you think your mom knows anything about this?"

He shook his head. "No. Whether your suspicions about him are true or not, she's the home maker and social director of their lives. She doesn't get involved in his business. I doubt she's even aware he owns all those houses on Falcon Drive."

"Good. 'Cause, I like her."

"I do, too," Peter understated, struggling with his emotions. "A-and I don't hate my dad. I-I just can't believe he'd do something like this. Yet, I-I sort of *can*."

"I know," she interrupted, empathetically. "I know. Okay... how do you want to work this for tomorrow?"

"Well, can we *please* keep this under wraps? Don't tell Father Fitz, or Maddie, or Clara, or anyone until there's absolutely no doubt whatsoever—"

"Of course," she assured. "Peter, of course! I took a leap of faith here. It's *because* I slept with you that we're having this discussion now. *Of course* I realize we're holding people's lives and reputations in our hands. Not to mention our own. *Of course* I'll be discreet."

Two minutes later, Peter and Goldie came out of the church. He mentioned that he had to interview someone near Denver for a story, but offered to buy her a quick cup of coffee. She declined, saying she was actually going to wander around and look at the stores with the intention of doing some Christmas shopping. So, Peter gave her a quick kiss goodbye, drove off, and she started walking toward River Street.

As Peter and Goldie came out of the church, Eli Johnson spotted them from a distance in his cruiser. Like

Peter, he had gone to the hotel looking for Goldie, and Maddie had told him that she was at St. Mark's. He watched them with a wrinkled brow, disturbed by the kiss, and wondered why she and Peter would be in the church since he knew Peter wasn't a parishioner. Something Goldie had said to him on Monday festered in his head, and he wanted to ask her about it. But now he thought maybe he should shadow her to see if it revealed anything. He watched her for a couple of hours, but nothing out of the ordinary happened. She briefly returned to her hotel, then came back out with a folder and went to Clara's Gifts, where she returned the notebook of gingerbread patterns. After that, she went to Miller's General Store and spent nearly an hour browsing and visiting with Zeke and Chad in front of the potbelly stove. Next, she stopped at a bookstore for nearly thirty minutes, and after that, she went to the post office and sat on a bench where she was admiring the community Christmas tree. Although she wasn't doing anything unusual, Eli found it hard to take his eyes off her. As he sat in his cruiser, a local woman approached him, asking for his help to locate a family dog that had escaped from her backyard. So that took him away for over half an hour. After that, a load of hay bales fell off a truck near the Sparkledove Arms, and that required his attention for over two hours. By the time the hay bales had been restacked and the snowy street filled with pieces of wet straw had been cleaned up, his sister, Dinah, showed up for a dinner date they had planned the previous Friday at the community dance. After a nice dinner and long talk, Dinah hopped in her car to return to nearby Brownsville. Once she was gone, Eli took a slow evening cruise down Falcon Drive to look at the houses with the red Sparkledove Realty signs.

In the intervening hours, Goldie had spoken to Maddie at the front desk, made a lengthy phone call in the phone booth, had dinner alone in the hotel's restaurant, then took a bath. A little before 10:00 p.m., she was debating whether or not she wanted to go for an evening walk or go to bed, when her thoughts were interrupted by a knock on her door.

When she opened it, she saw Eli standing in the hallway with the large pathos leaf wallpaper.

"Why did you ask, 'Why are you working for a man like Charles Banyan?'" he began, getting straight to the point.

"What?" she said, surprised to see him, especially at her hotel room door and at this late hour.

"Yesterday at my office, when you brought the flowers, your question suggested a problem with his character. Why?"

"Look, Sheriff," she said wearily, "it's late."

"May I come in?"

"No."

"Why did you say what you said about Harriette Noise?" he pressed. "She *does* happen to be ill."

"Then keep your boss away from her," she urged.

"What?"

"Why didn't you answer *my* question?" she fired back. "Why do you work for that man?"

"Because he gave me a job that no one else was ever likely to offer. Look at my leg, Goldie. I thought my life was over after Pearl Harbor and after..." his voice trailed off, not wanting to mention Lila Hemmings.

"Did you ever search around town for that black vehicle with a scratch of light tan paint on the driver's side?"

"Huh?"

"The one that ran Bucky Eggleston off the road?"

"I said it was a 'possibility' Bucky was run off the road. Not a certainty. I also said finding a vehicle with a matching scratch of paint on it wasn't very likely."

"Okay," she said, unsatisfied with his answer. "Well, like I say, it's late and I gotta go to bed. Why don't you go hang out with your buddy, Tully?"

"He's not my buddy," Eli replied. "He doesn't live in town, and I don't even know his first name."

"Uh-huh... but he and Crosby are sure here a lot, aren't they? Goodnight, Sheriff," she said, closing her door.

Eli looked at the closed door for a moment, raised his fist to knock again, but then decided not to. Frustrated, he walked away.

A few minutes later, Eli was cruising the quiet streets of Sparkledove, trying to figure out what Goldie was up to. He wondered about Harriette. He wondered if Goldie was keeping things from him because she was working on a story above and beyond the article she was supposed to be writing. Then he considered maybe there was nothing unusual about an elderly woman like Harriette feeling poorly, and he just had hurt feelings because he saw Peter Banyan kiss Goldie. Yes, he admitted to himself, he did like her and thought she was very attractive. But he also saw no possibility of a relationship. He also thought she was full of conspiracy theories, quick-tempered, and frankly, a little nutty. While he was considering such things, he found himself driving past Clancy's Bar & Grill and noticed there were four or five cars in the parking lot, including Tully's black pickup truck. So, he decided to pull in.

He saw there were two other black vehicles in the lot besides Tully's. So, he parked, grabbed a flashlight from his cruiser, got out, clicked on the flashlight, then examined the exterior passenger side of one car, then another, then Tully's pickup. There were no scratches on any of the vehicles, although he did notice there was a three to four-inch section of black paint on the front quarter panel of Tully's truck that didn't quite match the original paint job. It was close, but not a match.

Eleven minutes later, Father Fitzsimmons answered the front door of the rectory to see the sheriff standing on his doorstep.

"Eli?" Father Fitz said, surprised. "Everything alright?"

"Can I come in, Father?" he asked. "We need to talk."

Twenty-Seven

THE MOUNTAIN CODE

It was 6:20 a.m. the next morning when Goldie stepped outside the Sparkledove Arms to find Peter sitting in his idling station wagon with a cup of coffee for her. The temperature was thirty degrees, and the town wasn't quite awake. They hoped to avoid being seen in the early morning hours, since they intended to cut through the wire fence erected by the city. Both were dressed in warm clothes, hats, and gloves. Peter also had a backpack filled with items they might need. Besides wire cutters, he brought a flashlight, a thermos of water, rope, a first aid kit, a small hand pick, and a few other things. He admitted he hadn't slept much the night before, and Goldie admitted the same. He also said he had given Father Fitz his photo negatives for the article, and if her suspicions about his dad were true, he'd be the first to report it in *The Sparkledove Wing* and would back her 100 percent.

On the far eastern side of town, and going slightly around a mountain base, they crossed the river on an old wooden bridge with no guardrails, which led to a dirt road with three houses on it. The last of these was the Nelson property, where the mountain lion had been pilfering chickens. Just beyond the Nelsons', before the road came to a turnaround dead end, was a wooded area where Peter pulled over. They got out and walked about thirty yards inland to the fence, then Peter, wearing his backpack, began snipping away. Once they were through, they trudged their way uphill through some woods with a lot of exposed rock where the powdery snow had been blown away by the wind, so there was practically no evidence of their tracks. They eventually came up to the bend in the dirt road of the Maynard site, between the director of operations' house and the sealed-up mine entrance. As they quietly neared the mine, Goldie heard the generator and saw that the three short ore cart railroad ties, which had once been stacked up to look like part of the sealed entrance, had been moved aside.

"Oh my God," she quietly said, grabbing Peter's coat sleeve. "Somebody's in there!"

"Good," he said, unconcerned. "Time to get to the bottom of this."

She looked down the dirt road toward the chained gate that led to the covered bridge. The gate was chained tightly shut, and there were no footprints in the snow coming up the dirt road, other than a few windblown traces of her previous visit and encounter with the mountain lion.

"Whoever they are, they came up another way," she determined. "Let's go hide in the office and watch to see who comes out of the mine."

"They'll see the tracks in the snow going to the office," he observed. "Go wait there if you want to, but I'm going into the mine. I'll have the element of surprise."

"You're gonna leave me out here alone?" she protested.

"Then come with me," he said. He pulled his .45 caliber army-issue pistol out of his winter coat pocket. "Nothing's going to happen to you, Goldie. I promise."

"I'm gonna hold you to that," she said.

He put the weapon away, and they moved carefully toward the mine entrance as the day was getting brighter. They bent down, stepped over a couple of permanently affixed ties, and went into the mine.

"Whoa," Peter whispered, seeing the seemingly endless string of lit electric lights that hung from spikes on the left-hand side of the mine wall. "How far does this go?"

"Pretty far," she answered softly. "We'd better keep quiet. Who knows how much voices carry? Just follow the lights."

"Okay," he nodded. "Lead the way, since you've been here before."

They silently descended deeper and deeper into

the mine, passing a maze of interconnecting tunnels on either side for both miners and push carts with numbers painted on the walls outside of them. After several minutes, they came to a connecting tunnel where the lights turned left into tunnel "22."

"We just keep followin' the lights?" he whispered.

"Yes."

"The air's getting thin," he said, breathing heavier.

"Tough it out, Mary," she cracked. *"You're* the one who wanted to come down here."

After about a minute's walk in tunnel "22," Peter noticed little trickles of water dribbling down the rock walls to the wet ground.

"We're goin' underneath the river," Goldie quietly explained.

About fifty yards beyond that, she suddenly stopped.

"There are people up ahead," she whispered.

"Yes," he agreed in a normal voice. "Time to go meet them."

"Sshh," she urged, turning to him. It was at this point that she noticed he had pulled the pistol out of his pocket again. He cocked it, then pointed it at her.

"What're you doing?" she asked, still whispering.

"Move!" Peter said, sternly, gesturing with the gun that she should keep going.

Suddenly realizing she'd been betrayed by her leap of faith in Peter, Goldie expelled a deep breath, closed her green eyes, then reopened them with a wiser perspective.

"You're in this with your father, aren't you?"

"Uh-huh," he confirmed. "Keep moving. Let's go."

She shook her head regrettably, then continued on.

"Oh, Peter—and you were such a good writer."

"I still am. I'm just not going to be a poor one."

"What an idiot I was," she admitted. "You and Charles were playin' good cop, bad cop. You, the kind, considerate reporter who doesn't like to air people's dirty laundry, writes beautiful obituaries, and aspires to be a novelist, pitted against the autocratic father who bullies others and wants to prove to everyone that *he's* the boss."

"He *is*," Peter agreed. "And a very effective one. Under him, the town's tourism business has grown substantially."

"Not to mention, his pocketbook," she said, still walking. "Skimming from vendors, taking a little from historical society dues, maybe even taking a cut from the community dance, huh? But it all paled in comparison once that old geology report showed up, didn't it?"

"Got it all figured out, don't you?" Peter concluded.

"Yeah, pretty much," she agreed. "Except for a few details."

They fell silent until they met up with Charles, Tully, and Crosby standing near the entrance to tunnel "12" that turned left and went off into the darkness. Running across its entrance was the continuous string of clear lightbulbs. About ten feet beyond the entrance, continuing down tunnel "22," was the area where the tunnel floor had collapsed, leaving only that small ledge. Goldie knew from her previous visit that there was a several-hundred-foot drop from where the floor had given way. Tully and Crosby were wearing their usual blue-collar clothes, and uncharacteristically, so was Charles.

"Hey, boys," she greeted, mustering her courage. From her time with Markie, she knew tough guys were only incentivized by fear. So, she was determined not to show it. She took a stick of gum out of her winter jacket pocket, unwrapped it, then stuck it into her mouth. Charles looked her over with her black rubber-clip boots, blue jacket, and burnt orange stocking cap.

"Good morning, Goldie," he greeted. "I imagine, right now, you're pretty frightened."

"Not really," she said, cracking her gum. "I'm disappointed in junior over here, but glad to finally get some answers."

"Curiosity killed the cat," Tully observed.

"You've already met Tully," the mayor said. "His red-headed companion is Crosby."

"How ya doin'?" Goldie nodded with her distinct Bronx accent. She cracked her gum again and looked around. "Where's your other pal, Eli?"

"The Boy Scout? He's not a part of our little group," Tully huffed.

"Ah..." she said, thinking. "You just answered one of those details for me."

"Really? What was that?" Peter said, still pointing the gun at her while slipping off his backpack.

She looked at Tully and Crosby. "Well, I've seen the sheriff with you two gentlemen, so I was never sure if he was part of the gang." She turned to Charles. "But now I get it. You hired him because he didn't have any experience and was physically challenged. When he returned to Sparkledove, he was still usin' his cane. You could take advantage of his inexperience, mobility, and still get complimented by the community because he was a decorated war vet."

"You're smart, Goldie," Charles smiled. "Smarter than the average woman."

"She can't be all *that* smart," Crosby scoffed in his Scottish tongue. "Look where she is."

"I *am* sorry, Goldie," Peter admitted, "that I used you."

"Fuhgettaboutit," she shrugged. She looked at Charles. "So, when did you buy this old mine?"

"Right after I commissioned ore samples from not one, but two different out-of-state mining geologists," Charles answered.

She looked behind her. "And when did the floor give way?"

"According to the final geology report of 1882, some of it had fallen away even then," Peter said. "No doubt it was a reason to abandon the tunnel. But it's nothing a bridge can't fix with today's modern engineering."

Goldie recalled what Harriette Noise had told her. "The geology report came to the historical society in late 1939. It's nearly Christmas of 1942. So, you've been workin' on this scheme for a long time."

"Years," Charles admitted. "I've invested everything I have. There's no turning back."

"How much silver do you figure is down here?" she asked.

"Could be as much as a hundred tons," Peter replied.

She paused, calculating. "Wow, that's over $4,000,000.00 in 1942... $55,000,000.00 in current mon..." her voice trailed off. "If you hit gold, even more. And, of course, since you own a realty company and are the mayor, you knew how to keep the purchase quiet."

"We've answered your questions, Goldie, now answer one of mine," Charles said. "Who originally put you on the trail that something was going on?"

She took a couple of steps and looked beyond the men standing near the entrance of tunnel "12." Figuring she might try to escape down that way, Crosby warned, "Don't even think about it."

She turned back to the men. "Bucky Eggleston had been working a lot of long hours. There was a manpower shortage at his office because of the war. The day he died, he told his wife he'd been drinkin' coffee all day. So, he didn't fall asleep."

"He could've been drinking decaf," Peter suggested.

"He hated decaf," Goldie replied. "He even called Martha the day he died and made a joke about how he'd be up for days." She looked at Tully and Crosby. "You two pricks ran him off the road, didn't you? Charles knew he didn't have any life insurance because, as either the head of the historical society, his realtor, or as mayor, he knew the particulars of the Eggleston finances. If Bucky were dead, Martha couldn't hang on to the house." She looked at Charles. "You also knew from pestering them about upkeep, she probably wouldn't want to."

"Those are huge assumptions," Charles said.

"No," she countered. "Eli examined Bucky's car at the junkyard and suspected it could've been run off the road. He gave his findings to the state police. I also have a picture of Tully's truck with a scratch of light-tan paint on it. The same color as Bucky's car. In fact, my photo is in beautiful color."

"That's impossible," Crosby replied.

"No, it isn't. I snapped it with a flash while you two were breaking into Midland Elementary School Sunday night. A couple of friends took me over there with this great camera," she explained, referring to Josie, Dexter, and the borrowed camera from Dexter's father.

"That was before we painted it," Crosby said to Charles.

"Oh, did you paint over it?" Goldie asked, not knowing. "No worries. Eli used to work in a body shop. I'm sure he'll be able to spot the difference. Which brings to mind some questions: Why did you boys follow me to Midland Elementary? Why did you feel it necessary to return at night, break into the school, and steal a list of the employees? Why were you so concerned about who I saw? *Unless,* of course, you had something to hide?"

"Lupe," Charles muttered, now realizing she had been listening in on the basement stairs. "I'm going to kill her."

"You mean like how you had your boys kill Bucky Eggleston? You mean like when you killed Jason Shirk by poisoning him when he suspected what you were up to? How did that work, incidentally?"

Banyan hesitated momentarily, then decided he didn't have anything to lose by answering.

"Our late sheriff was even more of a Boy Scout than our current one. He was also more experienced as a lawman. He became too curious about too many of my business dealings. I couldn't allow that. But he was also a creature of habit. He ate breakfast at the same place every morning. A place where our friend Mr. Tully here worked as a short-order cook."

She looked at Tully, who smiled, then she looked at Peter. "You *did* say he worked in town for a while."

"I did," Peter confirmed.

"And now somebody's slowly poisoning Harriette Noise," she continued. She turned to Banyan. "Yeah, I know she's ill, Charles. You'll discover her kids will be picking her up and taking her to the hospital later today."

She looked around at the four men.

"Basically, boys—you're all fucked."

There were several seconds of silence where Charles, Peter, Tully, and Crosby looked at one another, beginning to realize that they were. Until Charles confidently smiled and responded,

"The state police closed the case on Bucky Eggleston, and I can arrange to have his car destroyed. I know from Peter that you talked to Evie Hines about exhuming her father, but what if we dig him up first? The cemetery in Idaho Springs is quite scenic, but isolated. Or maybe we'll have his body disappear from the mortuary? If Harriette Noise's kids are going to take care of her, wonderful. I wish her a speedy recovery and can't wait until she's back to work. It'll give me time to convince her that her house is too big for her. And as for the geology report at the historical society, that was my supposed motivation for all this? Artifacts get lost all the time. Especially with an elderly, forgetful caretaker like Harriette."

He took a step toward her. "Then there's you, Goldie. A nice, but slightly eccentric woman who seemed to be confused and disoriented when she came to town, as witnesses will attest. A woman who decided to go caving on her own. A woman who cut a fence, trespassed onto closed city property, and disappeared into this labyrinth of tunnels. As for me owning the mineral rights to most of what's under Falcon Drive, I can generously share some of my newfound riches with Evie Hines, Martha Eggleston, George and Susan Ash, and Harriette. I can give them all a one-time payoff, look like a hero, and still make a fortune." He smiled. "So you see? Everything you *think* you have—you don't."

"Enough of this!" Crosby said, agitated. "Let's toss the bitch into the cavern."

He took a step toward her, but Goldie held out a hand like a traffic cop.

"Bad idea, Carrot Top! What *I* know, my editor knows. So does a reporter for the Associated Press. So does a prominent citizen in town. I also left a note in my room sayin' I was comin' up here with Peter. I've additionally got photos of you and Tully's snowy boot prints from when you broke into the school, and photos of you two clowns wearing those *same* boots at the dance Friday night, standing right next to your boss, the mayor. I've even got a footwear expert who will verify the boot prints in my photos belong to *your* boots," she said, remembering Gerome's brother. "So, again, you're screwed."

"Dad?" Peter asked, concerned.

"Tully," Charles ordered, "go to her hotel room right now and retrieve the note before a maid cleans in there and finds it."

"But—"

"*Do it!*" Charles insisted. "And hurry! Go the back way around the mountain. Don't leave tracks in the snow and—uh—don't be bothered if you hear a ruckus behind you."

Tully didn't want to miss the fun of Goldie's death but reluctantly obeyed. As he did, Peter, holding the

.45 on her, warned: "You should learn to keep your mouth shut, Goldie."

"Not to mention, think things through," Charles added. "You took pictures of Tully, Crosby, and me at the dance as well as some footprints in the snow outside of a school? So what? Nothing was taken from the school. The lock wasn't even broken. It was picked. All that's missing is an eight-and-a-half-by-eleven-inch piece of paper, which is impossible for you to prove. It also doesn't matter if you contacted one or a dozen reporters, or who you spoke to in town. Without Bucky's car, the geology report, or Jason Shirk's body—all of which I can handle—you have nothing."

He stepped away from her, went over to the drop-off in the floor of tunnel "22," then turned back to her.

"You're going to have an unfortunate fall of several hundred feet. We'll take down all the lights, the spikes holding them up, and remove the generator. I doubt investigators will want to consider what you've told others and spend hundreds of dollars on core samples without that geology report. But even if they do, all it proves is that there is still silver in a mine that I legally purchased. And the mineral rights to the properties? They were legally purchased, too. So, checkmate. If no one considers your conjectures, then I'll let a respectable amount of time pass, build a bridge across the collapsed floor, and start mining. In the interim, you, my dear, will have become a distant memory. So, again, checkmate. There's no way this ends well for you."

"Time for a swan dive, lassie," Crosby said, coming for her.

Suddenly, there was a flash of light and a loud bang from the darkness of tunnel "12." A wide-eyed Crosby grabbed his chest, stumbled back a few steps, then, with a scream, tumbled backwards into the black cavern where the floor had given way. The sounds of the shot and scream seemed to echo everywhere as Charles and Peter looked at one another, astonished.

Goldie turned to Peter, confidently.

"Your team got here early. Mine got here earlier."

He looked at her, open-mouthed.

"How, how did you know—"

"That you were setting me up?" she finished. "I read one of your short stories Friday night while you were sleeping. Loved the one about the abandoned mine with all the core sample holes. Except, how would you even know what core sample holes *were* unless you researched them, or had recently seen 'em?"

With an impulse of fury, Peter raised his pistol at Goldie's head and pulled the trigger. Nothing happened. The firing pin just clicked. Surprised, he looked at it, then at her.

"I took your bullets yesterday while you were in the church checking out Father's pictures," she clarified. "I knew you kept your gun in your glove compartment. Right next to the whisk broom."

Peter looked at her for a few more seconds, then dropped the pistol, turned, and ran down tunnel "22," heading back the way they had come.

"Well, *that* was unexpected," she observed. "I didn't think he'd turn into a wuss."

With a sudden blood-chilling scream, Charles Banyan charged at Goldie with outstretched arms, intending to strangle her. But a second shot and flash of light came from tunnel "12," striking Charles in his left knee. With a painful yell, he collapsed to the ground in front of her and grabbed his leg. As the sound from the second shot bounced around the rock walls, she looked down at him, chewing and cracking her gum.

"You can't hurt people you were elected to serve, Charles. It's the mountain code."

"You bitch!" he screamed. *"You Goddamn bitch!"*

"Yada-yada-yada," she said, stepping over and picking up Peter's .45. She ejected the clip, dug into the pocket of her blue winter jacket, and produced a handful of bullets. As she reinserted them, one by one, into the clip, Paul McCaw slowly came walking out of tunnel "12" holding his Sedgley Springfield hunting rifle.

"Hey, Goldie," he calmly said, ducking to avoid the string of lights going across the tunnel entrance.

"Ay, Paul. How ya doin'?"

"Hey, Mayor," he said, looking down at Banyan. "Sorry about the knee."

"You shot me, you asshole!" Banyan painfully yelled.

"I hope you didn't have to wait too long," Goldie said, still loading bullets.

"Not too long," Paul said, straight-faced. "Saul

sealed up the entranceway behind me, and we was real careful about tracks. I had a flashlight and followed your instructions. I just hunkered down yonder and waited by them long planks on the floor. The lights came on about twenty minutes after I got here."

"Y-you waited in a dark mine to ambush us?" Charles asked between tears and gritted teeth.

"No different than waitin' in a duck blind or a deer tower. Besides, I had jerky."

Goldie put the last bullet in place, then slipped the clip into the handle. "What long planks?"

"There's a couple long planks in tunnel "12," and I figured people musta used them to get across the collapsed floor of tunnel "22.""

"Perfect," Goldie smiled, mocking herself. "*Now* I find out there were planks. Where's Saul?"

"Probably about to entertain Tully," Paul figured.

"Okay," she said, pulling back the chamber and cocking the revolver. "I'm gonna go after Peter. You mind babysittin' the mayor? Peter said there's a first aid kit in the backpack."

"Not at all. We're gonna need a new mayor, and I wanna pick his brain. I think I got the personality for politics."

"Well, you *are* a giver," she agreed.

"True," he said, unemotionally.

It took several minutes for Peter to emerge from the mine entrance. When he did, he was breathless and tired. Stepping over the railroad ties and tasting sweet air again, he paused, bent over, and took several deep breaths before he was even aware of what was happening around him. Over by the old mining office, he finally noticed that Tully had been bound and gagged by Saul McCaw. Tully lay on the ground, a scarf wrapped around his mouth, his hands tied behind his back, and Saul was just finishing tying his legs. As the captive grunted, Peter saw that Saul's rifle was leaning against the office wall. When Peter and Saul saw each other, Saul went for his rifle, and a burst of adrenaline kicked in for Peter. The younger Banyan ran down the dirt road toward the chained gate and the covered bridge; no longer thinking about leaving footprints in the snow, going a back way, or even the newly tightened chain on the gate. He just wanted to escape. Figuring he had to keep an eye on his prisoner, plus knowing Peter was too well known in town to hide for long, Saul decided not to pursue.

As Peter rounded the bend in the road heading toward the gate, he was totally unaware that just on the other side of it, the barefoot woman in the white summer nightgown who carried a rope with a noose was walking toward him. She passed through the wire gate like smoke through a screen door. The two passed by one another only inches apart; she headed up the road toward the director's house, leaving no footprints, and he chugged through the snow toward the fence. Coming to the chained gate, Peter rattled it frantically, then started to climb over. But he abruptly stopped when he saw Eli's black-and-white Ford come down the end of the covered bridge and make a sharp left turn to head up his way. Eli had the bubble light on top of his car on, and Peter knew this couldn't be good. Hopping down from the gate, he turned and started to run back the way he came. Within another twenty seconds, he unknowingly ran right through the apparition, still making her way up the road. When he did, a shocking chill ran through his head like a sudden brain freeze. With a yell, he stopped, fell to his knees, then to his hands with a numbing shortness of breath. Simultaneously, Eli's cruiser burst through the chained gate and slid to a snowy stop a few yards behind him. As the oblivious, sad, blonde-haired woman continued onward to her daily rendezvous with death, the sheriff jumped up out of his car with a revolver in hand and limped up the road to a shivering Peter still on all fours.

"Howdy, Peter," he drawled.

A few seconds later, Goldie appeared at the bend of the road, running toward them. She stopped, still holding Peter's .45, saw him on the ground, then saw Eli standing behind him. She also saw the woman in the white nightgown silently turn and head up the path toward the director of operations' partially opened front door. She watched her slip inside, then turned her eyes to Eli. He smiled, put two fingers to the side of his head, then saluted in her direction.

Seeing the corny cowboy gesture, a big smile started to stretch across her gum-chewing face.

Twenty-Eight

BREATHE

Ninety minutes later, and still early in the morning, Sparkledove residents were experiencing two unusual things simultaneously. The first was that an ambulance carrying Charles Banyan slowly made its way down the dirt road from the old Maynard Mining operation. It carefully turned, went through the covered bridge, then continued down Bridge Street heading for the highway. The second unusual thing was at the opposite end of town, in front of the sheriff's office. A state police paddy wagon was loading up Tully and Peter Banyan while a few curious onlookers wondered what was happening. Five minutes after the ambulance carrying Charles rolled onto Highway 70, Clara from Clara's Gifts and Chad Miller from Miller's General Store were in a car with Harriette Noise and also heading for the highway, intending to take her to the same hospital where the mayor was going.

Meanwhile, Goldie sat in one of the two chairs in front of Eli's desk at the sheriff's office, reading over a statement he had just typed up. Finishing, then nodding, she picked up a pen on the desk, signed it, and handed it to the sheriff.

"You misspelled 'tunnel' once, but other than that, it looks good."

"T-h-a-n-x," he spelled out. "You did a heck of an investigating job, Goldie: getting color pictures of the paint scratch, figuring out what was happening over on Falcon Drive, Jason Shirk being poisoned—everything!"

"You're not so bad yourself," she said, returning the compliment. "Knowin' the paint Tully used to cover the scratch was new, convincin' Father Fitz to tell you everything I told him, then gettin' to my room early this mornin' and findin' that note."

"After talking with Father, I wanted to get to your room at first light because I was afraid you were going to do something dangerous."

She took a tissue out of her purse and disposed of her gum. "And see? I didn't disappoint."

He looked down at the floor self-consciously. "Banyan hired me because he thought I'd be a pushover, didn't he?"

"It doesn't matter, copper," she replied, tossing her tissue and gum into a wastepaper basket. "You weren't."

"I-uh... I'm sorry you didn't feel you could trust me."

"It wasn't you personally. It's cops in general. I've, eh, I've sorta been conditioned to think they were the enemy unless they were on the payroll."

He paused, looking at her.

"You want to explain that?"

"It's a long story. Then, when I saw you, Tully, and Crosby at the tree lightin' ceremony…"

He shrugged. "Banyan just told them to help me with the barricades because of my leg."

"Yeah," she admitted. "I read too much into that one. I'm sorry. So, what happens now?"

He leaned back in his chair, feeling the weight of his duties. "I've got to have a tough conversation with Stephie Banyan, the city council has to be called for an emergency session, statements need to be taken from the McCaw Brothers, and I have to figure out who to call about retrieving Crosby's body. I'm not even sure it *can* be retrieved. I also want to keep up with Harriette Noise's kids about her condition. They're meeting Clara and Chad at the hospital."

"You think she'll be okay?" Goldie asked, concerned.

"Don't know. I don't know what she was given, and Banyan isn't talking until he sees a lawyer. She's in her eighties, so it's anyone's guess."

"Give me one minute alone with either Charles or Peter," she said. "*I'll* find out what was given to her."

"I said the exact same thing to the state police," he replied. "You've done enough. What're you going to do about your article?"

"I'm filing two pieces. One for the AP about Charles and Peter, and the other is exactly what you'd expect for *Adventure Escape*. The AP story will probably be co-authored by a true investigative journalist my boss knows, while my article for the magazine won't come out until next year's December issue. By then, the stink from the Banyans will have worn off, and you'll have a nice, positive story. At the end of the day, Sparkledove really *is* the perfect place for Christmas."

He rose from his chair. "I'd better get over to Stephie's before she hears things through the gossips, if she hasn't already."

"Her whole life changed this morning," Goldie acknowledged. "I know somethin' about that. Let me know if I can help."

"I want to revisit what you said about your distrust of law enforcement officers," he reminded. "You said it was a long story. Despite what happened today—I'll make time to hear it."

She shook her head. "I gotta make arrangements to go back to Columbus. I think I've done what I'm supposed to do here."

"Stay through the weekend," he suggested. "The Tour of Homes is really nice and, if you *really* want to help, like, talk with Stephie Banyan or Martha Eggleston, you can't do it if you're gone. Take some time to wrap things up and say goodbye to the friends you've made. You might be surprised just how well-liked you are."

She looked at him and smiled a little. "Maybe I will. There are still a couple of mysteries about this town that I haven't figured out, and—"

"Goldie," he interrupted. "Stand down. Breathe. Go hiking in the mountains, make a snowman, Christmas shop, or just go down to Miller's, sit in front of the stove, and chew the fat with Deke."

She considered for a moment that if she went to Columbus, it would be an existence totally unknown to her. What new questions, problems, and strangeness would she encounter? Maybe it was because she had gotten so little sleep the night before, but she was tired. She wanted to relax. As Eli had suggested, she simply wanted to breathe.

Twenty-Nine

SURPRISE MOVES

The next two days, Wednesday, December 9th, and Thursday, December 10th, were days filled with talk and aftershocks. Owen Mitchell made sure that his friend at the Associated Press coordinated with Goldie and got the entire story about Charles and Peter Banyan's alleged land grab scheme, attempted murder of Harriette Noise, as well as their suspected involvement in the murders of Bucky Eggleston and Jason Shirk. When the story broke in the *Denver Post* with a dual byline that included Goldie's name, the townspeople of Sparkledove were genuinely taken aback by Peter's involvement, but many were quick to believe Charles' guilt. People started coming out of the woodwork, revealing truer feelings of how Charles always rubbed them the wrong way with his dictatorial rules to homeowners and his superficial political smiles. "I always thought he was crooked about this," or "I always suspected something was funny about that," entered into a lot of conversations.

The city council unanimously voted to fire Charles Banyan as mayor. A special fire department rescue team from Denver explored tunnel "22," but after going down two hundred feet with men on ropes, determined Crosby's body was irretrievable. After being interviewed by both Eli and the state police, Stephie Banyan was cleared of any wrongdoing. Lupe and Margarita, as well as Paul and Saul McCaw, also gave their statements. During these two days, Goldie took an extremely grateful Martha Eggleston out to lunch and spoke over the phone with Evie Hines. In a surprise move to cut a deal with the prosecutor, Peter Banyan confessed that arsenic was the poison of choice used on Jason Shirk and Harriette Noise. Harriette's doctor diagnosed that although the former schoolteacher was very ill, he was cautiously optimistic about a recovery, and the entire town seemed to take a collective sigh of relief upon learning this, since she had taught three generations of citizens.

Goldie already had a level of notoriety in Sparkledove, but after the AP story broke, she couldn't go anywhere without people stopping and talking to her. Some were happy and grateful for her investigative efforts, while others were concerned about the negative impact the scandal would have on the city's tourism business. She told person after person that while she'd never want to do anything to hurt the economy of the town, the Banyans and their plans had to be stopped.

On Friday and Saturday, December 11th and 12th, the Sparkledove Tour of Homes took place. After purchasing tickets, people could visit the first floors of numerous Victorian homes from the 1860s to the 1890s, decorated in the spirit of those years, between the hours of 4:00 and 8:00 p.m. Homeowners greeted guests in period costumes, and electric lights on the Christmas trees were the only modern exception to otherwise period decorations. One homeowner played a harpsichord for guests. Another had an antique music box that played "O Tannenbaum" and "O Come All Ye Faithful." Still another homeowner made dozens of ginger snaps and offered them to guests until the supply ran out. As visitors moved from house to house, carolers from a local church serenaded them on a street corner. Meanwhile, downtown, the stores stayed open until 10 p.m., and like the tree lighting ceremony, River Street was closed off to traffic due to the numerous attractions and vendors set up on the street. Two of the biggest draws were a merry-go-round for kids and the opportunity to see Santa Claus sitting in a big red throne that sat in front of the community tree in the courtyard of the post office. Stu Frey played Santa and was a natural, considering his barrel chest, white hair, beard, and age.

Despite the scandal, or perhaps even because of it, the town was jammed packed with visitors Friday night. Members from the volunteer fire department acted as traffic cops, and the city council even allowed Eli to hire two off-duty state policemen to act as designated deputies for the night. In total, there were nineteen homes open to the public, and one of those was Stephie Banyan's. Although heartbroken, she decided to face any gossip head-on and support her community the best way she could. Many townsfolk viewed her decision as both brave and classy, and although it was too soon to tell, it seemed like the sins of Charles and Peter would not necessarily be held against her.

Dressed in slacks and her outerwear from Miller's, Goldie visited five homes on the tour, listened to carolers, bought a candy apple from a vendor on River Street, and watched the kids standing in line for their chance to tell Santa their Christmas wishes. She was alone as she moved through the town, yet she wasn't alone at all. She ran into Lupe and her family, whom she had met before at the Thanksgiving potluck. She stopped and spoke with Maddie and Dean, who were taking a twenty-minute break from their duties at the hotel to stroll among the crowd and absorb some of the festive fun. She saw Herb Pontz, who was taking the night off from the munitions factory in Denver, and met his wife, Sharon. Goldie asked Herb about where he had come up with the line: "It's been a hard day's night, and I've been working like a dog." But, like Ed Peterson, who quoted the Bee Gees at the community dance, he couldn't remember where he'd heard the saying. She didn't like this ongoing mystery, but she took it in stride. She was accepting that there were some things about Sparkledove she might never figure out.

About 8:30, she ran into Eli, who had been busy all night making sure everything was running smoothly. Even though it was one of the busiest nights of the year, he asked Goldie to hop in his police cruiser and said he wanted to show her something special. Intrigued, she followed him to a side street and climbed into his Ford sedan. He circled downtown, passing dozens of cars parked on the sides of streets, until he was just a few yards from Bridge Street. When they got there, she noticed Bridge Street was closed off, like River Street, but she couldn't see why. Eli parked his car in a space with a sign that read: Reserved for Sheriff. He turned off the engine, then told her to wait until he rounded the car to get her door. She liked the chivalry but didn't understand what they were doing.

"So, what's the deal?" she asked, getting out of the car and not having a clear view of the street from where they parked.

"When the town has some nice snowfalls and freezing weather like this year," he explained, "we do something special on Bridge Street."

They came to the street, and Goldie drew a sharp breath in delightful surprise. The street had not been plowed from the recent snowfall of the past few days, and there were horse-drawn sleighs taking folks for rides up and down the street. There were one-horse sleighs, two-horse sleighs, and all the houses on both sides of the street had lit candles in every window on every floor. With the beautiful, clear night, riders bundled in blankets, and the sleighs clanging with bells, it was like a scene from a Currier and Ives illustration.

"Wow! This is incredible!" she said, open-mouthed.

Eli walked her over to a single-horse sleigh, where the owner was holding the bridle of his horse and gestured for her to climb aboard.

"You arranged this for me?" she asked with a dazed smile.

"Research for your article," he replied. "With thanks to Bart, who owns the rig."

They got into the sleigh, pulled a blanket over their laps, then Bart, the owner, smiled and stepped aside as Eli took the reins. This was unusual since the other sleighs were being driven by their owners. As the horse slowly clip-clopped away, she felt self-conscious about all the other people waiting their turn for a sleigh ride, but she also loved being treated as someone special.

"So, how does this work with the people who live on the street?" she asked.

"You mean, with their cars?"

She nodded.

"They either put chains on their tires or park over on the next block," he replied. "Next weekend, weather permitting, a couple more streets will be left unplowed for sleigh rides." He looked around. "This is my favorite part of the town's Christmas season."

"I can see why," she smiled.

"You warm enough?"

"Perfect."

"Good. So, what did you mean when you said you'd been conditioned to think cops were the enemy unless they were on the payroll?"

She looked at him with an arched eyebrow.

"You really gonna do this? Interrogate me on a beautiful candle-lit street in the middle of a sleigh ride?"

"Um, yep."

She took a deep, reconciled breath. "My former boyfriend, the one I told you about, we kinda grew up together. When he was a teenager, he became involved with a large crime family in New York and never left it. I'm sure my years of mixing with the criminal element helped me to figure out what Charles and Peter were up to. Unlike Stephie Banyan, though, I can't plead ignorance. I-I knew who my boyfriend was and what he did."

Eli fell silent for several seconds while he absorbed what she shared.

"Were you—did you—" he began.

"Go on crime sprees with him? No," she answered.

"But—you're not with him now. You live in Columbus."

"Yeah, but we were together for a long time. We still would be if he hadn't dumped me. That's the kind of lousy person I am. I'm just a gangster's broad."

He thought for several more seconds, then shook his head.

"I don't buy it. Even if he hadn't dumped you, you wouldn't have stayed with him."

"You can't say that. How could you know that?"

"Because I know you. You're not a lousy person, Goldie. Maybe you stayed with him out of habit. You said it yourself, you grew up together. Maybe you were blinded by love. Maybe it was a little of both, but you *do* have a moral compass, and a good one! You had the sense to move away."

"About that," she started to say, "I didn't really have any control—"

"Plus, look at what you put a stop to in this town single-handed," he cut in. "Like you said, your past actually served you well. You sniffed out things nobody else did."

"Yeah, well... there's somethin' about this town that makes ya care, y'know? Sparkledove has been good for me."

"Then stay," he suggested.

She looked at him, surprised.

"What?"

"Stay."

"I can't do that, Eli."

"Why not? *The Wing* is going to need a new editor, it puts more distance between you and old problems, and the whole town knows and likes you."

"I can't stay."

"Why?"

"Because I have a job and a life in Columbus."

"Can you build a better life in Columbus than here? I bet not."

"I-I..." She paused, unable to answer the question because she knew nothing about Goldie Maraschino's 1942 life in Columbus, Ohio.

"Just think about it," he said. "Things happen for a reason."

The horse's hooves clopped onto the covered bridge, where volunteers had shoveled snow over the plank floor so the sleighs could continue. They passed another sleigh on the opposite side of the bridge, where the driver had stopped so passengers could look out the window at the downriver view. They slowed down to take in the upriver view, and by the time they reached the other end of the bridge and turned the horse around, the other sleigh had moved on, so they could stop next, since it was the better of the two views.

"Would you like to stop for a moment and look at the river?" he offered. "Or would it just remind you of Claude Bolton?"

"I would like to stop. It probably *will* remind me of that poor soul, but it's also a great view."

"That it is," he agreed.

They pulled up to the window and Eli called, "Whoa," as another sleigh approached on the other side of Bridge Street. Goldie looked out at the river and the beautiful night, then back toward the street. All the flickering candles in the windows on the first and second floors in the distance looked like dozens of golden fireflies.

"Thanks for arrangin' this," she smiled. "This is seriously cool!"

He reciprocated with a smile, then, in a surprise move, leaned over and kissed her. Although caught off guard, she didn't pull away. The embrace lasted about seven seconds, but in its tender warmth was the whisper of much longer implications.

After their mouths separated, Goldie squinted her green eyes and looked at the lawman, not knowing what to conclude.

"I've wanted to do that since the first moment I saw you walking around River Street without a coat," he confessed.

She cocked her head slightly, still squinting and thinking about the kiss.

He looked at her, unsure. "W-would you say something, please?" he urged.

"You used your tongue," she noted.

"Yeah. It was something I heard about in the service and wanted to try. But only with someone special. Sorry if it—"

"No. Tongue is good. I... I just..." she looked toward the approaching sleigh now coming onto the bridge. "We'd better go," she suggested.

Eli nodded, turned toward the horse, and jerked the reins.

It was mostly a quiet ride back to the end of the street. He wondered if he'd upset her, and she wondered if a subconscious attraction to Eli was a contributing factor to how she often felt bugged by him.

After what seemed like a long time, she asked, "If you've wanted to do that since I first came to town, why did you wait until I'm on the verge of leaving?"

"On your first day, the afternoon you sat down at my table in the hotel restaurant, you told me your boyfriend had cheated on you for several months, and you'd just found out about it the day before."

She thought for a moment, recalling.

"It makes more sense to me now because he was in New York, you live in Columbus, and are frequently on assignment," he explained. "But the wound was brand new, and there are rules about that. A gentleman doesn't play on a young woman's emotions when she's hurting. I wouldn't have kissed you now, except we're out of time and I was gonna bust if you didn't know how I felt."

She compared his answer with things that Peter said and did, and began to look at Eli in an entirely new light.

Thirty

CHOICES

Fifty-five minutes later, the Tour of Homes was long over, the stores were closed, and most of the street vendors were either gone or packing up their trailers. Only a few people still lingered on River Street while the local Boy Scout troop patrolled the streets to pick up litter. The two hired off-duty state policemen were taking down barricades, Eli was driving an inebriated city council member home, and Goldie was slowly strolling back to her hotel from the post office and community Christmas tree, thinking about the kiss Eli had given her in the sleigh.

As she was approaching the Sparkledove Arms, she saw Stu Frey putting his Santa costume in the back of his truck parked on the street in front of the hotel. It had two swing-open back doors, no side windows, and he used the vehicle for his meat deliveries.

"Ay, Stu," she greeted. "How ya doin'?"

"Hi, Goldie," he greeted, now wearing his bib overalls and coat with the wool collar.

"You made a great Santa tonight," she complimented. "I watched you with the kids. You really made 'em believers."

"Nice of you to say," he said, closing one of the back doors, then the other. "Maddie and Dean let me change clothes in their office behind the registration counter. Congratulations, by the way, on the big story you broke about the Banyans. Everybody's talking about it."

"I'm glad it didn't hurt tonight's festivities."

"Aw, Sparkledove doesn't rise and fall on the actions of a couple of bad apples. It's all the good apples that matter."

"I guess so," she agreed.

"So, will you be heading off to Columbus soon? Or would you rather go back to your own time in New York City?"

She looked at him as her eyes widened and jaw dropped.

"W-what did you say?"

"I said, are you going to head off to Columbus soon? Or would you rather go back to your own time in New York City?"

She looked at his scruffy white hair, barrel chest, white beard and swallowed hard.

"If you tell me you're the real Santa Claus, I am gonna totally lose it."

He smiled. "No. Not quite. But I *do* know who you are and where you really came from."

She looked at him with a dazed expression while he put his calloused hands inside the pockets of his winter coat and nodded in the direction she'd just come. "C'mon. Let's walk a little."

They turned and started to head back down River Street. She went along because he clearly possessed answers she wanted.

After several silent seconds, she asked, "Who are you? I mean, *really?*"

"To the townspeople of Sparkledove, I'm Stu Frey, rancher and supplier of meat. To you, I'm an angel who can answer some of your questions."

"An angel?"

"You were asking Father Fitzsimmons whether or not they were real in Clara's Gifts, remember?" he reminded. He held out an arm. "Want to pinch me to see if I'm real?"

"I believe you," she said, acceptingly. "There have been so many other weird things that have happened to me in this town, why not go walkin' with an angel who has a ranch and plays Santa Claus?" She looked at him, suddenly concerned. "Is this place real? Am I dead?"

"I assure you, this place is very real, and no, you're not dead. You're in Sparkledove, Colorado, on December 11th, 1942. But you're also in a coma back in twenty-first-century New York City, and have been for seventeen days."

"A coma," she realized. "I *thought* I could've been

in a coma! I mean, I considered it days ago. B-but, why here? Why now? How can I be in two places at once?"

"Where do you think people go when they die, Goldie?" he asked.

"I-I guess they go to heaven... or, or hell. I mean, if they go anywhere at all."

"Oh, they go somewhere. God said they would. For some, it's pretty clear. It's either paradise or eternal damnation. Then, there are people like you. Souls on the bubble. Staying with Markie Santina for so long was a bad choice. You enabled him. Supported him in everything from suggesting he buy a second condo in your building to hide things, to double-checking his books. Pretty damning stuff, Goldie. But then, you go to Vegas to help a grieving aunt. Or anonymously assist a burdened mother at an airport. Or you fight bigotry and preserve a man's dignity in a bus terminal. You even helped a young couple become more aware of unprejudiced bias. Nobody is ever totally good or evil. Still, the measure of a person's deeds usually points one way or another. But not you, Goldie. You're fifty-fifty. So, you were sent here."

"To 1942?"

"To purgatory, and a set of problems."

"W-wait a minute," she said, pausing. "Are you tellin' me—I'm in purgatory?"

"Where do you think purgatory is, Goldie?" Stu asked. "Some middle plane of existence between heaven and hell?"

"I-eh-I dunno."

"It could be anywhere... Detroit, Michigan, in 1954. Casablanca, Morocco, in 1870. Paris, France, in 1899. Or, Sparkledove, Colorado in 1942."

They started walking again and were silent for several moments while Goldie thought about what she'd heard.

"So, purgatory is different places on Earth at different times?"

"I didn't say that. I said purgatory could be anywhere. But it just so happens yours is in Sparkledove. And it also just so happens that this is my territory."

"You mean, like, you're a guardian angel?"

"I mean, like, this happens to be my territory."

She sighed a little, feeling overwhelmed. "I need a drink."

"I wouldn't mind one, myself," he agreed. "But it's cold, and that place is closer." He pointed down a cross street to St. Mark's.

"Uh, it's pretty late," she said. "I don't think the church will be open."

"Oh, it will be for me," he assured.

He started walking down the side street toward the church with Goldie a few steps behind.

"Yeah," she agreed. "For you, *sure*. I mean, since you're... unbelievable!" she muttered.

Stu came to the front doors of the church, tried them, and they were unlocked. He went inside with Goldie following. The place was moody and filled with flickering shadows from a half dozen lit votive candles as well as the red sanctuary candle. They walked about halfway down to the altar, then Stu genuflected and entered a pew. He pulled down the kneeler, got on his knees, made the sign of the cross, and said a prayer in silence. Taking his lead, Goldie did the same thing and silently said an "Our Father," one of the few prayers she remembered from her Catholic upbringing.

"Purgatory can be for the living or the dead," Stu finally said quietly, still on his knees. "Where or when depends upon the soul involved. You were dropped into a place and a set of circumstances that you either had to accept or not. You were given clues to problems that you could choose to see or not. Then, once you saw those problems, you could either try to solve them or not."

"Choices," she realized.

"Choices," Stu confirmed. "They define you. You made contradictory choices in your life in New York. You've made consistently good ones here, and they weren't easy ones to make."

"Spendin' the night with Peter Banyan was *not* a good choice," she admitted.

"But that's how you found out he was working with his father," Stu reminded.

She thought for a long moment, and the angel let her take all the time she needed.

"So, if I did good. Made smart choices. What happens now?"

"I've already clued you in on that. You can stay in 1942 and make a life for yourself, or you can wake up in a New York City hospital bed and go back to your life there."

"I'm not gonna die?"

"Sure you are. Just not today. But either way, Goldie, there are challenges. Back in New York, Markie still intends to marry Kristen DiVarno, you will still be estranged from your sister, and you will struggle to build a new life. Here, you've got no family, there will be hundreds of things you'll have to learn, and hundreds of modern conveniences you'll lose."

"I've got no family here?" she asked.

Stu shook his head. "The Goldie Maraschino of 1942 is, like you, from New York City, but she has no family. She was raised in an orphanage in the Bronx until she was fourteen and then adopted by a couple who happened to be college professors. They wanted to adopt because they, themselves, were orphans. They wanted an older child because they were middle-aged and didn't have the temperaments for an infant. They also understood that, at fourteen, Goldie's chances of finding a forever home were very slim. A year later, her parents took new teaching jobs at Marietta College in Ohio. That's how they wound up in the Buckeye state. The father died of a heart attack when Goldie was nineteen, and the mother died a year later from pneumonia. But by that time, her education was nearly complete and her penchant for writing well established. She worked for a newspaper for a couple of years, then moved to Columbus, where Owen

Mitchell hired her. If you stay, that's who you are, and I'll tell you more.

"If I stay, what happens to this other version of Goldie? Her being? Her soul?"

"A soul has incalculable value," Stu smiled. "The bible says so many times, and God loves his creations. But souls don't always remain in a body for a full, long life. If you stay, the Goldie of 1942 will be well taken care of, and you'll take her place. That's all you need to know. If you go back to New York, then your accomplishments here become her accomplishments. But if you go back, the good you've done here doesn't mean an automatic free pass to paradise. You've still got to make smart choices."

She got off her knees and sank back into the pew, thinking, then shook her head. "This soul swappin' stuff is a total mind fuuu—*twist,* she corrected, considering they were in church.

"'Soul swapping'" isn't exactly the right term," Stu noted, getting off his knees and likewise sitting. "But I understand why you'd assume that. Just remember what Father Fitz said to you in Clara's about God's wisdom being different than man's."

"First Corinthians," she recalled.

"Very good," he smiled.

"If I go back, will I remember what happened here?"

"Of course you will. You don't learn anything from all this if you don't."

"A-and if I choose to stay? Will I remember my life in New York?"

"Again, yes. That's part of the lesson. But you won't be allowed to use your knowledge of the future for personal gain. No betting on the World Series where you know who wins. Or buying stocks that you know will take off. Oh, you could try. But I'd know and it wouldn't work out."

She glanced around with a furrowed brow until her eyes fell upon the confessionals.

"Wouldn't it have been easier to just give me a clean slate in confession or somethin'?"

"Would you have learned anything?" he asked.

Her shoulders slumped. "P-probably not."

He looked her over.

"You okay?"

"I-I don't know."

"Any gut reaction to staying or going?"

"I don't know," she repeated.

He smiled a little. "If it helps, you're not the first to be in this situation."

"What do ya mean?"

"Others have shown up unexpectedly in Sparkledove before."

She paused for a moment, then her eyes widened with realization.

"Claude Bolton! And the woman in the white nightgown!"

"Her name was Agnes Dundee," Stu nodded. "Like you, both Claude and Agnes were souls on the bubble. Both were given the opportunity to make choices and redeem themselves through different circumstances. Both might've been given choices to stay or go as well, but neither could cope with being displaced."

"So they killed themselves," Goldie concluded.

"Purgatory isn't easy, Goldie," Stu affirmed.

"And God just keeps them trapped here?" she asked, annoyed at the unfairness of the notion. "So, they can kill themselves day after day? Year after year?"

"No. They're not caught in some continuous loop," Stu corrected. "They chose to reveal themselves to you the only way they could. But there are limitations to what they could do. By showing you what happened to them, they made you curious for answers. They were telling you to keep going. Not to give up. And see? You didn't."

She thought for a moment. "So, where are Claude and Agnes now?"

"Going home."

"What do ya mean?"

"I mean, they helped you, you prayed for them, and they're going home."

"I never prayed for—" she began to say. But then stopped and remembered what she said the second time she saw Agnes, the same morning she was chased by the mountain lion: "God, why don't you help these poor souls?"

"Go look outside," Stu suggested.

Skeptically, she rose and went to the front door of the church. Stepping outside, she looked around, saw nothing unusual, then glanced toward the clear sky. When she did, she saw two bright shooting stars, one right after the other. But they weren't falling to earth. They were going upwards toward heaven.

Smiling a little, she turned back toward the church, and her eyes lingered for a moment at the snow-covered nativity scene in the front yard that was illuminated by a floodlight. After a few seconds, Stu walked out the front door.

"Whether you realize it or not," he said, "you showed Claude and Agnes great empathy, and God answered that. Now, they're in paradise."

She nodded appreciatively. "Good! Thank you."

"Don't thank me," he replied, pointing upward. "Thank Him."

She looked up, said, "Thank you" sincerely. Then she looked at Stu and changed subjects. "Eli kissed me tonight."

He cracked a small, knowing smile. "I'm not surprised. He's liked you for a while."

They both fell silent for several more seconds. Goldie didn't know what else to say, so the angel offered one more suggestion.

"Why don't you go see Clara tomorrow?"

"Clara? Why?"

"Ask her about her life here since she decided to stay."

"You mean, sh-she's from another time too?"

"Go talk to Clara. Maybe she can help you decide.

He looked around. "I gotta get home. I have deliveries to make bright and early."

They started walking back toward the hotel and his truck.

"Stu, I'm sorry to repeat what you said, but I'm still tryin' to wrap my head around it, you're a rancher who sells meat *and* an angel?"

"Yeah, but only you and Clara know about the angel thing."

"And you're here every day?"

"Not every day. My ranch is out of town a ways. But, like I said, this is my territory, so I'm around a lot."

"H-how big is your territory? Did you have another life before you—"

"Let's stick to the immediate choice before you, eh?" he interrupted. "Where would *you* like to go? I'll give you tomorrow to decide. All right?"

"Yeah... okay."

They walked in silence until they were almost all the way back to his truck.

"Hey, Stu?" she asked.

"Yeah?"

"Just one more question: Are *you* okay? I mean, are you happy doin' what you're doin'?"

He looked at her and smiled warmly.

"A human asking an angel if they're okay. It's that kind of concern for others that tells me no matter what choice you make, you're probably going to do well—Goldie Maraschino, like the cherry."

Thirty-One

THE REST WILL TAKE CARE OF ITSELF

Not surprisingly, Goldie hardly slept that night. Although all of her questions had been answered about why she'd awakened in Sparkledove, Colorado, in 1942, she now had to absorb an entirely new set of facts. The biggest being that God was real. Angels were real. The afterlife was real. There was no question about it. Like billions of others, she had always drifted back and forth about God, most times believing, but sometimes doubting. Now, she had to stare it straight in the face. There would be judgment. Choices had consequences. Then, there was the choice before her: where was she going to live out the remainder of her life? She felt special yet humbled all at once. She suspected hers was a choice few others got to make.

The following morning, Saturday, December 10th, she was waiting on the plank sidewalk for Clara to open her store. At 9:55 a.m., Clara walked out of

Miller's, where she sometimes went to grab some coffee and catch up on the latest gossip with Deke and Chad Miller. Seeing Goldie waiting for her, she flashed a big smile and crossed River Street.

"There she is," Clara announced. "The talk of the town. How are you, honey?"

Goldie waited until she was closer before answering so nobody else would hear.

"I know you're not from this time, Clara," she began. "I also know Stu Frey's an angel."

The older woman paused briefly, surprised, but then recovered and smiled. "Say, you *are* a good investigator, aren't you?" She dipped a hand into her overcoat pocket. "You'd best come inside. I think I'm going to open a little late this morning."

She unlocked her front door and stepped inside, the wooden floor squeaking as she did. But she didn't turn around the sign hanging on the door's glass from "Closed" to "Open." Once Goldie was inside, she locked the door again, took off her winter coat, and carried it to the back room.

"I always thought you might've been a displaced soul," she said as she went. "Right from your first day in town. But, to his credit, Stu never gave you up."

"He wanted me to talk to you," Goldie shared.

"Stu?"

"Yeah."

"About what?"

"He gave me a choice to either stay here or go back to my own time."

"And what time is that?"

"New York City in the 2020s."

Clara nodded, hung up her coat in the back, then returned to the front of the store.

"The 2020s," she mused, shaking her head as if she hardly believed it, but she did.

"He said that others before me have been given the option to stay or go," Goldie continued. "Then he said I should talk to you. My challenge was the Banyans. What was *your* challenge?"

The mostly white-haired woman who always wore slacks started to move around the store, plugging in Christmas lights for various displays.

"I didn't wake up in Sparkledove like you. I moved here later. I woke up in Aurora, Colorado. It's on the other side of Denver, about sixty miles away." She plugged in some lights, then moved to another display. "Like Stu no doubt said to you, *my* good versus bad choices were very much fifty-fifty. I was only twenty-three at the time, but even then, my choices toward the light and dark were pretty contradictory. Maybe I'll tell you about 'em sometime. But what you asked is: What was my challenge? I discovered and foiled a bank robbery that also involved the kidnapping of three small kids. That was over forty years ago."

Goldie did some quick calculating in her head while Clara continued to plug in lights.

"So, you woke up in Aurora in the late 1890s?"

"1900 to be exact."

"And you decided to stay?"

"Yes."

"Did you replace another version of yourself in Aurora?"

"No. Stu's told me a little about how that can happen, but it's different for different people."

"Where did you live before you woke up in Aurora?"

"Stevens Point, Wisconsin," she answered, plugging in more lights. "I was in a car accident with a girlfriend. We were both pretty baked at the time and were driving back from a movie theater where we'd just seen *Saturday Night Fever*. That was in 1977. Is John Travolta still a big heartthrob?"

"Yeah, if you've got a pacemaker."

"Oh," she realized, "I guess he *would* be a lot older. You, uh, you want some coffee? Mine's not as good as across the street, but not half bad."

"No. I'm good. Thanks."

Clara looked at her and chuckled. "I can't tell you how strange it is to say 'John Travolta' out loud and have someone *know* who I'm talking about." She went over to the radio and turned it on. "Stu wasn't the angel in these parts back then. It was a woman named Ruth, but yes, I stayed. The Clara Dawson I left in Stevens Point, Wisconsin, never came out of her coma."

"Why'd you stay?"

"Oh," the senior one sighed, "lots of reasons. I wanted to remove myself from certain people and temptations, and I fell in love with someone here. Matter of fact, we're still together."

"Really?" Goldie asked. "Who is he?"

"*She* teaches music over in Golden."

Goldie nodded. "D-does she know where you really—"

"Oh, no," Clara interrupted. "That's against the rules. If you wind up staying, you'll get to know all about the rules. Like, if you tell people certain things about the future, it won't register in their minds. The origins of what they hear get fuzzy. For instance, I can recite song lyrics from my youth to people and they'll remember the lyrics, but not where they came from."

The tubes in the radio warmed up just as Kay Starr was singing.

"*You,*" Goldie realized. "You're the one responsible for me hearing lyrics from groups like The Jackson 5, the Bee Gees, and the Beatles."

Clara smiled. "It's my little way of messin' with the universe and keeping Stu on his toes. As you might imagine, it was difficult for a young woman to go from listening to Linda Ronstadt to Kate Smith. By the way, did the Beatles ever get back together?"

"Uh, no."

"Not even for one concert?"

"I, eh, I don't know what I'm allowed to say and not say about the future."

"Okay, honey. Don't sweat it... if you stay, I'm sure Stu will give us some guidelines. For now, just talking to someone like you is Christmas present enough."

The two women looked at one another for a

moment, then Clara walked over to the visitor and took her hand.

"You did good, Goldie. Believe me, I *know* what you went through. I tried to reassure you as best I could. But every soul has to find their own way."

"I understand," Goldie said.

Clara patted her hand, then went over and flipped the "Closed" sign to "Open" and unlocked her front door.

"Once you made your decision to stay," Goldie asked. "Was it hard?"

"Of course it was. Damn hard! No matter how much time you have to mentally prepare, you don't fully appreciate all the things you're giving up. Not just people, music, and familiar surroundings, but things that won't be invented for decades. I'd kill for my toaster oven, or my Princess Phone, or my cassette tapes. So, yeah, it's hard. On the other hand, because you know what you know, you're privy to some wonderful secrets and can help people in ways you never thought possible. You can warn a friend about the effects of smoking. Or teach people to be less wasteful and find new uses for things. Or talk someone out of investing their life savings into an idea that you know isn't going anywhere. Even educate folks about gay rights. Most importantly, though, in the darkest days of this war, you can give others hope and encouragement because you *know* we're going to come out of it on the other side. It's not being smarter than others, Goldie. It's just using what you know to make a positive difference."

"So, you don't regret your decision to stay then?"

"It was the right choice for me. It may or may not be the right choice for you."

Just then, a customer walked into the store.

"So, what're you going to do?" Clara asked.

"I don't know... but thanks for your insights."

After she left Clara's Gifts, Goldie tracked down Father Fitzsimmons and acquired the photography negatives she needed for her article. Then she returned to her hotel and spent several hours writing two drafts of a three-thousand-word article entitled, Sparkledove: A Small Town With A Big Christmas Heart." It was a homey and positive profile about a town that valued its heritage and offered lots of holiday activities from yesteryear, but welcomed guests with all the modern amenities anyone would need. She didn't write about Charles and Peter Banyan but focused on several other townspeople instead; from Maddie and Dean, to Eli, Clara, Deke and Chad, and even Saul and Paul McCaw, who she described as "generous and charming, but diamond tough, as mountain men of the Rockies should be."

It was close to 6:00 p.m. by the time Goldie took her article and negatives down to the lobby. Dean, working behind the counter, had an envelope to accommodate her materials, and Goldie addressed everything to Owen Mitchell using the address on one of her business cards. Dean promised to mail everything off for her, then Goldie thanked him sincerely for all of his and Maddie's hospitality. She had no sooner turned toward the restaurant across the busy lobby when Eli came through the front doors. Slipping off some gloves, he smiled and limped over to her.

"Howdy," he greeted.

"Howdy, Sheriff," she responded warmly.

"Uh, haven't seen you today."

"I was holed up in my hotel room for most of the day writin' my article. I just gave it to Dean to mail off to my boss."

Eli looked over at the counter where Dean was. "Does that mean maybe you've decided to stay a little longer? I mean, you could just return to Columbus and write your article there. But if you're mailing it in, then that could mean—"

"It means I've got another assignment," Goldie lied. "I-I'll be leaving first thing in the morning."

"Oh," he said, clearly disappointed. "I thought maybe you'd stay for the entire Tour of Homes weekend."

"Me too, b-but this new assignment popped up kinda fast."

Eli nodded and thought for a moment.

"So," he said, self-deprecatingly, "the kiss was that bad, huh?"

She glanced around the lobby. Like the evening before, the town was buzzing with tourists. Wanting a little privacy, she took him by the arm and walked him past the Christmas tree and over to a corner near the phone booth.

"The kiss was wonderful," she said quietly. "You know it was. But I've got another quick assignment and then I've gotta go home for the holidays. I'm not sayin' goodbye. It's more like, a 'See ya later.'"

That wasn't true. She was saying goodbye. But she also wanted to spare his feelings. Perhaps she should've been more honest, but with the lights from the nearby Christmas tree glowing, people smiling, and the radio behind the counter playing "Winter Wonderland," acknowledging that she'd never see him again seemed too hard and final.

Eli's blue eyes examined hers skeptically for a moment, then his face softened. "Look, if 'See ya later,' should turn into we never see each other again, I just want to say I really liked knowing you. You drove me a little crazy sometimes, but it was a good crazy."

"Thanks," she smiled sincerely.

"There you are," they heard a voice say. Both turned around to see Stu Frey in his winter coat with the wool collar. He was carrying a large cardboard box.

"Howdy, Stu," Eli greeted.

"Hi, Stu," Goldie said more timidly.

"Goldie agreed to help me get ready for my appearance as you-know-who," he said to the lawman. "Got the costume here, and Maddie and Dean let me change in their office behind the counter, but the boots are a little tight. You've got to practically bulldoze 'em onto my feet."

"You want a police escort to walk you down to your throne, Santa?" Eli asked.

"Yeah, that'd be great. Go get yourself a cup of coffee in the restaurant, and we'll be out in a few."

He looked at Goldie. "See you later?"

"See you later," she agreed.

A little smile flickered on Eli's face, then he turned and headed toward the restaurant. Goldie watched him go, then followed Stu around the counter and into the back.

"Help with your boots?" she asked quietly.

"Well, I needed to talk to you privately *somehow*, right?"

"Sure," she said.

They greeted Dean, who was working the counter, then went behind it and into a short hallway where there was a supply room, the hotel office, and a half bath. They went into the office, and Stu shut the door.

"So," he said, setting his box down and slipping off his coat, I heard what you said to Eli. I take it you've decided to stay?"

"No," she corrected. "I'm gonna go back."

He nodded slightly, then paused. "You realize you're going back to an injured body. It's going to hurt for a while."

"Staying here will hurt more. I'll miss my mom too much, and my sister, even though she hates me. I'll miss all the conveniences, the access to information. I never finished high school, Stu. Everything I know I've learned through the internet. You take that and social media away from me, and I'm just a dumb chick. I mean, dumber than I already am."

"You're not dumb, Goldie," he assured.

"I'm too much a fish outta water here. The water may be polluted back in New York. But at least I know how to swim in it."

"You sure?" he asked. "This is a one-way trip."

Goldie thought for a moment with moist eyes, but then nodded.

"Yeah. I'm sure. But I'm grateful, Stu. I'm truly, truly grateful and honored to have been given the choice. I'm amazed how generous the Lord's been with me."

"On His behalf, you're very welcome."

"I, uh, I *did* write my article. I put it in a package with some photo negatives and addressed it to my publisher. Dean is mailing it for me."

"Very good. I'm glad you're leaving with that buttoned up."

"Right... so, uh, what should I do now?"

He looked toward the restaurant as if he had X-ray vision and could see through the walls. "Eli's still in the restaurant. Hurry through the lobby and go up to your room. Then just hop in bed and go to sleep."

"Eh, it's kinda early."

"Oh, you'll go to sleep. I promise."

"Well, can't I, like, say goodbye to people?"

"You did what you came to do, Goldie. You won't be forgotten. People will carry your actions in their hearts whether you say goodbye or not. Considering the false hope you just gave to Eli, I think it's best if you just go upstairs and sleep."

"But, what about me packing, and checking out, and, and—"

"Are you going to stay?" he asked pointedly.

"Well—no—but—"

"Then the rest will take care of itself," he smiled with finality.

She paused, then remembered she was talking to a celestial being, no doubt capable of handling all remaining details.

"Yeah. Okay... thank you, Stu. For everything."

She turned and exited the office.

Coming out of the back hallway to behind the counter, she smiled at Dean, who was waiting on a customer, and said hi to Josie in the lobby, who was dressed in her elf costume and emptying a can ashtray next to the phone booth. Pausing and taking time to look around the decorated lobby of the Sparkledove Arms one last time, Goldie smiled affectionately, then slowly turned and went up the stairs that led to room number 9.

Thirty-Two

BACK IN NEW YORK

When Goldie's green eyes slowly flickered open in a private room at St. Vincent's Catholic Medical Center on West 12th near Greenwich Village in New York City, the first thing she noticed was that her entire body seemed to hurt. Then, she saw all the flowers and plants that had been sent. A half-dozen offerings were sitting around her beige room. Next, she noticed a cast on her right arm. Finally, she realized she was alone. In fact, she was awake and by herself for a good five minutes before she saw the nurse's call button on the side of her bed and decided to use it.

Within a minute of pressing the button, a man with a nice smile and green surgical scrubs came into her room.

"Welcome back," he greeted. "I'm Doctor Mark Zawicki, and you're at St. Vincent's on West 12th. Can you tell me your name?"

"Goldie—Karen Maraschino."

"Good. How're you feeling?"

"E-everything hurts," she moaned.

"I'm not surprised. You were doing a *Sleeping Beauty* routine for quite a while. But the good news is now that you're awake, I'm optimistic about a full recovery. You're an incredibly lucky young woman. Do you remember what happened?"

"I-I was crossing Mercer Street... it was snowing, I think."

"You were sideswiped by a passing car," the doctor said, taking her chart out of a plastic holder on the wall next to her bed. "It spun you around like a top, and you banged your head on the street pretty hard when you fell, which caused your brain to swell and the resulting coma."

He referred to her chart. "You've been out for eighteen days. You have a couple of lacerations on your face and a hairline fracture on your right arm, but you're healing nicely. You also had surgery to stop some internal bleeding. The procedure is called a thoracotomy. I made a small incision along your left ribcage to get at the bleeding, but everything went well, and in another year, you'll hardly notice the scar. The rest of your body is basically one big bruise, so hurting means you're healing. As I said, you were very, very lucky."

"I'm back," Goldie mused, looking toward the window but not really seeing anything except the rooftop of another building.

"Yes, you are," the doctor said, not aware of her total meaning. "You're hooked up like the *Bride of Frankenstein*. You've got a catheter, we've been feeding you through a tube, and you've got a saline drip going. We'll start to get you unplugged in a little while. But first, would you like some water? Ginger ale, maybe?"

"Ginger ale would be great."

"I'll have one of the nurses bring you some. And we'll notify your family and friends that you're awake."

"M—my friends?"

"Markie Santina and entourage. He wanted to be notified as soon as you woke up and handed out hundred-dollar bills to the nursing staff like Hershey bars to make sure that happened. He's also paying for all your expenses, considering you have no health insurance."

"So—that ginger ale is gonna cost about thirty bucks, huh?" Goldie joked.

Doctor Zawicki smiled. "Markie Santina, he's kind of a mobster, isn't he?"

"Where'd you get that idea?"

The physician shrugged. "*The Daily News, The Times, The Post,* the chief of hospital security, and my uncle, the cop."

"Don't believe everything you hear, Doc,"

The doctor looked at her with a half-smile of disbelief.

"Fake news, huh? Okay... you rest up. I'll see what I can do about that ginger ale."

Within an hour of waking up, Goldie had some

ginger ale and Jell-O, her catheter, feeding, and saline tubes were removed, and she'd been walked to the bathroom, where she discovered she had blonde hair on her head again. There were also some large scabs on her forehead and left cheek. As Stu Frey had promised, she remembered everything that had happened in 1942, but she was glad to be back in modern times and familiar surroundings. She'd awakened at 8:33 a.m. on December 12th, a Thursday. By 9:40, Markie Santina came into her room, accompanied by two bodyguards who waited outside the door. One of whom was Bruno Carmichael, whom she had last seen in the lobby of the condominium she had shared with Markie.

Markie breezed in wearing an expensive black leather waistcoat reminiscent of Tully's, a red silk scarf, and an olive turtleneck with black slacks. He also carried a dozen pink roses in a vase and had that Richard Gere smile that she traditionally found irresistible.

"There she is!" he greeted warmly with his thick Bronx accent. "How ya doin', baby? You scared the bejesus outta me, you know that?"

"Ay, how ya doin', Markie?" she reciprocated weakly, eying the roses. "Those for me?"

"And those, and those, and those," he replied, pointing out other flowers and plants in the room. "I mean it, Goldie. I was scared sick. But don't worry 'bout nothin'. I'm taking care of all expenses. Everythin'. You just concentrate on gettin' better."

He set the roses down on the windowsill, then

went over to the side of her bed, leaned over, and gently kissed her. She accepted the embrace, but was confused by it.

"So—what does all this mean?" she asked after the kiss. "The flowers, the private room... did you and The Queen of Frump from NYU have a fallin' out?"

"We spent seven years together, Goldie. I promised I'd take care of you, and I'm still doin' it. I also feel terrible about the way we left things the day you ran out. I feel partially responsible for what happened."

"Oh, don't feel that way, baby," she chided. "Feel *entirely* responsible."

"I *am* sorry, Goldie. Really and truly sorry."

She looked into his brown eyes and gave him the benefit of the doubt.

"Okay... thanks for keepin' watch over me while I was out of it."

"Sure. I called your mom and sister, and that plant over there is from Tom."

"My dad?"

"Yeah. He was here for a couple of days, but then had to get back to work in Pittsburgh. But I'm sure he'll be callin'. Everybody's been real worried."

She nodded. "I'll be sure to call him later. I, uh, I want you to know, Markie, that although I hate what you've done, I also think you're tryin' to make up for it in your own way. So, I ain't gonna be a problem. I'm gonna take your exit package and—well—exit."

"That's my girl," Markie smiled. "I knew you'd come around to seein' the smart way of doin' things."

He clasped his hands together. "Well, alright then, I'm gonna make sure your new apartment is all clean and ready for ya. I'll put all your favorite food and drinks in the kitchen and make sure your cable and the utilities are hooked up. Eh, the doctor give you any idea when you can get outta here?"

"No. We haven't gotten that far yet."

"Well, don't worry about it. I'm gonna take care of everythin'."

A wave of old affection came over Goldie. Or maybe it was just gratitude.

"Hey, Markie, y-you really gonna marry Kristen DiVarno?"

"Yeah... it's gonna be good for my standin' in the family... but you've made me very happy, Goldie. And who knows what might happen between us in the future, eh?"

She cocked her head at her former boyfriend quizzically. "What does *that* mean?"

"What?"

"Are you sayin' you're gonna marry Kristen, but you wanna keep me on the side? I thought you said she was the 'whole package.'"

"I'm just sayin' after your accident and everythin', the thought of you not bein' in my life was very upsettin'. *Really* upsettin'! As for the future, it's— y'know—unwritten."

"Yyyeah," she drawled, "I ain't gonna be no back-door babe like in a Stones' song."

"One thing at a time," he encouraged. "Now that

you're goin' to take the apartment, the car, and the bank account, maybe there's somethin' you can do for me."

"I'm in the hospital because you broke my heart. But, by all means, Markie, what can I do for *you*?"

"It's nothin' really," he understated. "A token of goodwill."

"What?"

"Your diaries. When the boys were packin' up your stuff, we couldn't find 'em."

"What do ya want with my diaries?"

"Ay, Goldie, c'mon now... we were together a long time. Who knows what you've written down in 'em."

"There's nothin' incriminatin' in my diaries. They're just full of girl stuff. Notes about clothes I bought. Movies we went to. Restaurants we ate at. Anniversaries, some of which you forgot."

"Then it won't be a big deal to let me look through 'em, huh?"

"It will be if you read about how many times I faked orgasms."

He looked at her, surprised.

"Not all the time," she qualified. "Not even most times."

"I gotta check out the diaries, Goldie. It's just a precaution."

"Yeah, I think I'm gonna keep their location private," she decided. "It's just a precaution."

He furrowed his brow disapprovingly. "I'm not likin' what I'm hearin' here."

"Markie, I loved you, and I'd never do anything to hurt you. My diaries are my private thoughts. But if their existence bothers you, good. Consider them an insurance policy that says you're gonna leave me and my family in peace. They're not at my mom's, or my sister's, or my dad's. They're in the same place where I keep the first corsage you bought me, the charm bracelet my dad got me, and the key to the hotel suite from our first trip to Mexico. They're with my personal, private treasures. And that's what they are, private!"

He looked at her for a moment as if he might understand, but then had to switch gears as Goldie's mother, Carla, arrived. She was forty-seven, was once a looker like Goldie, but had been worn down by a lack of education that never went beyond two semesters of junior college, a failed marriage, and a series of jobs that never paid more than thirty thousand dollars a year. She was a gigantic contradiction about her daughter's relationship with Markie. On the one hand, she knew he was involved in criminal activities. She didn't know specifics, but she knew they were bad, and this went against her Catholicism and sense of right and wrong. On the other hand, she liked that Goldie lived in a seven-figure condo, wore fine clothing and jewelry, and had been able to enjoy a more comfortable lifestyle than she'd ever had. So, she treated Markie respectfully. Like a mother-in-law who didn't approve of her son-in-law, but acknowledged that he made her daughter happy.

Markie and Carla chatted pleasantly for a few minutes, mostly about how relieved they were that Goldie was awake, then he excused himself so mother and daughter could catch up. He promised to visit Goldie again soon, but in the meantime, told her not to worry about anything for a third time. Once he and his two bodyguards were gone, Goldie briefly told her mother that she and Markie were on the outs, then apologized, saying she had to rest, which she did. She fell asleep, and Carla stayed in her room for the next several hours. She also spoke to Doctor Zawicki about Goldie beginning a physical therapy regimen to get her muscles back in good working order.

Thirty-Three

DECISION

On Monday, December 16th, Goldie was downstairs in the physical therapy department of St. Vincent's and walking briskly on a motorized treadmill. She wasn't quite up to jogging yet, but she'd been eating regular food for a couple of days, the scabs on her face were getting smaller, and her physical strength was improving. She was still going to have to wear a cast on her arm for four more weeks, but Dr. Zawicki had said he would probably release her that afternoon. Markie had come for a second visit on Saturday and brought her purse, cell phone, and the address and keys to her new apartment. He also gave her five hundred dollars for walking around money because he had canceled her credit cards since they were no longer together. But he reminded her that she also had a new bank account with fifty thousand dollars in it. During the visit, he asked again for her diaries, and she replied she'd think about handing them over once she was settled into her new place. He didn't particularly like being put off, but Goldie knew how to handle her former boyfriend with just the right combination of humor, sass, and ego gratification. He reluctantly agreed to postpone the subject, or so she thought.

She was in sweat clothes her mother had brought her, looking down at the step counter on the treadmill, when she heard a familiar voice behind her.

"Are you outta your damn mind?"

Still walking, she turned around to see her sister, Ellen, standing behind her a few feet away with her winter overcoat open and her hands impatiently on her hips. She was twenty-eight, three years older than Goldie, lived in Upper Montclair, New Jersey, and was married to a nice guy named Levi who managed a Verizon store. She worked part-time as a receptionist and had two kids: a three-year-old named Austin and a six-year-old named Trevor. She was good-looking like her sister, but with brown hair and a little heavier. She was also even more quick-tempered than Goldie.

"Ay, sis, nice to see you, too," the younger replied, a little sarcastically.

"Are you outta your damn mind?" Ellen repeated.

"Can you talk a little louder? I don't think the therapists and patients over in the corner heard you."

Goldie switched off the treadmill, then turned and stepped off the machine to face her sibling.

"*What?*"

"When I dropped Trevor off at school today, you know who was there? Bruno Carmichael!"

She was referring to the thick-necked, large-chested enforcer who worked for Markie.

"What was Bruno doin' at Trevor's school?"

"That's what *I* asked," Ellen replied. "He said he was payin' me a courtesy visit since we went to school together. He said that you and Markie are history, Markie's gonna marry some bimbo from Chicago, and that he set ya up in a nice apartment as part of a consolation prize. But he *also* said you've been keepin' diaries while you two were together, and Markie wants 'em. All of 'em!"

She looked at Goldie with open hands, perplexed. "You been keepin' diaries?"

"Yeah."

"What are you? Twelve?"

"Hey, Lady Gaga keeps a diary. So did the Queen of England."

"But they didn't live with Sonny Corleone! You're endangering my family."

"Did Bruno threaten you?" Goldie asked.

"Not exactly. He said it was a courtesy call. But he showed up at my kid's school."

"Markie isn't gonna do anything against you, or your kids, or Mom, or Dad. The family doesn't operate that way. I mean, they *do,* but not with people who aren't in the business." She shook her head. "Never in a million years did I think those diaries would be a stickin' point with me and Markie."

"Why did you even write them?" Ellen asked.

"Well, at first, it was because I *was* twelve. Then, it became a habit. Later, I started to like writing. After that, I didn't want to forget things, and some of the stuff I wrote down even helped Markie. Kinda like a stenographer."

"Is there incriminatin' stuff in them?"

Goldie grimaced as if embarrassed. "Wellll…"

"Jesus, Goldie!"

"Look, I know Markie Santina better than anyone, and I'm tellin' ya, your family is *not* in danger."

"Give him the diaries," Ellen ordered.

"You know he was unfaithful to me for eight months."

"Guess you didn't know him as well as you thought," the older one retorted. "Give him the diaries."

"I dedicated my life to that man."

"Give him the diaries!"

"I was in a coma for eighteen days because of his screwin' around."

"Goldie—"

"When I was in my coma, I had what you might call an epiphany—a word and its meaning I wrote down in one of my dairies, incidentally. It was a spiritual awakenin'. It's important that I make smart decisions from now on. Make amends for past transgressions."

"What does that mean?" Ellen asked.

"I'm not sure yet."

"Look, I'm glad you're gonna recover from your accident, and I'm glad you've had this epiphany, or whatever. But I'm keepin' my distance from you, and I want Markie and his boys to keep *their* distance from my kids."

Goldie looked at her with a mixture of hurt and anger.

"First, you don't wanna be around me because I'm livin' with Markie, and now that I'm not, you *still* don't wanna be around me?"

"You didn't leave Markie; he left you," Ellen reminded. "And you're playin' games with him by hangin' onto somethin' he wants."

"Well, they *are* mine," Goldie defended. "He never showed any interest in them ever, until now."

"When you've cut all ties to him, when you've made these 'smart decisions' you're talkin' about, when time has passed and I'm convinced Markie Santina's out of your life for good, then reach out to me. But that won't be while you're livin' in an apartment he's payin' for."

"What do ya want me to do? Move back in with Mom?" Goldie asked.

"Mom won't take ya. We've already discussed it."

Ellen turned and started to walk away. "You wanna do what's best for your family?" she called over her shoulder, "give Markie the diaries, get outta town, then get a job."

Goldie watched her sister leave the physical therapy department, knowing she was in a catch-22. If she wanted to have a relationship with her sister, she'd have to cut all ties with Markie. But if she couldn't move back in with her mom, those ties couldn't be cut just yet. She'd have to try to build a new life based in an apartment that he was paying for. At least for the next six months. She briefly considered suing Markie for alimony under a common-law wife argument. But a good attorney would quickly eat up the fifty thousand dollars Markie had put in an account for her. She had no savings of her own because her boyfriend had always taken care of everything. Her shoulders slumped slightly as she returned to her room and waited for Dr. Zawicki to release her.

She spent the next several hours using the hospital's WiFi and researching things on her phone. Sparkledove, Colorado, had its own website, and surprisingly, still looked much like it did back in 1942. The Victorian homes were still there, had been kept up, and were still a big tourist draw. So was the covered bridge. So was the look and charm of the stores on River Street. But the Old West plank sidewalks were gone, streetlights had been added, and the Sparkledove Arms was now a boutique hotel called the Silver Dollar, owned by Hilton. *The Sparkledove Wing* had been closed for decades, Clara's Gifts was now a Starbucks, and a general store was still where Miller's used to be, but it was no longer owned by the Miller family. The town's population had grown from 1,002 in 1942 to its current size of 3,016. Three national hotel chains just off the highway, a fishing expedition company, and a one-hundred-unit townhouse complex for Denver commuters had a lot to do with it.

Goldie Googled everyone she could remember from her time-traveling journey. But there were problems, partly because she only knew the first names of many people like Josie, Dexter, Maddie, and Dean, and partly because over eighty years had passed. She didn't find a thing on Sheriff Eli Johnson or the McCaw family, but she did find a *Denver Post* article about the trial of Charles and Peter Banyan. She learned that Charles, as well as an accomplice named Jack Tully, were sentenced to life in prison without the possibility of parole, while Peter was sentenced to twenty years. She also found an obituary for Father David Fitzsimmons, who, at the time of his death, was Monsignor David Fitzsimmons. He'd been dead for several years and passed away in a Denver area retirement home for Catholic priests. But this connection to her eighteen days in Sparkledove made her heart race. She thought about how good-natured he was, his photography skills, and the positive effect he would have on her life for years to come.

She was released from the hospital about 1:00 p.m. and took a cab to her new apartment on 53rd. The only memento she took from her stay was the plant her father had given her. Being back in Manhattan felt strange after her time in Colorado. As she rode, she noticed everything seemed dirtier than in the past: the litter on the streets, the snow plowed high into black mounds in parking lots, even the gray sky. The people on the street seemed different, too. Nobody smiled or made eye contact. She expected to be relieved once she was back in her own time. But she didn't feel that way. She felt anxious. As if another shoe was about to drop. She recalled what Stu Frey had said to her: building a new life wasn't going to be easy.

Her new apartment was in a three-story brick building that had been built in the 1950s and was once a soft drink factory. It was an 880-square-foot, two-bedroom with a couple of nice old brick walls, decent window views, new appliances and counters, and furnishings from Rent-A-Center. In the kitchen cabinets, she found dishes and glasses, canned soups, spaghetti, and mini ravioli. There was also bread, cookies, and other snacks. In the refrigerator, there was yogurt, wine, beer, bottled water, condiments, and sandwich meat, as well as frozen steaks, hamburger, and a pork roast in the freezer. A collection of cooking spices sat on a kitchen counter, as well as a checkbook, key fob, and directions to a parking garage a block away, where the car Markie had bought for her was waiting. Her clothes had been hung up in the closet, but there was still a lot of settling in to do. All of her artwork, photographs, albums, and ceramic masks were still in boxes, as were shoes, cosmetics, jewelry, underwear, and an extensive lingerie collection bought entirely for her by her ex.

Markie had done what he had promised, but it was a noticeable drop in lifestyle, and it would take time and effort for her to be comfortable in it. She opened the checkbook on the kitchen counter. The first entry was fifty grand, and an ATM card also sat inside. While she was looking at it, her cell phone rang. It was Markie. She switched the call to voicemail. Then, she went over to a box marked "LPs," opened it up, and searched through the box looking for a particular album. Plucking out *Dark Side of the Moon* by Pink Floyd, she opened the sleeve. In between the cardboard and the plastic liner that held the album, she pulled out a small key to a safety deposit box. Looking at the checkbook again, she made a decision.

By 2:30 p.m., she'd packed some clothes and had gone to the parking garage to get the car Markie had left for her. It was a Ford Fusion, a few years old but in good condition. After putting her bags in the trunk and hopping in behind the wheel, she paused, suddenly suspicious as a thought entered her mind. She popped the trunk again and thoroughly examined it. Then, she popped the hood and carefully looked under it, obviously searching for something. Finding nothing, she next felt under each of the wheel wells, and on the rear passenger side wheel well, she finally found what she was looking for. It was a small, magnetized tracking device.

Looking at it, she smiled to herself. "I know how you think, Markie Santina."

She put the tracking device and her cell phone under one of the Fusion's front tires and crushed both items as she pulled out of the garage.

Her first destination was a Citibank branch in

Midtown, where she emptied the contents of her safety deposit box. This included a copy of her birth certificate, her passport, a Smith & Wesson .22 10-shot pistol fully loaded, six volumes of diaries, and three thousand dollars in emergency cash. She originally intended the cash and the weapon to be for Markie should he lose all standing in the family and have to leave town in a hurry.

Next, she drove several blocks to a location of Chase Bank where she closed out the checking account Markie had set up for her. She put all of the money in a large Gucci tote, went to a 7-Eleven and bought a burner phone, then drove across the George Washington Bridge into Clifton, New Jersey, where she got a room at a high-rise Doubletree Hotel.

For the remainder of the day, Goldie considered her options. Although she never consciously considered using what was in her diaries against Markie, she acknowledged there was both a safeguard and a danger to keeping them. She kept track of important happenings in case Markie needed an alibi for one thing or another. She'd written down information he had casually shared so that facts wouldn't get distorted or forgotten. The diaries had proved to be of benefit on more than one occasion when she had reminded Markie about certain dates and places. But Markie never realized she was directly referencing from her diaries. If she surrendered them, she suspected he'd be angry about their detail and accuracy.

The longer she considered her options, the fewer options she seemed to have. There were nothing but problems with Markie. She'd lost her status and trust as a live-in partner, but she now also realized he intended to stay in her life. He'd already suggested that she be his mistress. She knew her mother and sister loved her, but she also knew they considered her a problem child, and neither one particularly wanted to be around her right now. Her father loved her too, but he had a different life and wife in Pennsylvania. Then there were her friends, the people she hung out with; they were all tied to the Lombardo family. Since Markie was going to marry Kristen, she knew exactly where their loyalties would fall. She had told Stu Frey that besides her family, she wanted to return to her own time because she was so dependent upon modern conveniences. But now, those didn't seem very important anymore.

About 5:30 p.m., as the sky was growing dark and Christmas lights began to dot the view from her sixth-story hotel window, a realization struck her.

"Oh, Jesus," she sighed to herself. "I shoulda stayed in Sparkledove! I was safe. I was wanted... Eli was a good man, and there were sparks. Oh, God, what've I done?"

She remembered a line from the old Christmas song, "Toyland," that brought tears to her eyes:

"Once you pass its borders, you can never return again."

Thirty-Four

Goldie decided to lie low at the Doubletree Hotel for the next three days. She only left her room to go to the exercise center twice a day, and she also went to an office supply store where she purchased some stationery and two small mailing boxes. She wrote a long letter to her mother, thinking it more personal than an email. She explained that she intended to make amends for her involvement with Markie and that, as a result, she would most likely be out of touch for a while. She apologized for any disappointment or hurt she may have caused her mom and thanked Carla for all of her hard work in trying to raise her properly. Then she used a mailing box, put the letter and the cash she'd gotten from her safety deposit box in it, and mailed it. She also wrote and mailed letters to her father and sister. She hoped these correspondences wouldn't be final farewells but knew it was possible.

On Thursday, December 19th, at 10:20 a.m., there was a knock on Goldie's hotel room door. Opening it, she saw New York Police Captain Shawn Corning standing in the hallway. He was forty-seven years old, in good physical shape, and had dark hair with thick eyebrows. He wore a suit and an overcoat with a tan scarf. He was in charge of the Organized Crime Unit, or OCU, for Greater Manhattan. The two knew each other and had met on more than one occasion, but not as friends.

"Ay, Captain," she greeted. "Thanks for comin'. C'mon in."

"Goldie," he nodded, walking into her room.

The cop looked around, then shrugged. "So, what's up? On the phone, you said the trip would be worth my while."

"Yeah... you want somethin'? I got a can of soda or can order some coffee."

"I'm good," Corning said. He went over to a chair at the wall desk and sat down. Goldie continued to stand.

"Th-this is a weird conversation to begin," she opened.

"Take your time," the officer said. "I'm in no hurry."

"Markie and me ain't together no more."

"I heard something about that on the street," he confirmed. "Is that why you're here? Are you hiding from him?"

"I've decided to make a clean break. Set some things right."

"I heard about him and Kristen DiVarno. I also heard you were struck by a car." He eyed the cast on her arm and the scabs on her face. "You okay?"

"I'll survive."

"Glad to hear it... so, what can I do for you?"

"You've taken Markie in for questioning too many times to count. Even charged him a few times, but you've never been able to make anything stick. What if I told ya I've kept diaries? Years of 'em filled with names, dates, and places. Evidence that would incriminate him and a lot of people in the Lombardo family."

A smile slowly crept across the captain's face.

"I'd say you were Santa Claus, and I must have been a *very* good boy this year. Frankly, when you called, I was hoping your reason for wanting to talk might be something like this."

Goldie hesitated, a little unsure, then sat down on the corner of her king-size bed.

"So—if I wanted to turn these diaries over to you? How does it work? What would happen?"

"First, I'd have to read them and determine their value. If they *are* incriminating, then I'd have to talk to the DA's office and see if arrest warrants are justified for Markie and anyone else implicated in any crimes. Next, there would be a trial in which you would play a role as a witness. If *you're* implicated in any of these criminal activities, the DA might offer a deal. Do you have an attorney?"

"No, but I didn't do nothin'."

"Knowledge and complicity of crimes is a crime in and of itself, Goldie. Don't think it isn't."

"Basically, what you're sayin' then is everything in my life changes with a snap of a finger."

"I'm not going to lie to you. Things will change. You'll need an attorney. You'll also need police protection and probably a new ID when this is all over."

"A trial could take months. Even years, couldn't it?" she figured.

"It would take a while," he confirmed.

She thought for a moment, then nodded. "Okay... what are the next steps?"

"Do you have the diaries with you?"

"No," she lied. "But if you meet me here at 5:00 p.m., I'll turn 'em over."

"Why don't I go with you and we'll get them right now, together?"

"If I'm goin' into protective custody, if this changes everythin' in my life, there are some things I need to wrap up. Loved ones I need to say goodbye to."

This was a lie as well because she'd already written and mailed off her letters to family, but Corning didn't know this.

"Goldie—" the cop protested.

"I want today, Captain. And it's not even a whole

day. It's, like, six and a half hours. I called *you*. Ya think I'm gonna change my mind. Run out?"

Corning looked her over, then nodded. "Well, have you at least got anything you can send me? Pictures of the pages on your phone, or—"

Goldie shook her head.

"Okay," he agreed hesitantly. "I can be back here at 5:00. You *be* here." He stood, reached into his suit coat, and produced his card. "Call me if you run into any problems."

She likewise rose. "Will do. And Captain, I don't wanna be tailed. I need this last day of freedom. If I see that I'm bein' followed, my offer's off the table."

"What's the big deal?" he asked.

"It's the principle of the thing. *Your* life isn't the one that's never gonna be the same again," she said with a pointing finger. "It's mine! Leave me alone until 5:00. That's not a lot to ask for what you're gettin'."

"Does Markie know about the diaries? Is he looking for you?"

"Yes, and yes. I ditched my cell phone and also found and destroyed a tracking bug he planted on my car. So, he doesn't know where I am. I've been out of touch for a few days and suspect he's nervous about the diaries."

Corning reluctantly nodded again. "All right... I'm sorry you got your heart broken and were physically busted up. But good things are going to come from this, Goldie. You're doing the right thing."

"Takin' down Markie won't stop the Lombardo family or organized crime, Captain."

"Maybe not, but my mom always says pulling the biggest weeds makes the garden better. I think deep in your heart, you know that's true."

Goldie cracked a small smile. "Okay, copper. See ya back here at 5:00."

Six minutes later, Corning was returning to his unmarked police car in the hotel parking lot, where one of his detectives, a chunky man named Wallace, was bundled up in his coat, leaning against the car and smoking a cigarette.

"You're not going to believe what just happened," the captain said.

"What?" Wallace replied, flicking his cigarette away, then the two climbed into the vehicle.

"You know Goldie Maraschino?"

The detective thought for a moment. "Markie Santina's girlfriend?"

"*Ex*-girlfriend. I just met with her, Markie's got a new squeeze, and Goldie is a woman scorned. She wants to turn state's evidence. She's got diaries. Years of 'em with names, dates, and I'll bet all sorts of juicy tidbits."

"Really? That's fabulous! Where is she? Where's the diaries?"

"I'm coming back here at 5:00 to pick up her and the diaries. She says she needs today to take care of some business with family."

"Uh, you think that's wise?" Wallace wondered.

"No. But that's the price of the opportunity. Listen, you know her on sight, right?"

"She's got a cute little ass that's hard to miss."

Corning looked around. "There's a Denny's over there that's got a good view of the lobby door. I want you to hang out there and see if you can get an ID on her car: Make, color, license. I can't get it from the hotel registry 'cause we've got no jurisdiction here."

"Let's call some friends at the Jersey State Police," the detective suggested.

"There's no time. I got the impression she'll be leaving very soon."

"How do you know she's coming out the lobby door?" Wallace asked.

"I don't. But I gotta do *something* to hedge my bet. She says if she sees she's being followed, the deal's off."

"Why?"

"Probably because she doesn't like cops and they're about to be in her face for, gee—I don't know—forever! Now get over to Denny's. I've got to go see the DA, set up a safe house, and try to find out if Markie's looking for her."

"Okay, Captain. You got it."

Wallace climbed out of the car and walked a short distance across the hotel's front parking lot to Denny's Restaurant. After Captain Corning had driven away and was out of sight, Wallace pulled out his cell phone and dialed a number. After one ring, someone answered.

"Bruno? It's Steve Wallace. I've got some inside information. Ask your boss if he wants to know where his old girlfriend is, and who she just had a meeting with."

Thirty-Five

A WELL-THOUGHT-OUT PLAN

Goldie had spent her time at the Doubletree looking at things from every angle. She wasn't surprised by anything Corning had shared, but she also knew that going into protective custody would be a mistake. The Lombardo family had connections in police precincts in all five New York boroughs, and while she knew Captain Corning was clean, she didn't believe he could keep her safe. She also knew that once Markie learned of her betrayal, he'd seek permission to put a hit on her. So, she used her days in seclusion to carefully plan out her moves.

Within a half hour of Corning's departure, Goldie used the second of her small mailing boxes. She packed up the diaries and left them at the front desk for the captain. To ensure that only Captain Corning received the box, she tipped the day manager five hundred dollars. Besides the diaries, she also included a letter. It had been written even before Corning arrived, explained that she wouldn't be safe in protective custody, and said that the diaries themselves would have to be enough for a conviction of Markie. She did, however, leave a small opening for further participation by suggesting she might follow up with him on a burner phone at some point in the future. She also asked the captain to tell anyone on his team that he might've spoken to about their visit that she had decided not to turn over the diaries and was going into hiding. This would perhaps slow down Markie's efforts to find her, and would therefore give her time to put distance between herself and New York. It would also buy Corning time to digest the diaries' content and determine their worth, as well as ensure that only a small number of people in the DA's office knew of their existence. In theory, this was a well-thought-out plan. But what Goldie hadn't foreseen was Detective Wallace being on the take and accompanying Corning on his visit to her.

When Wallace called Bruno Carmichael, Bruno was over an hour away in Manhattan, but he had a friend in Clifton, the town where Goldie was, who did the occasional favor for the Lombardo family. By coincidence, he worked at an electronics store less than ten minutes away from the Doubletree Hotel. Since Bruno knew what kind of car Markie had gotten for Goldie, and that it still had dealer tags, he described the car to his friend, and a second tracking device with a longer range was placed on Goldie's Ford Fusion a mere two minutes before she went out a hotel back door, hopped in her car, and headed for the Jersey Turnpike.

Although Wallace calling Bruno and him having a friend in Clifton was unfortunate for Goldie, she did catch a break. Markie had promised Kristen an entire uninterrupted day of Christmas shopping. This included looking at china patterns, linens, and furniture for their new home, which was important to Kristen. Markie promised she'd have his undivided attention until their day was over. So, he turned off his cell and went shopping without his usual two bodyguards. It wasn't until nearly 6:30 p.m. that Bruno finally reached him. By then, two pieces of information had been conveyed to Bruno from Detective Wallace. The first was that Goldie intended to turn over her diaries to the police, and the second was the nullification of that decision, and that Goldie was on the lam. Captain Corning agreed with the logic in Goldie's letter about the subterfuge of changing her mind, told Wallace about this reversal to cover all bases, and it had the desired effect. Instead of immediately seeing red and going into a rage, Markie decided to have Bruno follow Goldie to see where she was going. Perhaps, he thought, if she didn't have the diaries with her, she was going to where they were.

Thirty-Six

FINISHING UP

"Yeah?" Markie said, answering his cell phone.

"Markie, it's Bruno. How ya doin'?"

"So, where are ya now?"

"Outside of St. Louis. How long do I gotta keep followin' Goldie? I mean, Jesus, I'd like to be back before Christmas, y'know?"

"St. Louis?" Markie exclaimed, surprised. "She don't know no one in St. Louis. The closest she's ever been to St. Louis is drinkin' a Budweiser."

"Yeah, well, this is the wildest goose chase *I've* ever been on," the enforcer said, disgruntled.

"You keepin' your distance?"

"Yeah. The new tracker's workin' great. I'm keepin' at least a mile behind her."

"She showin' any signs of reachin' a destination?" Markie asked.

"No. She just goes on endlessly like NCIS."

Markie thought for a moment. "Why would she be drivin' across country? Wait—wait a minute—that aunt of hers in Las Vegas. Five will get ya ten that's where she's goin'. Hell, I even suggested she might want to make a new start out there. But I want the damn diaries!"

"She's probably got the diaries with her," Bruno concluded.

"Maybe. But what if she don't? What if she lied to Corning about bein' able to easily access the diaries and she took 'em out to her aunt's for safekeepin' after her uncle died? You stop her now, and we might never get 'em."

"I stop her now permanently, and it don't matter."

"Sure it does. What if somethin' happens to Goldie, then the diaries materialize? Through her aunt? Or a friend? She's too smart to leave 'em with her mom, sister, or father. Naw, we gotta let this play out."

"She betrayed you, man!" Bruno reminded.

"No. She *threatened* to, but changed her mind."

"Doesn't matter, Markie. After everything you offered her—the apartment, the cash, the car, payin' her medical expenses, she betrayed you by callin' Corning."

"You don't know women, man," Markie said. "Goldie's still pissed about Kristen, but she's not an idiot. I'm not gonna burn her just because she's hurt and wants a fresh start. But I *do* wanna see those diaries. So, just play your favorite road tunes, keep followin', and keep me posted."

It was now Saturday, December 22nd, and Goldie was headed for Sparkledove. She knew nobody in town would recognize her, but she wanted to return to a place where she was once known, liked, and made smart choices. She didn't expect to see Stu Frey again, but she hoped to kneel in a pew at St. Mark's and maybe feel closer to God. She couldn't return to 1942, but since she'd seen the town online and knew that many things were still the same, she felt like she was going home.

She finally arrived in the late afternoon on Sunday, December 23rd. She tried to check into the former Sparkledove Arms, now called the Silver Dollar, but there were no vacancies. It was odd being back in the same building. The lobby area was very contemporary, and the Christmas tree in it was small and filled with LED lights that were hard on the eyes. The registration counter was where the restaurant used to be, and the area where the 1940s registration counter and back office once were was now a gift shop. She found a room at a LaQuinta Inn just off Highway 70, where the community center once stood, and felt happy but sad at the same time.

By 8:10 p.m., Goldie had driven down Bridge Street, parked, and was walking toward the covered bridge. There was no seasonal roping affixed to its sides, and the three overhead lights that once lit the interior were gone. But the glassless viewing windows were still there, and there were still candles in most of the windows of the houses on Bridge Street, although they were electric. There was only a light dusting of snow on the ground, so there weren't any horse-drawn sleighs, but she did see a group of young carolers going from door to door. She heard them from a distance as she walked onto the bridge and stood at the window where Claude Bolton killed himself. She looked out at the same beautiful view of the river, starry sky, and the mountains of eight decades ago and prayed: "Dear Lord, thank you for givin' me the guts to leave New York and do what I did with the diaries. Maybe it won't make much of a difference in the grand scheme of things, but it was the right thing to do. By the way, even though I've read December 25th is more of a ceremonial date than the real thing—happy birthday."

Just then, she heard something and suddenly turned toward Bridge Street. At first, she thought it might have been Claude Bolton, but it was just a man walking his dog.

The following morning, December 24th, Goldie slept in late. She took a shower with a plastic bag over her cast, then put on a turtleneck with a cut sleeve for her cast, some Merrell boots, and a down vest. Taking a stocking cap and gloves, she decided to get thoroughly reacquainted with Sparkledove. She began at Clara's Gifts, which was now a Starbucks. Then, she walked up and down both sides of River Street, examining the stores. The sidewalks were busy with last-minute shoppers, and she was delighted to see that the stores still catered to tourists. She was likewise pleased to see a tall community Christmas tree standing once again in the brick courtyard of the post office. She went into Miller's General Store, now called Sparkledove Mercantile, and looked around. She inquired about the Miller family, but the store manager was young and unfamiliar with the people who started the original business. Goldie then asked if he was taking employment applications, and, liking her looks, he said he was. So, she spent some time filling out an application with bogus information she hoped wouldn't be checked. Next, she went a few blocks over to St. Mark's Catholic Church. It looked exactly the same, except the nativity that had once been in the front yard was now replaced with a glass-enclosed sign that had a listing of services. The church was locked, but there was a 7:00 p.m. Christmas Eve Mass, and Goldie decided she'd attend. After that, she walked down Falcon Drive. All of the houses looked pretty much the same and were beautifully decorated for the holidays, but the old Eggleston house had been remodeled on the inside to accommodate multiple apartments, and there was an "Apartment For Rent" sign in the window. She knocked on the front door, met the current owner, and took a tour of a one-bedroom apartment on the second floor. She really liked it but said she wanted to look around and see what else might be available, and informed the owner she'd follow up with him after Christmas.

Wherever Goldie went on this Christmas Eve, Bruno was watching her from a distance. He'd seen her the previous night strolling on the covered bridge. He saw her filling out what looked like a job application through the front window of the Sparkledove Mercantile. He observed her going into a house on Falcon Drive where an "Apartment for Rent" sign was in one of the front windows. It seemed to him that Goldie was not headed for Las Vegas but had already reached her destination, although he had no idea why it was Sparkledove, Colorado. He had tried to call Markie the evening before, but the call went straight to voicemail. He had tried several more times this day, but the attempts likewise went to voicemail. He didn't know what to do. But he had convinced himself that Goldie had the diaries, and he was going to get them.

Finally, a little after 4:00 p.m., just as things were starting to get dark in town from the sun setting behind the mountains, Bruno's cell phone rang. It was a number he immediately recognized.

"Hello?" he said formally.

"Bruno? It's Frank Lombardo. How are ya?"

Frank was head of the Lombardo family, Markie and Bruno's boss, and the final word on all operations in New York.

"I'm fine, Frank," Bruno said. "To what do I owe the pleasure?"

"Listen, I know you're doin' some last-minute shoppin' today, but you need to finish it up." He was speaking in a type of code because he knew how easily cell phone calls could be monitored.

"Has somethin' happened?" Bruno asked.

"Yeah. Markie's been arrested by the DA's office.

Our attorneys don't think they can hold him for long, and that the evidence is circumstantial, but you never know. As a friend, I'm sure he'd appreciate you bein' here for moral support. We all would. So, finish things up, will ya?"

"Yeah, Frank. Sure. I just got one more thing to check off my list, and then I'll come see ya."

"Make sure you do. Talk to you later and Merry Christmas."

"Yeah. You, too."

Disconnecting the call, Bruno pieced together a scenario in his mind: Goldie had turned over her diaries to Captain Corning after all, and her cross-country trip was an attempt to disappear until she'd be needed as a key witness for a trial. If she were eliminated, however, the things written in her diaries would go unsubstantiated. Frank Lombardo had just issued a death sentence for Goldie, and Bruno Carmichael, upset about being away from his family for the holidays, was more than ready to carry it out.

At 5:15, Goldie was roaming through Sparkledove's only cemetery on the edge of town. The cemetery was in a secluded area, wasn't very big, and had a four-foot-high wrought iron fence around it. Within just a couple of minutes, she found a plot for the Miller family and saw both Deke and Chad Miller's graves, along with their spouses and other family members. She found Maddie and Dean and learned their last name was O'Rourke. She likewise came across Lupe and her husband and learned their last name was Estevez. She located Horace Mason, buried next to an apparent second wife named Michelle. She discovered Ed Peterson, whose car was shot up so badly by Horace. It was incredibly sad to see all these people gone, yet it was somehow comforting at the same time. There were lots of old friends she could always visit.

Just as it was nearly impossible to read the gravestones due to the lack of daylight, she finally spotted Eli Johnson. He was buried in a double plot, but there was no headstone for the grave next to his. This could've meant he never married, or had a wife buried somewhere else. Her green eyes became moist as she sank to her knees, took off one of her gloves, and ran her fingers across the chiseled letters of his name. Then, she looked down at the date and saw that he had passed away fifteen years earlier, when he was in his nineties.

"Oh..." she sighed. "I-I'm so sorry, Eli. I shoulda stayed. I shoulda explored what coulda been... I shoulda built that new life."

Her thoughts were interrupted as she suddenly realized someone was behind her. Turning, she saw Bruno Carmichael standing behind her, wearing gloves and holding a Glock .9 millimeter with a silencer.

She was surprised, but only momentarily. Then, she rallied her courage.

"Ay, Bruno. How ya doin'?"

"Ya gave your diaries to the cops, didn't ya?"

"Yeah. I did."

"They were in New York all the time," he figured.

"Yeah. They were," she confirmed.

"Big mistake, Goldie."

"All depends on how ya look at it," she replied.

He glanced around. "What the hell are ya doin' here? Why're you in this town?"

She thought about the .22 Smith & Wesson that she'd left in her car, then looked up at him and smiled bravely while tears filled her eyes.

"I-I'm goin' home for Christmas... and you're the conductor who's gonna punch my ticket."

The big man cracked the faintest of smiles for a few seconds, then pointed the Glock at Goldie's head and fired. She fell quietly to the ground next to Eli, then Bruno fired again.

After glancing around, he bent down and searched her pockets. Finding her key fob, he got up, turned, and walked to her Ford Fusion that was parked just outside the cemetery's fence. Opening the truck, he found her Gucci tote bag holding her gun and Markie's cash. Grabbing the tote, Bruno closed the truck, then walked away, leaving Goldie's body where it had fallen.

Thirty-Seven

AT THE JOHNSON'S

When Goldie's green eyes slowly opened, she had no idea how much time had passed. She remembered that she had been kneeling in front of Eli Johnson's grave when Bruno Carmichael came up behind her with a gun. She recalled they spoke for a few seconds, then there was a flash of light, but after that—nothing.

Now, she was lying on her back, and her eyes were slowly focusing in on an overhead light fixture in a plaster ceiling that she recognized. The lights were off, but there was enough daylight peeking in from the edges of the drawn curtains to give her an idea of the place. As she became more alert, she slowly propped herself up on her elbows, looked at the patchwork quilt covering her, then around at the familiar room. She was back in room 9 of the Sparkledove Arms.

"Oh my God," she muttered. "It's 1942 again! H-how did I... Stu said that I couldn't..."

Not finishing her thought, she threw the quilt off her body and hopped out of bed, wearing the same ivory slip she'd worn when she first awoke in the room. She ran over to the rounded mirror above the dresser and looked at her hair. It was dark brown, and there were no bullet holes in her head.

"Oh, Lord. I don't know what's goin' on, but thank you! *Thank you!*"

Six minutes later, she was hurrying down the stairs to the bustling lobby of the hotel, wearing one of the three original dresses that she had found in her suitcase when she first arrived. It was 10:00 a.m. on Christmas morning. The lobby with its nine-foot Christmas tree and candle sconce lighting on the walls was just the same as when she left. In front of the tree were the same guitarist and violinist who had played in the lobby at Thanksgiving. Maddie was behind the counter, wearing her glasses with the silver chain and a red cardigan sweater with Christmas trees embroidered on it. Seeing Goldie approach, she smiled.

"Merry Christmas, Goldie!" she greeted.

"Maddie!" Goldie called, hurrying over to her. "I, uh, I-I'm havin' one of my short-term memory losses. When did I get here? When did I come back?"

The proprietor looked at her for a moment, then smiled acceptingly.

"You got in yesterday afternoon. By sheer coincidence, we had a last-minute cancellation, and your old room was available."

"Did I say why I came back?"

"You told Dean that you wanted to settle here. Personally, we're delighted."

"I did?"

"You did. You said when you got back to Columbus, you tried to pick up with your life there, but ultimately decided to quit your job, come back here, and see who you could talk to about taking over the *Sparkledove Wing.*"

"I did?" she asked, smiling with moist eyes. "Brilliant! That's great! Thanks, Maddie! I gotta go find Eli!"

She started to hurry across the lobby toward the front door.

"Goldie!" Maddie called.

The younger one stopped and turned. "Yeah?"

"Take a coat, dear," she reminded.

Goldie looked down at herself and realized she needed one. "Oh, right," she said, heading for the stairs again.

Within another five minutes, she was out on the street with her overcoat on and running down the middle of River Street toward the other end of town. As she ran, she was practically a female version of George Bailey in *It's A Wonderful Life,* calling out to stores:

"Hello Clara's Gifts... Hello Miller's General Store... Hello Summit Grocers... Hello you ol' Historical Society..."

Finally arriving at the sheriff's office, she was disappointed to find it closed and Eli's police cruiser nowhere in sight. Turning to return to her hotel, she spotted Stu Frey's truck at a stop sign on a cross street a block away. Giving a loud whistle like a foreman on a loading dock, she caught Stu's attention, and he waited. So she ran down to where he was while he rolled down his window.

"Hey, Merry Christmas!" he called as she neared. "What're you doing?"

"Looking for Eli," she replied.

"He's with his folks today in Brownsville. You want me to run you over there? It's not that far."

"Yeah. That'd be great. Thanks!" she replied, knowing their meeting wasn't by chance.

She rounded the passenger side of the truck, climbed in, then Stu turned right onto River Street and followed it down, intending to turn right again in front of the Sparkledove Arms and head toward the highway.

"How come I'm here?" she asked, getting right to the point. "I thought you said I couldn't come back."

"What I said was: 'Your decision is a one-way trip,'" he corrected. "That was true. You were *always* going to come back. It just took you a little while to figure that out."

She squinted her eyes. "That sounds like a trick."

"No. That sounds like a God who believes in first, second, and third chances for those who aren't afraid to go after them."

"So, you *knew* I'd want to come back?"

"I didn't, but He did."

Stu's truck turned onto Highway 70, and the vehicle began to pick up speed.

"I love my family, Stu. Y'know? I always will. But I can't do anything for 'em, they've got their own lives, and they can't do anything for me, either."

"God helps those who help themselves," he observed.

"Now that I'm here, is the other Goldie—I mean—will her soul be—"

"Her soul will be fine," Stu assured. "I promise. Your family will be fine, too."

She thought for a couple of moments.

"Are my efforts back in New York goin' to help nail Markie? Are the diaries by themselves gonna be enough to convict?" She paused for a moment. "You know about the diaries, right? I mean, I'm assumin' you do."

"The diaries without your testimony won't be enough to convict. But Bruno Carmichael left your ID with your body in the Sparkledove cemetery, and that was sloppy. Markie won't be convicted because of the dairies, but your death begins a series of events where Markie loses his standing in the Lombardo family, and those events eventually cost him Kristen. Don't worry, Goldie. Justice will come to Markie Santina. Bruno Carmichael, too, for that matter."

She nodded, neither happy nor sad with the news, and looked out at the day. It was windless and overcast, as if it might snow.

"So, what do I do? How does this work?" she asked anxiously.

"Live your life," he advised. "Just live your life. And realize I'm not going to reveal any big things to you about God, Jesus, soul swapping, or mysteries of the universe. I can't intervene in most things, either. I'm not God, and there's a natural order to things. What you already know, what you've already been given, is a tremendous gift. One that should last a lifetime. Don't waste it, Goldie."

"I won't," she promised.

"Uh, and please don't go reciting song lyrics to people by artists who aren't even born yet. The containment is bothersome."

She smiled. "I'll talk to Clara about it."

"Between the two of you, you *could* do a lot of good in town. You could become great friends and help champion some progressive thinking about all sorts of things. You two could help spread a lot of love, peace, and optimism."

She looked at him, amused. "You sound like an old hippie."

"How do you know I'm not?" he teased.

"S-so what's goin' on here? Did Harriette Noise recover?"

"Harriette's going to be fine. The Banyans are still in jail, a trial date has just been set, and it could be the town will have a major new benefactor in Stephie Banyan. That is, if the tunnel you found out about has a vein as rich as Charles thought."

Within another five minutes, they got off the highway and went into Brownsville, which was a town even smaller than Sparkledove. They arrived at a modest but nicely painted blue-and-yellow two-story wooden house on a quiet street corner. As Stu pulled over, Goldie saw Eli's police car in the driveway.

"There you go," he said.

She hesitated for a moment.

"What if he hates me for running out on him like Lila Hemmings?"

"Then it's a long walk back," Stu figured. "'Cause I can't hang around. It's Christmas."

She nodded while an idea came to Stu. He reached behind Goldie's seat into the cab of his truck, opened a nearby ice chest behind her, pulled out a package wrapped in brown paper and tied with a string, and handed it to her.

"Here. Take this as a Christmas gift for Eli's mom."

"What is it?" she asked.

"Two ribeye steaks."

She took the package and looked at it.

"You're an angel. You couldn't have pulled out a nice bottle of Mondavi?"

"You don't want 'em? Give 'em back," he said, holding out a hand.

"No... I'll take 'em... thanks."

"Steaks are expensive these days," he reminded. "It's a nice gift."

She nodded again, repeated her thanks, then climbed out of the truck as some snowflakes began to descend. She walked up a short sidewalk, then up a few steps to the front porch. As Stu drove away, she knocked.

A few seconds later, Mary Louise, Eli's mom, opened the door wearing her best dress.

"Goldie," she exclaimed. "W-well, my goodness."

"Hi, Mary Louise," she said. "Merry Christmas."

"Merry Christmas. I thought you went back to Columbus?"

"Yeah. I did, but—"

The appearance of Eli in the foyer stopped her in mid-sentence. He was wearing a suit and tie. The same one he'd worn at the community dance.

"Howdy," she said.

"Uh, howdy," he answered, surprised to see her.

There was an awkward moment of silence, then Mary Louise said, "Please, come in."

"Thanks," Goldie replied.

As soon as she stepped into the house, two more people came into the living room that was immediately off the foyer. One was Eli's sister, Dinah, also wearing a dress, and Eli's dad, who, like his son, was wearing a suit and tie.

"Here, let me take your coat," Mary Louise offered.

Goldie set her wrapped package on top of a cabinet radio just inside the living room that was playing the Tommy Dorsey Orchestra's version of "March of the Toys," then slipped off her coat. In a corner of the living room was a lit Christmas tree decorated with glass bulbs, but also trimmed with rows of strung popcorn and cranberries. Opened presents were also underneath it.

"Uh, this is my sister, Dinah," Eli introduced. "And my dad, Seymour."

Goldie shook hands with both of them while Mary Louise hung up Goldie's coat in the front closet. When she was finished, the visitor retrieved the package from the radio and offered it to her.

"Stu Frey gave me a ride over here and thought you might enjoy these," she said, being honest. "They're two ribeye steaks. I would've brought somethin' as well, but to tell you the truth, my return to Colorado was very spur of the moment."

"Well, I'm glad you did," Seymour said. "It gives me the chance to say how grateful people are about what you discovered about Charles and Peter Banyan. Lord only knows what other kind of damage they could've done in Sparkledove."

"Very true," Mary Louise concurred. "And thank you," she said, referring to the steaks.

"We just got back from church. Dinah's boyfriend will be coming over a little later for dinner, and you'll stay, too, of course."

"Well, I..."

"Yes, that'd be great," Dinah encouraged.

"Yes, please stay," Seymour echoed.

"Yeah," Eli agreed. "Then, maybe you'll tell me what in the Sam Hill you're doing here."

Everyone looked at Goldie for an explanation. She emboldened herself, then looked at Eli's father.

"Seymour, *somebody* told me that I could build a new life in Sparkledove, and it could be better than my life in Columbus. Somebody *also* told me I might be able to take over *The Wing* as its new Editor-In-Chief. Then, that somebody kissed me and used his tongue. Now, wouldn't you say that was practically a proposal? And if that somebody in question is surprised that I'd turn up on Christmas morning, then, wouldn't you say he was a cad? That he was cavalierly playing with my affections? Toying with my heart?"

Seymour looked at Eli, then at Mary Louise, then back to Goldie, who had an impish twinkle in her eye.

"Uh, w-well," he stammered.

"*I* certainly would," Dinah said, liking Goldie immediately and taking her side.

Mary Louise looked at her son. "Did you do all that?"

Eli's face turned red as he fiddled with the knot of his necktie. "W-w-well—yeah—but there was lots of other stuff in between."

Mary Louise suddenly made some decisions.

"Seymour, go set another place at the table. Dinah, get some more potatoes from the pantry for mashing. I'm going to put these steaks away and get going on some extra cranberry sauce."

Mary Louise, Dinah, and Seymour all left the living room to attend to their various tasks with subtle smiles. Eli looked at Goldie with his blue eyes shining. Her surprise appearance was the best Christmas present he could've ever imagined, and she felt exactly the same way.

"You, eh, sure you want to stay?" he asked in his slow cowboy way.

"Positive," she answered. Then, she hesitated. "Don't you want me to?"

"Oh, I absolutely *do,*" he confirmed. "But you know, there are a lot of food shortages going on and, in these parts, that includes turkeys."

"So, what's your mom makin'?" she asked.

"Pot roast," he replied.

Timothy Best is the author of seven other novels, all of them award-winning. He's also a Creative Director-Copywriter in the advertising business and has written for Fortune 100 companies like Allstate Insurance, Coca-Cola, GM, Honda, Toyota, Walmart and many others. Readers can connect with him on his Goodreads page at:

https://www.goodreads.com/author/show/6092023.Timothy_Best

When he's not writing, he plays drums in rock & roll and blues bands throughout the Atlanta area.

Thank you so much for reading the Sparkledove. If you enjoyed it, please leave a review on your bookseller's website.

About the Publisher

Harbor Lane Books, LLC is a US-based independent digital publisher of commercial fiction, non-fiction, and poetry.

Connect with Harbor Lane Books on their website www.harborlanebooks.com, TikTok, Instagram, Facebook, X, and Pinterest @harborlanebooks.